IN IT
TO
WIN IT

ALI CURTIS

First paperback edition February 2024

Book design by Yummy Book Covers

Editors: Dawn Alexander; Britt Tayler, Paperback Proofreader

Proofreader and Copy Editor: Brooke Crites, Proofreading by Brooke

ISBN 979-8-9880530-0-2 (paperback)

ISBN 979-8-9880530-1-9 (ebook)

For D.
Every day with you is the best romance of all.

IN IT
TO
WIN IT

CHAPTER 1

EMILY

New York's bitter air whips me right in the face as I exit the revolving door. An icy drizzle falls from the sky as the temperatures drop steadily, and I'm grateful the bar is only a few blocks from my office.

The windows are fogged up so I can't see inside, but I'm pretty sure the girls are already there. I know Josie and Lucy were planning on happy hour tonight, and Smith's Cave has been our go-to place for as long as I can remember. Some would dub it a dive, but it's one of the few places I feel comfortable in my skin. Sawdust on the floor, an old pinball machine, and two pool tables in the back. It's one of those "long and deep" layouts: looks like nothing from the outside, but inside, you might as well be in the charmed wizarding tents from *Harry Potter*.

Stepping inside, I stomp the moisture off my boots as I look around for my friends. The bar's packed and charged with that familiar Friday energy synonymous with knocking another workweek off. I scan the crowd and find Josie talking animatedly to Lucy, arms flailing and face flushed, before she sees me and abruptly gets to her feet.

"Emily?" She shoots a glance down at her watch then back up to me. "Emily!" She's grinning, and when she yells my name over Luke Bryan telling all the country girls to shake it for him, she manages to pull the attention of half the patrons in the bar.

My cheeks burn and I duck my head, contemplating pulling my jacket's frost-covered hood over my face. Before I even have the chance to set my things down, Lucy yanks me into an embrace, eyes filled with concern, and asks, "Is everything okay? Why are you here so early?"

Josie chimes in, "Seriously, did someone die? If someone died, we should probably settle our tab."

I laugh as I take my coat off and add it to the stack of jackets and bags in the corner of our booth. "I know, I know. Shocking that I'd show my face before eight o'clock on a Friday."

Josie sips her margarita and nods. "If the shoe fits, Cinderella."

I playfully stick my tongue out at her.

"Speaking of Cinderella, I'm loving the sparkly gold sweater, babe. Fancy."

"Thank you," I dip in a half curtsy. "Every now and then I break up the all black wardrobe with some sparkle. And thanks for the concern, ladies, but I'm actually here with good news." I sit down, scoot next to Lucy, and then lean over to grab the pitcher and an empty glass. "Guess who was just told she'd be leading one of the pitch teams for the Imperial account?" I stop to take a long chug, dragging out the anticipation. "This girl!" I give them a little shoulder sashay, the tequila already working its way into my blood.

"Holy shit, Em! I heard DMG was one of the finalists. That's amazing!" Josie says, holding up a hand for a high-five. I smile and slap her palm.

"Are you serious? That's amazing, Em!" Lucy adds, leaning over and giving me a side hug. "If anyone deserves a shot at this, it's you. You've been burning the midnight oil there for years. You're going to kick ass and take names."

I take another big swallow of my margarita. "I still can't believe it myself. After they announced the finalists this afternoon, Josh called me into his office and told me the good news. Sounds like Imperial is living up to their reputation of being as needy as an overtired and hangry toddler, because they told us we only have four weeks to deliver everything."

Josie scrunches her nose. "Perfect, so half the time of a normal pitch. Love that for you."

I nod, leaning over to dip a chip in guacamole. "Yep. So, work will be even more insane than it has been, hence why I'm here so early. This will probably be my last night out for at least the next month. But on the plus side, if we win the pitch, there's no reason I won't get promoted to Account Director." I cross my fingers and tilt my head back in a show of praying to the dingy bar gods. "If that happens, it'll be intense for a while, but the dwindling dollars in my bank account will very much appreciate the extra company."

"And we very much appreciate your company tonight!" Lucy raises her glass in a toast. "Pencil us in for celebratory drinks when you land the account"—she gives me a pointed look— "*and* the promotion."

"Thanks, Luce." My stomach knots thinking about just how dire my finances are. I've always prided myself on being responsible and accountable. But I'm *this* close to officially living on PBJ, and the girls don't even know how bad it is. This promotion could not have come at a better time. This pitch is a gift from the universe and I plan to take full advantage of it. "But anyway, no more talk about work or overtime or anything to do with Imperial." I throw her an easy grin and clink her glass. "So, what's today's good thing?"

"Luke, actually! He just finished a big case so we're meeting for dinner to celebrate." Lucy's very close with her twin brother Luke, which means we are too by default, although we don't see him much because of how busy he is with work. Josie starts peppering her with questions while I take the time to scan the crowd.

The whole place is buzzing, and I wonder if it has anything to do with the forecasted snowstorm promising a day on the couch and in sweats tomorrow. I know that's my plan. The weather's been mild for late February, but meteorologists are making it sound like we'll be getting all of winter at once this weekend.

I turn to Josie and waggle my brows. "So, are you going to fill us in on last night? How was your date?"

"You guys won't believe this one… So, we've been texting for about a week, nothing too extensive though because he asked to meet for drinks basically right away."

"Nice. Direct and to the point. I appreciate that." Lucy nods her approval.

Josie continues with her story and I let out a deep breath, sinking into the leather back of the booth. I close my eyes for a moment, laughing at Josie's commentary. When I finally sit up and open my eyes, they lock on a pair staring intently back at me. Goose bumps crawl up my body and send the hairs on my arms rising to attention. I freeze, unable to tear my eyes away.

The rest of the bar blurs as I stare at the most flawless face I've ever seen—square, chiseled jaw covered with the barest hint of a five o'clock shadow. Thick brow line. Sparkling, crystal blue eyes the color of the Caribbean Sea at sunrise. Strong hands grip his pint glass as he brings it up to his lips for a sip. Kissable lips. As if all that wasn't perfect enough, whatever his friend whispers in his ear makes him smile, and without taking his eyes off me, deep dimples pop up framing his grin.

My face heats to the tip of my chestnut brown hair, and I take a moment to be grateful I actually washed and blew it out this morning or else I'd have nothing to hide behind. I let it fall like a curtain around my face as my blush moves down my chest and heat swirls in my stomach. I chug the remains of my margarita and release an audible exhale.

Josie follows my line of sight and sighs. "Finally. Blue Eyes over there has been staring you down since you walked in. I was wondering how long it would take you to notice."

"Hm, Blue's what?" I drag my attention to the girls and feign innocence. "Geez, why does Hank have the heat turned up so high?" I fan my sweater to let some of the cool air circulate against my flushed skin. "It's not snowing in here," I grumble.

"Emily"—Lucy leans into me and pats my forearm—"this is your last night out before you're more married to your job than you already are. That guy is hot. And he's clearly into you. Go talk to him, live a little." She lets go of my arm and settles back against the booth, smug as anything.

I wave a hand in the air. "He's probably mixing me up with someone else and trying to place me. Anyway, you guys know more than anyone that the last thing I need right now is a distraction. The biggest opportunity of my career is kicking off on Monday." And every alarm in my head is blaring that old Blue Eyes over there would be a *major* disruption.

His broad shoulders are straining against his striped button-down and his rolled-up sleeves expose toned forearms. My stomach takes another tumble because, forearms. If he smells half as good as he looks, I'd be a total goner. Stick a fork in me, I'd be done.

I outwardly cringe at my cheesiness. *How the hell am I in advertising?!*

Josie flips her hair for dramatic effect, and I'm not sure if it's for my situation or to get the attention of Blue Eyes's buddy. He's wearing jeans and a flannel, and she's always been a sucker for the rugged lumberjack look. "Yes, but that's Monday.

Today's *Friday*. Forget about work for a couple of days. It's not going anywhere."

It does sound tempting, and Blue Eyes is definitely stirring something inside me that I buried a long time ago, right around the time I tossed Greg out with the wedding invitations we would no longer need.

It's probably the margaritas speaking, but maybe for one night only, and only because the girls are leaving me basically no choice, I can throw caution to the wind and feel like my old self again. Live in a bubble. Toss off the weight from my shoulders. Lord knows the confident Emily from before has been MIA. In fact, I replaced her with the stress of a lease I can no longer afford and a savings account dipping precariously close to zero. Old Emily was fun, flirty, *fearless*, and she could banter with the best of them. Come Monday, the blinders will be securely back in place and my goals will still all be within reach. If I'm being honest, just the thought of what could happen tonight makes my insides flip upside down with giddy anticipation.

"That may work for you, but let's be honest. That guy couldn't possibly really be interested in me. He looks like that, and well"—I look down at my barely-B-cup chest and move my hands in a circular motion—"there isn't much here for the taking."

Josie flicks my arm to snap me out of my self-deprecating moment. "You know, Em, one of these days you'll have to put your big girl panties on and do this yourself, but I'm feeling rather generous tonight." She stands up and hands me her empty glass. "We need another round. I'll be right back."

Before Lucy or I can think to stop her, she's sauntering over to Blue Eyes and his friends. A path clears for her like she's Moses parting the Red Sea, and there's little question why. Standing at five-nine, Josie is all curves, blonde waves, sun-kissed skin, and sparkling blue eyes. The quintessential California girl. And now, perched on the edge of my booth seat, I watch as she seamlessly joins their conversation, cursing myself for never learning how to read lips. I watch Josie eye the lumberjack like the last slice of pizza after a rowdy night out as she turns in slow motion and flips that hair one final time.

Then she proceeds to strut back to the table like a runway model. "Give it five minutes. They'll be over."

"What did you say?" I whisper-yell between my clenched teeth in case, unlike me, Blue Eyes is a lip reader.

She grins and cocks an eyebrow. "Don't you trust me?"

I flop back against the booth and stare at the ceiling. "Not in a situation like this," I groan dramatically. "I could be at home finishing the latest Ali Hazelwood I started last night."

"Oh." Josie snaps her finger at me. "You mean the one where the love interest is as tall as a Redwood and has a penis the size of a pirate ship?"

"Isn't that all of them?" Lucy deadpans, and we all laugh.

"Ladies, don't hate. We love our Steminists and their love stories." I turn to address Lucy and continue, "Especially you, our favorite, and only, environmental engineer friend, saving the world one climate project at a time."

"Listen." Josie picks up the new pitcher the waitress dropped off, refills her glass, and raises it for a new toast. "I didn't say anything you won't thank me for tomorrow." She shrugs but her eyes are mischievous. Her glance jumps from Blue Eyes back to me. "To Emily, popping her one-night-stand cherry. Lord knows it's about time."

Lucy shrugs like *Meh, good enough*, raises her glass, and drains the rest of her drink. "Oh man, I wish I could stay and watch this with a vat of popcorn, but I have to go meet Luke." She stands up to put on her coat, pausing to address me. "Just remember, my dear, men are into angels in the streets and tramps in the sheets. Use a condom!"

I laugh as she drops a kiss on my cheek. She starts heading to the door and looks back when she passes Blue Eyes, stopping right in front of him. To my utter humiliation, she proceeds to place a hand on his chest and then, if body language is to be believed, appears to issue a warning. To his credit, he takes it all in stride, eyes never wavering from mine. Finished with her third degree, Lucy looks back at me with a wink, then disappears in the crowd on her way to the door.

I face Josie, eyes wide and mortified, my mind pulsing like a blender as I try to imagine the possibilities. I turn to look back at him, but he's no longer standing still. He's walking toward us. He's easily six feet tall, and even in the dim lighting, I notice how effortlessly his dark jeans hang off his slim hips.

"Hi." He's now standing at the end of our table and it's clear he's addressing me.

I glance at Josie, who is smiling like a Cheshire Cat behind her glass, obviously not picking up on my panic.

"Uh, hi," I stutter.

"I'm Matt." He sticks out his hand for me to shake it.

I stare at it for a beat before I reach mine out. "Emily." His hand swallows mine, and a charge ripples up my arm when we touch. He holds my hand longer than necessary and I shiver when he releases it, feeling cold without his heat on my skin.

"Emily, I don't normally do this," he starts, and I can't help but chuckle at the cliché. An impish grin lights his face as he shakes his head and looks away briefly. "I really don't, but I need help with something, and your friend"—his eyes dart to Josie—"made me think you might be up for it?" He motions to the lumberjack at his table. "My brother and I have a long-standing pool rivalry. I'm undefeated in the last five games and he's itching to take me down, but the rule is that we have to play mixed doubles. Which means... I'm in need of a partner." He pauses briefly to let me digest his confession before tilting his head, brows raised, and asking, "Any chance you'd be up to help a guy out?"

I try to play it cool while my entire body bubbles like boiling water. Shit like this does not happen to me. Josie, yes. Me? No. I see the neon sign flashing *Danger!* over his head and I know it's a bad idea. But the drinks are going down easy and spending time with my girls has relaxed me, so I dig deep to excavate the old Emily, just for tonight, shrug a shoulder, and reply, "Why not? I'm feeling charitable tonight."

He blows out a relieved breath and holds his hand out again to help me up from the table. "Lead the way," I say, smiling. As he walks us toward the pool table, I glance back at Josie over my shoulder, my eyes bulging as I prepare myself for what lies ahead.

CHAPTER 2

MATT

One Hour Earlier

"Little brother, it's good to have you here," Ryan says, slapping my back. "The city has never been more alive, and the women have never been hotter. Although, you may want to ease into it, considering you're not in Kansas anymore. Wouldn't want you getting burned by any big-city girls."

I roll my eyes at him. "*Chicago* is the third largest city in the country, jackhole. The women there can definitely hold their own." Not that I would know, considering there hadn't been anyone since Stella and I broke up, but *that* is a minor detail Ryan doesn't need right now. "I'm not worried about the ladies."

He raises an eyebrow, not buying my act. "Care to put a wager on that, Matty?"

I shake my head but laugh. Classic Ryan, always trying to up the stakes with friendly competition.

"Aw, are you scared you might lose?"

I sip my beer and shoot my eyes to Ben, giving him my best *Can you believe this shit?* Look. "Scared? No. Wise enough to know it's not worth engaging with you? Yes. So it's a no to the bet, but please, enlighten us."

Ryan leans over and clasps my shoulder. "I'm just looking out for you, trying to make sure you haven't lost your touch, that's all." He stands up straight, a sure sign he's just getting started.

I wave my hands in a circle. "Continue, please. You have me curious now."

Ryan puts his beer down and rubs his hands together. "Okay, what I was *going* to say is if you can make the next girl who walks into the bar fall for you, I'll buy you floor seat playoff tickets for the Knicks. But I'm not talking just for a make-out session in the back bathroom like high schoolers. No, it has to be panty-dropping, meet-my-friends, fall for you hook, line, and sinker."

"Oh shit! You know he never would've been able to say no to that. How many nights did he practice three-pointers and try to dunk on you pretending he was John Starks?" Ben lets out a slow whistle, loud enough to be heard over the music in the crowded bar, and if I wasn't so shocked, I'd probably mirror his reaction.

Still laughing, Ben slaps my shoulder. "I have to head back to the office, but it's great to have you back in town, my man." He raises a chin to Ryan then leans his head toward me. "Try to keep him out of trouble."

After Ben leaves, I decide to play it cool and feign indifference. "That would've been a decent payoff, sure, but Knicks tickets don't need to be on the line to prove I still got it."

Ryan leans back and crosses his arms, sights set on the front door. When it opens, he waggles his eyebrows at me. I scrub my hands down my face, afraid to look.

I must be owed a favor from a past life because when I look up, a brown-haired beauty walks in and my body immediately responds.

Deep within my stomach, desire dusts itself off and stirs to life. *Jesus, Matt, cool it,* but it's the first time in a long time I remember feeling such raw, instant attraction. I notice her bright green eyes from across the room, and when she smiles at whatever her friend has said to catch her attention, they light up like sparklers on the Fourth of July. She smirks and bites her bottom lip, and I immediately imagine what it would feel like to suck on it. I watch as she winds through the crowded tables. Simultaneously, my breath stops and my cock swells... She is absolutely mesmerizing.

Like I said earlier, it's been a while, but that's nothing Ryan needs to know. He's been trying to help me get back in the game for a while. And yeah, there have been a few women, but it always felt like I was just going through the motions. No real spark. No exciting connection. But just looking at this woman has completely thrown me off balance.

For the next thirty minutes, I can't take my eyes off of her. She's focused on her friends, and much to my dismay, unaware of anyone else. I know I'm staring but I can't look away, hoping at some point I'll get another glance of those emerald eyes.

More than once, one of her friends catches me. When one of said friends has finally had enough, she slaps her hands on the table, stands up, and starts walking our way. Before I know it, she's leaning into me, finger pointed directly into my chest, and while I try to mask it, I'm grinning big at the turn my night has taken.

"Listen, Blue Eyes, either man up and come talk to my friend or stop salivating at her like a dog whose too-short chain is keeping him from reaching a T-Bone." Pausing, she lifts her chin in a challenge for me to deny it. "Her name is Emily, and you will never find a better person with a bigger heart. So grow a pair already, but remember that if you crush her, I'll crush you." Turning to Ryan, she purrs, "Now *you* can salivate at me all you want, big guy." With a wink at my brother, she turns around, and I swear I see a tornado funnel in her wake.

Ryan's eyes are wide and his shoulders are shaking as he tries to stifle his shock and, more likely, awe. "Forget any bets on my end, but it looks like you have to do something now. I wouldn't want to get on her bad side." He tilts his head toward our new friend—surely she's a friend after that smack-down, right?—and grins mischievously. "Plus, I think we're overdue for a game of Davis Doubles."

I place my glass on the table next to us and blow out a breath before walking over to them. Nerves ricochet in my gut and I pray I don't crash and burn. A jolt zaps through me when she grabs my hand. "Lead the way," she says, smiling up at me. "Let's kick some ass."

I am the awkward middle-schooler leading the hot cheerleader to the gym floor for a slow dance, silently praying my hands aren't sweating while wondering where the fuck my mojo went. The current game is finishing, so we have a few minutes to get better acquainted. She hops up on a stool and focuses on the weather warning flashing across the TV screen, currently interrupting the Knicks game. I order a fresh beer and once I have it, I take the opportunity to study her behind the rim of my glass.

She was striking from across the bar, but up close, she radiates an energy that magnetically draws me in. Her sweater highlights the gold specs in her deep green eyes and the lightest sprinkle of freckles dust her nose. If I had to guess, I'd say she was wearing maybe just the slightest bit of gloss on her full lips. She's a natural beauty and she's taking my breath away.

Stella was a big fan of blood-red lipstick that tasted like chalk whenever I kissed her. She was tall, thin, and cold. Emily is petite and curvy in all the right places, and my pulse picks up thinking about her thighs wrapped around my waist. My hand swallowed hers when I grabbed it earlier, and the instinct to protect her immediately flared. *Wow, that escalated quickly.*

"Ugh! It's like they don't know what a rebound is," Emily yells, pointing at the TV and effectively snapping me from my thoughts. Between Ryan egging me on and Josie's lecture, I worry for a split second that I'm in over my head. Now that we're only an arm's length away, the chemistry I'd been feeling since she blew through the door only intensifies. My fingers are itching to run through her hair and brush it back from her face. *Get a fucking grip, you amateur.*

I clear my throat, but my voice comes out hoarse anyway. "So, Emily, on a scale of *Never picked up a stick* to *Pool shark*, where do you stand?"

"I've played around with some sticks and balls in my time," she jokes, demurely batting her eyelashes and biting her bottom lip. Yeah, she knows exactly what she's doing. I stare at that bottom lip and wonder if I would taste the salt from her margarita if I kissed her. I'm picking up the faintest trace of coconut and I find myself inhaling a little too deeply when she stands up from the stool.

"Just remember: stroke it, don't poke it." I wink at her, finally finding my mojo and reprimanding it for falling asleep at the wheel. A blush creeps up her cheeks as she walks toward the cue rack mounted to the wall and—fuck me, I'm hard just thinking about how many other ways I could get that blush going.

"Oh, is *that* how it's done?" She widens her eyes, play-acting the saucy ingenue like an Oscar-nominated actress. She grabs a stick from the wall and starts chalking the tip. "Maybe you can show me. You know, to make sure I don't mess up."

I seriously want to kick my own ass at how much she's affecting me. You'd never guess it was sixteen degrees outside with the beads of sweat gathering at my hairline. She holds up her cue and tilts her head, beckoning me to the table.

I lightly chalk my own and then start my mini lesson. "The key is to stay relaxed and keep a loose grip on the stick. You never want to grab too tightly, or you won't have room to move back and forth." I lean over the table and demonstrate.

Emily bites back a smile and her eyes sparkle. "Okay, so tight grip, bad. Room to move back and forth, good."

I smile back at her. "Exactly."

I motion for her to lean against the table to set up for her shot as I walk up behind her, placing my hands lightly on her hips. "You want to hinge at the hips so your weight is in your legs and feet, not your arms."

"Like this?" She grins over her shoulder and pushes her ass right into my crotch. For the love of all things holy, this woman is something else.

I lean over her, placing my hands over hers, and take a minute to note how soft her hair is against my cheek. She stills, and I hear her take a quick inhale as our bodies line up. We don't move for what feels like an hour, but in reality is probably only a second or two.

"Your streak dies tonight, little brother. Prepare to go down!" Ryan bellows as he and Josie approach the table. I jump back and notice the tension in Emily's shoulders when I do. Ryan, oblivious to the moment he just interrupted, grips Josie's waist and pulls her close to his side as she leans in to hear him over the noise of the bar. She throws her head back and laughs, playfully swatting his shoulder.

He makes a beeline for Emily, who is now leaning against the wall. I can't tell whether she's breathing heavily or if I'm just hyperaware of the rise and fall of her chest. "Don't let his dimples distract you, sweet pea. He's a wolf in sheep's clothing, and he sucks at pool."

Emily raises her eyebrows and looks up at him with faux indignation, not letting his six-two frame ruffle her feathers. "Actions speak louder than words, Lumberjack. Rack 'em and let the best team win."

I laugh out loud at her taunt as Emily, aka my new favorite person in the world, comes around the table next to me. Putting her hand on my shoulder and standing on tippy toes, her breath tickles my ear as she whispers, "I grew up playing pool at my uncle's bar every afternoon after school. We got this."

I'm left speechless as she squeezes my shoulder and walks to stand next to Josie. When I was warned off hurting this girl, she was made to seem fragile, almost naive. This Emily who is flirting and talking trash? Yeah, she's nothing but confident. And if I'm not mistaken, she's also about to hustle my brother.

CHAPTER 3

EMILY

I focus on Ryan racking the balls, distracting myself from the fact that touching Matt made my entire body tingle. I haven't felt this light in a long time. Hearing myself flirt is an out-of-body experience, each word out of my mouth more brazen than the last.

Matt's blue eyes and dark lashes that would be the envy of any cover model definitely help to draw me out, not to mention the fact that he does indeed smell as good as he looks. It's a mix of driftwood and soap, fresh and clean. He's got that subtle charisma that makes me want to know more.

He's shorter than his brother by a few inches and not as built—which is a plus in my book, because at five-two, anyone over a foot taller than me doesn't fit right. Where Ryan is all brawn and biceps and clearly spends a lot of time in the gym, Matt has the body of a soccer player—muscular, but in a less in-your-face sort of way. He's comfortable in his skin, and for damn good reason.

Josie wanders over to me and whispers, "You can cut the tension between the two of you with a spork. You need to tap that tonight."

I roll my eyes, trying to calm the triple back handspring my stomach does at the mere thought of something happening with Matt. "Josie, we're playing a friendly game of pool. There will be no *tapping* unless you count you and the lumberjack tapping out when we kick your butt. You'll be getting the action tonight. He can't stop undressing you with his eyes."

Josie looks down at me and winks. "You know I'm going after that. He's so my type, even if he's drinking watermelon beer." She lifts her shoulders and holds her hands up in surrender before joining Ryan again.

I shake my head and laugh. I wish I had a fraction of Josie's confidence. I used to, but that girl hasn't been around for a while.

The crack of the balls from Ryan's break draws my attention. *Right*, I tell myself, *I need to get my head in the game*. I have one final weekend before it's time to hunker down, and while Matt is a recipe for disrupting said focus, he looks positively delicious for a one-night-only tasting menu. I can do this. Hell, after months with only battery-operated company in my bed, a warm, breathing body would be a nice treat, even if it's only a temporary one.

Ryan sinks the three-ball on his break, and then easily pockets the five-ball. He's good, I'll give him that. This is going to be fun.

"Oh, I think I get it." I look up, wide-eyed and enthusiastic.

"You shoot in order of the rainbow, right? So next is the yellow ball?" Matt chokes on his beer and hides his grin behind his palm. He's already enjoying this, and I'm just getting started.

"No, sweet pea, that's not how it goes." I can almost see Ryan's chest puff out as he starts to innocently mansplain the way of billiards. "We're *solids*, so we'll try for all the full-colored balls, and you and Matty are stripes. If I miss, then you'll get a chance to hit." Ryan drops the two-ball in on a bank shot, but then misses his next attempt. He looks at Matt with a shrug. "You're up."

Not moving from his stool, he says, "Ladies first," and looks in my direction with a grin that sends a shiver down my spine. Ryan's eyebrows hit the ceiling, clearly confused that Matt is risking bragging rights.

I excessively chalk up my cue and study the table. "So I definitely don't go for green, right?" Ryan looks at Matt as if to say, *Is this chick serious?* and patiently repeats his instructions that I'm supposed to be aiming for the striped balls. I lean over and gently tap the nine-ball, sinking it into a corner pocket.

"Yay!" I jump up and run to Matt, slapping his raised hand for a high-five. Ryan looks surprised and mumbles something about beginner's luck. I hand my cue to Matt. "Your turn!" I say, and this time he's unable to hide his laugh.

"No, sweetie, you get to go again since you made it."

"Oh, okay." I giggle. On the next shot, I sink the twelve- and fifteen-balls in quick succession. At this point, Ryan starts to get a little suspicious, looking back and forth between Matt and me. Without saying a word, I knock in three more balls back-to-back. Ryan leans his head back and groans, realizing he's getting played.

The ten-ball is the last of the stripes and I sink it, leaving just the shiny black eight-ball for the win. I call the side pocket. It's a beautiful drop shot, and the next thing I know, Matt is lifting me off the floor and swinging me around.

"Respect, sweet pea, respect." Ryan is there to fist-bump me as my feet hit the ground. "There's a lot of power in that little body, huh?"

Matt moves behind me and settles his hands on my waist. I lean back and he tightens his grip. "Hey, Ryan, you were always better at spelling than me. Remind me, how do you spell hustled?"

For all his bravado, Ryan is a good sport, his spirits also being lifted by Josie draped all over him, making sure he isn't too disappointed. We're all laughing like old friends—sickeningly *coupley* friends—when the waitress comes over to ask if we need refills.

"We'll take two margaritas," I say, pointing between Josie and me. "He'll have another IPA?" I ask, turning my head to look back at Matt. When he nods, I continue, "And one watermelon beer for my girlfriend over here," I say, pointing at Ryan.

Matt barks out a laugh and pulls me in even tighter. "This one's a keeper," he says, laughing at his brother's expense, his breath warm against my ear.

One-night-only tasting menu, Emily. One night only.

Drinks in hand, we grab a high-top and stools near the pool table. Two more games and another round of drinks later, Ryan and Josie are failing miserably at keeping their hands to themselves. When they stand and start gathering coats and bags, my stomach drops. I'm not ready for the night to end and immediately feel disappointed, wondering if Matt's also ready to call it.

I stay seated and focus above their heads, concentrating on the SportsCenter closed captioning like it holds the secret to life's greatest mysteries in a lame attempt to stall. He's casually talking to Ryan about their dinner plans tomorrow night and not making any move to leave. I'm paralyzed with awkward indecision about what I should do, not wanting to seem desperate but also more than interested in staying back with him.

Matt finally turns toward me. "Up for another round?" he asks, arching an eyebrow.

All eyes are on me as they wait for my response. I nod. "But just a club soda." I'm just enough buzzed and want to keep my wits about me. Josie launches into mama-bear mode.

"You"—she points at Matt—"make sure she gets home okay." She turns to face Ryan. "We can trust him, right?"

Ryan slides his arm around Josie's shoulder. "I'd trust Matty with my life, and yours too."

She considers this as she stares him down. "Fine. But, Em, I want a text as soon as you're home." Then she looks at Ryan and says, "Let's go, big guy, you're walking me home."

"As you wish," Ryan says, bowing his head. Josie looks at me and winks.

"So, Matthew."

He visibly stiffens. "Matt, not Matthew. Matty even, but never Matthew."

"Okay, *Matty*, then. What's your story?"

"Hmm... let's see." He looks up, and I try not to salivate as he pulls his lip between his teeth. "I just turned thirty-four, I'm an Aquarius, I don't like piña coladas but I'm okay getting caught in the rain." His eyes crinkle, and there come those dimples again.

"And you love long walks on the beach?" I add with a smirk.

"Definitely enjoy long walks on the beach," he answers, his eyes darkening.

I shake my head in jest. "The real story, please."

"Okay, okay. My story... I have an older brother, who you just hustled—totally awesome, by the way. We grew up outside New York City. My dad worked all the time, my mom stayed home. I played lacrosse at Northwestern, stayed in Chicago after school, and just moved home last week. Pretty cookie-cutter."

He says it with a small smile, but I sense some tension underneath the breezy description. I know the game of glossing over the heavier parts, but I don't want to ruin the vibe, so I don't push for more.

"And you, Goldie?" he asks as he rubs my sleeve between his fingers, "Besides being an undercover pool professional?" he asks.

I chuckle at his question. "I don't know if I'd go that far."

"I would. That was an impressive show. But the real story please." Matt gives me a teasing look, throwing my words right back at me.

"I'm thirty. Only child. Grew up in a small town upstate. My parents split up when I was young, so it was mostly just me and my mom after that. Lamented for many years that I was a mere Muggle. Went to college locally and couldn't wait to move here when I graduated. I watched one too many rom-coms glamorizing big-city life, so it was impossible to stay away."

He quirks an eyebrow. "Muggle?"

"Yeah, I was pretty introverted growing up and spent many nights escaping to Hogwarts, wishing I was at least a Half-Blood."

Matt lets out a soft chuckle and scratches the back of his neck, which causes his shirt to tighten around his bicep. Not that I'm noticing or anything.

I sit up a bit straighter. "Are you a fan?

"Guilty." His hand drops to the table and I follow the movement, watching his fingers tap excitedly on the wood surface. He has great hands. Big hands. Long fingers and neatly trimmed nails. As I stare at them, tempted, I let my mind wander, thinking about what he could do with them. My skin tingles imagining them exploring my body. He picks up his beer, snapping me back to attention.

"I've read the full series a few times. It was an escape for me too." He tilts his head, rubbing his jaw and studying me. "Let me guess..." He pauses to think for a few moments. "You're a Hufflepuff. Loyal, hardworking, patient. I'd say fair, but seeing how you just schooled my brother, I'm not sure about that one. But yeah, definitely a Hufflepuff."

I purse my lips and nod. "Loud and proud." His blue eyes are playful, flirty. He's easy to talk to. Charming. Carefree. *Distracting.* For the second time in minutes, my thoughts wander into dangerous territory. I take the opportunity to examine him closely under the guise of guessing his Hogwarts House, shaking my head in mock disappointment. "You're too easy—total Gryffindor. Brave, courageous, loyal."

He leans in, and the hairs on my neck stand at his closeness. His lips graze the top of my cheek as he whispers in my ear, "Don't forget chivalrous too." Of course, this captivating, confident man wouldn't be anything else. My heart pounds beneath my too-hot sweater and I wonder if he can hear it.

The bar is starting to empty out a bit and the music's slowing down. The first few bluesy notes of Chris Stapleton's version of "Tennessee Whiskey" comes on, and Matt stands and holds out his hand for the second time tonight.

"Dance with me."

I stand and place my hand in his, and this time it's shaking slightly from the intensity in his darkening eyes. He leads me to the makeshift dance floor and drops his hands on either side of my waist. We start to sway to the music, my arms settled on the grooves of his shoulders, and it occurs to me how perfectly molded we are like this. Heat courses through my body while I stare at the buttons on his shirt, not trusting myself to look up. *Inhale, exhale. Stop acting like you've never been kissed before.*

I lock my hands around his neck and plead with my nerves to relax. Matt, apparently having none of these anxious thoughts, tips my chin up and splays his palm flush with my neck. His Adam's apple bobs with a deep swallow, the only indication that maybe he's feeling a little shaken too, but he just continues to stroke my jaw with his thumb.

I hang my head back and raise my eyes to his mouth. He takes it as his cue to run his hands through my hair, stroking it away from my face. For those few moments, I feel adored. He parts his lips and gently skims his fingertips down my jaw, almost like he's afraid to break me.

Matt's eyes never leave mine as we let the music guide us, swaying side to side. He's in no rush, letting the moment settle, and it feels like the slow climb of a roller coaster to its first big drop. Nervous anticipation has me restless, and my hands wander from his neck across his sculpted shoulders and down his lean back, tracing every curve and loving the way he tenses when I reach his sides. I watch his eyes transition from a clear blue to a deep dark gray as his pupils dilate like the shift of the sky when an unexpected storm rolls in. I finally look down to his lips and let myself wonder what they would taste like.

Ever so slowly, he leans closer, stopping a few inches from my mouth, giving me a moment to pull away if this isn't what I want.

"This okay?" he asks softly.

I brace myself and nod once before he dives in, brushing his lips over mine in a featherlight kiss. When I lean ever so slightly toward them, he responds by framing my face with his hands and deepening the kiss. All self-control crumbles as his tongue traces my lips, teasing them open. He tastes like the orange slice from his beer, and it makes me wonder why I haven't been eating oranges every day of my life. His other hand trails down my back, landing on my waist and pulling me closer to him. I can't remember the last time I was held like this as strong arms tenderly embrace me. I feel his arousal against my stomach and a faint whimper escapes me. Surrounded by his smell, his taste, and the heat of his body, I subconsciously register that we're still in the middle of Smith's Cave, but I'm incapable of pulling away. Any sense of propriety has evaporated. I move closer, wanting to be connected to him at every possible point—*needing* to be.

Matt groans as his tongue teases mine, stroking and retreating, and he tilts my head for better access. My hands stroke up and down his back as I stand on my toes, pushing into him, melding our bodies together. I have never been kissed like this before, and I definitely don't want it to stop.

CHAPTER 4

MATT

I don't know how long we stay like this, slowly moving to the music. The more we kiss, the more I need to taste her; the more our hands stroke, the deeper I want to feel her skin on mine. Not since the early days of dating Stella have I felt such a visceral attraction to someone, and even then, I don't remember it taking me down like this. Her touch ignites a fire inside me, and all I want is *more more more*, but I know that won't happen standing in the middle of the bar.

I painstakingly tear my mouth away from hers, panting like I just sprinted to catch a closing train door. Her hypnotic green eyes bore into mine and her breath is uneven, letting me imagine she's feeling the same connection as I am. I can't allow myself to imagine anything else.

"Hi." I look down and twirl a piece of her hair around my finger.

"Hi, back." She smiles wide.

I lightly kiss the corner of her mouth and drag my nose from her temple to her ear. "Emily, I don't want to be too presumptuous, but I'm nowhere near ready to say goodnight. I live a few blocks from here, and I'd really like for you to come over. No expectations... I just want to keep hanging out. There's a ton of boxes, but the couch and TV are set up." *And the bed*, I think as my stomach tenses, waiting for her response.

A blush runs across Emily's face as she takes a small step back, her hands falling slack at my waist and her shoes circling in the sawdust on the floor. Her thoughts are moving at warp speed, that much is clear, before she finally sighs deeply.

"Hey—" I tilt her chin up to properly see her. "Care to share what's going on in that pretty little head of yours?"

A flurry of emotions scatter across her face—desire, hesitation, uncertainty—battling to convince her what to choose. "It's the age-old battle of *want* versus *should*. I want to go to your place with you, but I *should* go home." She rolls her eyes. "I have a huge career opportunity coming up, and I can't really afford any distractions."

I laugh, but not mockingly. Nodding, I tell her I understand. "I get it. I start a new job on Monday and should be unpacking and preparing for that. But I haven't enjoyed myself this much in a really long time. Can we live in the bubble for a little longer—no work talk, no 'should' talk—and just see what happens?"

Emily squints her eyes and I see the last bit of her resolve softening. "How do I know you're not a secret serial killer or something?"

"You don't, but I understand where you're coming from." He tucks the hair he's been twirling behind my ear. "Do you want to text Josie my address and send her a picture of my license?"

She taps her bottom lip. "That's not such a bad idea… I'll think about it." Still, she doesn't move. I hold my breath, feeling my stomach clench in anticipation. "Okay. Bubble it is." She steps back and holds out a hand to shake on it. I exhale, grinning as I shake her hand. She lets out a happy little squeal when I pull her toward me and capture her sweet mouth in another kiss. This kiss is hungrier than our earlier ones, my fingers sliding through her silky strands, and I groan as I pull away, wanting to get her anywhere but here.

Her hand clasped in mine, I lead us back to the table with all our stuff. Emily's quick to zip up her coat and put on a bright pink hat with an oversized pom-pom flopping around on top. The woman is full of contradictions. A few moments ago, she was sexy and passionate, and yet here, all bundled up, she looks perfectly sweet and innocent.

My breath catches as we step outside. The snow is coming down harder now, a few inches piling on the sidewalk and making it a little trickier to navigate. The streets are peaceful with the flakes muffling the chatter coming from those who, like us, aren't ready to call it a night. Rarely do these moments exist in the city. Manhattan looks magical, like a real-life snow globe.

Lit up by the glow of street lamps, the clean, crisp snow falling like weightless fluff you could trust-fall into and not feel a thing. The brownstones lining the streets are mostly dark, and the tree branches are glistening with ice, like nature's disco ball lighting up the night. If not for the wind, it would be quite the romantic stroll.

But as we walk against it, it bites and blows, forcing us to tuck ourselves into our coats and making it impossible to have a conversation. I squeeze her hand now, mirroring the tightness I feel in my stomach at the possibility of her in my bed tonight, even if just for more of those drugging kisses. She looks up, smiling, and I wonder if she's thinking the same.

It's not long before we get to my place, which could in part be from the eager pace I set. We rush through the revolving doors, stomping the snow off our boots as soon as we're inside.

We half run, half walk down the hall, grinning at each other, and I open my apartment door in record speed. My cheeks hurt from smiling so much tonight. It's a foreign feeling, but man, it feels good to just be completely present—and totally happy—in the moment. As soon as the door's shut, I push her against it, kissing her relentlessly, teasing her lips with my tongue and cradling her face in my hands, craving skin-to-skin contact.

Emily's right there with me, working through the buttons of my shirt and pushing it off me with lightning speed, letting her nails skate across my skin. Desire intensified by her touch, I grab her ass and hoist her legs around my waist, walking us to the couch and slowly laying her down. I throw the back cushions and throw pillows to the floor, giving us more space, then stand there with my hands on my hips, chest heaving as I force myself to catch a breath. I silently thank the Pottery Barn associate who convinced me I needed this couch-turned-twin bed. I climb over her, bracing my weight on my arms next to her head.

Her eyes meet mine as she smiles up at me. There's no more hesitation now that she's made her decision. Something deep in me stirs at just how happy *she* looks, knowing I had something to do with it. That possessive feeling from earlier in the night creeps back in, and I feel a strong urge to be the person who gets to claim and protect her.

She closes her eyes and pushes her hips up to meet mine. Back in the moment and more ready than ever to take what she's offering, I nibble my way from her lips to her ear and kiss the shell down to earlobe, playfully nipping at it. Her hands are all over my back and in my hair as she keeps pressing up into me. My lips never leave her soft skin, trailing from her ear, down her jaw, across her neck. My tongue traces her collarbone, swirling in the hollow of her neck, and I lick the supple space between her breasts, following the path of her V-neck sweater.

Yeah, this is nice, but it's going to have to go.

I work at inching it up and over her, then pause to stare at her chest. My breath catches at her perfect handfuls, lush and spilling over the top of her pale pink lace bra. She braces herself on her elbows, and I lower my mouth, teasing her taut nipples through the lace.

"You still with me, Goldie?"

Her eyes twinkle at the nickname while she shyly bites her bottom lip. "Yes." She arches up even more, giving me room to stretch my hand underneath her to unclasp her bra and pull it down her arms.

"Fuck, yeah," I feel my grin stretch. "But remember, you're in control. If you want to stop, we stop."

She brushes the hair off my forehead. I close my eyes and press into her fingertips. I like her touching me like this. "I know."

Chest to chest with nothing between us, our lips and hands are everywhere. Emily's moving her hips so seductively underneath me that the past few months of my self-imposed celibacy rears its ugly head, threatening to send me over the edge before I've managed to work through what I plan on doing with her... to her. My cock is straining against my jeans, and Emily's writhing beneath me is not helping in the slightest.

Slow your roll, Matt.

I start to recite the alphabet backward in a desperate attempt to gain some control.

Meanwhile, Emily's in a zone of her own. She rocks against me, eyes closed and head dropped back, a look of pure bliss on her face. I welcome the opening and suck on her neck, wanting to leave my mark on her. Her knees tighten around my hips and her hands grab at my waist to guide my movements, chasing the friction. I follow her lead, rocking back and forth, watching her abandon any inhibitions as she takes what she wants. She's so fucking beautiful as she directs me through ragged breaths. *"Yes, right there. Please, don't stop."*

I feel her grip even tighter around me as her back bows, yelling out as I feel her crash around me. I can't remember ever being this turned on, and I'm helpless to control myself, watching her lips part, body quivering, face and neck flushed...

Yeah, the alphabet can go fuck itself.

My cock is so hard I can almost hear it throbbing. I thrust against her, starting to feel pressure building from my legs and racing up my spine. As she comes down from her high, I move against her one more time and see stars as heat bursts out to my limbs. And then, hand splayed against her waist for support, I bury my face into her neck and collapse against her as I explode.

Several deep breaths later, my thoughts catch up to my brain and I turn my face to press an open-mouthed kiss to the patch of skin beneath her ear. My face flushes for a whole new reason.

Oh my God. Did I really just dry hump her like the 40-year-old virgin?

Mortified, I bite my lip and try to stifle a horrified laugh. I feel Emily's chest rock with giggles as she runs her fingers through my hair. Within seconds, we both burst out into full-blown laughter. I turn and lean against the back of the couch, my arms locked around her waist, and wonder how, in just a few hours, this woman has managed to completely bewitch me.

CHAPTER 5

EMILY

Matt's face is bright red, and I'm not sure if it's from exertion or embarrassment, but I'm right there with both emotions myself. I'm shocked at how freely I lost control under him, but also amazed at how safe I felt. *It's just the margaritas, don't go overthinking anything.*

I turn to look at him. His eyes are closed and his dimples are on full display, thanks to his sheepish smile. *God, this guy is gorgeous.* I lazily run my fingers through his soft wavy hair, and when he opens his piercing blue eyes to look at me, I lose all function over my breathing. And this is just my reaction to his face. His forearms were enough to turn me on, but he is pure lean muscle everywhere, down to his washboard abs.

"So, um, yeah..." He scrubs his hands down his face. "That hasn't happened to me since I made out with Jenny O'Leary in her basement sophomore year."

"Ah, that Jenny, she was such a temptress." A boyish grin appears as I continue to run my fingers through his hair. "Sophomore year of high school, right?"

He laughs as he moves over me again, bracketing his arms around me. I'm wrapped by the scent of ocean air, and I tug his shirt to bring him just a little closer. "So pretty and such a sassy mouth," he whispers, leaning down to press light kisses on my lips, nose dragging down to my jaw, lingering over every sensitive part like he's savoring me.

Greg never took his time like this. He'd lose patience and blame me for my body not being responsive, saying I was at fault, that I had issues. I researched how to have an orgasm like a dissertation. As time passed, I got more and more tense in bed, and Greg got more and more frustrated. That translated to us hardly ever having sex toward the end, even when I'd try to initiate it. He was quick to rebuff me. I felt broken, defective, and it would get worse whenever I tried to fix it—fix *myself*. I felt inadequate and undesirable, and finding Greg cheating on me was just the cherry on top, solidifying those feelings and locking them in a keyless safe. That's when I really started to throw myself into my work, piling on the projects to numb the pain, and hiding from the possibility of further rejection.

But my body needed no time at all to get turned on by Matt, as it just proved. There was no thinking, no strategizing or worrying if he was enjoying it, because his touch, his sounds... They mirrored all of mine.

"I bet you had a lot of girlfriends in high school. Let me

guess—prom king, football captain, most likely to succeed… Am I on the right track?"

Matt rolls onto his back and hums, eyes on the ceiling. He combs his fingers through his hair and says, "Prom king, no, but lacrosse captain, yes." He looks over at me to gauge my reaction. I circle my hands for him to keep going.

He lets out a heavy sigh. "Listen, I worked hard at everything I did. Despite some people thinking otherwise, I earned everything I achieved. I was lucky that I didn't need to live in the library, but I put in time studying. I loved sports, so I was always training or working out. I took nothing for granted and tried to pay it forward as much as possible. I loved coaching the younger kids, giving them tips and extra attention after practice. Ryan was two years ahead of me and *he* was the prom king, the big man on campus, so my social life was great by default.

"But no girlfriend? That seems hard to believe."

"I hooked up a bit, but I was so focused on lacrosse that I didn't want a girlfriend. I ended up with one senior year, but we fizzled after graduation and haven't spoken since. I think she's married with twins now."

I turn on my side to face him. "Clearly you've kept up your workout regime," I joke, squeezing his bicep and trailing my fingers down his arm.

Matt shakes his head as he leans in to kiss me. Within minutes, we're both breathing heavy. Pulling back, I run my fingers over his stubble. I'm trying to soak in everything I can, knowing it'll have to sustain me for the foreseeable future.

Sure, I've dated a bit here and there since Greg left, but it's been easy to avoid sex because no one's held my interest for more than a few drinks. Nothing like this. Matt feels dangerous in that way. From the minute he introduced himself, it was all instinct, wanting to be near him, hoping he would touch me, needing him closer. It's like he's a charge I've been missing, a current I needed to get my stagnant heart beating again.

Seriously, Emily? Ease up there, Jane Austen.

A loud honk from a snow plow startles us. The sky is pitch-black except for the faded glow from the streetlights below. Matt shifts and sits up, looking outside. "The snow is really starting to come down." He gets up and heads for the window, leaning a palm against the frame. "It's so strange to see only a few cars out." His body silhouetted against the window is a sight of its own as he turns around, and the light casts shadows over the deep V melting into his unbuttoned jeans. He walks over and gives me a soft kiss.

"I'll be right back. Don't go anywhere."

As if he has anything to worry about in that regard. Given that it's close to 3:00 a.m., I'm not sure if I could even catch a cab right now, especially with the snow still coming down. Plus, contrary to all rational thinking, I don't want to go. Matt's apartment may be filled with boxes, but it already feels lived in, homey. Most of his furniture is set up—small high-top dining table, desk in the corner of the living room, flat-screen TV mounted above a dark pine entertainment center. There's a coziness to it, especially the deep-cushioned navy-blue couch I'm lying on, so I grab a throw blanket from the oversized lounge to my right and drape it over myself. Matt emerges from his bedroom in blue plaid pajama pants and a light gray T-shirt that molds to his chiseled chest. *How is it legal for someone to look so good in pajamas?* He comes over to the couch and sits beside me, brushing my hair from my face with light fingers, exactly how he did at the bar. I forgot how good physical contact could feel, and it hits me how long I've gone without it.

"Hi."

I smile and snuggle into the blanket.

"Hi, yourself."

"I don't think you'll have much luck getting an Uber in this weather. Why don't you stay and we can figure it out in the morning?"

The want versus should battle rages briefly but is resolved much quicker than before. "Okay," I agree, pulling the blanket tighter around me.

Matt stands up and holds out his hand. "My bed is a lot more comfortable, come on."

Immediately, my mind goes into overdrive on the short walk to his bedroom. *Shit, am I really doing this? When was the last time I shaved my legs?*

Two seconds later, we're facing each other in his room, next to his very big bed. It smells like Matt as I peruse the room and take a deep inhale. Masculine. Fresh. His bed is perfectly made, a navy-blue duvet pulled tight on both sides. There's a nightstand with a phone charger, lamp, and a stack of hardcover books with a pair of black-framed glasses on top. I internally groan. In my book, glasses are a very close second to forearms.

He drops my hand and looks at me. He's fidgeting and scraping his hand through his hair. "So, I had a lot of fun tonight. I hope you did too." I nod, uncertain where he's going with this and wondering why he seems uneasy all of a sudden. He rubs down the back of his neck. "I want you to know that I don't expect anything else to happen just because you're staying. We don't have to do anything else, or anything you don't want to do. I mean, unless you *want* to do something, and then I would be totally fine with that too. More than fine." He drops his hand with a deep sigh.

I bite my lip to try to hide my smile. Does he realize this display of jitters is only making him infinitely more attractive? The push and pull between us feels so well-balanced. We're Yin and Yang, one of us confident while the other isn't, feeling secure when the other is wavering. It's uncanny, feeling so emotionally intertwined with someone like this, especially someone I just met.

I bite my bottom lip and nod while stifling a giggle, not wanting him to feel any more self-conscious. Matt slips away to grab a T-shirt from his dresser and hands it to me. I drop the blanket that's still wrapped around me and put it on, holding his gaze while I unbutton my jeans and slide them off, shivering once the cold air touches my skin.

"Come on, Goldie. Get in bed before you freeze to death." He folds the duvet back for me to slide in and comes up right behind me, bringing his body flush against mine. He gently nudges one arm under my neck, acting like a pillow, while his other hand settles across my stomach. He softly kisses the exposed spot between my neck and shoulder, and I snuggle in closer.

CHAPTER 6

MATT

It doesn't surprise me that she fits perfectly in my arms. I feel her melt into me as she drifts off to sleep, her breathing slowing down and evolving into tiny snores. Warmth wraps through my chest knowing she feels safe and comfortable enough to sleep so deeply in my arms.

I wish I could sleep like that, but my head's buzzing a mile a minute, replaying how I ended up here with Emily. Meeting someone was the last thing on my mind when I met up with Ryan and Ben tonight, but I was powerless to resist her. Her eyes, her laugh, the softness she tries to cover up with sass. It's not innocence per se, but there's something fresh and good about her that grabbed me immediately.

And her body... She set me on fire. Feminine. Curvy. With silky skin that smells like lavender. The way she responded to me, the sounds she tried to swallow... It was the hottest experience of my life, and that's saying something considering most of our clothes stayed on.

Eventually, my eyes are too heavy to keep open, and it feels like I just fell asleep when an incessant buzzing wakes me. A slew of incoming texts from Ryan blow up my phone, asking if I got lucky. I run a hand down my face and type a message to say I'll call him later, then delete the texts so Emily won't see them. I'm glad I didn't take Ryan's bet. While the tickets would be awesome, I would've called it off after last night. She deserves way more than to be part of something so trivial.

As I'm putting my phone back on my nightstand, it hits me. *What the flying fuck is happening here?* Yesterday, the possibility of playoff tickets would've made my month, my *year*.

I guess this means I'm finally getting my shit together, doing what I need to do to move on. Now that I'm back in New York, I need to stick to my plan of getting in and out of my dad's company as quickly as possible. I'll work on figuring out what I'm doing with my life after that. This couldn't be worse timing. I don't need a love interest creeping into the equation, and I certainly don't need to be feeling this lightning bolt of attraction that's making me wonder when I can see her again even though she's lying right next to me.

I quietly climb out of bed and head to the kitchen to put some coffee on. The snow is still coming down and at least a foot is piled up on the parked cars below. There definitely won't be too much going on today, which is just fine with me.

I pour two mugs when the coffee's ready, add some milk, then search my cupboard for sugar, not knowing how Emily takes it.

I like this feeling of taking care of someone. Stella was always hyper-independent and would very rarely let me tend to her. In fact, she went out of her way to prove she didn't need a man around. From a young age, I always knew I wanted a wife and family. I'd carve my own path and make a point not to follow in my father's footsteps. No working all the time, no pressuring my kids to meet unrealistic expectations or cutting them down to try to make them tougher.

Emily stirs at the sound of the bedroom door creaking, a tiny moan coming out of her as she rolls to her back.

"Morning." I smile down at her as she arches up into a deep stretch.

"What time is it?" she asks.

"Around 10:30."

"Oh, wow. I haven't stayed in bed this late in a long time." She sighs as her arms land back on the bed.

"Did you sleep okay?" I ask as I put her coffee mug on the nightstand.

"I don't think I've slept that well in over a year."

"I believe it, between your snoring and the drool on my chest."

"What?" Emily's eyes fly open only for her to squeeze them shut again. "Please tell me you're joking."

I chuckle at her response and shake my head.

She pulls the comforter over her head and then peeks out. "Uh, um. Sorry?"

I gently pull the duvet down from her face, quietly laughing. "I had a lot of fun last night. I'm glad you stayed."

"Mmmm." Emily lets out another moan and closes her eyes as I sit on the bed next to her, leaning against the headboard. She's warm and sleep-mussed, and I hold my mug on my lap to camouflage how quickly my body reacts from simply seeing her in my bed.

"Do you drink coffee?" I ask, turning toward the nightstand to grab her cup.

"Is Hermione's favorite place the library?" She smirks and sits up next to me to take it. She reverently holds it between her hands and inhales deeply. "Is it still snowing?"

"Yeah, there's already at least a foot on the ground. It's supposed to let up mid-afternoon. I think the city that never sleeps is collectively hitting snooze."

She sips the coffee and sighs. She's beautiful in the morning light, wearing just my ratty Blackhawks T-shirt.

"That actually sounds perfect. It's nice to have the world stop for a few hours."

I nod in agreement. "Are you hungry? I was about to get breakfast going."

"Yeah, I didn't eat much last night. Breakfast sounds great."

I stand and go to my dresser, grabbing a pair of pajama pants and a hoodie and tossing them on the bed. "You're going to have to roll these up a bit, but at least you'll be warm. I'll be in the kitchen when you're ready."

I haven't done a full grocery haul yet, but thankfully I have enough basics to whip up some pancakes for breakfast. I put on some music and search for the cookware I'll need in the mess that's my half-unpacked kitchen. This is definitely not how I thought my Saturday would start but the snowstorm's suspended time and my stomach tugs realizing how content I am right now.

When she walks in to join me, I bark out a laugh. Emily is drowning in my clothes, looking more adorable than she did last night in her hat. The thought of her scent lingering on my clothes flashes through my mind and my smile widens before I quickly brush a hand over my mouth and remind myself to cool it.

She sits on a stool and looks around my apartment as I heat up the stove and melt some butter in a pan. There's a small box of frames in front of her on the island and she reaches over to grab the one off the top. It's a picture of Ryan and me in front of the Eiffel Tower.

She holds up the frame. "When was this?"

"Right after Ryan graduated law school. We took a few weeks and backpacked through France and Switzerland."

"Very romantic," she says with a hum.

I laugh. "Have you ever been to Paris?"

A dreamy look dances in her eyes when she says, "No, but it's actually the top thing on my bucket list." A smile lights up her face, crinkling the skin around her eyes. "My mom and I always talked about it, saying it would be our big adventure. We'd go to museums and eat croissants and go to the top of the Eiffel Tower at night. We could never afford it, so it was always a far-off dream, but one day I hope to make it there. My ex always laughed at me for it because he thought it was so cliché." Her shoulders fold in, and I wonder if she's aware she's made herself small at the mention of him.

"Well, he sounds like an ass. And he's wrong. Ryan and I loved it. It really is the most romantic place I've ever been."

"Are you and Ryan close?" she asks, hands still cuddling her mug. I like how she looks in my hoodie, in my kitchen, all cozy and cute.

"Yeah, we're pretty tight. Don't get me wrong, he was—and always will be—a jackass big brother to me, refusing to pass up any chance to call me out or egg me on. But he has a big heart, and he cares deeply."

I turn off the stove and bring the pancakes to the table. Emily sits down as I pour us both more coffee and grab the syrup and utensils.

"It's not Paris, but Bon Appetit, madam," I say as I bow my head and she giggles.

I shake my head as I sit. I wait for her to take a bite, watching her eyes flutter closed as she chews, and then dive into mine.

We fall into easy conversation about everything and nothing and it feels like this is something we do all the time. We finish eating, our bellies full, taking a moment to digest. The conversation lulls and then, Emily abruptly stands, takes our empty plates to the sink, and starts washing them before I can stop her.

I grab the syrup and put it back in the refrigerator before leaning against the counter to face her. "You don't have to do that."

She turns to me quickly, wet plate in her hand, inadvertently splashing soap suds on my face. "Oh shit!" she exclaims.

I look down, lifting the hem of my T-shirt to wipe my eyes, and she drops the plate in the sink. She raises her hand to wipe the drops off my face with the sleeve of my hoodie right as I turn my head and she hits my nose instead.

"Oy." I pull back and she jerks her hand back as if she burned my skin.

"Ugh, I'm sorry." Her face reddens as she clenches her hands together, avoiding eye contact.

I chuckle at the absurdity of our interaction. "What just happened?" I'm grinning as I continue to wipe my face.

She groans, hiding her face in her hands. "I don't know. I just got nervous all of a sudden. I mean, we're sharing secrets over pancakes while I'm still not positive you're not a serial killer." She looks at me through her fingers.

Moving toward her, I'm unable to hide my grin as I wrap my arms around her shoulders. She rests her forehead on my chest, still hiding from me. "I get it. It's a little strange to me too about how comfortable it feels between us." I rub her back for a few minutes and she looks up at me, her chin resting on my chest. I shrug my shoulders and pull her closer. Kissing the crown of her head, I tell her, "It's the benefit of living in the bubble."

She's smiling now, bright green eyes twinkling, and pressure spreads in my chest as she looks up at me. I rub my thumb along her bottom lip. I feel her cheeks heat as she ever so slightly opens her lips. Her tongue slips out, licking the pad of my finger, and I inhale a sharp breath, dipping it deeper in her mouth as she pins it between her teeth.

My voice is hoarse as I say her name and brush my lips against hers. She tastes like maple syrup, and I savor each stroke of her tongue against mine. Her hands slide down my chest and stop at my waist. She fists my T-shirt to pull me closer and stands on her toes to deepen the kiss. We finally pull back, breathing heavy.

"Hi."

"Hi back," she whispers.

A battle rages in my mind as we stand in my kitchen. I know she doesn't want anything because of work, and quite honestly, I should be thinking the same thing. But I don't want her to leave. Not yet. Maybe it's the snow, or maybe there's something to all this 'living in the bubble' talk, but I'm still not ready to say goodbye.

"I doubt there's too much going on today," I start as she links her hands behind my back. A tremor of nerves rolls through me. "I wouldn't mind staying inside the bubble a little while longer if you want to stay and watch a movie?" I turn to the sink to finish washing our dishes, feeling surprisingly vulnerable. I glance at Emily over my shoulder, trying hard to play it cool.

She pulls the sleeves of my hoodie over her hands, a small tell she may be nervous too. "Yeah, I can stay a little longer."

We settle on the couch, sitting close but with a slight awkward space between us. Yawning, I grab a blanket and drape it over us as we start a movie. Exhaustion from our late night wins out and the next thing I know, I'm opening my eyes to the scrolling end credits and Emily's sleeping head on my chest, our legs intertwined, and... my heart full. I rub my eyes with my palms and expel a loaded breath.

It's been less than twenty-four hours, and this girl is already under my skin. *I'm so fucked.*

CHAPTER 7

EMILY

I try not to smile as the cab pulls away, but it's a lost cause. The snow eventually stopped and Matt had to meet Ryan and his mom for dinner, so I'm heading home for more couch time. I tell myself I'll allow the warm and fuzzy feelings for one more night, then squash them with tomorrow's sunrise.

My thoughts swirl and the buildings blur as we drive down Second Avenue. Manhattan is beautiful during a snowstorm, but the aftermath is less than stellar. Huge snowbanks line street corners and are already turning black, like the city opened its mouth and heaved a hacking, sooty cough. And yet, despite the dull and gray scene outside my foggy window, I can't stop smiling and shaking my head in silent laughter as I replay my night.

The cab drops me on Irving Place, one of my favorite blocks in the city. When I saw the listing for my apartment I knew a place in this neighborhood wouldn't last long on the market so we made an appointment to meet with the broker the next morning. As soon as we opened the door, I felt deep in my bones that it was meant for me. The broker told us he'd received close to fifty calls in just a few hours about this specific unit, and he didn't need to say anything more. In reality, I was sold before we even stepped foot in the entryway. I gave Greg my best puppy dog eyes and we left with an iron-clad two-year lease and a mutual assurance that we'd make the slightly higher-than-affordable rent work between the two of us.

Now, thirteen months later, Greg is out of the picture and I am barely managing to scrape by even with dipping into my savings and cashing out some of my 401k.

Along with our inflated lease, we'd had to put first, last, and an extra month of rent down for a security deposit. When he moved out, Greg said I could keep the security since I'm now funding the apartment, but that money won't be in my hands until the lease runs out. After months of covering it on my own, I know I can't make it through without a raise, and I'll lose that deposit if I break the lease. This Imperial pitch really couldn't have come at a better time.

I still resent Greg for everything he shattered—my dreams, my confidence, my bank account—but I'm reminded of how grateful I am for life's twisted games every time I step inside my cozy, quiet oasis where I can refuel and escape from the world.

Today though, everything feels just slightly dimmer as I go through the motions of collecting my mail and waiting for the elevator. *God, I sound pathetic.* It was one night—plus a sweet, snowed-in morning—with a random guy. Sure, he made me laugh and his kisses were mind-blowing, but seriously, this has to be the effect of reading one too many romance novels.

I put my mail down on my solid maple console table, toe off my slush-lined boots, and hang up my coat. The temperature dropped again during my trip home and the wind outside makes me grateful for my furry Ugg slippers I keep by my shoe stand.

My bra immediately comes off and I change into my flannel pants and a hoodie. I'm nestling under my favorite crocheted afghan when my phone lights up with a text.

Josie: Spill it, sister <eggplant emoji>

Lucy: We need details.

I chuckle and do a giddy little dance. I sent a thumbs-up message to the group chat this morning to let them know I was alive and well and to call off any search party they'd been planning, but I knew they'd be buzzing for the tea.

Me: <zipped lips emoji>

Josie: Shove it. I've been desperate for an update.

Me: You first, did Ryan poke you with his cue?

Josie: Ha-ha. Don't quit your day job. And don't deflect! This isn't about me.

Me: Eye for an eye...

Josie: <eye roll emoji>. Ugh, fine. He was a total gentleman. Walked me home, stayed for a little bit, and then went on his way. Very PG.

Me: I guess you really can't judge a book by its cover. Interesting.

Lucy: I think it's kind of nice he was a gentleman.

Josie: Anyway, Em, we're waiting.

Me: Let's just say Matt may not have been a total gentleman... in the best way possible. <wink emoji>

Josie: GOOD FOR YOU! Look at you getting some lovin'

Lucy: Yes!!

Me: Yeah, yeah. So now I'm exhausted, but it was fun. Lord knows when I'll come up for air next once this project kicks off. Brunch tomorrow?

Josie: You know it. Get some sleep and be prepared to share the juicy details<fist bump emoji>

I'm chuckling when I reach for the remote and hear my phone ping again. Shaking my head, I pick it up, expecting a funny meme from Josie.

Magic Matt: Hi!

Goosebumps prickle up my arm *When did he program his name in my phone?*

Me: Who dis?

Magic Matt: It's Matt.

Me: MAGIC Matt?

I may be rolling my eyes, but I'm giggling like a schoolgirl.

Magic Matt: At your service for all your needs <wink emoji>

Me: <eye roll emoji> Terrible <laughing emoji>

Magic Matt: Ryan was grilling me before my mom showed up. I revealed nothing, but apparently he and Josie had a good night.

Considering the information I just got from Josie, someone isn't telling the truth. I'd put my money on Ryan.

Me: She just blew up my phone too. How's dinner?

Magic Matt: Food is delicious, and while I love seeing my mom, I'd rather be back on my couch watching movies with you.

My chest tightens and I rub my fist against it.

Me: I wouldn't mind that.

Magic Matt: Music to my ears. Gotta go, just wanted to say hi.

Me: I'm glad you did. Have an extra dessert for me.

Magic Matt: Sleep well, Goldie.

I groan. *Talk about timing.* Matt is quickly getting under my skin, and I can't find it in me to mind. Truth be told, I know it isn't just because he gave me my first non-battery-operated orgasm in who knows how long. I mean, it was pretty spectacular, don't get me wrong, but he had my attention way before that. He's playful and fun, sweet, and sexy. He's exactly what I *don't* need in my life right now.

I'm finally starting to feel like myself again. I no longer wake up every morning with a pit in my stomach, wondering how my life has veered so far off track and scrambling to pick up the pieces. I have a new, perfectly predictable routine. I'm befriending this new version of Emily and learning her ins and outs. And now, in a matter of 24 hours, my life went from the straight and narrow to charged and unexpected. Matt offered an incredible night of no-frills fun, there's no doubt about that, but as I look around my apartment—the one I am determined to stay in—I force myself to accept that the fun can only last so long.

CHAPTER 8

EMILY

I wake up on the couch with an infomercial talking head shouting that I can get free shipping if I order in the next ten minutes. I remember my eyes getting heavy but don't remember falling asleep. I sit up and stretch, stiff from the couch and head to the kitchen for some much-needed coffee. It's no longer snowing and the bright sky is clear, but I'm a seasoned New Yorker at this point and know all about the bone-chilling cold and whipping wind that await me.

Mornings like this make me nostalgic for when I didn't live in solitude. I can honestly say I don't miss Greg, but I do miss the presence of *someone*. I miss being in a pair, the us-against-the-world feeling that hits particularly hard on winter mornings when you can snuggle deeper under the covers and have a warm body there to hold you. Thinking of Greg holds none of the gut-punch feelings it used to, which can only mean progress. The self-doubt is still potent though, which is another reason why I need to distance myself from Matt's heady presence. I'm not anti-love/relationship/coupledom or anything. I've seen it work for many of my friends and co-workers and I'm actually a bit of a hopeless romantic, as a glance at my bookshelves proves, but I just don't think it's in the cards for me anymore. I can flirt with the best of them, and I did have fun with Matt, but when the shine fades and *real* life creeps in, I'll once again be left gluing the pieces of my heart back together.

I take a big gulp of coffee and shift my thoughts to the week ahead as I dress for brunch. I have never been more ready for an assignment. I don't know much about the auto industry, but I do know this is an opportunity to try something different. It's time for car manufacturers to take women seriously. We all drive cars—well, everyone outside of the city. Imperial has broken so many barriers in the auto industry overall, and I'd love if they could break barriers for women too.

I pull on a pair of black leggings and my favorite oversized off-shoulder sweatshirt, then throw my hair up in a practiced bun, not even bothering to smooth my flyaways. Sunday brunch attire at its finest.

We're meeting at an old beat-up diner off Union Square. The girls have been great about accommodating my strict budget and are always happy to hunt for a more off-the-beaten-path (read: cheaper) spot with me. Josie and Lucy are already in a booth when I push the glass door open, and I take a deep breath, preparing myself for the grilling I'm sure to get.

"Sooooooo?" Lucy asks, grabbing on to my arm as soon as I sit down.

"Can you believe how cold it is? The snow will never melt!" I rub my hands together and blow hot air onto my fingertips.

"Nice try, not happening." Josie points at me and demands, "Talk."

"I don't know what you want to hear. We hung out after you guys ditched us. I went back to his place, we hooked up, and that was it." I wave to the waitress and ask for some coffee. I'm intentionally downplaying the night, because if Lucy and Josie catch on that I'm into Matt in any way, they won't leave it alone.

"Em, he is smoking hot and was clearly very into you. He seems really nice too... Why wouldn't you go for it?" Lucy asks, ever the cheerleader.

"Because you guys know what this promotion means for me. I can't let a guy distract me right now. He's hot, yes, and we had a lot of fun. But it was just a one-time, weekend thing. Plus, he just moved back to the city, which means he will most likely move on to the next cute girl he sees."

"Emily, we know Greg did a number on you." Lucy reaches over and circles my wrist. "But if you could only see yourself the way we do. Greg is the loser in the breakup, not you. I know it's not easy to bounce back, but you have to believe that."

"Thank you." I tap her hand, hoping she knows just how soothing her words are. "I promise to work on it for my homework." I take a deep, cleansing breath and shake my head. "Now can we please talk about something that I'm positive is juicier?"

I lean toward Josie and point my finger. "I think *you* have some explaining to do."

The waitress comes by with our coffees and takes our orders. I need to hear about Josie's night, given what she told us versus what it sounded like Ryan told Matt.

"Honestly, I thought Ryan would be a sure thing, but like I said, it was very PG. He took me home, stayed for a drink, and we only made it all the way to first base." Josie feigns irritation with an eye roll.

I laugh to myself, thinking that those brothers need to get their games out of high school.

"He was loud and rowdy in the bar, whispering raunchy things in my ear, the works. Handsy, too. But once we were alone, he was kind of awkward. Then we made out and both burst out laughing. It was like kissing a cousin or something, all the attraction just disappeared. Total disappointment."

We sulk with her for a total of thirty seconds before our classic brunch banter takes over. Between Lucy's descriptions of the stodgy engineers in her firm and Josie's stories about her class of fifth graders, I laugh until my stomach hurts and am so grateful for these two women in my life. In a city that can be cold and heartless, we created our own sister crew.

Once the bill is paid, I grab my coat, turning to put my arm in and I see Ryan standing by the hostess stand talking to a very pretty brunette. She's tiny, maybe slightly over five feet, and reminds me of a cute cheerleader. The girl-next-door that is impossible not to fall in love with. A real-life Kelly Kapowski. They're huddled close, laughing, and there's a familiarity between them as she puts her hand on his arm to emphasize a point.

My heart drops wondering if Josie has noticed him yet. They may not have had sparks last night, but it still wouldn't be great to see, especially just a day after they hung out. I keep walking until my steps falter. I was so busy worrying about Josie that I didn't notice Matt standing next to Ryan. My breath catches at the sight of him, and I think this casual version of him may be my favorite so far. He's wearing a backwards baseball hat, worn jeans, and a royal blue fleece vest that makes his eyes shine. He's undeniably handsome; if KK is the girl-next-door, Matt perfectly complements her as the town heartthrob. My stomach starts bubbling with nerves as I watch him walk over to Ryan and Kelly *(as she will now be known)*, put his arm around her, squeeze her close to him, and kiss her on the crown of her head, not letting go of her.

The bubbles in my stomach start to boil. *What the actual hell is this?* In a flash, self-loathing stirs inside me. How stupid could I have been to think Matt would be interested in me? No guy looks like him and has the effortless, charming personality he does just to settle down the minute they move back to town. My pulse picks up and my face flushes as the urge to hide washes over me. I watch the hostess motion for them to follow her. She's walking directly toward us and as soon as Matt faces me, our eyes lock.

He grins like he just rolled triple 7's on the slot machine and picks up his pace. He still has his arm around little Kapowski and I'm outraged at his cocky confidence, assuming he's congratulating himself for last night's conquest and his prey for today in the same room.

When they reach us, Matt drops his arm from KK's shoulders and stands in front me. "Hi," he says softly as he shoves his hands into the pockets of his jeans, a boyish exuberance all over his face. "So funny running into you here."

I don't trust my voice, so I simply nod. Telling myself to ignore his smooth, deep voice and hypnotic blue eyes, I try to play off nonchalance, but the icy frost vibrating from my body is nothing compared to the freezing temperatures outside. Matt senses it right away, looking at me with both concern and confusion. "Emily, is everything okay?"

I continue to nod. "Yeah, funny coincidence." I say, trying to will my voice to not shake.

Somehow I register Ryan introducing Kelly—who is actually named Carly—to Josie and I turn to listen, grateful to have something to shift my attention away from Matt. I feel his eyes on my profile as I watch Josie shake Carly's hand and hear Ryan say, "Our cousin."

Relief crashes through me. *Cousin.* She's his cousin. But as soon as my blood pressure evens out, shame takes its place. My internal dialogue had me acting like a jealous girlfriend... after one night. This can't be good. It hits me then how little I know about the guy. I don't even know his last name for Pete's sake. Now that I think about it more, he's the one who suggested we live in the "bubble." I cringe at how stupid I was to even go home with him. I rely on my gut instinct a lot, and while it told me I could trust him, I'm realizing now that my gut was referring to my physical safety. This misunderstanding proves my emotional well-being is unprotected when it comes to him. I want to shake myself.

I give Matt a tight smile, feeling like my brain is short-circuiting from the cascade of emotions I experienced in the past five minutes. Determined to get as far away as I can, I muster an easy, "I have to go. Enjoy brunch," then I glance back and tell the girls I'll call them later, heading straight for the door.

CHAPTER 9

EMILY

I'm breathing heavy, the cold air not even registering as I exit the restaurant and head toward my apartment. I walk as fast I can through Union Square, which is surprisingly mellow for a Sunday. The playground, normally packed during the weekend with families enjoying leisurely mornings, is empty, piles of slush obstructing the slides and swings. My rapid breaths match my quick steps as I try to convince myself the run-in at the diner was actually a good thing. A favor of sorts. If a quick misunderstanding could knock me so far off my feet, what would happen when he inevitably walked away?

Safe at home and back on my couch, I silence my phone and lose myself in *Friends* reruns. The sun finally starts to set and I jump in the bath, readying for a quiet night of reading, when my phone buzzes. My chest squeezes as I berate myself for simultaneously hoping it's Matt but also dreading if he calls me out on my behavior this morning.

Magic Matt: Hey.

I see the three dots moving, so I wait to see what else he has to say before I respond.

Magic Matt: I'm not sure what happened earlier, but I was really happy to see you. I hope everything's okay.

Me: Hey.

Way to ease right in there, Emily.

Magic Matt: Hi

Me: Sorry if it seemed like I ran out.

Magic Matt: I was looking for the 5-alarm fire you were sprinting from.

Magic Matt: Did I do something?

I sink deeper into the tub, the hand holding my phone sticking up from the bubbles like a flagpole. Now that I've had a few hours to process the situation, I can admit I overreacted.

Me: You didn't do anything. It's just me.

Magic Matt: You?

Me: Yeah, it's me. I'm the problem.

Magic Matt: All right, T Swift. Exactly how are you the problem?

Just rip the Band-Aid off, Emily.

Me: I was surprised to see you.

Magic Matt: I was surprised to see you too, but it was a happy surprise for me. Not sure for you?

Not exactly ripping it off there, Em.

Me: It just surprised me to see your arm around another girl after spending half the weekend together.

I scrunch my face together and close my eyes, scared of how he'll react.

Magic Matt: You mean Carly? She's my cousin. She, Ryan, and I were super close growing up and today was the first time I saw her since I moved back to the city.

Me: Yeah, I heard Ryan introducing her to Josie.

Magic Matt: So you assumed I was with you both Friday night and Saturday during the day and then just moved on to someone else last night?

Me: Um, something like that?

I'm now submerged in the water up to my chin, eyes nearly shut as if I'm watching the dumb girl run up the stairs when the murderer breaks in.

Magic Matt: Were you jealous?

Yes, yes I was. Not that I will admit it.

Magic Matt: I would've been if our roles were reversed.

Okay, not the response I was expecting, but I'll take it.

Me: Yeah?

Magic Matt: Damn straight. I had a lot of fun with you. In case it's not clear, I'd like to see you again.

I don't respond, fighting the urge to tell him I also had a lot of fun but it doesn't change anything.

Magic Matt: Did I lose you?

Me: No. Just feeling a little embarrassed over here about it all. Sorry I assumed the worst.

Magic Matt: You know what happens when you assume, right?

Me: Yeah, ass out of u & me, blah blah. Although I was the only ass there today.

Magic Matt: Well, it's a good thing your ass is so cute then <wink emoji>

Relief is my friend once again, and it's like a cement block has been lifted off my chest as I exhale and sit up a bit. When did the bath get cold? I yank the plug with my toe and then step out onto my fuzzy bathmat, watching the water disappear down the drain and feeling more relaxed than I have all day.

Me: <eyeroll emoji>

Magic Matt: So, were you hoping to use a vanishing spell on poor Carly?

Me: No, but maybe I could use one on you right now. I apologized and you accepted. Let's just drop it. K?

I put my bathrobe on and sit on the edge of the tub.

Magic Matt: You're very cute when you're jealous.

Me: Can we please move on?

Magic Matt: Okay, okay. Moving on. What are you wearing?

Ummm, this is something I really wasn't expecting. But... I'm kind of here for it.

Me: What?

Magic Matt: I'm thinking of your sweet ass, so now I want to know what you're wearing.

Me: I'm actually in a robe... I just got out of the bath.

Magic Matt: Hmm... now I really wish I were there.

Me: Yeah?

Words are hard, okay? Don't judge me.

Magic Matt: Yes. I meant what I said... I had a lot of fun with you and I want to see you again. Next time hopefully walking toward me instead of with sparks trailing you as you sprint away.

Me: That does sound like a better plan.

Magic Matt: Are you around this week? Can I take you to dinner?

My stomach swirls at the thought of seeing him again, but it's better to quit while I'm ahead.

Me: I am... but remember I said I'm about to jump into a huge project at work? It starts tomorrow and I'm basically going to be in the office around the clock until it wraps. I really don't have time right now.

Magic Matt: I remember. Are we still in the bubble or can I ask about your job?

Me: You can ask. I'm a strategy manager at an advertising agency. We're pitching a new account in a few weeks and I'm leading one of the teams. It's a new industry for me, so I'm pumped, but also a little stressed.

Magic Matt: I get it. I respect it too, but I can't say I'm not disappointed you want to end before we begin. What's the new industry?

Me: Auto.

Magic Matt: Cool. What agency is it?

Me: DMG.

There's a long silence from Matt, which has me scratching my head. I move from the bathroom to sit on my bed. Waiting. Before I start spiraling again—as I tend to do—I see the three bubbles pop up.

Magic Matt: I think I've heard of them.

Me: It's a small firm so all eyes will be on me. I'm confident we can win. And when we do, it will hopefully include a promotion for me. <crossed fingers emoji>

I hit send before I can consider adding the dollar-sign-eyes emoji. I've probably bored him to death with my work talk. He did ask though, so that's on him.

Magic Matt: I get it. It sounds like you have a lot going on, so I'll let you go. You know how to reach me if you change your mind.

Me: Thanks for understanding. Maybe in a few weeks once things have calmed down?

Not likely, but he doesn't need to know that.

Magic Matt: I'm not going anywhere.

Magic Matt: Good luck tomorrow.

Me: Thanks.

And that's it. I don't hear from him for the rest of the night. I can't shake the feeling that something shifted when we started talking about work. I realize I didn't ask him anything about his new job and kind of blabbed on about myself, but again, he was the one to ask. Maybe that's why he felt a little cold at the end? Not cold, exactly, but something... I shake my head and tell myself to stop feeling paranoid.

I'm relieved things ended on a good note with him, but the

whole day was eye-opening.. If seeing him with his *cousin* got me this upset after one night together, there's no telling what seeing him again will do to my central nervous system.

With that in mind, I start my Sunday night routine. I put on my favorite flannel pajamas, slather on a mango-scented face mask, and start the kettle for peppermint tea. When the water is ready, I fill my favorite mug and add a splash of milk. Setting it on my nightstand to cool, I rinse off the mask, brush my teeth, and climb into bed. I manage to get in a chapter of the latest Sarah Adams book before I start to doze off, imagining myself rebuilding brick walls around my heart.

CHAPTER 10

EMILY

My eyes are already open when the alarm goes off. I'm wired in that fizzing-from-the-inside way, and I haven't even had a sip of coffee yet. "Let's do this," I say brightly to the ceiling of my dark bedroom, throwing back the covers and swinging my feet to the floor. I brace my arms on each side, take a deep inhale, and push myself up.

I attempt a pep talk while I brush my teeth. "Listen here, Emily Cooper. You are smart, you are capable, Imperial would be lucky to have you lead their account. You. Can. Do. This."

I spit in the sink and when I come up, my arms are on my hips in a superhero pose. I feel like a world-class idiot but have to begrudgingly acknowledge that maybe there is something to the positive affirmations my mom made me recite when I was a little girl.

And yet, for all the good she tried to instill in me, my mom never realized how confused she left me, given the gap between what she said and how she acted. She preached confidence, strength and independence as the ultimate trifecta. I was the golden child that was supposed to possess all three, meanwhile my mom was afraid to be alone, jumping from one bad relationship to another until they all inevitably ended with the *men can't be trusted* speech. My father was at the core of her relationship woes, but despite him breaking her heart, she got up every day, went to work, and took care of me. Outside of that, it was a very long time before she recovered from his absence. She cried whenever we talked about him. She dated men like my father who only let her down and disappointed her. If only she could've drunk the Kool-Aid she spent years selling me.

I shake my head free of the trials and tribulations of Maria Cooper, hop in the shower, and start going through my checklist for the day. I need to meet with Heather to get a full report on all the current research they have for the auto market, including consumer psychographic and demographic breakdown. Imperial is a status symbol, but it extends beyond the money. People who drive Imperial cars care about status, but also about the environment. They care about the newest model and how it'll look pulling up to the exclusive restaurant's valet, but also about how their purchase will impact the future generation. Or at least that's what they want people to believe. *Do good for yourself with a luxury vehicle, do good for the world at the same time,* and all that.

They've been focusing so much on the status side of things,

targeting the men who golf at the country club, that they're missing out on the women who consider Imperial for sustainability. That's the sweet spot I want to pursue.

I wonder if I would get to pick my own team for the project, and I begin thinking of a second list of questions for Sheila. I open my closet door and look through my neutrals-heavy wardrobe, wondering which black or navy combination it will be today. Josh will be introducing me as team lead in our meeting first thing, so I want to look the part. I pick a black sweater dress that's belted at the waist and flares out at my knees. I pair it with tights, knee-high boots, and my signature gold hoops. Professional and stylish. I feel like I'm donning my armor and preparing for battle. I do my second superhero pose of the morning, readier than ever to slay any dragon that gets in my way.

Popping my earbuds in, I step out onto 16th Street and head toward the subway. I'm relieved to see Marty and his coffee cart made it despite the snow and stop to grab a blueberry muffin. He fills my thermos with coffee and I instantly feel a surge of joyful contentment. I am a creature of habit, and it wasn't easy finding my balance after everything fell apart when Greg left. But I created a new routine, a new way of being, and it feels good to realize that, for today at least, I'm feeling confident and in control. Today is already a good day.

I spot my boss Sheila as I enter our building and wave as she waits for me by the elevators. Eight a.m. is a very early start for the advertising world, so it's just the two of us.

"Today's your day, Emily. Are you ready?"

"More than you know. I can't thank you enough for your support. I know I can nail this account, and I can't wait to get started."

"You earned this. I have full confidence in you." She smiles and gestures me into the elevator. "It's going to be some long hours though, so I hope you were able to relax over the weekend."

Thoughts of Matt slink in and a blush creeps up my face. A montage of us—bent over the pool table and slow dancing in the bar, exchanging heated kisses under the covers and flirty texts last night—scrolls through my head like the CNN ticker.

"Ah, earth to Emily, you still with me?" Sheila asks, leaning over to catch my eye.

I try to laugh off the fact that I have no idea what she just said. "Sorry, yep. It's nothing. I'm here."

"Looks like wherever you just went was more than *nothing*. I guess it was a fun girls' night out?" Her eyebrows dance, eyes bright.

"Um, ha, yeah. It was a really fun night, plus all the snow." I wave my hand around like *Weather, am I right?* in an attempt to get my shit together.

Sheila nods her head, not buying my mumbling. "Uh-huh. Snow. Anything more riveting to share?"

I laugh and give up. Sheila has a way of extracting information, but it doesn't really bother me. I trust her. The elevator reaches our floor and we walk out, heading toward our respective offices.

"Okay, fine, yes. His name is Matt and he just moved here from Chicago; he was out at the same bar as us." We stop outside her office and I grab her forearm. "Sheila, he was straight out of a romance novel. Dimples, forearms, and *so* charming." I mentally gush about how he smelled like freshly cut firewood on a dewy morning, and thinking of his lips on mine causes my heart to skip a beat. "Sadly, I had to let him down easy, given Imperial and my very bleak social future. Anyway, he's starting a new job today as well, so it is what it is—one amazing night."

"I don't know, Em. You're vibrating with energy—and don't you dare say it has anything to do with *work*." She gives me a look at that and I have to choke back a laugh, as she is my boss after all. "It suits you. People balance work and relationships every day, there's no reason you can't do it too."

Sheila walks into her office, leaving me with that thought. For so long I've been focused on my career, getting promoted... being the independent woman my mom willed me to be. Can I have both? What would that even look like?

My life is finally in order. This pitch is my top priority right now. One thing at a time or else it gets too messy. Not to mention how much thinking about putting myself out there scares me. It took a while but I finally put all the pieces of my heart back together.

I hang my coat behind the door of my office and sit down with a heavy sigh. I can't think about it now and push any thought of Matt out of my head. I want to take advantage of the quiet to jot down my thoughts from this morning and the information I'll need to build my case around targeting women.

I'm so engrossed in my solo brainstorming session I don't realize it's time for Josh's meeting until Sheila knocks on my door. Most people think a Monday morning meeting is an act of cruelty, but they help me prep for the week and I love catching up on everyone's weekend, if only to live vicariously through them. My weekends usually don't look like this past one. Most of the time they're filled with work, romance novels, and an hour or two with the girls when I can manage it.

I grab a seat next to Brian, our head copy editor and the world's biggest Knicks fan. His hilarious commentary on the state of the team is always good for a laugh.

"So, should I even ask your thoughts on the double OT Friday night?"

"Em, Em, Em. Ugh! Did you see it? Terrible. They disappeared in the paint and my six-year-old could have rebounded the ball better than they did. Disgraceful. I don't know if the Garden will ever see the playoffs again, let alone a championship."

My back is to the door as I face Brian and listen to him animatedly retell the OT fiasco. I try not to think about watching it with Matt standing behind me, the warmth of his chest lingering as I let myself lean back.

Josh walks in then and clears his throat, cutting Brian's story short. "Can I have everyone's attention? This is going to be a short meeting because we all know it's heads down on the Imperial pitch for the next several weeks."

I drop my pen and lean under the table to grab it as Josh continues.

"Emily Cooper will be leading one team, and I want to introduce the newest member of DMG, Matt Meyer. He'll be leading the other team. Matt just moved to New York from Chicago, where he worked at State and Clark, overseeing their auto business."

I freeze as I slowly straighten up. *What are the chances? It can't be him.* I'm moving in slow motion as if under water, and Josh's voice is marbled as I pick up bits and pieces of what he's saying.

"He's also worked on a handful of successful pitches so that experience will be critical for us."

I emerge from under the table and freeze.

Matt.

Brilliant blue eyes. Soft, kissable lips. Chiseled chest hiding beneath those buttons.

What. The. Fuck?

I lock eyes with him. Neither of us moves a muscle. Matt, who has dominated my thoughts and whose kisses I can still taste on my lips, is the leader of the competing pitch team. My Matt... is *this* Matt? The newest DMG employee? An auto industry veteran? I close my eyes and shake my head. Shit like this doesn't happen in real life.

I open my eyes and—nope, still the same Matt who slept with his arms around me during our afternoon nap and made my body explode with an orgasm. My hands ball up in fists on my lap, and it registers that we've resumed our stare down. His face is expressionless as Josh wraps up his announcement, asking everyone to give Matt a warm welcome.

"Between Matt's and Emily's leadership, I'm confident we'll bring Imperial home to DMG in no time."

Matt never takes his eyes off mine and smoke starts to come out of my ears. If looks could kill, he would be a bloody puddle on the floor. My brain finally starts functioning, firing questions rapidly through my head. *Did he know?* If he did, how could he not have told me? I rambled on about my job, this opportunity, how much it means to me… and he just took it all in. Now he's the competition? He's an auto account *expert* and is going to just waltz in here and threaten all my hard work and sweat equity?

"Our priority and focus for the next month is Imperial and Imperial only. Sheila and I will meet with Matt and Emily later this morning, and we'll share assignments with you all by end of the day. Stay tuned for more."

Everyone starts shuffling out the door. Matt, Sheila, and Josh move to a corner of the room to sidebar. Sheila calls me over, but I just shake my head and keep walking.

She rushes out of the conference room to catch up to me. "Emily, what's wrong?"

"Nothing, sorry. I just wasn't expecting someone new to be joining the team."

"It was a bit of a surprise to us as well, but I met Matt on Friday and I think you two will get along really well. He has great experience, and his previous office in Chicago raved about him."

"I'm sure they did. Awesome." My sarcastic tone is not lost on Sheila as she follows me into my office and closes the door.

"I don't know what I'm missing here… Why are you so upset?"

I look intently at Sheila, willing her to understand so I don't have to say it out loud. "His name is *Matt*, he just moved from

Chicago? He was starting a new job today...?" I roll my hands in a circular motion as if to say *Are you picking up what I'm putting down?*

The last piece of the puzzle clicks for her. "Oh. My. *God.* That's the Matt you met on Friday night..." It's not a question, but still I nod, pursing my lips and widening my eyes. Sheila closes her eyes. "Oh shit, Em."

"Yep, oh shit. He never mentioned a thing, and I went on and on about how important this job is for me. I can't believe this... How could I be so stupid!" I moan and flop down in my chair.

Sheila leans her hip on my desk. "Let's take a deep breath and think about this for a minute. Is there any chance he didn't know? Maybe he's just as surprised as you?"

Just as I drop my head back and groan, there's a light knock on the door. Sheila opens it and steps aside for Matt who's standing there, hands in his pockets, shoulders bunched up, giving me what I imagine are his most sheepish eyes.

"I'll leave you guys to get acquainted," she says, giving me a look as she shuts the door behind her.

"I can explain—"

"You can take your explanation and shove it," I say, cutting him off before he can further ruin my day. "You completely deceived me. You let me go on last night about DMG, meanwhile you knew you were starting here. This is your new job. And *of course* it is. How could I be so fucking stupid?" I hiss the last part, because as pissed off as I am, I'm also at work. And despite how much this has thrown me off-kilter, I value my co-workers' respect around here.

"Emily, I know it looks bad."

"You're damn straight it does."

"Please just let me explain."

"Honestly, I couldn't care less. I know we have to work in the same office now, but as far as I'm concerned, you're nothing but the new guy who I don't need to know. You stay in your lane and I'll stay in mine."

I get up with such force my chair slams against the wall behind me. I walk up to Matt and we stand toe-to-toe. It takes all my willpower not to wax poetic about the turquoise depths of his eyes or how perfectly his shirt hugs his broad shoulders. Throwing up my hands and groaning in frustration at myself, I push a finger into his chest, which was a bad idea because now I'm trying to ignore how solid it is while remembering how smooth his skin was underneath my fingertips.

"You know what? I don't care that you're an auto expert, I'm going to win this pitch and you can sleep with your losing record at night. You'll be sorry you ever stepped foot in this office." I give his chest another shove with my finger, trying to move him toward the door.

Unfortunately for me, he's got about a foot and seventy pounds of muscle over me and doesn't budge. Instead, he wraps his palm around my finger and gently pushes it down. Widening his stance and crossing his arms, he looks down at me and growls, "Fine, if that's how it's going to be, then I'm sorry I wasted your time by coming in here to try to make you understand. I gave you the benefit of the doubt when you ran out of the diner. How about you show me the same courtesy?"

An awareness of his body makes me wonder when we started to move toward each other. We're standing so close my chest brushes his with my quick breaths. My wrist vibrates, my Apple Watch reminding me to breathe because my heart rate is spiking. We stare each other down like champion boxers at weigh-in before the big fight, willing the other to step away.

The spell is broken by Sheila's knock, reminding me that we have another meeting. With a final glare, I step back, grab my notebook, and leave without a word. Matt turns and watches me walk out.

This is not how I imagined today would turn out.

CHAPTER 11

MATT

What the actual fuck just happened?

I knew Emily would be angry that I didn't tell her my new job is at DMG, but I just found out last night she worked here when we were texting, so it's not like I hid it from her the whole weekend. I understand why she's angry, but man, she is *pissed*.

I saw her passion Friday night in my apartment, and she was breathtaking when she let herself give in to it, but a mad Emily? Her eyes turn a deep green, like the pine needles of a fresh Christmas tree or—probably more fitting—like Oscar the Grouch during one of his diatribes. I know she thought my inability to form coherent sentences stemmed from being the object of her ire, but what made my stomach plummet wasn't her anger... No, it was how much it turned me on. It took all my self-control not to kiss her right there in her office. At ten o'clock on a Monday morning. I'm so screwed.

And I'm not oblivious. I could tell from the second she mentioned her job that it meant everything to her. It wasn't my first choice to come here to New York, but I have no say in the matter right now. Once again, my father, the great Roger Davis, does what he does best—and that's make my life miserable.

Unfortunately, I owe him. And I owe him big. When he told me DMG, his agency, was pitching Imperial, I knew it was time to pay up. It was the final push I needed to move back to New York. But of course, he couldn't help himself, throwing in a snide remark, questioning whether I could cut it here. It was my mistake in thinking that he might, I don't know, support me like a father should? So now the account actually means less than the desire to prove him wrong and win this pitch. After that, I'll finally be free.

Regardless, I'm here now, and this would be a huge accomplishment for the agency. It benefits us all if DMG gets Imperial, and that means Emily too. Win-win. I just have to figure out how to manage this tension. I've been through agency pitches like this before, and drawing a line in the sand, treating the other team like an enemy... That's the worst scenario possible.

In an ironic welcome to my father's agency, I'm unable to log in to my computer because I apparently don't exist in the system. After twenty minutes of rebooting and trying various usernames, I give up and call IT. I'm on the phone with them when I hear a knock on my door. I look up and see Sheila.

She steps into my office. "Hey, Matt. I'm just checking to see that you got the invite for our meeting with Josh? It's starting now."

"Shit, no. I'm locked out of my computer." I stand up and grab a notebook and pen, telling IT I'll call them back later.

Sheila gives me a warm smile. "We're really happy you're here. I know this morning was a little tense, but I'm confident we have the right people working on this."

I nod, grateful for Sheila's show of support. This was definitely *not* how I envisioned my first day going, and while I had more warning than Emily after she revealed she worked for DMG last night, I'm still stunned that the one woman who made me feel a spark again is the one I'm now technically competing against. To make matters worse, this "competition" means everything to her and almost nothing to me, beyond settling the score with my father.

I stop and motion for Sheila to lead the way. The office is buzzing the way an agency floor should—loud chatter and laughing, groups congregating around shared spaces, and bursts of color everywhere. Campaign swag and signage line the walls and the tops of cubicle cabinets. Those seated at their desks have headphones in to block out the noise. This place is nirvana for young creative types who still think they can change the world with an ad campaign and a catchy jingle. Which isn't to say it's not possible, it's just not the place for me. I suffocate in this environment.

If I only had the courage to go after what I wanted, I'd be a practicing physical therapist already. Give me some scrubs and massage tables, some weights and resistance bands, and I'm happy. Years of suffering through injuries and the general beating my body took playing D1 lacrosse, it's the one place off the field that I feel comfortable. I love the physical part of it—pushing through when you don't think you have anything left—and the way therapy connects the mind and body.

I'm so in my head I don't realize Sheila stops at the door to Josh's office and I have to pull back to avoid bumping into her. Of course Emily is already sitting in there, waiting, and catches my clumsiness. She smirks and cocks an eyebrow, her eyes slowly trailing down my body, and I feel like I'm a Rembrandt being analyzed before an auction.

"Come on in." Josh stands and waves us into his office. He circles his desk and takes a seat on the chair next to a coffee table and plush linen couch. Sheila settles on the sofa lining the back wall and I follow, sitting down next to her.

"Imperial is anxious to move quickly through this process. They want to have their campaign ready for summer, which doesn't leave us much time to execute when we win." He winks at us to make sure we caught the confidence in his statement. "They also don't want a big dog and pony show, so while we'll be presenting an integrated plan, they only want the strategy team pitching to them. This means they'll work solely through us and expect things to be as streamlined as possible."

Emily bites the corner of her bottom lip as she digests his words. She opens her mouth and closes it a few times before saying, "Will the other teams be willing to give us ideas if they know they won't be pitching? I can't see the PR group being happy about that."

Josh sighs but nods his head. "They know they have to be team players, and Imperial makes the rules. Roger Davis personally spoke to the head of PR and social to make sure they were on board. They know how much this account would mean to the agency, so everyone has agreed to play nice in the sandbox. For now at least."

Emily sits up straighter. "Great. Do we get to pick our teams now?" She glances over at me. "Not that Matt would really know who to pick, being that he just joined today, but I already know who I'd prefer to work with on this." She smiles sweetly at me, as if she didn't just cut me down in front of our bosses.

Sheila tries to hide her smile by looking down at her notebook. Josh outright laughs and nods his head. "Sure thing, Emily, you can pick your team."

"I'd like Sarah, Rachel, and Naomi." She turns to me with a saccharine smile plastered across her face. "Matt, any issues with that?"

She knows damn well I won't object considering I have no fucking clue who those people are. I tilt my head and swing out my hand as if to say *They're all yours*.

"Okay, Emily, that's your team. Matt, I'd recommend Priya Kaur for insights, Jeremy Broome for Associate Strategy Director, and Jose Serrano for Creative. It's a top-notch team, and Priya and Jose have some auto experience. They've all been with the agency a while, so they can help you get up to speed quickly."

Now I'm the one with a sugar sweet smirk on my face, and Emily's eyes narrow in on me as I shine it her way.

"Sounds great, Josh. I'm confident the four of us can knock it out of the park. It'll be great to combine their knowledge with my fresh perspective and deep industry experience. I couldn't be more pleased to get started." I sit back confidently, crossing my arms over my chest.

Emily takes a deep breath and gives an unintentional, spot-on imitation of a cartoon character whose face turns red and smoke comes of out of their ears, anger bubbling over and consuming her. This may be more fun than I bargained for.

"We're done here for now. Matt, hang back a second and I'll introduce you to your team."

Emily stands, straightening her shoulders and marching out of Josh's office without another look.

I spend the rest of the day with Priya, Jose, and Jeremy. Auto accounts are second nature to me, so my concern isn't the category. At the core of a successful pitch is authentic chemistry between the team because we're facing long, intense hours, which means I have to catch up on years of office camaraderie.

I hate to admit it, but DMG is a well-run operation. From what Josh has told me, my dad spends most of his time holed up in his office or flying to meet clients, so most of the credit for the tight-knit atmosphere goes to Josh. It's smaller than the more well-known agencies who always make the cover of *Ad Age,* but over the past few years, they've built a solid portfolio. And just in case the pressure wasn't high enough, winning Imperial will put them firmly on the map.

When Emily texted last night and revealed where she works, my stomach plummeted eighteen floors to the basement of my building. I was naive to think we could find a way to work together, but now I'm worried about simply surviving being in the same meeting room with her, let alone coordinating projects.

My phone pings as I walk back into my office. It's not the text I want but one that I was expecting.

Dad: Your mother would like you and Ryan to have dinner at home on Friday night. Be there at 8.

My shoulders immediately tense at the chill in his words. The only takeaway is that I'll have a reprieve from having to face him right away, even if it's just four days.

CHAPTER 12

EMILY

I salvaged the rest of Monday brainstorming with Sarah, Rachel, and Naomi after the shock of Matt wore off. I picked them not just because they're women, but because they're the right women for this account. None of them are car junkies, but they're creative thinkers, which is what I'm hoping will give us an advantage. Imperial doesn't need another standard car campaign, and it's definitely not what we're going to feed them.

I filled Josie and Lucy in on my nightmare with lots of texts in all caps in the afternoon, and they responded by showing up at my apartment with my favorite Thai takeout to strategize. I hardly slept last night, tossing and turning nonstop. I gave up around four a.m. and resorted to yoga for some calming strategies. That lasted all of fifteen minutes until I called time of death and made a cup of strong coffee instead.

Me: I'm heading into work. Tell me again I can do this because I'm shaking and I can't tell if it's nerves or anger. I'm pissed that it might be nerves.

Lucy: Inhale-Exhale (and I know you want to give me the finger for saying that, so put all your anger into it and flip the phone off).

Me: Ha, at least that made me laugh.

Josie: Repeat after me: I will crush the fucker today. He's a mere fly falling victim to my swatter.

Me: Swatter?

Josie: LOL sorry. It's insect month at school.

Lucy: Insect month is a thing?

Josie: It is if you're a 5th grader. It's actually made me appreciate the crawly critters a little more.

Lucy: Ew, not sure there's anything endearing about insects.

Me: PEOPLE. Can we FOCUS?

Josie: Sorry. I just feel like maybe we're missing something here. He really didn't seem like the world's biggest douche canoe the other night.

Me: Not helping. Swatter was better.

Lucy: Josie, stop talking. Em, this is YOUR job. Just keep remembering that.

I slip my phone into my bag and chuckle at their words of encouragement, managing to feel a little better by the time I get to the office. In a very mature, not-petty-at-all move, I waltz in easily a half hour earlier than usual to claim our war room. Armed with a fresh cup of coffee from the Keurig in the kitchen, I turn the corner to see Matt coming out of the copy room. *What. The. Fuck.* Did he sleep here? Early mornings and late nights at the office are my thing. It's bad enough I'm going to have to see him for most of our working hours, but now during my quiet hours too?

He doesn't hear me coming, so when he looks up and finds me marching toward him, his face lights up with a genuine smile and those goddamn dimples come out. "Hey, you're here early."

"Thanks, Captain Obvious. It's been my thing for three years. Please don't tell me it's going to be *your* thing now too."

He stops in front of me and lets out a breath. "Alrighty then. I'll just get out of your way." He steps to his left and I step right, putting us chest-to-chest. Frazzled, I move the opposite way only for us to collide again. I roll my eyes.

"Sorry about that." Almost as if in slow motion, we both decide to shuffle apart and—you guessed it—his warm body connects with mine, and this time I bring my hand up to his waist to steady myself. Not that I need any reminders of just how solid he is. We're so close I can notice how his eyes are more of a gray-blue with specks of yellow today and—*arrgghhh. Fuck off already, you and your stupid pretty eyes.*

"Uh, did you also learn how to walk two minutes ago? Stop moving and stand here"—I emphatically guide him to the left—

"so I can walk around you."

Matt puts his hands up as if I'm about to arrest him but stands still as I walk past him. "By the way," I yell to him without turning around or stopping, "this is our war room, so feel free to find a different one for yourself." Then I slip into the conference room and lean back against the door, huffing a sigh.

I put the coffee on the table and brace my hands on a chair to catch my breath. The contradicting emotions swirling through me are making me dizzy and things haven't even kicked off. How am I going to survive this?

We have our project-wide strategy meeting during lunch, so I know there's a chance I'll run into Matt again. This meeting is always packed because they give out free food and it's great for catching up on all the office gossip.

I was held up on a call so the lunch line is snaking out of the conference room door when I arrive. Most of the chairs are filled or claimed with notebooks and phones. I spot Naomi and she waves furiously, pointing to a chair with a pink scarf folded over it. I smile and take my spot in line, my eyes immediately landing on Matt—or rather, the back of Matt's head. He's at the front of the line grabbing utensils as he talks to a tall blond in skinny jeans and a tight red sweater. She laughs at something he says and then grabs his forearm like she can't breathe from the exertion of it. I mean, sure, he's cute and charming, but she's carrying on like he's Jimmy freaking Fallon in his prime *Weekend Update* years. He turns to try to find a chair, but she won't let go of his arm. In fact, it looks like she's growing talons, staking her claim. The line moves again and it's getting congested because there's only so much space between the seats and food table.

"Matt, over here, we saved you a seat," Jose yells over, and the briefest flicker of relief crosses his features. He slides on a smile before anyone can notice, but I caught it. I caught it because I felt it too. Relief that he was moving away from Talon Tracy over there. I don't even know who she is—which is rare, considering how much time I spend in the office—but we have guest speakers and visitors for this meeting all the time. Matt leans in to say something else and she nods, finally releasing him from her vice-like grip. Her friend joins her and she giggles as her eyes bulge and I see her mouth, "So hot!"

Bile climbs up my throat as I finally make it to the front of the line only to find scraps left, so I grab a water and head to the seat Naomi saved for me. Right behind Matt and Jose. If it wasn't so sad, I'd laugh.

"Hey, Nay, thanks for this," I say, lifting the scarf and draping it over the back of her chair.

"No problem. Did you get anything?" She's looking between my empty hands, her mouth turned down at the corners in a pout.

I shrugged. "Nothing left. I'll grab a slice from Gino's between meetings if I can." I check my watch. "Hopefully this won't run long and I can do it before my next call. Otherwise, I'm in back-to-back meetings till four."

Naomi leans over to Jose. "Hey, did you grab any extra chips or anything? Emily didn't get any food."

Jose looks back at me and my lonely bottle of water. "Sorry, no. It was slim pickings to begin with."

The next thing I know, Matt's holding out an unopened bag of pretzels, offering them to me with a timid smile. He's probably scared I'll rip them from his hand like She-Hulk. I can't quite blame him. "Here, take these to get through the meeting." My stomach picks this moment to growl so loudly it'll be obvious I'm being spiteful if I refuse them. He smiles and pushes the bag a little closer. "Please, take them. I wasn't going to eat them anyway."

When I lean over, I'm immediately transported back to our first night together as his fresh, woodsy smell reaches me, tugging at my resolve. Why am I mad at this guy again? *Shit*—no. I clear my throat and feel the crinkly plastic under my fingertips, but not before they brush his. The contact sends a charge surging up my arm and then between my legs. Matt tilts his head, and that's when I know he feels it too. His eyes lock on mine, and with the navy Henley he's wearing today, they're a deep sapphire blue.

"Thank you," I whisper, my neck flushing as I look away from where I can feel his eyes searing into me.

He nods once and turns around, right as Josh kicks off the meeting.

♥

The meeting runs long and I have to duck out to make my next call. So much for a real lunch. I was hoping to stay late to work on our outline, but I'm starving and feeling light-headed already.

I'm on my third call after lunch when I hear a very slight knock on my door. I switch off my video and lower the volume.

"Come in."

I'm surprised to see Matt at the door.

"Hey." He glances at my monitor and drops to a whisper. "I don't want to interrupt, but I got you something." He disappears back into the hallway, leaving me even more puzzled about what's going on. Then he's back, holding a white paper bag horizontally in one hand and a fountain soda in the other. "I grabbed you a slice from Gino's while I was out."

I open my mouth to say something but close it without uttering a sound. That was very thoughtful. Almost too thoughtful and I'm immediately suspicious. Suspicious is good, great—better than getting all soft about the gesture.

"Did you poison this?" I ask, hesitantly reaching for the bag. My stomach roars as the smell of hot, gooey cheese reaches it.

Matt shakes his head and laughs. "Today's special: cyanide-free."

I begrudgingly smile. "Well, thank you."

"Consider it a favor for the team. I can only imagine what a hangry Emily is like." He smiles wide, eyes crinkling at the corner and those damn dimples on full display.

"It's definitely not a pretty sight." I inhale and blow out a breath, knowing I need to say something. "This was very kind of you, Matt." I start to open the bag and take a sip of the soda.

"You're welcome. I'm glad I could help." His sincerity sparks the image of us lounging on his couch after our nap, my feet in his lap as he rubbed them. He'd said the same thing then. *Glad I could help.* I remember getting the distinct and powerful impression that this was Matt to his core. Always willing to help, to lend a hand. He seems like the type of guy who would give the shirt off his back to a stranger. But thinking about Matt being kind, or Matt smelling good, or Matt and his soft and tender kisses isn't going to help right now. Or ever.

But *especially* not until we know who's pitching to Imperial.

CHAPTER 13

MATT

The days have all blurred together as it's been nonstop meetings. I'm grateful to have made it to Friday still standing.

The biggest challenge hasn't been the information overload. Nope. It's the fact that Emily and her team were in the room with us the entire day and not once did she look at me. I couldn't stop watching her. She was engaged, asking questions with intention, and tossing out thoughtful ideas that gave me the excuse to continuously look her way. But not one glance was returned. Add discipline and self-control to the list of qualities that make her so attractive. That's assuming, of course, it took self-control to ignore me. Could be wishful thinking on my part.

I should be relieved the day—scratch that, the very long week is over, but it's Friday. The day I've been anxious about all week. There's no TGIF today. My most dreaded appointment of the week is about to begin: dinner with my parents.

I walk into their apartment and give my mom a hug. She hands me a glass of wine that I gladly take, knowing I'll need the liquid support to get through this meal. Ryan's already in the living room, talking to my dad. I brace myself as I join them.

"Well, I'm proud of you, it's so nice to see you excelling at the new firm."

Dad has a hand on Ryan's shoulder, and I feel like I've walked in on something when I see him squeeze it before turning to me. My muscles tense under his scrutiny.

"Hello, Matthew."

I grit my teeth. The sound of hearing him call me by my full name puts nails on a chalkboard to shame. He's the only person who calls me that, and it's because I make damn sure no one else does. He's ruined it for me, the sound dripping with disappointment every time it comes out of his mouth.

"Hi, Dad." I lift my chin, ready to go into battle.

"It's nice you could make it; I know this'll make your mother happy." He gives me his back and fills his glass with ice by the bar cart, pouring himself a generous scotch.

My dad is the type of man who can cut you down with one look. His presence is felt the minute he walks into a room, despite his slender physique. It's his disposition that precedes him. Roger Davis doesn't walk, he saunters. He doesn't look at you, he's constantly sizing you up (and makes no attempt to hide it). He wears literal rose-colored glasses so there's always the illusion that's he's not really there, or at least not paying attention. Always dressed to the nines, fighting desperately to ensure his rapidly receding hairline doesn't fully disappear, Roger Davis is always right.

I have to begrudgingly admit that the man does deserve some of the swagger. He started DMG from a two-room office in his parents' basement and built it into one of the top independent ad agencies in the States. He's rejected any attempt for merging and laughed in the face of any big conglomerate that tried to make him an offer. His blood, sweat, and tears live in every nook and cranny of our offices, and I can't dismiss that.

But Roger Davis, the father? He's a total shithead. At least to me. Ryan can do no wrong in his eyes, though. He wanted Ryan to follow in his footsteps at DMG, but somehow he was able to avoid the pressure *and* be on the receiving end of Dad's pride and joy with his success in corporate finance. I naively thought going into advertising could be the olive branch so desperately needed between us, the impetus for him to finally acknowledge something positive about me. Instead, it fueled his criticism, honed his dismissal of my abilities.

Ryan coughs, bringing me back to the room. I take a long sip of my wine, draining half the glass as I digest my warm welcome. Death by a thousand paper cuts couldn't be more accurate in describing what it's like to be in the same room as my father. I'm the one bleeding, and it doesn't matter if I sit complacently or push back, it all ends up with me sliced up and drained dry. It's taken almost thirty-four years, but I've become a master at translating his backhanded compliments. Ryan stands quiet in the corner, knowing the best way he can help is to fade into the background.

I'm saved from small talk when my mother lets us know dinner is ready. I need to defuse this, at least for my mother's sake. I've caught her fighting tears on more than one occasion, and I'm committed to doing all that I can to keep the peace.

I stand aside to let my father lead the way to the dining room. Ryan follows and raises his eyebrows as he passes me, silently alerting me that we're in for a bumpy ride tonight.

"So, Matthew, how are you settling in at the office?" my father asks without looking at me.

"Everything's going well. Josh has been a big help. The team seems great—strong creatives. You've built up a good group of people, and everyone seems happy within their roles."

"Well, why wouldn't they be? All the money we spend on the crap millennials need these days—free breakfast and ping pong tables and quiet rooms to think. When I was working my way up, I was lucky we had coffee in the office. It's ridiculous how much coddling and help this generation needs to get by. Although it shouldn't surprise me considering..."

He stares at me, leaving the sentence hanging but his meaning implied. I am one of those "millennials."

"How is the young girl leading the other team doing? Ellen something or other? Josh has a lot of confidence in her, but I'm not exactly sure why."

"Her name is Emily. Emily Cooper. She's been at DMG for years and is extremely skilled and qualified. Why would Josh's confidence raise questions for you?" I try to keep my voice steady, but

I feel myself walking toward a cliff, knowing the only way out is down. I reach for my glass of water, hoping that having something to wrap my hands around will keep me from roping them around my dad's neck.

"Well, first of all, a woman leading an auto pitch?" My dad scoffs as he cuts his steak. "Ridiculous, if you ask me, but then again, that's all the rage these days with equality and whatnot. Anyway, let's hope you keep your focus on the task at hand."

I cough as I take a drink of water. "Um, I'm not sure I'm following?"

"There's a lot riding on this. Your only priority should be bringing Imperial to DMG. I hope you don't lose sight of another golden opportunity being handed to you and let a girl get in the way of the one task you're being asked to do."

"Roger, please," my mom chides him with a *Don't start* slant to her voice. "Can we talk about something other than work?"

"No, Mom." I slice my hand into the air to interrupt. "I would actually love to hear exactly what Dad has to say about this 'golden opportunity' that was 'handed' to me." I feel a vein in my neck pulsing from the anger coursing through my body.

"Matthew, watch your tone with your mother," he warns.

"I'm not staying for this." She gets up and walks out of the room with tears in her eyes.

I ignore the warning and keep staring at him. "I'm waiting. Exactly what did you mean, Dad?"

He sighs, exhausted, as if I were a toddler tugging his shirt sleeves for the umpteenth time, asking for a lollipop. His tone is condescending and impatient.

"Come on, Matthew. You cost your client millions of dollars and almost caused your entire team to be fired. Luckily for you, I saved your ass, first by not revealing *you* were the one who fucked up and then by paying him back the money." I feel the room start to cave in around me, the collar of my shirt pulling tighter around my neck. None the wiser, he forges on, his own face reddening. "Now, years later, that same client—who holds you in such high regard because *I* kept your secret—needs a new ad agency to head his auto campaign. And he specifically asked if *you* would participate. If that isn't a lay-up, I don't know what is. I shouldn't need to explain any of this to you."

"Excuse me?"

"It's about time you saw the pattern we all do, Matthew. You coast through life expecting opportunities. It's always been the same story. On top of having an in with the client, your college roommate is the VP of Marketing, helping Imperial to decide which agency to choose. Not to mention you're pitching against a female lead. I mean, it'd be harder to take candy from a baby." My father ends his diatribe and sits back, taking a big sip of his scotch.

The silence is deafening. Ryan glares at my father and stands up in disgust, following my mother's path out of the room.

I look at my father, sitting there smugly in his chair, alienating everyone around him. Cold ice runs through his veins. I made a point to never ask for anything once I started high school and realized he was keeping score between Ryan and me. If I could pay back every lacrosse league registration and every cent of my college tuition to be free of this man, I would. I'd walk away and never look back.

But... that would break my mother's heart. That, on top of the debt I owe—which is apparently at the forefront of his mind—makes it feel impossible to break free.

The most ironic part of it all is that I never wanted this life. All I've ever wanted was to work with athletes, with my hands, and heal people. But his taunting drove me crazy. I wanted to show him he was wrong about me, maybe even earn some of his respect. I've wasted so much time trying to get something out of a man who I now see will always have blinders on.

I toss my napkin on my plate and stand.

I find my mom in the kitchen, her eyes brimming with tears. She's defenseless against him. For whatever reason, she stays with him, but that doesn't mean I have to. I put my arm around her shoulder as I lean in to kiss her cheek. "I'm going to head out. Thanks for dinner. I'll call you tomorrow."

This day—this week—needs to end. Dinner was a disaster and now her tears... I need to go before my heart cracks in two. I can't be mad at her, because I know she has to live with the man. I just have to work for him for the next few weeks.

My only goal is to win this account, and then I can finally break free.

CHAPTER 14

EMILY

My eyes pop open way too early on Saturday morning. I was hoping to sleep in, but no such luck. What a difference seven days can make. Just last week, the city was covered in snow, I woke up in Matt's bed, and work was my happy place. Now, I feel like I'm stuck in the upside-down.

When I finally got over the initial surprise of Matt working at DMG, I avoided him as much as possible. When that wasn't an option, I diligently decided I'd pretend he was an imaginary figure in my periphery. Adult behavior? No. Sustainable? Certainly not. But here we are. So now I'm both exhausted and wired from the shift in my carefully curated routine, and I'm not sure I have anyone to blame but myself.

I've planned to spend the day in the office. I want to get a run in, get ahead while the office is quiet, and then melt into my couch for a mindless marathon of reality TV. Exciting life, but hey, someone has to do it.

In typical March fashion, temperatures have shifted from freezing cold to the first signs of spring in the span of a week. I throw on a pair of leggings, sports bra, and long-sleeved tee, lace up my sneakers, put my apartment key in my pants pocket, and head out. Despite the early hour, the city is already stirring to life, full of promise and anticipation, while store owners sweep the sidewalks before they get too crowded.

Zoning out, I run to the Brooklyn Bridge and turn around. The sun bounces off the silver skyscrapers, and these are the moments when you realize just how massive this city is. Millions and millions of people on this 22-square-mile island. It makes you believe it when they say if you can make it here, you can make it anywhere.

But there is one big, unfortunately very attractive obstacle in my way of making it. And now I'm unsure if my blood is pumping from my run or from thinking of Matt.

Seeing him the past week in the office has been confusing to say the least. On one hand, I am so angry at him for disrupting things. He's blurring the lines I've had etched in stone: work, life, and now even my heart, which was supposed to be the most locked down. He's making me feel things I don't want to feel... *can't let myself feel*. On the other hand, when he gives everyone, including the interns, his full attention when they speak, or he makes sure everyone on his team has a chance to weigh in, it's clear he's a great leader and has a quiet, confident intelligence. Any ounce of resistance I have goes to shit when I find him staring at me across the conference room table, blue eyes boring into mine like he's trying to see down to my soul.

Listen, I get it. He didn't know where I worked at first. But the minute he did, he should have said something. Even though I can begrudgingly see why he didn't, it's beside the point, because I feel betrayed and hurt. Mad at the situation, and by association, at him.

I'm mad at myself too. After Greg, I swore I wouldn't let my guard down. He'd been charming and had completely swept me off my feet. He promised he would never hurt me like my father hurt my mother. Swore I was all he ever wanted or needed to be happy, that he loved all of me. I fought it until I didn't anymore, and then I got burned. When I caught Greg cheating, it was like someone ripped my heart straight from my chest and stomped it into pieces. I was completely shattered.

Even though the wounds have scabbed over, I still haven't fully forgiven myself, and that's why I won't let it happen again. Fool me once, shame on you. There's no room to fool me twice, even for someone like Matt Meyer.

I take a long, hot shower, trying to wash any thoughts of Matt away. Since it's Saturday and no one will be in the office, I dress in my normal weekend wear: black leggings and a cropped hoodie. I throw my hair up into a bun, strands already slipping out, and swipe on a layer of mascara to mask my tired eyes.

I treat myself to a vanilla latte and take a deep breath in the elevator. I love the office on Saturday mornings. It's when I'm most productive. I have an inch-thick file of notes that need organizing, and I want to draft the outline for our presentation. I can't believe I'll be presenting to Roger Davis! This is so huge.

The elevator dings and I walk off toward my office, jump straight in, and only come up for air an hour and a half later. Leaning back in an obnoxious stretch, I feel the satisfaction you can only get from checking off a big chunk of a to-do list. I'm making progress, but my coffee has gone cold, so I head to the kitchen to reheat it. I'm not paying attention as I turn smack into a wall. I look up, startled, and see it's not a wall at all. At least not one made of stone. It's just a rock-hard chest that could pass for one, with tight abs behind a T-shirt that smells like clean soap and driftwood.

The scent that belongs to the one person I've been trying to avoid.

"Whoa, slow down there!" he warns as he lightly grabs my arms to steady me.

"Hey! Watch the latte!"

Matt steadies my arm with the cup. "I know people love their coffee, but you're protective on a whole other level," he jokes.

"Yeah, well, I only treat myself to this once in a while, so it's special," I reply, chin tilting in defiance. Spending five dollars every day on a cup of coffee isn't in my budget. Matt doesn't need to know that specific fact, he just needs to make sure he doesn't make me spill it.

He chuckles. "No messing with the latte. Noted."

"What are you doing here anyway?" No longer surprised at his presence, my body starts tingling from his proximity. I look up as he takes a deep swallow. I tuck some hair behind my ear, silently cursing myself for not making more of an effort this morning.

"Uh, I work here?" He grins, his hands still on my arms. I look down and hone in on those beautiful, corded forearms. I want to lick them, graze my teeth along the length of them.

Rein it in, Emily.

I give a half-hearted laugh and step back from his touch, putting space between us to collect my thoughts.

But now I'm cornered. My senses are on high alert. All I smell is Matt and I want to wrap myself up in him. I drop my eyes and stare at his black sneakers, not trusting myself to look directly at him. Like a good yogi who stands up slowly, one vertebra at a time, I take in his dark jeans and the faded blue T-shirt that hangs loose at his waist but snug around his chest. I lick my lips, thinking of the ridges and valleys in all the right places behind that piece of cotton.

I stop at his neck, the day-old scruff that I can practically feel scraping my skin, the strong jaw, the full lips that were the softest I ever kissed, and finally look into his eyes. Eyes that are the same color as his shirt, that same Caribbean Sea-blue I noticed the first night at Smith's Cave. Eyes that aren't blinking as they search my face. His hair is mussed, like he's been running his hands through it, and my body hums. I close my eyes, wondering if he'd notice me leaning in to take another sniff for sustenance.

I open my eyes and Matt's still staring at me, one eyebrow cocked and a smirk on his face like he knows exactly what I'm thinking. His words finally register in my brain—he *does* work here now—and it's the splash of cold water I need to knock me out of my daydream.

"Yes, I remember," I coolly reply. "I *meant*, what are you doing here on a Saturday?"

He dips his hands in his jeans pockets and he shrugs. "Probably the same as you? Catching up, prepping for Monday. I wanted to have some quiet time to sort through my first week."

I did manage to notice that Matt is very thoughtful about his work, conscious to take a moment to think before he speaks. I'm not surprised he would want to catch up without too many distractions.

The silence lingers and my initial anger starts to soften when I remember what it's like being the new guy.

"It was pretty intense," I comment, an attempt at civility.

He takes a deep breath. "Yeah, you could say that." He laughs. "It's funny pitching an auto account in the city though, since pretty much no one here drives or has a car."

I nod my head and offer a tiny chuckle. "This is very true."

We both look away in opposite directions, the awkwardness of finally being alone taking shape. All I have to do is twist my body a little bit and walk away, but he's not moving and so my body refuses to either.

"The Knicks looked good last night," I say at exactly the same time he asks, "Did you see the new Harry Potter store finally opened?"

We lock eyes, amusement swirling in his pools of blue. Matt bows his head as if to say *You first* and then waits for me to speak.

"I did see that it finally opened. It looks amazing. I'm hoping to get there once the pitch is done. Did you watch the Knicks game?"

"Yes! Ryan and I actually went to the game. I haven't heard the Garden that loud since I was a kid watching Patrick Ewing play." He lights up like a little kid talking about—well, his favorite basketball team. "They're finally showing up in the paint and playing some defense, which is what we need. Jones was on fire, sinking three-pointers. It's way more fun to watch when they're in a zone like this."

I grin alongside him, his energy contagious. We fall silent again and I exhale. "Well, I'm going to get back to it." I tilt my head toward my office. "Good luck with your work today."

"Thanks, Emily. Same to you." I feel his eyes follow me before I finally turn the corner out of his sight.

Two hours pass, and I'm about to start packing up when my phone rings. It's my landlord. *Shit, shit, shit.* I know he's calling to ask where my rent is, but we don't get paid until next week and my bank account has never been this low. The timing couldn't get worse. I just need to get through this month and get that promotion.

I take a deep breath for courage and hit Accept.

"Hi, Mr. Marino."

"Emily, where's your rent? It's a week late."

"Yeah, I know it's late, I'm really sorry. I don't get paid until next week, so can I *please* have one more week? I can pay you half now."

"Emily, I can't keep doing this. You signed a lease. I should be raising your rent, not making concessions. This is the last month. If it happens one more time, you're out."

"I know I've been late, but you can't just kick me out, can you?"

"I can, and I will. I've been plenty patient. I should have taken the rest of your deposit a while ago."

"Mr. Marino, please. You know Greg moved out, and I've been trying to cover this on my own. Is there anything I can do? Can I find a sublet to take over the apartment?"

"Emily, you know the rules. There is no subletting of leases. We've been over this."

I feel my bottom lip start to tremble but vow to hold it together, at least while I'm on the phone. I tell Mr. Marino I'll have it to him as soon as I can, but panic grips me. I have no idea where I'll get the money. I haven't told my mom about the situation because I didn't want her to worry. Plus, I don't want to take any money from her. I hang up the phone and the tears start. Normally, I wouldn't cry at work, but Matt's office is on the other side of the floor and no one else is here.

The pressure of work, money, and the loneliness I feel, sitting here in my office with no one to confide in, gets the best of me. I sit in my chair and let the tears flow, giving me the release I need.

CHAPTER 15

MATT

I stop a few feet away from Emily's office door when I hear her talking. I'm meeting Ben for a late lunch near the office but want to say goodbye, savoring the silent truce from the kitchen. For that brief moment, I was back with the Emily from the bar—the one from my bed—and I didn't realize how much I was craving any glimpse of that version until she was in front of me. Not to mention how delectable she looked walking away from me in her leggings.

I didn't expect to hear her in tears. I feel guilty eavesdropping, but she sounds so desperate. She said she has a lot riding on the pitch and the potential promotion that comes with it, but this is more than I expected. She could lose her apartment? After seeing her in action all week, there's no doubt Emily is buttoned-up and responsible. I can't see her putting herself in such a position to be this under water financially. I have to be missing a piece of the story.

Guilt creeps up my stomach and clogs my throat. I need to win this pitch to finally be free of my debt, but I don't need it to avoid getting evicted from my apartment. This isn't even about the work like it is for Emily. She loves advertising. Part of me wants to confess everything, but why throw gasoline on the embers of her hatred for me when they finally seem to be cooling? She wouldn't understand, and I wouldn't blame her. This pitch, this job, is her livelihood. It's what she's worked so hard for the last few years. My callous feelings about it would only pour salt on her open wound.

I quietly turn around and head to the elevators. I realize just how little I actually know about Emily's life, even though I feel like I know so much about who she is. I know her soft moans of pleasure and how she fits perfectly in my arms. I know how her eyes crinkle when she's genuinely smiling at someone, and how the room shines brighter the moment she walks in. She brings light to anyone lucky enough to be in her orbit and has no idea how captivating she is.

I don't know much about her family though. She's mentioned her mom, but nothing about her father. I don't know where she's from or why she can't afford her apartment anymore. I know feelings and emotions, but I don't know any facts, and right now, it seems there are a lot of those facts causing her pain. All I want to do is walk into her office, take her in my arms, and reassure her that everything will be alright. That I'll help her figure it all out.

But since I'm pretty sure that's the last thing Emily wants, I leave to meet Ben for lunch.

I walk into the bar and see that Ben's already grabbed us a table. The bar is packed for March Madness, but thankfully we're in a back corner where it will be quieter.

"Hey, man," Ben says, nodding up at me. "You look like shit."

"Thanks, dude. Appreciate that." I nod back as I take off my jacket and sit down. I actually do appreciate that Ben notices and I won't need to bullshit my way through lunch pretending I'm not preoccupied with the gorgeous girl I just left in tears.

"Who died? Why the face?" he asks, pushing a full beer toward me. Have I mentioned how much I love my friend Ben?

I take a sip, sit back, and let out a long breath. "Nothing really, just work. New pitches are always high pressure, but the added element of Roger Davis is just getting to me a bit."

Ben is silent, letting me settle in. He's had a front row seat to the complexities of my relationship with my dad. "Do you regret agreeing to this?" The waitress drops off a plate of wings for each of us, both ordered by Ben before I got there.

I think for a moment as I bite into a wing. Do I? On one hand, I resent my father for basically blackmailing me to do this. But then there's Emily. I regret how it all came out and that she no longer trusts me, but getting to be near her every day is worth it.

"I didn't really have a choice. When my dad heard Nolan was running point for Imperial, he jumped on it. It's just that Emily was completely unexpected." I shake my head. "In some ways, it's a good thing because I get to spend time with her, even if most of it is spent with me trying to thaw her iciness."

"That's right, she works there." He finishes a wing and grabs a napkin to wipe his hands. "Not awkward at all," he says, laughing and shaking his head at me. "She cut off your balls yet?"

I squirm in my seat at that thought but laugh, immediately grateful there aren't many sharp objects in our office.

"I'm sure the thought has crossed her mind." I drop my head in defeat, grabbing another wing. "It's safe to say she was the complete and total opposite of happy to see me in the office my first day. It was a major fuck-up on my part, but what are the chances that she works at my dad's company?" As much as I know she's mad at me, I have to admit I look forward to seeing her every day.

"Don't get me wrong, she still avoids me like the plague, but every day I feel a little less hostility. Every now and then she'll refrain from her deathly glare, and she actually cracked a smile one time, but then I realized someone was standing behind me and it was directed at them."

Ben chuckles and shakes his head. "Only you, man. Only you would get yourself into a predicament like this. But it's good to see you actually caring about something—some*one* again. You're finding your old spark through all of this, and it's the first time I've seen something matter in a while. She may want your balls on a platter, but she brought you back to life, so I'm a fan."

I sit back and wipe my hands, taking another sip of beer as Ben's words sink in. I do feel alive again, and hopeful, which is strange considering how much Emily resents me right now. Despite her anger, she ignited something in me that I thought left with Stella and was never coming back. Sure, I've hooked up with women and had a handful of short-term relationships. They never penetrated the surface though, and the women always knew I wasn't looking for anything serious. With Emily though... That all blew up the minute she walked into the bar and I felt my heart start to beat again.

And now she's about to get evicted and needs this promotion much more than me. Yet if my father even had an inkling that I threw the pitch because of a woman, I would never hear the end of it. It would be the death blow that permanently knocks out any possibility we could civilly coexist for the benefit of my mother. He would be even more relentless.

"Yo, you there? I lost you." Ben tilts his head down to catch my attention.

"Yeah, sorry. Just thinking about work. Winning this pitch means way more to Emily than me. This is her career, and everything she's worked for the past few years is riding on this chance. Plus, she's hinted how much the promotion will help her financially. Hell, she doesn't even know my dad owns the fucking agency. I hate hiding this all from her, but I can't just waltz into her office and confess that my daddy made me do all of this and I'm leaving soon anyway."

"How has it been with your dad?"

"What you would expect: fucking miserable. But I'll give him credit that his jabs all happen outside of work. He's actually left me alone in the office. It was the one stipulation for me taking the project, and he's respected that, thankfully. But being there day in and day out has only reinforced that I'm ready to put all advertising behind me."

"So you're wondering if there's any way to win this pitch *and* still get the girl?" Ben asks.

His delivery is nonchalant but he hits the nail on the head with that one simple question.

I let out a long exhale. "That's the crux of it, yeah. My dad or the girl, I guess I have to choose."

"Do you, though? Have you thought about just telling Emily the truth? Instead of keeping it from her, maybe you should tell her what's going on. The whole story, so she has the full picture."

I hang my head and groan. "Yes, I've thought about it. I think about it all day, every day. Do I think it's a good idea? I have no fucking clue. I don't know if the truth will make things better or worse. Things will get really awkward really fast if it's not well received, and I don't want anything to hinder her chance to run the account."

Ben quietly stares at me. He slowly takes a sip of his beer and lets the silence hang.

"You are so fucked. I don't think you ever had it this bad for Stella. Throw in the cards now, my man, because this girl has you hook, line, and sinker."

I hold Ben's stare and then bang my forehead on the table. "I know, dude. God damn, don't I know it."

CHAPTER 16

EMILY

Having four weeks to pull together a fully integrated business pitch is pure insanity. It leaves little to no time to organize and strategize—both things key to how I work best.

This type of pitch includes bringing together multiple departments to create one team for the client. While the Strategy team usually spearheads everything, each specialty would have its own lead, and those leaders would meet with the client early on in the process for what is called a chemistry check.

But Imperial—and Hunter Holt specifically—does things differently. He wants everything to flow through the Strategy team. So, only we will be presenting the final pitch, meaning the pressure is on us—me, Matt, Sheila, and Josh—to nail the chemistry check. This is the first real test DMG has to pass, and if anything goes wrong, it could impact the entire selection process. If the check fails or we do anything to stir up doubt, we'll have more than just ourselves to answer to.

Given this pressure, sleep has evaded me the past few nights. I head to work unusually early, even for me, and am mentally scrolling through my to-do list when I enter my office and stop in surprise at what I find on my desk.

There's a large to-go coffee cup sitting there. It's from Charlie's, the coffee shop around the corner from our building. *What the hell is that doing here?* I definitely didn't have Charlie's yesterday, and even if I did, I wouldn't leave the cup there.

I move around the desk to sit in my chair, eyeing the cup like it could detonate any second, then see a Post-it half-stuck on the side.

E-

**A weekday treat to start
a big day on the right foot.**

-M

I put my hands on the cup and find it's steaming hot, the undeniable sweet vanilla scent confirming it's a latte.

Matt got me a vanilla latte.

I slump back in my chair, my head a whirlpool of questions. He remembered what I said on Saturday? I don't think Greg ever paid that much attention, and I thought we'd be married one day. Matt has been patient with me the past week and a half. He's not once pushed back on my bad attitude, he's winning over everyone working on the pitch, and he seems to want the agency to succeed, not just his team.

I close my eyes and sigh. I'm not used to someone looking out for me, and I don't want to like it as much as I do. Continuing to give him the cold shoulder when he's trying so hard to connect makes me the bad guy in this current situation. And with everything we all have on the line, the only bad guys we should be worried about is the other agency pitching Imperial.

I take off my coat and grab my phone.

Me: Hi.

Magic Matt: Hi!

Me: Thank you for my latte.

Magic Matt: You're welcome. Life's too short to wait for a special occasion for a good cup of coffee. And today is quite the occasion.

Me: The coffee will do me good. I didn't sleep much last night, thinking about lunch today.

Magic Matt: Same. At least we're in it together.

Together. I pause, not knowing how to respond to that. My brain knows he means as colleagues—and in some broader sense, teammates—but my stomach flips thinking about how Matt and I were together the first weekend we met. All the togethers are becoming hard to pull apart.

Me: True. Thanks again for the coffee. I'll see you for lunch.

♥

A knock on my door tears my gaze away from my screen. It's 12:10 and Matt is standing in my doorway, wearing his coat.

"Ready to go?"

My breath catches as I discreetly drink him in. He's wearing black boots, dark jeans, a navy-blue-and-white-checkered button-down, and a navy jacket. All the blended blues succeed in making his eyes sparkle like stars against a midnight sky. He's so damn handsome, and this reaction—flutters in my belly, a nibble on my lower lip—worries me. My resolve to keep distance between us is slowly deteriorating.

"Uh, yeah, let me grab my jacket." I stand up and feel the warmth of his eyes grazing up my body. I say a silent prayer of thanks to Zara for this dress, and also to my dry cleaners for helping me keep it in good shape after so many wears. He flattens himself against my door to make room for me to pass, and the smell of the ocean air hits me as my shoulder brushes his chest. His hand finds the small of my back to guide me, and I turn back in surprise.

"Shit, sorry." He pulls his hand off me and holds it up in surrender.

I give him a close-lipped smile. "No worries. All good," I reassure him, willing the goose bumps forming on my arms to go away. I have a coat on, for Pete's sake—how the hell can his touch affect me like that through layers of cotton and wool?

We walk in silence, my stomach clenching with nerves, thinking about both lunch and the closeness of Matt. There's the usual anxiety about meeting a client for the first time. I'm relieved there's a small group of us and not the paralyzing pressure of one-on-one conversation, but I'm still preoccupied with the out-of-control feeling that accompanies new situations.

My thoughts are interrupted as we join the crowd waiting for the elevators. Every Wednesday, midtown is swarmed with tourists trying to eat before their two p.m. Broadway shows, and it can be a bitch to navigate. Most of us slip out to try to beat the pre-matinee lunch rush, which causes its own congestion.

I shuffle side to side and clear my throat. "Have you been to Bistecca before?"

"Not here. They have a location in Chicago that was terrific, so I'm expecting a decent meal at the very least." He shrugs his shoulders.

"I'm too nervous to even think about eating."

"Hey." Matt's toe taps mine. "Hunter would be lucky to have you on his account. He'll realize that." I feel the full force of his attention on me and am momentarily tongue-tied.

Thankfully, I'm saved by the elevator arriving. Matt holds the door open for everyone to pile in and I'm the last to enter before him. People are still shuffling around, hitting floor numbers and trying to find personal space, when I'm pushed to the side. Matt shifts behind me and anchors his hand on the railing to my left. He's standing so close I can feel his warm breath on my neck. I tip back ever so slightly remembering how much time he spent exploring that spot with his mouth and squeeze my legs together, willing my body to stop reacting. We stop at the floor below us and three more people try to squeeze in, forcing me to take another step back and leaving no room for even Jesus Christ himself between us.

I turn my head and look up at him. "Sorry, I know it's tight in here."

He smirks down at me. "That's what she said."

I roll my eyes but can't hold back a laugh when we stop at the next floor and more people shuffle on and off. I squeeze closer to Matt to avoid getting knocked out by an oversized backpack and my hip pushes his hand against the elevator wall. He turns it slightly so it's now resting on said hip. My skin burns at his touch. I instinctually lean into him again, like I'm one of Pavlov's dogs being trained for specific behavior. Touch, lean. Good Emily.

I look over my shoulder at him. "I don't think anyone else can fit in here, so hopefully we're in the clear until we hit the lobby."

His lips brush my ear as he murmurs, "I don't mind. With you this close, I can smell your coconut shampoo. It makes me wish the scent still lingered on my pillow." He squeezes my hip once, then pulls his hand away. My heartbeat pulses in my ears. I thought that night was living rent-free only in my head. I don't know whether to be appalled Matt brought it up, impressed that he had the balls to go there, or turned on by his deep, gravelly voice. I settle for a combination of all three, heavier on the latter for sure.

The elevator doors open to the lobby and I feel the lightest brush of his fingers on my lower back as we exit. "And we're off to the races." Matt winks at me and I *hear* my breath catch.

For the first time since he showed up, we're on the same side instead of competing against each other. Our shared goal today: woo the client so they choose us. Like he said this morning, we're in this part together. It's not lost on me how the thought of Matt and I as a team makes me feel safe, protected.

I feel feverish, and the fresh air is a salve on my flushed cheeks and the fire kindling in my belly. As we approach the restaurant, I see Sheila a short distance ahead of us and I speed up to reach her, mainly to put some distance between Matt and me.

Hunter Holt's reputation precedes him. He's known as one of the toughest negotiators, doesn't take shit from anyone, and has a poker face that would make a Navy SEAL break down. The man fears no one yet given the groundbreaking accomplishments he's made in the auto, tech, and aeronautics industry, he's revered. He's a trailblazer, a risk taker, and a brilliant engineer. As tough as his reputation is, he's also known for his fairness.

"Nice to meet you, Mr. Holt," I say as I hold out my hand to shake his. His handshake is firm as I maintain eye contact the entire time. He tilts his head as he sizes me up. Without another word, he turns toward Matt.

"Good to see you again, Matt."

Matt nods. "Hello, Hunter."

Excuse me, what? See you *again*? Matt never mentioned he knows Hunter. *What. The. Fuck*? That would have been good intel to have coming into this. And yet, Matt left out an important detail—a really *important* detail—which makes my blood simmer.

I fight the urge to kick Matt in the shins under the table as we all sit down. He takes the spot next to me but is avoiding looking at me. He dives straight into a conversation about the Knicks with Josh and Hunter, and I wonder if he saw my surprise when Hunter greeted him.

The waiter comes by and takes our orders. Once he leaves, we sit in that awkward silence among strangers who are sizing each other up and wondering if there's a connection to be made. Like a group first date. I start racking my brain to come up with something interesting and witty to say, which only makes my mind go blank, and my temple starts throbbing the more the situation feels out of my control. Josh thankfully interrupts the spiral.

"Emily, why don't you introduce yourself to Hunter first?"

All sets of eyes turn toward me, and my mouth goes dry.

"Hi." I lift my hand and awkwardly wave. "Emily Cooper. I've been at DMG for five years. I've worked on both the creative and strategy side of things, most recently leading Strategy for health and personal care brands for Peters Grant, and before that I led Creative for Lantern's soda brands."

"Those are some major brands. Have you ever worked in the auto industry?" Hunter asks.

"No, I haven't. But I've worked on major consumer brands when they were breaking through to the market or targeting new customers. My strength is translating insights into action and finding the emotional connection with a target audience. I look at the fact that I haven't worked in auto as an advantage, because I'm approaching the account with fresh eyes and new perspectives."

Hunter sits back and crosses his arms over his chest as if he's sizing me up based on my answer. He gives nothing away, giving me a polite nod as he turns to Matt. Does this mean I failed the first test? I certainly feel dismissed.

"So, Matt, I heard you left Chicago. I hope things are going well here." It comes out as more of a question than a statement, and I feel like I've been sitting at the kids' table too long because so much is going over my head.

Matt nods. "It was bittersweet leaving the Aura team after all we did to launch in Europe and Australia."

"That launch campaign was very impressive. If I remember correctly, it won a few awards as well."

"That's right. We won a Cannes Lion and a Clio for the launch campaign." Matt gives his reply with little emotion, like he hasn't just acknowledged he's in possession of two of the most prestigious awards in advertising. His humility is not lost on me.

Hunter addresses me next. "Emily, have any of your campaigns won awards?" There's a challenge in the question, but it doesn't come across condescending, and I appreciate his directness.

"Actually, two. A Cannes & two Effies."

Hunter folds a finger over his lips, studying me. "What were the campaigns?"

"One was for the Lantern Europe launch, and one was for feminine products from Peters Grant."

"Feminine products," he repeats, still giving nothing away. "That's..." He trails off. "Very different than cars."

"True, but we built a groundbreaking campaign based on psychographic research, and isn't that what you would want for Imperial?" I volley back. "We took the insight that young girls are struggling to process the media's messages about their appearance and ability, and we provided them with a clear one—that it's okay to be different, to be strong, to feel confident, and to believe in yourself. Not only were we able to inspire the younger generation of women to believe they're more than what the patriarchy wants them to believe, we also connected girls across the world to support each other."

"So you opted to tug on heartstrings rather than talk about the product?"

"Excuse me?" I didn't mean for that to come out so loud. That campaign is one of the highlights of my career so far. Hundreds of thousands of products went to girls in third-world countries thanks to its success.

I feel Matt's hand grab mine under the table, likely sensing my rising anger. He gives me a slight squeeze, and I'm grateful for the distraction. He doesn't let go, reassuring me he's there. With that one touch I feel supported. He's making sure I don't combust in front of the client even though it could have given him an advantage if I did. He chose to help me instead. I squeeze back as I take a breath before I say something I know I'll regret.

"We didn't set out to tug heartstrings; we set out to make a tangible impact. There are millions of girls across Africa who are forced to miss school because of their periods, putting them at a disadvantage to progress through their studies and secure jobs. Our campaign enabled us to supply enough product to ensure over a million girls were able to remain in school and graduate on time. It hit an emotional chord because it was truthful and authentic, and it won awards because it created a movement. I assume you want the same approach for Imperial—to find unexpected insights and surprise consumers with it."

The table is eerily quiet. Thankfully, our food arrives to give us something to focus on. The silence lingers as we eat until Hunter finally speaks.

"You are correct in that I want to surprise and delight my customers, Emily. But like most men, I lean toward facts, not emotion. Imperial produces superior cars in the luxury bracket, and the men who buy our cars understand that. After his years leading auto accounts, Matt can agree that when it comes to cars, men want something sleek and fast and powerful. Don't you agree?" Hunter fixes his gaze on Matt.

"I believe there's room for both," Matt replies in a firm but even tone. "What Emily is saying about finding a unique and unexpected insight is spot on and is what great advertising is built on. You want the audience to feel the right emotions, otherwise your product won't rise above the clutter. You never want to rely fully on one attribute because that alienates so many other possibilities. The best work balances emotions. If we want to bring new buyers to the brand, we need to find the right mix of playing up the power, like you've so rightly pointed out, while making a personal connection, like Emily suggested. It'll be a challenge, but one that I'm confident we can meet."

I don't know how he managed to do it, but in a handful of words, Matt was able to support me without disagreeing with Hunter, expertly defusing the rising tension. His gaze drops to mine, those deep indigo eyes reassuring me. *Together.* I'm safe. He gives my hand another quick squeeze before pulling it away, and I feel its absence as the cold air hits my palm.

"Well, you both are certainly passionate about your craft. And admittedly, Emily, you've given me something to think about. We've yet to consider the emotional side of Imperial." He wipes his mouth, drops his napkin on the table, and stands. Our plates haven't even been cleared yet, but apparently Hunter is done with lunch. "Hopefully that will translate to what you present. I have a meeting downtown so I need to cut this short, and I need to push up the presentations to two weeks from today due to some business overseas. I met with the PR team this morning to make them aware." He looks over at Josh. "Nolan will reach out with the meeting details."

Once he's out of the restaurant, I exhale the breath I'd been holding. Josh looks at Sheila, Sheila looks at me, I look at Matt—and we all burst at once. "He wants us to be ready in two weeks?" comes from Shelia, and "Is he for real?" rips from Josh. I turn to Matt and pin him with a glare, though it lacks the vex it held before the events of lunch. "And you *know* him? Don't you think that information would have been helpful to share ahead of time?" Matt is about to respond when Josh puts a hand up to cut him off. "Regardless of all that, we have to deliver a pitch in fourteen days." I don't miss the anxious undertones in his voice. "You both ready for this?"

Matt nods and I look at Josh, offering what I hope will boost his confidence. "Never been more ready. Bring it on."

I'm silent as we walk back to the office, choosing to listen as the others discuss timing and rearranging meetings. I'm shaken, but more so from uncovering another secret that Matt kept from me. We pause once we enter the revolving doors of our building.

"Listen, I know Hunter is tough, but this account could be career-defining for all of us," Josh says. "I know we have the talent and the right ideas to take Imperial to the next level. Let's forget about Hunter and just put our heads down over the next two weeks."

Josh checks his phone. "Sheila and I have to meet with PR, so we'll catch up with you later to map out the revised schedule." They walk off, leaving the two of us to face each other.

Once they're out of earshot, I finally unleash. "How the hell do you know him? And why didn't you say anything?"

He blows out a breath and looks up. "I led the account when Hunter was CEO at Falcon, before he started Imperial."

"What was all the talk this morning about being in this together? Together means not blindsiding your teammate on the field in the middle of the game. Or did they not teach that in your fancy lacrosse camps?"

Matt steps back as my comment lands. It was a low blow, but my anger got the best of me. He hasn't approached this pitch, or me, like the competition I've made it out to be. He didn't intentionally seek out DMG and this assignment just to take it from me. But he also strategically omits information, and a lie is a lie no matter what package it comes in.

"Wow, all right."

"Matt, I'm sor—"

"No, no. I appreciate the honesty," he cuts me off, jaw clenched. "In retrospect, I probably should have mentioned that Hunter and I know each other, but I could already see how nervous you were about this lunch. I know how you've built Hunter up in your mind, and I didn't want to give you any additional stress. I was concerned you'd think my knowing Hunter would give me an advantage, but I can assure you it did not. There's no such thing as an advantage with Hunter."

"I see that now, but a warning still would have been nice."

"I get it, and I apologize." He takes a deep breath. "While we're on the topic, I also know Nolan Fields."

I suck in my lips and nod my head, not sure what to make of all of this. Matt knows everyone. How is it possible I feel even more threatened?

"It's a small industry, Emily. But it doesn't change anything. In the end, we both want DMG to win the pitch, right?"

I can't argue with that. Regardless of who runs Imperial, it would be a huge win for all of us. Plus, I haven't forgotten how Matt backed me up with Hunter today.

"Yes, that's right."

Matt stays silent and nods.

"Can we just promise no more blindsides?" I motion between us. "I know this hasn't been easy, but if we're going to win, we have to be in sync in front of the client. No surprises."

"No more blindsides." He holds out his hand for me to shake. I place my hand in his, watching it get swallowed up. I shiver as he ever so lightly rubs his pinky finger against the side of my hand. Neither of us moves to let go until a group of suits breaks the spell with their laughter. I pull my hand back, cupping it discreetly with my other to soothe the aftershocks of our contact.

We walk to the elevators with silent tension circling us. I'm not entirely sure if I can trust Matt, and I can't shake the unsettling feeling I've had since his arrival. Yet, there was nothing I wanted more than for him to keep holding my hand under the table. Battling through these emotions feels like an insurmountable task. With the new deadline Hunter just sprung on us, there's way too much to get done, and expending energy on trying to figure Matt out won't help anything.

CHAPTER 17

MATT

It was Hunter and his previous company—Falcon—that almost cost me everything and why I'm in this situation in the first place. Yet, I've always had a decent relationship with Hunter Holt, even if he can be tough at times. But when he initially challenged Emily, I was momentarily stunned as a fierce protectiveness dug its nails into me. I wanted to shield her, keep any and all hurt away from her. Ironic, considering I managed to do that myself by sidestepping the fact I know Hunter, but hindsight's a bitch—lesson learned.

Even with my fuckup, it feels like Emily and I have inched a little closer to each other. I don't have any time to dwell on it, though. The accelerated schedule and our internal creative challenge—the meeting where we present our ideas to each other and see what bubbles to the top—have been pushed up as well. Everyone stayed late last night in the hopes we wouldn't have to pull an all-nighter leading into tomorrow's challenge. It's 6:30 p.m. and my goal is to have everyone home by ten so we can get a good night's sleep. I decide to order dinner and grab some beer, stopping by Emily's office to see if she has any special requests.

I know I don't need to do this—I *know*. But ever since lunch, I've found myself looking for any excuse to see her. My mind constantly wanders back to how gracefully she stood up to Hunter when he tried to downplay her achievements. She was brilliant and beautiful, even more so because I felt her shaking under the table. It's getting harder to deny the pull she has on me, and I'm so exhausted from the hours we've been working that I can hardly even try to fight it. So off I go, under the guise of the all too important and urgent question of sausage or pepperoni.

Her office door is ajar. She's making notes on a presentation, brows creased and murmuring to herself. She bites on her lower lip and I have to stifle a groan. Those lips. Remembering how soft they are keeps me awake at night. How good they tasted.

I clear my throat to get her attention, and she looks up and smiles. Can I take that as a good sign? Or is it how she initially greets everyone—look, see, smile? Even so, it's much better than *look, see, sneer,* which is what I was getting last week. I'm buoyed with confidence and step into her office as she tilts her head and removes her headphones.

"Hey."

Let me note for the jury that she is *still* smiling.

"I'm ordering some pizzas and beers for the team. I'm hoping to send everyone home by ten so we can be fresh for tomorrow.

Any preference for toppings?"

"Pizza's a great call. Make sure to order from Angelo's." She digs into the top drawer of her desk and hands me a menu. "They have the best garlic knots."

"Thanks for the tip." I reach out to take the menu and my fingers overlap with hers. Emily stares at our hands, paused midair, and then quickly pulls away.

"Anything else besides garlic knots?"

"I'm good. I trust you to pick." Her smile is a little stiffer and I notice she's rubbing her fingers on her legs. "I'll grab a slice when it gets here." She pops her ear buds back in and gets back to it, not so subtly dismissing me.

Thirty minutes later, both teams are in a conference room, and I feel the collective pressure deflate as music is cranked and everyone digs into the pizza. A promo for a Julia Roberts movie marathon plays on the muted TV. Julia is standing on the fire escape as Richard Gere pulls up in his white limo, arms extended, holding the black umbrella and long-stemmed red roses.

"Now that," Priya exclaims, pointing at the television, "is one of the greatest movies of all time."

"Oh, one hundred percent," Naomi replies, high-fiving Priya across the table. As she sits back down, she starts belting out how it *must have been love, but it's over now…*

Rachel and Jose join in, lamenting about how they lost it somehow.

"Please, Jose, spare us," Jeremy jokes as he launches a crumbled napkin in this direction. He looks at Priya. "You want an epic movie-montage love song, look no further than *Armageddon*. Aerosmith. Bruce Willis. Everyday heroes rescuing the world from an asteroid on a collision course with earth? Now *that* is cinematic perfection."

Naomi tilts her head in consideration. "Toxic masculinity themes aside, I can accept that. It's a classic for sure."

"Well, if we're going to talk classics, you can't forget the Voice, Miss Whitney Houston." Rachel stands and pulls Jose up, serenading him with "I Will Always Love You." Jose pretends to wipe tears with the napkin Jeremy launched at him, and everyone applauds as they sit down.

"Wait a second," Emily shouts from the back of the room where she's sitting on the cabinets lining the wall. "Has no one seriously mentioned the Canadian Queen? Did you all not grow up watching Jack and Rose? Celine Dion and 'My Heart Will Go On' must be on that list." Everyone nods their agreement. "And for the record"—she lifts her finger and points up at the ceiling as if to say *I'll have you all know*—"there was plenty of room for Jack on the door. Such a shame." Emily's laughing as she shakes her head in mock disappointment. This might be the most relaxed I've seen her since the first night we met. She's radiant. Her brilliant emerald-green eyes are dancing under the fluorescent conference room lights.

I stand up from where I'm leaning against the door. "I have to say, as the new guy, I'm kind of disappointed that y'all missed the most epic, most iconic, most addicting love song from a movie." I feel all eyes on me as I look down to my phone and scroll through my music app. "Before I hit Play and this song becomes permanently stuck in your head for the next forty-eight hours, I say *You're welcome*." I take a bow and crank up the volume on my phone.

The first few notes play as the girls cheer and stand up to sing along about having the time of their lives. The guys are groaning and shaking their heads, but Jose rises and whips out a cha-cha that would give Patrick Swayze a run for his money. Everyone is singing as they start to clean up and bag the garbage. I look over at Emily, smiling wide, and manage to catch her eye. I hold her stare and wiggle my eyebrows twice, just to test the waters. Her cheeks turn pink and she looks down, her hair swinging loose and covering her face. She jumps down and turns her back to me as she starts to pile up the empty pizza boxes.

Priya surveys the long conference room where she's standing next to me by the door. "Hey, Emily," she shouts. "I bet you could run and do the *Dirty Dancing* jump with Matt."

"Very funny, Priya, but we don't want Matt to throw out his back. We have a pitch to deliver." Emily winks playfully, but I see that her face is becoming increasingly flushed.

"Booooo," Jose hisses, heading for the door. "If we win this, Emily, you owe us a jump!"

She's laughing as they all start filing out of the room. "Sure thing."

Everyone clears out until we're the only two left. Emily finishes cleaning off the table and joins me on my end of the room. The urge to be near her, to touch her, is so strong I fold my arms to keep them in place.

"It's nice seeing everyone blowing off some steam," I say, leaning my shoulder against the wall to face her. Truthfully, it's more like blocking her from leaving. The Emily before me is the one who hustled my brother and ran through the snow with me. She didn't have a care in the world, watched movies and napped with me on a lazy Saturday afternoon. I plan to steal as many moments as I can with her.

"Definitely. Pizza was a good call." She stands next to me, her back touching the wall, and turns her head in my direction.

"How are you feeling about tomorrow?"

She tenses at that, pushing off the wall and squaring her shoulders. The change is subtle, but just like that, she has her armor back on. I want to kick myself for reminding her that we're still essentially in competition.

"Really good, actually. I got a second wind after lunch with Hunter. I almost owe him a thank-you for challenging me because now I want to not only impress the shit out of him, but I want to show that you can be emotional and award-winning without defaulting to"—she puts her hands up in air quotes—"tugging on heartstrings."

"I have no doubt that if anyone can get him to acquiesce, it'll be you."

She looks over at me with a tight smile and nods, like she's not sure if it's a compliment or a challenge.

"Thanks for ordering pizza for everyone. I'll let us both get back to work." She turns and takes a big step around me, avoiding any chance of touching me on her way to the door.

I watch her walk out, frustrated with myself for not being able to break through the wall any further. I've managed a few small cracks in her composure, but she's still guarded, and I can't imagine she trusts me any more than she did when I first arrived at DMG.

I meet my team back in the war room and we work until I start to see more and more yawns hidden behind palms. I call it a night when I spot Jose with his head on the table at 9:30. I'm confident we're in a good place and have enough to wing it if questions come up. Everyone packs up pretty quickly and I set up Ubers for everyone on my corporate card, much to their delight.

I'm bringing the last of the beers to the kitchen when I pass the other war room. I expect it to be dark, but the light is on, illuminating the back of Emily's head, slanted in contemplation and staring at the screen. It's an unspoken rule that you never enter the other team's war room, so I stand back, put the beers on an empty desk outside the room, and lean against it. I can only see her now, not anything on the walls or the whiteboard, so I'm technically not breaking any code.

"Emily?" I ask to get her attention.

She angles her slender neck back and looks out over her shoulder. "Hey, Matt. I didn't realize you were still here."

"Just cleaning up and then heading home. Are you calling it a night soon?" Much like a hunter on a bright morning in a quiet forest, I have to step carefully to not spook her.

Emily groans and shifts in her chair. "I don't know. Yes? No? I keep running through our presentation and all I hear is Hunter's voice nitpicking and tearing everything part." She puts her forehead on the table. "If I think about him anymore, he'll turn up in my dreams and then I'll be billing him for my therapy."

"Well, we most definitely can't have that." I laugh, even though deep down I've never been more serious. The thought of Emily dreaming about Hunter makes my stomach crawl. I grab two beers and hold one out to her. "I have yet to see the infamous DMG game room. Tell me, Emily Cooper, are you as skilled with a ping-pong paddle as you are with a cue stick?"

Her eyes open wide for a minute, no doubt thinking back to the night we met. It seems like a lifetime ago. A forgotten lifetime that hasn't been discussed but is never far from my mind. Heat warms my chest when I think about how peaceful she looked sleeping next to me. I somehow knew that type of peacefulness was a rare thing for her and knowing her better now only confirms that assumption.

She rolls her chair over and accepts a beer. "Well, my uncle's bar didn't have a ping-pong table, but I'll still kick your ass." The late hour and her utter exhaustion are apparently enough to humor me.

"Let's go, killer. Game on." I hold my hand out, and much to my pleasant surprise, she takes it. We lock eyes and, again, it's as if I'm back at Smith's Cave, holding my hand out to her and feeling the buzz of anticipation course through me. As my hand closes around hers, I'm reminded just how right it feels in mine.

Emily quickly pulls her hand away and stands up. It takes every ounce of willpower I have to not snatch it back. Doesn't she feel any of this? Whatever *this* is?

DMG's headquarters take up an entire city block, and its game room is legendary in the advertising world. Running from one side of the building to the other with a wall of floor-to-ceiling windows facing south, it showcases the exquisite Manhattan skyline like nothing else. Foosball and ping-pong tables are set up in the middle of the room. Against the memorabilia-covered wall opposite the windows is a worn-in leather couch and love seat with a dozen or so bean bags scattered around. At the back is a fridge, a game cabinet, and state-of-the-art stereo system. The pride and joy is a vintage Pop-a-Shot basketball game, decked out in Knicks' logos and colors.

I turn the radio on to a mellow country station as Emily looks for paddles in the game cabinet.

"No dice," she says, shrugging a shoulder. I finally have her alone, relaxed, and I'm not about to let the absence of some paddles blow this opportunity. I take a long sip of my beer and wander over to the other end of the room. I pick up one of the basketballs and take a few shots. "How about a game of HORSE instead?"

She's at my side now and I notice her glance down at her watch. "I think that'll take too long."

"PIG?" I offer instead, holding the ball out for her.

She takes the ball and faces the basket. "Who you calling a Pig,

Meyer?" she says, draining a shot like Stephen Curry from the three-point line and winking at me.

I lift an eyebrow suspiciously. After Emily hustled Ryan so easily, I don't trust her naiveté at bar games one bit.

She sways her hips side to side in a victory dance as she sinks another shot. I line up in the row next to her, ready to shoot. She blows out a breath. "Actually, how about a break from all the competing for one night?" she says softly, turning to look at me. Picking up her beer, she tilts it toward me like an unspoken olive branch.

"No arguments here." I clink her bottle and our eyes hold for a few beats as we each sip our beer. I see a little more of the armor crumble down. Not wanting to push too hard or too fast, I put all the balls back in the basket next to the game. Emily rubs a thumb along the neck of her bottle and starts to peel off the label, heaving a long sigh through her nose.

"How are you settling in to being back in the city?" she asks.

"It feels like I never left—in a good way. Still surrounded by boxes, but it's better than expected. All that's left to do is head back to Chicago in a couple of weeks to grab a few things I left in storage, then I'm here for good."

I run back through my words and realize that "here" could be interpreted a few ways. I mean New York, but I see the wheels turning in Emily's head as she thinks I mean DMG.

She turns to look out the windows. It's a clear night and the city is alive. The New York Harbor looks like black silk beyond the twinkling skyscrapers, and it feels like the Statue of Liberty is within arm's reach. I put my beer down and walk behind her, our reflections staring back at us in the glass. We're closer than we've been in the past couple of weeks and I'm afraid to breathe in case I disrupt the equilibrium.

The first few chords to "Yellow" come on over the speakers and I see the change in the way her chest moves up and down with her breath. This song was playing when we woke up together that Saturday morning, lazing in bed and stealing kisses without a care in the world. It almost makes me laugh to think that the biggest problem I had that morning was figuring out whether I should tell her about Ryan's failed attempt at a bet. Now I'm trying to just find some common ground.

I take a step closer, carefully watching her reaction in the window. Our eyes stay connected as she takes another sip of beer.

"Emily," I rasp, all the desperation I've been feeling seeping out in that one, breathless word. She remains still aside from her chest rising and falling. My hands are burning holes in my pockets, and I drop my head back with an inward groan. I give in—of course I do—and tentatively place my hands on her shoulders, eyes never leaving hers. I feel her suck in a breath, which pushes her back against me. Neither of us moves an inch as my grip on her shoulders tightens ever so slightly. I turn her so she's facing me, her eyes on the ground, on her beer, on anything but me.

She's so close her chest is brushing against mine. So much is riding on this moment, like I'm at the free throw line with :03 left in game seven of the championships and the Knicks are down by one. *If I sink the first shot, we have a chance. I miss, and it's all over.*

"Em, look at me."

She doesn't move. I don't even see her breathe. *I bounce the ball on the free throw line, taking my time, because tying the game keeps our hope alive.*

"Please." *And I lob the ball up...*

She stays still, her attention rooted on our shoes. Just when I think it'll bounce off the rim and be game over, she glances up at me through heavy-lidded eyes.

Nothing but net..

"Matt." Her voice is so soft I have to strain to hear it. "We can't."

"Why not?" I whisper, my heart hanging out of my chest. "This situation is temporary. It's not always going to be like this."

She closes her eyes and shakes her head, looking down again. *Up goes the game-winning shot. It's all on the line, now or never. If I lose her here, if she pulls away, time runs out.*

"God, Emily, if you knew how badly I've wanted you..." She looks up at my confession and I cup my hands around her face, stroking her cheeks. "I know that sounds insane because we haven't known each other very long, but I know you feel the connection, and to think work could prevent anything else from happening is destroying me." I take a step closer and she doesn't pull away. She looks up at me and licks her lips.

I rub my thumb over her bottom lip. "I lay awake every night thinking about how smooth your skin is, how badly I've wanted another taste of these lips." I skim my hands to her temples. "I dream about running my fingers through this soft hair." Slowly

I comb through the strands, pushing them away from her face. Her gorgeous, perfect face and those magical eyes.

Slowly tracing her nose with my own, I murmur, "Tell me you don't feel it and I'll walk away. As much as it'll wreck me, if you don't want this, I will never bring it up again. But if you feel even a fraction of what I do, please trust me. Trust this. Trust *us*." It's a whispered plea, a 50/50 shot that could break me if she says no. *The ball arches up and sails toward the hoop in slow motion.*

After a few moments of nothing, of her just searching my eyes, she finally nods.

Swish.

That nod, that slightest movement I would have missed if I didn't have all my senses targeted on her, makes me feel like I just won the NBA championship, the Super Bowl, and an Olympic gold medal in every damn sport at the same time. Relief rushes out of me like a flash flood, surprising me at how much I let ride on her answer. It has taken Herculean effort to keep myself away from her, my fingers constantly aching from holding back. She's intoxicating, hypnotic, and with the way I'm slipping under her spell, it doesn't matter if she's spitting vitriol at me or reluctantly nodding at something I say, I crave her. No matter how much my common sense is trying to tell me to stop, I'm physically incapable with her in my arms.

I lower my head and test the waters, lightly brushing my lips over hers. The fullness of them makes me groan. *Go easy, pal.* Heeding my own advice, I plant slow, soft kisses on her lips, feeling her hands grip my shirt and drag me ever so slightly against her. I trail kisses on her cheek, up to her temple and across her forehead, repeating the pattern down the other side of her face, worshiping her with my lips and silently praying she feels what I do. My hands are glued to her cheeks as I worry the slightest movement will disenchant us.

I pull my face back to look into her eyes and see the last of her armor crumble. Her hands tighten around my waist as she leans into me. I lower my mouth to hers, lightly stroking my tongue against her bottom lip, willing her mouth to open for me. When she relents, my fingers grip the back of her head, holding her in place to try to show her how much I've wanted her since she hasn't let me tell her with my words.

She presses into me, surrendering to the kiss. My constraint breaks as her hands run up and down my sides and I walk her backward toward the couch. Our lips never break apart, even when I turn around and sit, bringing her on top of me to straddle my legs. Her hair spills around her shoulders, over my hands, and when she lifts her head, I see the smile that rocked my world the minute she walked into Smith's Cave a few weeks ago. It's the smile that's been haunting my dreams, leaving me to wonder if I'd ever be lucky enough to be on the receiving end of one again.

CHAPTER 18

EMILY

A soft whimper escapes me as Matt's tongue glides across my bottom lip. My legs tighten around him as one of his hands trails down from my shoulder to my ribs, slipping behind my waist to lightly squeeze my ass and pull me further against him. His other hand is on my jaw, holding my lips to his. I feel his smile against my mouth, his calloused hands caressing my cheeks. The contrast of soft and hard spins me in the most glorious circle. I nip his bottom lip and suck on his tongue, tasting the orange of the IPA he loves so much. His moves are cautious and careful yet probing and testing, waiting to see how I reciprocate.

My heartbeat slams against my chest and I'm sure he can feel it through my clothes. I'm breathless but don't want to separate from him for the oxygen I need. I've fought this thing, yes, but I've craved his touch, and I'm tired of resisting. I'm drained from it. So at this moment, nothing else matters but Matt's hands on me—not the promotion, not my apartment, nothing at all.

Still cradling my face, he pulls away and rests his forehead against mine. He tucks my hair behind my ears with a tenderness that makes me sink deeper into his lap. "You have no idea how badly I've been wanting to do that." His fingers trail over my face like he's trying to memorize every detail. He pulls me back to his mouth, one hand sliding to the back of my neck and the other gripping my hip.

He's holding on to me for dear life, like he's afraid I'll slip away.

He tilts my head to deepen the kiss and I grind the length of him, hard and straining against his jeans. He kisses the underside of my jaw, lightly nipping at it, and I'm drowning in his taste, his smell, his touch. My core pulses as he pushes up to create more friction between us. He drags his teeth along my neck, sucking at the hollow of my throat like he's trying to mark me, and then licks across my collarbone.

We continue to make out like teenagers in heat, reliving our dry hump session from his apartment. My body responds to him like it never has to anyone else. I weave my hands through his hair and tug him closer. I don't ever want to stop. In fact, I'm questioning all my life decisions that've kept me from kissing him every night since we met. I would stay here all night if I didn't have the creative challenge tomorrow.

The creative challenge.

Tomorrow.

My team versus Matt's.

The same Matt feasting on my mouth like it's his last meal.

Matt.

I'm kissing the enemy.

I jump off his lap, wiping my mouth with my sleeve to erase the taste of him—even though it feels sacrilegious to do so. *What the fuck am I doing?*

"I, uh, I have to go. We can't be doing this. I'm sorry. I need to leave." I'm stuttering and looking around like I forgot something. I'll tell you what I forgot: my common fucking sense. I need to be at the top of my game tomorrow, and with the way things are going, I'm teetering on the point of not caring at all.

"Emily, wait." Matt stands, reaching for my hand, but I pull away too quickly.

"I can't, Matt. I can't do this." I sprint out of the room and down the hall to my office. Grabbing my bag and my coat, I pull my arms through the sleeves as I speed walk to the elevator. As soon as the elevator doors ping open to the lobby, I run out, yell goodnight to the security guard, and hail a cab. I don't think I've ever reached the street from my desk as quickly as I did just now.

I didn't sleep very well, fighting the memory of Matt's lips on mine, his touch, the way my body responded just being near him. The intense chemistry I've never felt before, almost like I can see the electricity buzzing between us. As I laid awake, I wondered if I should throw caution to the wind and give in to it, in to him, if only to release the pent-up tension. But it was throwing caution to the wind that snowy night that put me in this position in the first place. I need laser focus on this pitch. No distractions, and Matt is a ginormous one—with or without his hands or lips on me.

The rare times my thoughts didn't default to him, the slides for our presentation were on a continuous loop in my head. This day can't begin—and then end—fast enough.

I get ready for work at six a.m., given I'm already up, and run through the presentation in the shower and as I dry my hair. I predictably dress in all black but go a bit more casual today—black skinny jeans, a wide mock-neck black sweater, and black booties. Comfortable and agency-professional. Gold hoops, my David Yurman statement ring on my middle finger—in case I need that later—and I'm good to go. The armor is on.

The subway is quiet and quick and I'm at my desk by eight a.m., greeted again by a steaming hot latte.

E–

Just because.

–M

My stomach swirls. This is the shit that will throw me off my game and make me soft. I don't need sweet, thoughtful, charming Matt. I don't need him to tell me he's thinking ahead and ordering pizza and beer because everyone has been putting in such long hours. Or that he put everyone's Ubers on his corporate card last night to ensure they had a safe way to get home. And I really don't need him to publicly support what a romantic masterpiece *Dirty Dancing* is by acknowledging that it has one of the most classic love songs to ever be sung. The next thing you know, he'll be telling Hunter no one puts me in a fucking corner.

Focus, Emily. This is the first time I'll be presenting to Roger Davis, and it needs to be flawless. Impeccable. Thankfully Roger is in L.A., so he won't actually be in the room, but he'll be on video conference. Both teams will be in the room, and just knowing Matt will be there fills me with jittery anticipation.

It's a quarter to two when Sheila pops by my office as my team heads to the conference room. She looks rested and fresh: hair pulled back in a tight ponytail, eyes bright and ready for the day. Her ability to always be calm and controlled is total life goals.

"How are you feeling?" she asks from my door frame.

"Like I'm going to vomit, but that's normal, right?" I let out a self-deprecating laugh. "If I go through this presentation one more time, it'll be tattooed on my skin." Sheila laughs as she takes a sip of her coffee. "How are you always so calm and collected? You never look frazzled."

"Train for marathons on a continuous basis and you'll be too tired to think about anything else too."

"Yeah, hard pass on that one." I laugh and roll my eyes at her.

"I'm confident that you're ready and in great shape based on what we went over yesterday. This is your moment, Em. I know you'll shine."

My breath catches as I feel my gratitude for her swell—she is a boss, yes. But she's also a mentor and a true friend. "Thanks. That means a lot," I respond with a full heart. "But you need to leave before you get me all emotional and flustered." I smile and shoo her out of my office after giving her a quick hug.

I shut my door and take a few deep breaths, then check my teeth in the small mirror on the back of my door. I give myself a strong nod of approval. It's showtime.

The conference room is full. Matt's huddling with Jose and Priya as Jeremy checks their slides on his laptop. His back muscles flex against his thin sweater as he leans over and taps on the keyboard. My face heats and I press my thighs together at the memory of last night. Matt must sense my presence because he looks up and finds me immediately. As if reading my thoughts, he licks his lips and nods once, acknowledging me in the most professional way possible, but his eyes, full of hunger and dark with desire, reveal that his thoughts mirror mine.

I walk over to Sarah, Naomi, and Rachel as they scroll through our slides on Naomi's laptop. Josh is talking to our IT guy to set up the video conference, and it looks like they're having some sort of technical difficulty, but that's the last thing I need to focus on right now.

"Ready, ladies?" They all turn to look at me with big smiles on their faces. This is the first time an all-female team is pitching a new account, let alone a car account. Josh and Sheila were surprised when I told them who I wanted, but I knew the best way to break through with new ideas was to put together a renegade group. I'm proud of the work we've done, and while I'm nervous, I'm also excited. I believe in our approach.

Josh turns to the room. "We're having some issues with Roger's video. He can see the screen and us, but for some reason our video isn't connecting to him. So we won't see him, but Roger will see and hear everything."

Perfect. Seeing Roger Davis was going to be the hardest part for me, as I've heard his poker face is notorious for throwing people off.

"Emily, your team is up first, so whenever you're ready." Josh walks to his seat and everyone sits down, all eyes now on me.

I'm in a room full of people who I know, who know my work, and who will always have my back. Yet my heart is pounding so hard I'm worried it will burst through my skin. The presentation clicker vibrates in my shaking hand, my armpits are damp, and my chest is starting to feel heavy, like someone's pressing down on it. *I can do this.* I take a deep breath. *I am as prepared as I could ever be. I can do this.* I close my eyes and slowly exhale.

"Thanks, Josh. Hello, Mr. Davis, hope all is well in Los Angeles." *Fuck.* My voice is rattling like an old beachside roller coaster, only making my heart pound harder. I clear my throat.

"I'd like to introduce my team. I'm Emily Cooper, Strategy Director. Sarah Chen is our Creative Director, Rachel Bergman leads our Insights, and Naomi Jackson is our Media Director." I'm talking so fast I don't have time to inhale.

I pause. *Don't blow this, Emily. Breathe.*

"All women on an auto pitch," Roger mumbles, but we all pick it up perfectly. "This should be interesting."

Um, what? Roger Davis's misogynistic attitude snaps me out of my panic. *Not today, Satan.*

"Actually, Mr. Davis, I made that decision very strategically."

My voice comes out a little steadier as I concentrate on slowing down and breathing. "Imperial is known for breaking barriers and taking an unchartered approach to the automobile industry. They're the first to have a fully electric SUV, they are pioneers in self-driving technology, and their factories were net zero before the term became mainstream. We feel strongly they could benefit from a new approach to telling their story. Imperial is not just a brand, it's a feeling and a lifestyle. Yes, it has power and sleekness, but with Imperial, you get more than that. With Imperial, you're making a difference. By driving an electric vehicle, you're not harming the environment; in fact, you're protecting it, because every vehicle is carbon-neutral at the production phase. You're celebrating a company that is making the right impact. Through driving an Imperial car, you're making an impact too."

The room is silent. My girls are beaming at me. So far, so good. I take another deep breath.

"The automobile industry has notoriously ignored women in their advertising. The few times women have been featured, they're shown as haggard soccer moms, carting around multiple kids to events in a practical minivan. I would say it's similar to how dads are only shown in sitcoms as bumbling fools, which we all know is a misguided stereotype that needs to end.

"Women influence over 80% of automobile purchase decisions. In fact, they influence almost all household decisions. Outside of their family's health and happiness, the top issue women are concerned about is the environment, what the world will look like in fifty years if we don't all start taking more conscious measures to protect it. Driving an Imperial car alleviates any concern that she's hurting the environment. Driving an Imperial car actually takes that worry off her plate, and show me any woman who wouldn't appreciate that—especially a mother who's running a household while managing a career."

That's Rachel's cue to dive deeper into the insights. I did it. It could have been better, and I could have been less nervous. I missed one part of the script I wanted to nail that I should have reviewed more, but it was concise and everything worked the way it was supposed to. I'm still trembling when I turn my focus on Rachel, doing everything I can to keep my eyes away from Matt. As much as I want to see his reaction, I couldn't bear it if there was any disappointment in his eyes.

Rachel finishes her section and tosses to Sarah, who walks them through our digital mood board and aesthetic that brings the look and feel to life. Sarah nailed the vibe we wanted to convey perfectly—clean, light, uplifting. No added clutter. She walks through a few storyboards and hands it to Naomi, who brings it home with a very targeted media plan featuring more digital, social, and influencer promotion as our insights show us where, what, and how working women consume media.

When Sarah's done, I drive it to the finish line. My voice is back, strong and no longer wavering. "We know this is an unexpected approach and turns the brief on its head. But we strongly believe if Imperial wants to break out from being a niche brand, this is the right way to go."

Naomi clicks to the end slide and I look around the room. A

flush creeps up my cheeks as my adrenaline comes down. My eyes snag on Matt's and he's staring at me with a mix of pride and regret. His lips are in a thin line and the dimples are nowhere in sight, but his eyes say all I need to know. That this whole situation sucks.

I turn back to Josh and the rest of the room. They ask a few follow-up questions but not too many because damn, our presentation was flawless. Smiles and nods all around the table.

We take our seats and wait for Matt's team to load up their presentation. Once it's up and we confirm Roger can see the new set of slides, we wait. I realize I'm holding my breath for the second time today, but I can't decide whether it's from concern about the competition or how much I care about it.

CHAPTER 19

MATT

Emily nails her presentation. Not that I expected anything different, but I could tell she was nervous when she first started speaking. Like a true champ though, she powered through and commanded everyone's attention. Her passion is unmissable, but more than that, she was poised, confident. *Beautiful.* I could listen to her talk to me about horsepower and clean emissions all day long. I had to shift a few times in my seat to keep my physical response to her under control because, while I swear I was listening, my eyes kept wandering to her lips, calling to mind the taste of her kisses from last night.

Even my dad grunted his approval, though I'm sure he's probably rolling his eyes at her female-slanted pitch. He's always been a misogynistic prick. Jeremy tells me our slides are ready to go and I blink away my thoughts. I'm not usually nervous before big presentations but this moment is different. It's the first time

I'm presenting to my father as a professional, and I know he'll be scrutinizing every detail like the judges at the Westminster Dog Show. That's exactly how I feel—on display and ready to get ripped apart for one wrong move.

I take a deep breath and jump in.

"Hi, everyone. Thank you for joining us, especially from California." I don't address my father in any specific way, conscious not to draw attention to any connection between us.

"Let's start with introductions. I'm Matt Meyer, Strategy Director. Jose Serrano is our Creative Director, Priya Kaur is our Director of Insights, and Jeremy Broome is our Media Director."

"Luxury goods are aspirational, high quality, and symbolize affluence. They are also expensive and, for most of us, unattainable. That's what makes them so desirable. You want what you can't have. You want what is perceived as the best. What is better than associating yourself with the cream of the crop? That's why you see so many fake designer bags sold on Canal Street and celebrities dripping with branded attire and jewelry. The halo association gives credibility, allure, and often drives a desire to be in that exclusive company."

I've practiced this so many times I don't need to look at my notes. I also know luxury and exclusivity are the backbone of my dad's greed, so I know I've piqued his interest without needing to see his face.

"Imperial is one of the top brands synonymous with luxury. Sure, that's what their brief told us, but we wanted to explore further. Priya will take you through some of the independent research we did. The numbers will show that when consumers—and potential buyers—think of Imperial, they think of the highest quality, the finest product, and status. They think excellence, and they expect it too."

I click through our slides, a mosaic of sleek black-and-white photos embodying a life of luxury. The montage includes the finest jewels, yachts, and beautiful people. Above the images are two words: *Expect Excellence*.

"Sure, being environmentally sound is important, but perspective buyers already know this about Imperial. That's their reputation—cutting-edge, high performance luxury. But it's the luxury part that brings them in. It's the *excellence* they long for. They don't have to sacrifice to be socially conscious. They get the best of both worlds. They become excellence."

I pause for the effect I'm hoping to get. The entire room is silent and all eyes are on me, waiting for me to continue. I avoid looking at Emily because the last thing I need is the distraction she always serves as for me. I'm in the zone, and I hope my father is paying attention.

I finish my part and hand Priya the clicker, taking my seat next to Jeremy.

I look over at Emily. She's biting her bottom lip and giving me a slight nod as if to say *I see you and that was good work* and it hits me like a jolt of energy when I realize I'm not only vying for my father's approval but Emily's too. Like Ben said, I am so fucked with how deeply this woman has hooked me.

CHAPTER 20

MATT

Priya, Jose, and Jeremy close out their portions of the presentation before I jump in to wrap us up. "We're happy to take any questions."

Josh and Sheila peppered questions throughout the presentation, so the only questions would come from my father. The silence is deafening until finally Josh speaks up.

"Roger, any questions?"

I hear my dad sigh and it sounds like he's shifting in his seat. "Thank you to both teams. The presentations were well researched, and I know it was under a tight timeline. They're very different, so I defer to Josh and team to determine which makes more sense. I'm not sure either is a home run, but at least there are some ideas to play with." He hangs up without saying anything else.

Classic Roger Davis. Confusing, backhanded feedback. Unclear direction. Leaving us all to question if there was anything positive in our presentations.

Josh again speaks up. "I strongly disagree with Roger's feedback. This was incredible work, especially with the deadline constraints. You all should be proud of yourselves, as I know I am of you."

Shoulders relax and tentative smiles flicker across the room. My father needs to triple Josh's salary.

"For now, it's been a full day and a killer week. Let's take a breather before we determine which pitch will resonate the most during the Tissue Session meeting on Monday. Remember, Nolan will be joining us for that. Until then, you've all been working long hours and I don't want you to burn out. How about some drinks on me to toast to a great challenge?"

A collective cheer is heard around the room as people stand and start gathering their things. Josh tells us to invite anyone who touched the presentations we just gave and anyone from our larger teams. There's an anticipatory buzz in the air as we exit the conference room.

"Where are we going, Josh?" Jeremy calls out as he turns and walks backward toward his desk.

"Let's hit up Smith's Cave. I'll ask Paul to call and reserve us some tables." Josh stops at his assistant's desk as he hands him his message slips.

My stomach dives at the mention of Smith's Cave. I haven't been there since the night I met Emily, and the ground we've covered between then and now is already so unsteady. All I want to do is get her to unwind and forget about this stupid competition between us. I would gladly give it up for her if I didn't have to pay back my father. It's like I've been stuck in quicksand for years, unable to claw my way out because my father's hovering with both hands on my shoulders. If we can just get this pitch completed—and won—then I can bow out and explain everything to Emily. But until then, I can't see a way out of this. Not until DMG wins the account and I'm finally free to move on.

"Yo, you ready, boss man?" Jose says as he taps my door. Jeremy is right beside him and together they have the energy of two kids who've just been told they're going to Disneyland. I don't blame them—they've been working their assess off and nothing tastes better than free beer.

"I told you a million times to stop calling me that, dude. We're a team." I give him a pointed look.

"Sorry, *Matt*. It won't happen again." He throws his hands up in the universal *I surrender* position and laughs. I throw my laptop in my backpack and grab my jacket as they pull out their phones and start talking about tonight's Knicks game.

I give Jose a playful shoulder bump as we walk toward the elevators and see Emily, Priya, Sarah, and Naomi walking toward us. It feels like high school with the girls on one end of the hallway and the guys on the other, that same end-of-year energy. I blow out a big exhale—I haven't felt this loose in a while. I know part of it is from finishing the presentation, but mostly it's from the girl walking my way right now. Just knowing we'll be in the same place tonight helps me breathe easier. This perfect excuse to see her outside of work and the buffer of our colleagues is my gift of manna from the heavens.

I cough in an attempt to tone down the ridiculous smile on my face while we gather by the elevator bank. Emily's laughing with Priya, and the tension that was so visible in her shoulders earlier is now gone. Separate conversations start as more people join and wait. Emily and I gravitate to the back and I fight the current that is pulling me to touch her. I put my hands in my pockets to stop myself from pushing a stray hair behind her ear.

I lightly bump her foot with mine to get her attention "Great job today. It was unexpected, but smart. If Imperial has any brains, they'll realize it's a winning strategy."

She bites her bottom lip and looks down at the toe of her shoes. A slight pink hue tints her cheeks and she looks up, pushing that loose strand back herself. "Thanks, Matt. I appreciate that. I know it was a risk, and who knows what Josh and Mr. Davis will decide, but I feel good about it. It was empowering to take a chance on something I really believed in and to be able to stand up and share it."

The air between us is buzzing and I wonder if she's feeling it too. We shuffle through the revolving doors into a warm March evening, the smell of the first flowers in the air. You never know what weather you'll get this time of year, and these early spring days are enough to put the entire city in a good mood. For me though? It could be dark and storming and I'd still feel just as light with the possibility of what tonight will bring.

The bar is crowded when we arrive, but our group has pushed

a few tables together and already pitchers of beer are being passed around. Luke Combs is singing that ice cold beer never broke his heart and a waitress approaches us with a tray full of shots. Josh gathers us and waits until everyone has one in hand. Emily's standing next to him when he calls me over to join, and I move to stand behind her, so close all I smell is coconut, and the back of her legs brush against my thighs. I hold my shot up with one hand and ball my other into a fist, my fingertips screaming at me to reach out.

Josh raises his shot. "I said it earlier and I'll say it again… your ideas, your preparation, your critical thinking and thoughtful answers to the brief blew me the fuck away." A few cheers go up—Josh is not one to swear in the office. "I'm proud to work with each and every one of you. I'm proud of what you create, and more than that, I'm proud of the people you are. I know we're going to blow them away next week. But for now, drink up and have fun." He slams back his shot and we all follow with a round of cheers and high fives. Josh turns to Emily and squeezes her shoulder, slapping my back a few times with his other hand. "Dream team over here. The two of you make magic." His phone rings and he walks away, leaving me to face Emily.

"Matt, you in for pool?" Jose calls over to me just as I'm about to double down on Josh's assessment. Her eyes widen at the mention of pool, and I know we're both remembering our first night here.

"Maybe I'll jump in later," I call out to him without breaking my gaze from the woman in front of me. The crowd around the table thins and I motion to a chair for her to sit. "Join me for a beer?" She hesitates for a second but then nods and takes a seat at the head of the table. I'm facing the wall with my back to the bar. Feeling bold, I hook my foot under her chair and pull it closer, wood creaking from rusty hinges.

"Sooo… come here often?" I ask with a cheesy grin, hoping to defuse the awkwardness between us.

"Only when I feel like whipping some unsuspecting butt in pool. It's amazing how much a small girl gets underestimated at bar games."

"Ah, yes. You do indeed know how to set the record straight." I laugh, reaching for two empty pint glasses and pouring us each a beer.

I hold out my glass to her. "Cheers again. Great job today."

"Cheers to you as well."

There's a heavy silence as Emily sips her beer and scans the crowd, careful to not meet my eyes. I take another sip and look to the TVs mounted above us, hoping the anchors will tell me what to do. *Get it together, you dipshit.* I take another sip for courage, and when I look back at Emily, I find her eyes on my mouth.

"So, any big plans for the weekend?" Her bouncing leg is the only sign that maybe she's just as nervous as I am right now.

"Not much, really. Probably play some basketball. Try to tackle another couple of boxes. Ryan and I are taking my mom to brunch on Sunday. It's been nice to see her more now that I'm back in town."

"But not your dad?"

I swallow the bile that rises in my throat just thinking about him, which gives me the pause I need to think through what I want to say. I fight the urge to tell her everything—who my dad is, how I'm stuck in this unbearable situation because of him, but I hold back even when I remember how irked she was with me at lunch the other day with Hunter. This is neither the time or place, and it's still too risky.

"My relationship with my dad is… complicated." She gives me a silent nod, encouraging me continue. "I try to limit my time with him if I can, more than anything so it's easier on my mom. We are oil and water and unfortunately, I can do nothing right in his eyes. He attributes any success I earn to Ryan paving the way for me or because it was handed to me thanks to all he provided. Nothing was ever because of my own hard work or ability. So we inevitably butt heads and I know she hates when we argue so much. He's been traveling a bit, so I've been able to see her a few times while he's out of town. I probably should feel bad about how much I go out of my way to avoid him, but I don't. It keeps the peace."

"I can imagine. Not that I would know too much on the subject," Emily mumbles, almost more to herself than me.

"What do you mean?"

"Ah, nothing." Emily blows out a breath and shakes her head. She studies her finger as it traces a random pattern in the glass's condensation. I watch as she folds into herself, shoulders slightly hunched and chin dropping at the mention of her dad. There's a story there, and it doesn't sound like a good one.

"Em?" I look at her with a silent question. "Everything all

right? Something up with your dad?"

"Ha, I wouldn't even know if there was." There's a hardness in her voice. Her mouth sets in a line and her eyes narrow as she continues to stare at her glass.

"You've never mentioned him. What's he like?"

"An asshole," Emily responds quickly, looking toward the door as if she's deciding if she wants to say more. I give her a moment without any pressure to continue. She takes a sip of her beer and turns back to me. "Actually, who knows, maybe he isn't an asshole to his new family. He cheated on my mom when I was five and left us to be with his girlfriend, who's now his wife, and they started their own family. He sent a few birthday cards when I was younger, but I ignored them until they eventually stopped. When I turned thirteen, I reached out to him just to see if maybe we could try again." She makes a *womp-womp* sound and laughs, but it doesn't reach her eyes. "I never heard back. So, it's always just been me and my mom against the world. She was a mess for a while, kept jumping from bad relationship to bad relationship because she was scared to be alone. But she always made me her priority. She worked two jobs for a while because my dad didn't give her any help and she never wanted me to miss out on anything."

"That's rough, I'm sorry you went through all of that."

Emily shrugs her shoulders and waves a hand, dismissing the heaviness of her confession. "Eventually she started moving up in one of the jobs and was able to be home more. She stopped dating dirtbags and a few years ago actually found a good guy.

But we both have a lot of scars even if we don't talk about them."

The mood's taken a nosedive, and while I would happily listen to Emily talk about anything and everything, I doubt this is the conversation she wants to have in the middle of a bar after an intense workweek.

"To better versions of our dads. May you find one and may I be one." I hold my glass out to her to toast.

"I'll drink to that." She finishes her beer and I refill her glass from the pitcher. "Is that something you want? To be a dad someday?"

"Absolutely." I refill my own glass. "I always pictured myself coaching my kids' sports teams, a house in the suburbs, hosting BBQs over the summer, driving a gas-guzzling, oversized SUV, but don't tell Hunter that." I wink at her.

"I can so see it!" Her face lights up with a smile as she slaps the table. The heaviness she's been carrying lifting ever so slightly. It's the smile I want to swim in, the one I want to claim for only myself. "You're definitely the little league coach and the dad with all the random *My kid did this* bumper stickers on his car. And you would be the king of bad dad jokes."

I laugh in agreement. "I do love a dad joke." I take a long sip of my beer. "I actually thought I'd have a kid by now, but what's the saying? Make plans and God laughs? I've experienced that firsthand."

"How so?"

And here is a moment of truth. Emily knows I went through a breakup in Chicago, but not that it was a divorce. I feel like

I'm balancing on the precipice tonight. She's relaxed, she's open. She's *here*. She's not running away and I'm panicking that any small misstep will send me tumbling over, permanently away from Emily. I don't know if it will affect her view of me and for the slightest moment I wonder if I should tell her about Stella. But there are enough secrets already and I don't want anymore. I just hope it isn't something that will put more distance between us.

"I'm actually divorced." I sit back and watch as she processes the information. Her eyes show surprise for a moment but quickly shift to compassion.

"Wow. I wasn't expecting that."

I shrug my shoulder in response. "It's not something I really talk about."

"I'm sorry, that's not easy to go through," she says without a hint of judgment.

I scratch the back of my neck. "It wasn't easy, that's for sure. I met Stella in college and proposed a few years after graduation. It felt like the next step, and she seemed happy. Everything was meticulously planned, but once the wedding was over, things went... downhill, I guess. I don't know if she even thought about the important part—the actual *being married* part. She was thinking of the party and the attention. I tried everything to get us back on track, but she wasn't interested. It was tough coming to terms with the fact that it wasn't about me or the relationship. She just wanted to move on to something new."

"Jeez, Matt, that's terrible. This was all in Chicago?"

"Yep. We officially divorced almost two years ago, but the relationship was over way before that. Probably right when we got home from the honeymoon."

"I guess I got off easy then," she comments under her breath.

My brows crease. "How so?"

"I was engaged, but we never made it to the wedding," she confesses around a heavy sigh.

I close my eyes and shake my head. "Nothing about that is getting off easy."

She puffs out a breathy chuckle. "True. It all sucks. Especially the girl I found sucking Greg off while we were engaged."

I groan and scrub both hands down my face. "Jesus, Emily. Who the fuck does something like that? And to someone like *you*? You dodged a bullet in the form of a world-class asshole."

She presses her lips together and sips her beer. A big cheer lets out by the pool table and we see a few of our coworkers celebrating.

I turn and nod toward them. "It's a really good team at DMG."

She smiles, and this time it reaches her eyes, crinkling the soft skin around them. "It is. You seem to fit in well."

I seize the moment and hook my foot around the bottom of her chair again. I lean my elbows on my thighs, our knees touching. Emily stares at where our legs meet and her chest begins rising with quicker breaths. The air is thick, so much unsaid, but our bodies say it all with how close we are. The raw chemistry between us is undeniable, but it's more than physical attraction. We just talked for who knows how long without stopping once to look around us or acknowledge anyone else in the bar.

I grow bolder and tap my finger on her knee. I know this is even riskier than the other night in the game room because of the people we know scattered across the bar. It's darker in here now that the sun has set and my back is shielding us somewhat, but it's still a risk. Yet she has responded to everything I've thrown at her tonight with care and compassion. I might be pushing too far with this physical touch, but I'm a gambling man, praying the odds are in my favor.

She looks from my finger to my eyes and back to our legs. Her pupils turn black, outlined by her eyes that are now a deep hazel, gold and brown specs scattered across the green. Her olive skin, her spray of freckles. God, she's gorgeous. She squeezes her knees together and rubs her thighs. I draw my finger up and tap her hand, hooking our pinky fingers. Right when I'm about to say something, I see her eyes rise and feel someone bump into my shoulder. She stiffens, almost like she's seeing a ghost, and she yanks her hand away from mine.

A smooth voice that immediately screams *douchebag* says, "Hey, Em. Funny running into you here."

She slowly stands and smooths down her jeans, combing her hand through her hair and pushing it back from her face. *This can't be good.*

"Greg. What are you doing here?"

I rise, standing protectively next to Emily and angling myself in front of her. My guess is that this is the same Greg she just mentioned. He's a few inches shorter than me and he's thin. Not the type of lean you get from the gym, but lankier, more wiry. His dark blonde hair is slicked back and his shirt is unbuttoned too low. He looks like the type of sleazeball who gives single guys a bad rap because we're grouped in with jerks like him.

Greg nods over his shoulder to a table in the opposite corner. "I'm here with some guys from work and our clients."

Emily visibly pulls back, biting her bottom lip when it starts to tremble.

He reaches out and pushes a strand of her hair away from her face. I'm grinding my teeth so hard I wouldn't be surprised if they're down to stumps. I'm itching to grab this jackass by the collar and physically remove him from her presence. But I'm following Emily's lead here and letting her dictate what happens next.

She pulls away from his touch. "Greg, please don't touch me."

"Come on, Em. It's me. We haven't seen each other in forever." He raises his hand back toward her face, clearly ignoring her request. My hand clamps down hard on his forearm. "She asked you not to touch her." I hardly recognize the growl coming out of me.

He rears back. "Who the fuck are you? Her bodyguard?" Emily's face flushes in embarrassment and I will myself to calm down so I don't make things worse for her.

"Only if she wants me to be. But for now, I'm just here to make sure that if she doesn't want anyone touching her, then no one fucking touches her. Especially you."

The arrogant prick rolls his eyes. I have zero concern if he tries to hit me. My adrenaline alone right now would knock him out.

Emily gently touches my forearm, nudging me to stand back. "Matt, it's not worth it." She turns to Greg. "It's none of your business who he is. And I have nothing to say to you, so I suggest you go back to your *clients* and get on with your night."

Greg shakes his head and blows out a laugh. "Wow, I thought you would have chilled out over the past year, but I see you're as uptight as always."

This guy is fucking unreal. I step up to him, sucking in a breath and slowly, through gritted teeth, make my warning clear. "I suggest you turn around now and don't look back, you pathetic piece of shit. If you speak to her like that again, you'll have to deal with me, whether she asks me to step in or not."

Greg puts his hands up, backing away. We watch his back as he retreats to his table. I take a few deep breaths to calm myself down and swear under my breath.

When I turn to Emily, hurt is painted across her features as she stares at the back of his head. Naomi and Rachel rush over. Naomi grabs her hand as Rachel asks, "Are you okay? We didn't even see him come in."

Emily brushes her hair back from her head. "Yeah, yeah… I'm fine. Just a shock seeing him, that's all."

Naomi gives the back of Greg's head a death glare. Remind me never to get on her bad side. "Matt, we saw you grab him. What the hell happened?"

"He was going to touch her after she asked him not to." My jaw tics as I hold back from adding that I wish I broke his arm.

"I wish you would have broken his arm," Rachel says. I knew I liked her. She looks at me. "Thanks for having our girl's back." Naomi's rubbing Emily's back when Jose calls that it's Rachel and Naomi's turn in pool. "You sure you're okay?" Naomi asks Emily.

"Yeah, I'm good. Thanks for checking on me." She forces a smile out. They both eye her then give her a quick hug, reluctantly heading back to their game.

"Are you sure?" I lean down to force her to look at me.

She sighs but nods. "Yeah, I think so." She looks over my shoulder at him and then back at me, a grin dancing on her lips. "I think maybe you're right, I dodged a bullet. And I think that bullet might also be balding."

CHAPTER 21

EMILY

I sit back down in my chair and Matt follows, scanning my face. I don't let my thoughts stray to how we've somehow gotten close enough for our chairs to be practically welded together.

"Really, I'm fine. That was bound to happen at some point." I look into his eyes. "I'm actually glad you were here. Thank you for standing up for me." I rub my hands over my eyes, suddenly exhausted, then clasp them together in my lap, watching as I rub my thumbs back and forth over each other.

Matt slowly lifts my chin to get my full attention. "I'm glad I was here too. No one should ever—and I mean *ever*—speak to you like that. But more importantly, he's so wrong in every way about you. You're *far* too good for him.."

My eyes water and I will myself not to cry. I'm not sad about Greg, I'm more so just feeling overwhelmed at what Matt's saying and all the ways he has been slowly showing me he's different. That I can trust him. He might be cheesy about it, but it's enough to pull me out of my head.

I take a moment to really look at him. His kind eyes. His tousled hair. Dimples. I think of how watching him growling at Greg was one of the sexiest things I've ever witnessed. The boy next door goes dark. For me. No one has ever even gone to bat for me before. This is a new sensation, this feeling that someone really does have my best interests at heart.

"Emily, I can't stop thinking about you, about the other night, about our weekend together. I can't turn this off… I don't *want* to turn it off. Greg has to be the biggest idiot I've ever laid eyes on because he let you go. I don't want to be that idiot, Emily. I see you. I see how amazing you are."

I mean, at any other time, on any other day, in any other lifetime, that speech would have melted me into a big sappy puddle on the floor. But it's smothering me right now. The tension at work, the pressure of winning, the long hours, not sleeping, Greg pulling up buried emotions… It's all too much right now.

The room suddenly feels really warm and the lights are too bright. The cheers from the pool table grate on my nerves. It's too loud all of a sudden, like a fire alarm going off in the middle of the night. I feel like I'm suffocating and just need to get out of here. Away from everything that's been stirring up inside of me since I first met Matt in this bar.

"Matt," I plead with him, "Please, just… don't. I'm not sure what *this* is, but I can't process any of it right now. It's too much." I pull away and grab my coat and bag from the pile behind us.

Matt's standing now, watching me bundle up. "I'm sorry, I really am. I have to go. Please say goodbye to everyone for me." Glancing down, I step around him and walk to the door without looking up until it shuts behind me.

My hand is up to hail a yellow cab before I even reach the curb. I need to put space between me and that bar and everyone inside of it. No—not everyone. Just him. If I wasn't failing in my resistance *before* Greg showed up, the way Matt reacted and the things he said blew it up entirely. But we're so close to being picked to pitch in Texas, which means I'm that much closer to the promotion.

He heard what Greg said. I'm uptight. I'm difficult. Unlovable. In the end, Matt will figure that out. I remember all too well how sweet Greg was at the start of our relationship and look where that ended up. I can't go through the inevitable heartbreak again. Matt is tempting, but I have to resist him. Since our kiss, I don't know what box to fit him in. He's throwing everything off balance and my equilibrium is nowhere to be found.

I exhale my relief as the cab pulls up to my building, anxious to get into my apartment and climb into bed where I can block out the rest of the world. I pass Mr. Marino's door on the way to the elevators and cringe. It's the reminder I need that I can't afford one more slip-up on rent.

This place is more than just four walls. It's a symbol of how far I've come. My entire body relaxes as I walk through the front door and lock up for the night. I sometimes even forget that Greg lived here for a short time. When he moved out, I tossed any and all reminders of him. Josie and Lucy spent that weekend helping me repaint and redecorate, framing prints we ripped out of magazines, and helping me re-upholster my couch with fabric and a staple gun (don't knock it—it actually worked out well). I nursed my broken heart and slowly started to put it back together here. The fractures have healed, now protected by a hard callus. I won't risk it breaking again.

After changing into pajamas, I pour myself a glass of water and head to the couch when my phone buzzes from the counter. I glance at the clock on the oven. *11:35?* My thoughts reel when it registers how fast the time flew at the bar. Thinking it must be Josie or Lucy, I grab it and swipe the message open.

Magic Matt: Hi.

My heart—traitor that it is—skips a beat.

Magic Matt: I just want to make sure you got home okay.

This is why he's trouble. Why can't he just be a thoughtless asshole?

Me: Hi. I just got home. Sorry I ran out so fast.

Magic Matt: I'm sorry I upset you.

Me: It's fine. You didn't do anything wrong.

Magic Matt: I feel like I did and I feel terrible. I'm sorry if I pushed.

Me: It's fine.

Magic Matt: Every guy worth his weight knows "fine" is thinly veiled code for "not fine."

That makes me laugh as my heartbeat starts to return to its normal rhythm.

Me: LOL, that is true.

Magic Matt: I'm sorry. You've asked for space, and despite what happened tonight, I've been trying to respect that. I got carried away. You have my word it won't happen again.

Me: Thank you. We're getting down to the wire. Let's just focus on Monday's Tissue Session.

Magic Matt: Can I ask you a question?

Me: Sure

Magic Matt: How do you make a tissue dance?

Me: ?

Magic Matt: You put a little boogie in it.

I groan as I roll my eyes but smile despite myself, feeling grateful for his cheesiness. Somehow he makes it work.

Me: Practicing the dad jokes already? Terrible.

Magic Matt: Well, I wasn't thinking that, but now I am. How about a poem?

Me: Sure?

I worry my lip as I watch the three bubbles pop up, not sure what to expect but confident it'll probably make me laugh.

Magic Matt: Don't kiss your honey, when your nose is runny.

Magic Matt: You may think it's funny...

Magic Matt: ...but it's snot.

Me: Awful. You don't need practice. You just need to stop.

Magic Matt: I nose those weren't too good.

Me: OMG

Magic Matt: I hope that's a good OMG?

Me: I don't know what it says about me or my sense of humor, but yes, it's a good OMG.

Magic Matt: GIF of little boy in hockey jersey pumping his hands with a very serious YESSSS

That also makes me laugh out loud.

Magic Matt: I didn't want you to go to bed sad.

Me: I appreciate the effort.

Magic Matt: I appreciate your appreciation.

Magic Matt: So... any big plans for the weekend?

Me: Matt...

I roll my eyes yet again, but who am I kidding? My cheeks hurt from smiling at this point.

Magic Matt: Yes?

Me: What was that you were saying about my request for space?

Magic Matt: <face palm emoji>

Me: Yes. I have plans this weekend.

I see the three bubbles pop up and disappear a few times, like he's editing his response. Finally, his text pops up.

Magic Matt: OK. I won't push. But Em?

Me: Thank you. And yes?

Magic Matt: Just remember. If you were a booger...

Magic Matt: I'd pick you first.

Me: Okay, okay, one more and you'll really blow it.

Magic Matt: Ah!!!!! See? I knew I sniffed out what makes you laugh.

Magic Matt: I'm going to quit while I'm way behind. Sweet dreams, Goldie.

I fall asleep with a smile on my face after rereading the text chain four more times.

CHAPTER 22

EMILY

I didn't tell Matt my plans were me, my couch, and a big stack of books. I wake up emotionally drained on Saturday morning and declare it a do-nothing day. I don't run, I don't do any errands, I just get lost in a favorite romance and take a long nap. On Sunday, Lucy gets called in on a case so I meet Josie for yoga and bagels and get sucked into a *Bachelor* marathon for most of the afternoon. All of the relaxing does my body and mind good, because I wake up feeling refreshed for the first time in a long time.

I dress more casually than usual on Monday morning because I know tissue sessions—the meeting where we dissect all of the ideas together—will be a full day without too many breaks. I'm in a pair of baggy boyfriend jeans with a frayed hem, black sneakers, and a fitted charcoal gray sweater.

I giggle to myself thinking of the word "tissue" and all of

Matt's corny jokes on Friday night. My stomach swoops and bottoms out every time I think about how it felt talking to him, how much it meant having him stand with me when Greg was there. The situation could have blown up into something monumentally awkward, but thankfully it didn't. I appreciated that Matt heard me and gave me the space I requested. Especially because today is huge.

The floor's quiet as I step out of the elevator. I head to my office to drop off my jacket and bag, checking the time to make sure I can run to Charlie's before everyone else shows up. Tissue sessions fall into the "special occasion" category and call for the biggest and strongest coffee imaginable. As soon as I open the door to my office, I breathe in the strong smell of espresso and bite my lip to hold back a smile.

E—

I nose you need one of these today.

—M

I have to hand it to him. While veering on the side of *too corny*, Matt's ability to own it outright is endearing.

I hang up my jacket and plug my laptop into my monitor. I'm leaning down to grab my lip gloss from my purse when Sheila pops her head in, her own steaming coffee cup in her hand.

"When did you get in? I didn't see you at Charlie's this morning."

I shut my laptop screen down and pile my notebook, pen, and phone on top of it. Standing up, I jam everything in the crook of my left arm as I grab my coffee with my right, waving it at Sheila. "That's because this was waiting on my desk when I arrived this morning."

She tilts her head with a knowing smirk. "Oh, was it now?"

"Yep. The man sure knows how to pile on the charm."

"Well, it didn't look like you were minding it too much on Friday night. You two looked a bit... cozy, shall I say?"

Technically, because Matt and I are on the same level, any sort of romantic relationship wouldn't be a problem. Plus, I know Sheila is supportive of work relationships as we've had a few at the agency recently. Does that keep my cheeks from heating though? Absolutely not. It *was* cozy, and I didn't mind it. Matt was sweet and attentive. Protective. A flush of warmth fills me thinking about how he towered over Greg.

"Ugh, don't bring it up. Did you happen to see Greg show up? Matt was next to me and totally put him in his place. And before you say anything"—I hold my coffee hand up and level her with a look—"we just talked. Nothing happened. Nothing will happen. I'll admit he's growing on me, and while I still intend to wipe the floor with his ass during the tissue session, I'm warming up enough that I'd lend him a hand up from said floor."

Sheila laughs. "That's definitely progress. But honestly, Em, I don't know why you're being so quick to write him off. I mean, it's not like coworkers dating each other is unheard of. You know Josh met Steven when they were associates here."

"Yes, I know, but it's not how I operate. I don't know if I'd ever get comfortable enough for that. We would be under a microscope and I'd feel like everyone was watching our every move. Like Taylor and Travis during football season."

"Riiiight... exactly like that," Sheila replies, and we laugh as we walk down the hall to our war room to meet with Nolan.

We're all seated around the table with Josh and Sheila at the head. Matt and his team sit opposite us, as if we're about to start the college debate championships. The screen flashes on and we all turn toward it.

Josh holds his hand up and waves enthusiastically. "Hey, Nolan, great to see you. Thanks for clearing out your morning for this."

Nolan is the perfect balance to offset Hunter's no-nonsense demeanor. Where Hunter is tall and broad, Nolan is thin and has a warm, welcoming face. His smile is wide and his teeth sparkle against his dark skin. I can easily imagine he and Matt being friends, as they have the same calmness about them. "Hey, Josh. No problem, I'm anxious to hear your ideas. Hunter's sorry he couldn't make it."

I'm not sorry about it. His absence is better than having the single winning ticket of a $1B Powerball jackpot.

"And is that the legendary Matt D—" Nolan starts to ask no one in particular, but Matt quickly cuts him off. "Hey, man, good to see you."

"My man! I heard you left Chicago. It's great to see you. You're a sight for sore eyes."

"So how do you and Matt know each other?" I blurt out. Thanks to his warning after lunch with Hunter, I was already aware that Matt and Nolan knew each other, but this feels more than just as work colleagues. *A sight for sore eyes?*

Nolan is shaking his head and smiling. "Oh, we go way back. Roommates and teammates at Northwestern. But we haven't seen each other in a while." There's a pregnant pause as if Nolan wants to say more but knows this isn't the forum to do so. Matt clears his throat.

Déjà vu kicks in as Josh turns to me. "Emily, do you want to kick us off and introduce your team to Nolan? Then we can jump right into the creative ideas."

Almost three hours later, each team has presented to Nolan. Not surprisingly, he loves both ideas. He was engaged through both presentations, asking questions, and brainstorming with us along the way. But since they're so different, we're at a crossroads. He likes the mom angle and has done his own research on how women are leading car purchase decisions for families. But he also likes the idea of luxury becoming synonymous with Imperial's electric vehicles and elevating the category overall.

Josh stands up and stretches. "We've done some great work so far and I feel like we're getting closer. How about a short break?"

"Sounds good." Nolan leans in toward his screen. "I'm going to grab a coffee. See you in fifteen." His screen goes dark as he turns off the camera.

There's a mad dash out the door to the bathrooms and kitchen. I turn in the other direction, walking as fast I can to the elevators. I need fresh air and I need space to think with the promotion hanging in the balance here. Matt's team did a great job presenting to Nolan and could easily sway the campaign their way. There's also the whole *We go way back* thing. Screw my budget—I'm hitting up Charlie's.

The brisk air is a shock to my system as I exit the revolving doors. Our spring teaser last week is over. I forgot my jacket in my rush, so I cross my arms tight across my chest to stay warm. My attention is on the ground as I hop over puddles on my way toward Charlie's. I'm mid-jump by the time I see a pair of black Converse, and it's too late to swerve out of the way before said Converse cut me off and I'm bumped off balance. My face snuggles into worn-in cotton and I'm transported to a bonfire on the beach, all crackling wood and salty sea air. I know that smell. I've dreamt of that smell. I woke up surrounded by that smell and that solid muscle curled against my back.

"Shit, I'm so sorry. I wasn't paying attention," Matt exclaims as I reluctantly pull back from him.

I peek up at him and blow my hair off my face. "No problem. It's not like I haven't done it to you before."

"Really? I hadn't noticed." He smiles down at me. Matt lightly grips my biceps and moves us a few steps out of the way of the door. He sees me shivering and starts rubbing my arms like a parent would warm up a small child. How very... *platonic* of him.

"Where's your jacket? You're shivering."

"I didn't think and just ran for the elevators. I had to get some fresh air. I didn't realize how chilly it'd be." Matt pulls me closer, and just being near his body heat is enough to warm me up. He continues to rub my arms and it's hypnotic, calming my nerves, quieting my thoughts. I step closer and burrow into his embrace, nuzzling my face into his neck, and a contented sign escapes me before I can catch it. I feel him inhale a breath before he squeezes me once.

"Come on, let's get inside." The temperature must have dropped ten degrees in the three minutes we've been standing here because cold seeps through my bones, chilling me to my core, when Matt releases his grip and steps back.

He keeps his hand on the small of my back as he opens the door to usher me inside. The blast of warm air feels stale and sticky and it takes all my willpower not to turn around and snuggle back into Matt's arms.

We stare ahead as we wait in line, careful to keep a little distance. Now that my brain and limbs are starting to thaw, my body flares in embarrassment that I snuggled into Matt like that.

Matt turns toward me. "So the session seems to be going well. It's nice not having Hunter there."

"It is, but we'll have to face him if we end up going to Texas. I didn't realize you were personal friends with Nolan..." I try to keep any accusation out of my voice.

"Nolan is a good friend. As you heard, we played lacrosse together and were roommates in college. We double dated a lot because our girlfriends at the time were close. He's actually married to Ava now, and they have three-year-old twins. Ava stayed tight with my ex and we lost touch. I guess you could say I lost Nolan in the divorce too." Matt puts his hands in his pockets and rocks on his heels. I'm suddenly mad at Nolan, at his wife, for choosing Stella over Matt, and at the same time I'm jealous as all hell that they even had Matt like that in the first place.

Thankfully, the barista interrupts and calls us up to the counter.

"Hi, Matt, what can I get you?" She smiles big and gazes up at him with heart eyes. "The usual?"

"Hey, Nicky. Yep. A large long black and a large vanilla latte, please."

Nicky bubbles under his attention, and girl, I get it. I just sniffed the guy. I think she actually giggles as she flips her long ponytail around. I want to flip my hypothetical one with Matt ordering for me like we're a pair, joined together on one tab. It does something to my insides and quite honestly, it's a new sensation. I never got a buzz over a joint coffee order with Greg.

What in the ever-loving hell has gotten into me today?

Matt winks at Nicky. "How's your day today?" She giggles again.

Um, hello! I'm right here, you fool. Why are you openly flirting with this girl?

But that's just it, right? He can flirt with anyone he wants. He can date whomever he wants. He's not mine. He's a gorgeous guy. If I were Nicky, I'd be writing my number on his cup every day. Jealously is a new emotion for me. I never felt jealous if Greg talked to someone else. Looking back, that was poor judgement on my part and I probably should've been more suspicious, sure. But with Matt, I understand why people call it a green-eyed monster.

I clear my throat to alert Matt that I am, in fact, still present.

Nicky tears her eyes away from him and bites her lip, looking down at the register like she just got caught with her hand in the cookie jar. "That will be $12.70."

Before I can open my phone to pay, Matt pulls out a crisp $20 and hands it to her. The barista places our cups on the counter as Nicky covers Matt's entire hand to grab the money.

Paws off, sister.

"Keep the change. I'll see you tomorrow morning." Matt grabs both cups and turns toward me, holding his hands out in a gesture that says *After you.* He's failing miserably to hide a smug smile and I cross my arms and glare at him. He knew exactly what he was doing and clearly enjoyed watching me squirm.

I look at him over my shoulder. "The usual, huh?" I ask in a sing-song voice, trying to imitate Nicky's giggling question.

Matt chuckles. "Yes, *your* usual. I can stop befriending the staff if it bothers you that much."

"It doesn't bother me," I say with a little too much force, speed walking once I'm back outside.

Matt is still laughing behind me. "Come on, Emily. You can't really be mad."

"Mad? Me? At that?" I tilt my head back toward Charlie's. "No," I lie through my teeth. "I have bigger things to worry about. Namely, the rest of the day with Nolan."

We're inside the building now and Matt stops to hand me my coffee.

"It's good that Nolan likes both ideas—it means we're on solid footing. At this point, we should focus on which has longevity and which lends itself to the best storytelling techniques."

Matt's right, even though I hate to admit it. It's about securing the win for DMG, and I resist the urge to pull a Meredith Grey and beg Nolan to "Pick me! Choose me!"

"You're right, but it's hard to do that without throwing one idea under the bus." I jab my finger in his chest. I may as well be jabbing my finger against a statue. "But it's not going to be my idea."

"Hold on a sec, Goldie." I hate how my stomach does a triple back flip at the sound of my nickname. Traitor.

He holds my finger against his chest. "Maybe there's a way to compromise."

I lift my eyebrow and hold his gaze. "And how exactly do we do that?"

"The women you're focusing on. Some are mothers, some aren't. Some are professionals, some aren't. Right?"

"Yes, these women are from all different walks of life, but they're smart and savvy. Environmentally conscious. One will be using this car to cart her kids to after-school activities and another will be driving to work or a night out on the town. We can't generalize."

"I agree. These smart, savvy women… They also want luxury,

right? They don't want to sacrifice style. Why do we have to differentiate that from men?"

I stand taller and nod. "They do, and we don't. They want to do right by the planet so they're considering electric vehicles." I pause, collecting my thoughts. "But that doesn't mean they have to give up the other things they want—the power, the luxury. They can still get *excellence* and save the environment. They get the best of both worlds with Imperial. And husbands, dads, whoever it may be, still get their speed and sports car-like qualities."

I'm on my tiptoes, one hand braced around Matt's bicep to keep balance. I don't hear any of the foot traffic around us or the elevators beeping. He's grinning at me as an invisible force field holds us in place. Chest to chest, eyes locked. Matt grips my waist and lightly tugs me closer to him. "I think we just got ourselves an excellent compromise and one hell of a campaign." His eyes look down at my lips and I instinctively lick them.

"Nolan will love it. Let's go win this thing, Em.

"We figured it out!" I say to no one in particular when Matt and I burst in the conference room. Everyone turns to us.

Nolan pops back up on the screen, sipping a steaming mug, and asks, "Who figured what out?"

Matt looks at me and nods, and it's my cue to continue. He's giving me the spotlight to share the idea, even though it was something we figured out together. I hold his eyes and nod back, promising I'll unpack how that makes me feel later, with the support of a glass of wine.

"We can combine the best of both campaigns."

Josh sits in his chair, motioning to us that we have the floor and should continue. I fill them in our idea and the room is silent. I feel Matt step closer, his arm brushing my back in solidarity.

Nolan finally speaks. "I love it. It balances our two best attributes and is unexpected with the pitch to include women. Speaking to them as the primary audience will elevate the brand in their eyes. It's brilliant."

Holy shit. This is way beyond spit-on-your-neck fantastic. Nolan likes—*loves*—our idea. For a moment, I'm stunned, so still I don't even feel myself blink. Relief and happiness wash over me and I stumble backward a bit. Matt's hand is firm on my lower back, supporting me. Like he has been since the beginning.

Naomi is the first to jump in. "There are great opportunities to deliver this over social as well. We can create profiles of each woman and post videos of their day, highlighting how Imperial helps them get through it—both looking and feeling better."

Jeremy snaps his fingers and points across the table. "Naomi is spot on. We know which sporting events skew a female audience so we can strategically place ads."

Jose and Sarah are huddled together, whispering to each other, and flipping through boards, already collaborating on the aesthetic plans. I see the two teams combine efforts seamlessly, without a hint of pushback, and my chest fills with pride. This rush of knowing we have a great idea and the sense of camaraderie is energizing. This is why I love advertising—it's late nights and high stress, but it's just as much creativity and chemistry.

Matt's hand drifts up to my shoulder and he squeezes it, smiling at me. "You did it, Em. There's no doubt they'll love it when you pitch it in Texas next week. You're going to win this account for DMG."

I close my eyes and, for the first time in weeks, I exhale as tension releases from my body. The first step is done. I think we may actually have a shot at this. I'm elated. I'm also suddenly so exhausted, but there's no time to think about that. As if they sense it, the team jumps in, allowing me a moment to collect myself.

I turn toward Matt, scanning his face, and see nothing but pride. This good, solid man has done nothing but try to get to know me. To protect me. Help me. Make sure I'm okay. Yes, he's beautiful, but it's his heart that's his most attractive feature. "No, we did it. I didn't come up with this idea on my own and I won't take sole credit for it. It was a team effort. The best of both of us."

Nolan clears his throat, drawing our attention. "I need to get to another meeting, so I'll leave you to it. I think you have something really strong here. Matt, Emily—looking forward to seeing both of you down here next Thursday." With that, Nolan signs off and silence blankets the room.

"That actually brings up a good point," Josh says, looking at Sheila. "We couldn't have reached this point without the effort and passion from the two of you." He turns to me and Matt, who is back to standing behind me and sending his body heat rippling through my sweater. "You should both present in Texas next week. It's the only idea that makes sense."

CHAPTER 23

MATT

Over the next week, our teams throw themselves into preparing revised research, media plans, and creative executions, while Emily and I hammer out the slides and script, talking through every point as teammates. We bring in experts from public relations and content production and drill them on anything that has the potential to be questioned, taking copious notes so we'll be ready for whatever Imperial throws at us. We role-play the client with each other to practice our responses. The two of us are so focused on the work and fall into such a rhythm that I don't think Emily notices how in sync we've become. Leaning over each other's shoulder to read emails, bumping thighs under the table when we're both working on our laptops. We order in lunch and dinner, her signature coconut scent invading my space as she leans over to steal something from my plate.

I am miserably in heaven. Heaven because the wall between us is now crashing down, barriers and blockades fading with every hour that passes. I'm learning more about Emily than I would've thought possible given her apprehension at diving into whatever it is between us.

I already know her coffee order, but I learn she doesn't drink a drop after four p.m. unless she wants to be up all night. She never orders her own fries but always asks me to place a large order for myself so she can have a few. She twirls her hair when she's listening intently and bites the left side of her cheek when she's absorbed in her reading. She always gets cold around 3:30 p.m., she stands when her watch commands it every hour on the hour, and if she doesn't have enough time to take a walk around the block, she'll do a few laps of our floor for a hit of adrenaline. Her laughter—especially when she's a bit punch-drunk—is contagious, and her eyes turn bright green when she's happy.

We call it quits at eight o'clock the night before we're due to fly to Texas. We'll have enough time after we land to run through everything before presenting first thing on Thursday. We're as prepared as we can be, and although I was already aware how dedicated Emily is to her work, seeing her in prep mode this past week inflates my respect for her like a helium hit to a foil balloon. She's full of contradictions. She has boundless energy and inexhaustible patience with those around her. Yet, if she makes a mistake or forgets a point she wants to make, she's ruthless with her self-criticism. She makes perfectionists look like bumbling fools and drill sergeants look like coddling mothers the way she dissects and tears herself apart. Not only is she harsh with herself, but she's wrong. So wrong. She's flawless. She remembers every detail, she has enough passion to keep us all going, and she glows under the spotlight of everyone coming to her for questions and answers. Emily is the visible leader of this pitch. Her opinion is the one that matters. Sure, I'm part of the process, but Emily is the one in charge.

Ryan: You leave tomorrow for Texas?

Me: Yep. We present Thursday. Then…

Me: Mel Gibson Freedom gif

Ryan: Idiot

Me: Possibly. You never know what Roger will pull at the last minute to try to torture me with

Ryan: The deal was you win Imperial for DMG and then you're set free, right…?

Me: Technically

Ryan knows as well as I do that *technically* doesn't apply to our father. Roger Davis makes his own rules, and that is exactly where this undercurrent of anxiety blossoms from as I amble around my apartment packing for Texas.

Ryan: Part of me can't believe he held that shit with the Super Bowl over your head for so long

Me: Well, he covered for me so I could save face with Hunter. Paying him back for the spot wasn't cheap

Ryan: No, it wasn't, but I'm still shocked he didn't write it off with the company

Me: He said it was too risky.

Ryan: Well, for what's it worth, I hope you kick ass and win. And get the girl <wink emoji>

Me: Ah, the girl

Ryan: What's the latest there? Have you finally told her who Dad is and what's going on?

I tense at the thought of that conversation. I'm relieved this trip is here and I will finally have the chance to come clean. I'm also terrified she won't hear me when the time comes, but I'm hoping she'll give me a chance to explain.

Me: Not yet. Once Hunter pushed the presentation date up, I couldn't do that to her—it would have completely thrown her off. I'm hoping Thursday goes well so I can tell her once it's over. It'll feel like a 100-pound weight off my shoulders.

Ryan: May the odds be ever in your favor.

Me: I need all of them. Not for DMG—our presentation's solid and I'll be shocked if we don't win. But me? I need all the favors. I need Dad to finally say we're even. And I need Emily to understand why I kept it from her so she doesn't tell me to fuck off out of her life.

Ryan: Good luck with both, little brother. I'm pulling hard for you.

Me: Thanks, dude. I'll let you know how it goes.

When I was kid, I thought I wanted to be a pilot. I loved airports, airplanes, the thought of being free up in the air and the miniature world below too far away to affect me. Being in an airport meant something was happening—you were going somewhere or coming home, and within that, adventure awaited. All of my favorite things were packed away. Anticipation and excitement coursed through my body. For a few years, I wholeheartedly dedicated myself to the quest of piloting planes. I would practice my take-off speech, study diagrams of cockpits, learn about the aeronautics. I could spout off stats on how much safer flying is than driving, or just about anything else on the ground with humans in charge.

Traveling also meant a break from my father. He would physically be in the same location as us, but his mind was preoccupied with everything happening at DMG. He spent most of those days pacing, cursing and barking orders on the phone, and while I felt sorry for whoever was on the receiving end of his wrath, I reveled in the fact that—for that week at least—it wasn't me. Those vacations were the highlight of my year.

That excitement still buzzes through me now when I travel, whether I'm flying for a few days on a beach or for a three-hour meeting and turning around the same afternoon. Airports signify possibilities. Clean slates. Being in the air cleanses you. Landing is starting over. I want our landing in Texas to be our chance to start over. Once we're done with the pitch, regardless of the outcome, we can restart. Possibilities. Only possibilities.

Optimism courses through me when I notice Emily slowly walking through the bookstore by our gate. She's holding an oversized bottle of water in one hand and reading the back of a hardcover in the other. The sight of her catches my breath. This is my favorite version of Emily: comfortable, effortless, natural. She's in the same cropped hoodie she was wearing the first Saturday I ran into her at the office and the leggings that outlined every one of her perfect curves. Curves I've thought about more than I'd ever admit, especially late at night in my bed where I imagined how it would feel to run my hands all over them.

But for now, we have a pitch to dominate. I walk up behind her. "Good morning!"

She startles, completely oblivious to the world around her, and it's only when I'm standing right in front of her that I realize she's gripping bottle to the point of bursting.

She puts the book down and taps her sternum. "Jesus, you scared the shit out of me."

I've seen Emily tense before, guarded behind her armor and ready to attack. But something in her expression is different. She's pale and has small beads of sweat by her hairline. The hand on her chest is trembling. Dark circles line her eyes, but they're alert, almost fearful. Something's not right.

"Sorry. Are you okay?"

"Yeah, I'm fine. I was just startled. No worries." Her tone is clipped. She's looking around, focusing on anything but me. The nervous energy around her buzzes like a hungry fly circling a picnic on a summer afternoon.

"I didn't expect security to be so quick. Want to grab lunch since we won't board for a while?"

She stares at me as if translating what I said into English. After a brief pause, she nods and puts down everything in her hand. "I can grab a water after we eat." She motions for me to lead the way but given her jumpiness this morning, I put my hand at the small of her back and nudge her forward. "Ladies first."

We grab two seats at the bar closest to our gate. Emily crosses her legs only to start jiggling the one on top. She runs her finger up and down her silverware, adjusting the utensils until she deems them perfectly straight. She then looks at the silent television screens above us, shifting to look around at the tables behind us. I'm getting dizzy watching her.

"So, how much coffee did you have this morning?"

She turns toward me again with a startled look on her face, shocked to find me sitting here. "Just excited for our trip!" Her smile is so forced and awkward it makes a second grader's class picture look like the Mona Lisa. Her eyes drop to her menu and she taps her phone to check the time. "I'm going to get a drink. It's five o'clock somewhere, right?"

"They do say time stands still in airports."

"They do?" She turns to me, nose scrunched.

"They being me. Worst case, we take a nap during the flight."

"A nap?" She looks at me like I just suggested we blindfold each other and ask the pilot for a turn to fly the plane at 35,000 feet. "I don't sleep on planes. I don't want to miss any import-ant announcements. I never sleep on planes." She's robotically punctuating every syllable, adorable in her attempt to convince herself it's a wise plan more than make sure I believe what she's saying.

I've never seen her act this agitated. I rack my brain through the events of last night and this morning. All she did was text me at dawn saying she would meet me at the gate because she liked to get to the airport very early and likes to do things a certain way. Why would she be so rigid?

Then it clicks.

"Em, are you afraid of flying?"

"Me? What? No. I'm fine. Everything's fine. Let's get that drink." She scoffs a bit too aggressively, again like she's trying to convince herself.

Emily orders a glass of sauvignon blanc and I order a pint of their darkest draft, a plate of nachos, and a side of fries to at least get something in her stomach. She drains a third of her glass with her first sip and visibly exhales. It isn't a relaxed breath, but it's progress. I realize it's the first time she's taken a full one since I met her in the bookstore.

She turns to me, foot shaking so violently she could knock herself off the stool. She starts talking really fast in a voice an octave too high. "So, for tomorrow, I think we should open the presentation with a joke. Do you know any good jokes? A joke might loosen them up. But not a booger joke. That won't work."

I tentatively place my hand on her forearm, taking care to

move slowly. "Emily."

She's fixated on the TV screen above us, draining another third of her glass.

"Emily, please look at me," I say, my voice gentle enough to lull a newborn to sleep.

"Hmm?" She keeps her body facing forward and tilts her head toward me.

"Can you take a deep breath for me?"

"Why do I need to take a deep breath? I don't need to take a deep breath."

"Emily!" I say a little more forcefully now, desperate to get through to her. "Please look at me."

She stops shaking. She finally turns, her body still.

"I'm not going to tell you not to be afraid of flying, but I want you to take some deep breaths. I'll be with you the whole time. I've got you."

She finishes her glass and takes a deep breath. Then she whispers like a frightened child, "I'm sorry. I really don't like flying."

This is not the time to mock her. She has a serious phobia, and we have a long flight ahead of us. I'm consumed with the need to pull her into my lap and rub her back. I've never felt such a primal desire to protect someone—not even Stella. My only focus for the next several hours is Emily's well-being.

"I'm here. What do you need?"

She blows out a defeated sigh. "I don't know. Nothing works. I've tried medication, I've tried meditation, I've tried running miles and miles the morning before a flight to exhaust myself.

Nothing works. I just have to grit through it."

She nods toward the bartender and points to her empty glass. "The wine is helping. Please don't judge me. I understand if you don't want to sit with me, but I beg you—don't judge me. I hate myself enough for being such a scaredy cat." She crosses her arms on the bar and puts her head down. My heart breaks at her vulnerability and how, at a time she needs the most compassion, she's berating herself and finding fault.

I rub small circles on her back. "Emily, I could never hate you, and there is nowhere in the world I want to be other than sitting next to you during this flight."

She peeks out from under her arms and gives me a tight smile. "Thanks, Matt."

The bartender brings our drinks and food and we eat in silence. She doesn't need chatter or distractions. She needs to do things her way, and I'm happy to oblige.

The gate attendant announces that boarding will start shortly. Emily finished two glasses of wine and is now nursing her third. She's visibly calmer, but nervous energy still hums around her. I signal for the check and pay it while Emily stands and goes through what I guess is a pre-flight checklist. I don't think she realizes she's mumbling out loud.

"ID, check. Boarding pass, check. Water, check. Gum, check." She takes a deep breath through her nose and blows it out hard and fast. She gulps all the wine remaining in her glass and gives the bartender a strong nod, as if finally accepting her road ahead.

I wait for her to move so she won't feel rushed or pressure. "Ready?"

She nods and puts her bag on her shoulder. I then take it off her shoulder and put it on mine. If I can't carry her mental load right now, the least I can do is take the literal load off her shoulders. I would take it all if I could. I want to sweep her into my arms, but something tells me that would trigger a new spiral, so I do the next best thing and hold her hand. A spark of static jumps between us and it charges right up my arm to my chest. The tension radiating out of her body could power our flight to Texas and back. I squeeze her hand, wishing I could do more, wanting to absorb all that fear. The third glass of wine seems to have calmed her enough to accept my help. "Let's go." I take a step and wait for her to walk with me. We move slowly, hand in hand, toward the gate.

Emily takes the window seat, and I'm in the middle praying to the airline gods that no one sits next me. I don't care if I'm smushed between Emily and the Mountain from *Game of Thrones*, I just want her to have some privacy and space. Thankfully, the gods are on our side and the seat remains empty as we hear the captain tell the flight attendants to prepare for takeoff.

Emily looks at me in fear and her foot tremors are level five on the Richter scale. I gently place my hand on her bouncing thigh and grip her chin with my other hand, tilting her face toward mine. "Em?" I whisper, holding her gaze.

"Hi," she whispers back, trying to break eye contact but failing.

"Hi, back." I smile, wondering if she remembers the same words we said our first night together. Her shoulders drop an inch, and for the first time in two hours, she smiles. The plane starts to taxi toward the runway.

"Em, this is what's going to happen. First, I'm going to check your seat belt to make sure you're as secure as you can be. Then I'm going to lift the arm rest so you can scoot closer to me if you want." I follow both these steps with precision until our legs and shoulders are touching.

The plane turns a corner and I know we're about to speed up for takeoff. "I'm going to hold your hand. You can squeeze as hard as you need to. I won't let go. Squeeze all of your energy into crushing my fingers like you've been trying to crush me in this pitch." That earns me a breathy laugh.

Emily squeezes my hand and a rush of affection fills me knowing she's letting me take care of her. "If you want to lean into me, go for it. If it'll help for me to rub your back, I can do that too. I won't do anything until you tell me. The only thing I'm focused on is helping you feel better."

Emily leans into me in response and I put my arm around her. "This good?" I wait for a nod before placing my hand down. I slowly drag my nails up and down her back and murmur reassurances as we accelerate down the runway and tip into the air. Emily's as still as the human statues who line Times Square for tips. The only proof I have that she's still with me are the intermittent squeezes of my hand. We level out after a few minutes and I look down when I hear soft snores. She's clutching my shirt with her free hand and sleeping soundly. I lean down and kiss the crown of her head, hoping she'll stay like this the entire flight. I'm content to hold her and let her dream, ideally of being back in her happy place with two feet on the ground.

EMILY

I feel soft caresses in my hair and snuggle deeper into my pillow. I'm immediately confused because my pillow feels like... denim? I peel open my eyes and am staring at the cover of a book on baseball statistics sticking out of a seat back pocket. The crackle of a loudspeaker and a man's voice directing flight attendants to prepare for landing fills in the blanks. *Holy shit*. I must have passed out. I knead my fists into my eyes, adjusting to the dry air, and try to wake myself up. Turning my head, I look up to see Matt smiling down at me, still running his fingers through my hair.

"Good morning, sunshine," he murmurs, keeping up his stroking rhythm.

"Have I been sleeping this entire time?" I try to stifle a huge yawn, but my effort is futile. My eyes get heavy again. *Stroke. Stroke. Stroke.*

"Yeah, you passed out right after we took off. The wine knocked you out."

"I can't believe I passed out like that. You're a pretty comfortable pillow," I tell him as I sit up and stretch.

"I'm glad to be of service."

I shift to my own seat, tightening my seat belt as I look out the window. Everything seems so peaceful. That is, until I feel the first dip of our descent and my stomach churns. I grip the arm rest and close my eyes. When I open them, Matt is staring at me.

"What? Do I have something on my face?" I wipe at my cheeks and try to make out my reflection in the window.

"You're beautiful, Emily. Don't ever think otherwise."

My hand stills at my cheek. I answer with a barely audible, "Thank you."

"Emily, I need to tell you—" Matt leans into me with urgency, but he's cut off by the pilot letting us know we'll be landing in a few minutes. He's been so kind to me today. He could have dismissed my fears or sat somewhere else. Instead, not only did he hold my hand and talk me through my anxiety, he let me sleep on him the entire flight. He didn't go anywhere. He stayed right by my side like he said he would.

Sweet, thoughtful, protective Matt is way more dangerous than the auto-industry charmer who could swipe that promotion from right under my feet. This Matt could steal my heart before I even noticed it was gone. It's getting harder and harder to resist him. Not when I feel my stomach freefall thinking about how he played with my hair for a three-hour flight. Not when he turns those turquoise eyes on me, so clear and warm that I could swim in them.

"Matt..." I reach out and touch his arm. That damn forearm that's all corded muscle and strong veins. All strength and warmth, just like the rest of him. *Emily, shut this shit down.* "Thank you for helping me through the flight. I really appreciate it. But let's just get through the next two days, yeah?"

His stare is intense. Scanning. Looking for something. It sounded like he had something important to say, but anything that doesn't have to do with Imperial wouldn't do us any good right now.

He doesn't break eye contact and I can feel how hard he's thinking. He thins his lips and nods once, accepting this time-out. This Matt is the biggest threat to my heart. The one who wants to tell me something important but puts those feelings aside for me. Who doesn't push for what he needs but chooses to take care of me instead. Again.

"What do you mean there isn't a room for Emily Cooper?"

My pulse is pounding in my ears and I feel my shirt start to stick to the newly formed sweat running in rivulets down my back.

"I'm very sorry, Ms. Cooper, but we don't have a reservation under that name."

I blow out a breath. *Keep it together.* "Okay, I understand. I'll take whatever room is available."

"I'm terribly sorry again, Ms. Cooper, but we are fully booked for the next three nights. I don't have any spare rooms."

This can't be happening. The most important day of my career tomorrow and there's no room at the fucking inn? Am I the goddamn Virgin Mary? I hang my head in defeat. I'm this close to exploding, imploding, falling apart.

Matt squeezes my shoulder and leans in to talk to the receptionist. "Hi. Can you check for my reservation please. Under Matt Meyer?"

Closing my eyes, I concentrate on breathing in through my nose, out through my mouth to keep my composure.

"We have a room under that name. Two nights, checking out Friday morning."

I snort. "Of course they have your room."

"Are there two double beds?"

"Just one king, Mr. Davis." I hear Matt sharply inhale as he tries to tackle this problem.

"Is there a couch?"

The concierge stands taller, all proud of herself for being able to answer one question the right way. "Yes, there's a couch."

"Great. Thank you." He turns toward me and gently pulls me away from the counter. "Em, I'll sleep on the couch. You can take the bed in my room. We'll be rehearsing most of tonight and the meeting is early tomorrow, so we'll hardly be in there. It makes the most sense."

He's not wrong, but it still *feels* wrong. It feels like playing with fire. Dancing with the devil. This is most definitely flirting with danger. But what choice do I have?

I huff out a breath of air. "Fine, it's not like we have any other options." Matt thanks the concierge, grabs the key card, and ushers me to the elevators. He's remarkably calm, which unfortunately isn't rubbing off on me. How can he be so practical and level-headed?

We stand outside the door as Matt fumbles with the room card, trying to make that magical green light click. When it does, an expansive room greets us—almost as big as my entire apartment. The blend of beige and cream neutral touches is meant to be soothing, but my mood is shot. Only one bed. Granted it's a large bed, but it's still singular.

"Ugh, I can't believe this!" My frustration gets the best of me. I'm nervous enough as it is, and now we have to have a slumber party.

Matt cocks an eyebrow. "Come on, Em. It's not that bad. It's not like we haven't slept in the same bed before."

"Not. Helping," I growl.

He grins. "That's fair. But we're grown-ups. We can get through this."

I look at the couch. It's small. More like a loveseat. "I can take the couch. I'm smaller."

"Don't be ridiculous. I'm taking the couch."

"Matt—"

"Emily," he cuts me off and puts both of his hands on my shoulders. Leaning down to look in my eyes, he tries yet again to convince me. "It's all going to be fine. Trust me."

I'm done arguing. I'm over this whole situation. I grit my teeth and haul my bag to the other side of the room. "I'm going to take a quick shower and change, then we'll do a dry run."

The shower makes me feel moderately better. I know I'm driving Matt a bit bonkers with how much we're practicing, but it has to be perfect. We spend the next two hours role-playing through the questions we're anticipating, trying to think of everything that the client might ask so we're ready. We hit a wall around six, the Dallas sunset casting a glow through the floor-to-ceiling windows being our only indicator of time passing and place an order with room service.

"I have to say, I've never been this prepared for a pitch. I'm feeling really good. I can't see how they won't love our ideas." Matt takes a bite of his burger and wipes the corner of his lip.

I spear a cucumber with my fork. "I hope you're right. I don't think I've ever prepared this much myself. It's actually taken some of the fun out of it."

"Really? It seems like you've been thriving, like you were made for this type of work."

"Don't get me wrong, I want to win this, and I need the promotion. But I'm not thrilled at the prospect of Roger Davis watching my every move, waiting for me to mess up somehow." I take a sip of my water, waiting for Matt to finish chewing.

Matt chuckles to himself. "Oh, do I know what you mean."

I'm not quite sure what that means so I file it away for later. "The only thing that excites me about all of this is bringing the ideas to life. Giving the spotlight to women. Portraying them as the strong, independent individuals they are. Not stereotypes and clichés. I'm way more passionate about that than cars. It's why I had such a good time working on the Peter Grants campaign. I love empowering women and young girls to believe the possibilities are limitless. Now if I could do that full time..." I trail off, stealing a fry off of Matt's plate.

"Why can't you do it full time?" he asks.

"Well, for starters, I don't choose our accounts or our strategy. Josh believed in this, but you heard Roger. *All women on an auto pitch... Piss off, old man.*"

My impression of Roger Davis causes Matt to spit out his beer. I grin at his reaction.

Ironically, Matt's been the exact distraction I needed today. After pushing him away to avoid his charm, it's the one thing that's kept me calm. "Anyway, what about you? Are you living your grand dream?"

Matt scoffs and the sound slithers down my spine. "Not even close. I stumbled into advertising by chance, but it's not really where my heart is. My dream has always been to work with athletes, rehabbing them. It's actually what I studied in my undergrad."

I pull back in surprise. "Seriously? I can see you doing something like that, but if that's what you really want to do with your life, then why are you here? What happened?"

Matt coughs into his napkin and mumbles something. I'm not entirely sure, but I hear the words "my dad" before he says a few more that I can't make out.

He crumbles his napkin and puts it on his plate. "After my divorce, I wanted to take classes to make the switch to physical therapy, but it didn't work out. It's—"

"Complicated," I finish for him.

Matt chuckles. "Yeah, I guess I've mentioned that, huh?"

"If it wasn't so complicated, how long would it take?"

"Two years. I have enough saved to get all the pre-reqs done and study full time. I'd be able to cover expenses and the first few years before I establish myself. Or I should say I should have enough; I'm still working out some details about a few things."

I give him a quizzical look.

"Let's just say I'm waiting to catch a break." He takes a big breath and blows it out with a chuckle. "We probably shouldn't let Hunter or Nolan know neither of us actually care about their cars."

"Hey! I care. I need this job. I'm surprised though, I thought this was what you wanted."

"I want DMG to win the account. More than anything. But I don't need to run it. I'd happily step aside for you to do that. I want to make sure I do all I can to help DMG come out on top."

I try to hold in my shock but my eyes bug out. *He doesn't want to run the account?* He's been working just as hard as me to make sure DMG wins. Why wouldn't he want to run it? And if he knows for sure he doesn't want to run it, does that mean that it's automatically mine if we win? My head is swirling. It's too much to process and once again, this is not the right time for any of it.

Staring at Matt, I try to connect the dots. He's talking in grays, leaving details out on purpose, but I can't figure out what or why. I just hope that whatever it is, it doesn't backfire on us somehow.

CHAPTER 25

EMILY

We run through everything one more time until exhaustion creeps in, and by the end, we're skipping over parts of the script.

Matt stretches in his chair, making the edges of his shirt ride up with the movement. A sliver of flat stomach and smooth olive skin catches my eye, a small trail of hair leading beneath his belt. It's bad enough I've had to stare at his biceps straining the fabric of his T-shirt all day. But now I'm fixated on where that hair leads to, remembering how good he made me feel.

God he is sexy. He moans as he leans in to the stretch and I want to climb onto his lap and feel those arms around me. Desire courses down my chest and a kaleidoscope of butterflies take off in my stomach. My mouth waters. It literally *waters* because this man before me is edible. He stretches his arms high and leans further back, revealing more of his chiseled abs. He pats those abs with one hand as he straightens, and I am now jealous of a hand… Great. If I don't get up and do something, I'll be all over him in five seconds flat.

I abruptly stand and start stacking our plates on the room service tray. "So that was a decent meal for room service, eh?" And now I'm Canadian. I hear the shakiness of my voice and cringe, feeling as transparent as a freshly washed window.

"It was great. I needed that beer too. I'm hitting an Imperial-sized wall."

Matt stands and grabs the tray, walking it outside the door. He comes back into the room, and I must be doing a horrible job of hiding my ogling because he stops, arching an eyebrow. "You okay over there?" His smile starts playful but then his eyes turn dark, like the clouds over the sea when a storm rolls in. I feel the thunder inside of me and know this storm would be electrifying if I gave in to it.

"I'm fine." I cough to camouflage the squeak in my voice.

"Do you mind if I check the score of the Knicks game? I think we're done for now, right?"

"Be my guest." I hand him the remote and sit against the headboard on the far side of the bed. He makes a valiant effort to turn the TV to face the couch, but it won't budge, so he sits diagonal from me on the other end of the bed as he flips through the channels.

Finding ESPN, he leans back on his elbows to watch. When the halftime score flashes that the Knicks are losing, he flops back onto the bed and throws his arms out, groaning. "This team is seriously going to be the end of me. I don't know why I torture myself." He turns and lies on his stomach, now facing me. My brain is short-circuiting, and I blame my full belly for lowering my inhibitions. I sit crisscross applesauce and shove my hands down to prevent myself from moving toward him.

"How about one episode of *Friends* and then we call it a night?" he asks, oblivious to the inner turmoil wreaking havoc on me.

I swallow, barely able to squeak out a response. "Sounds good."

Matt flips channels until he finds it and sits up. There's no way he's comfortable after the long day we've had, but I know he won't scoot back without my invitation. "You can sit back here if you want."

"You sure?"

"Yeah."

Oh my god, what's with the awkwardness, Em?

He slides back to the opposite side of the bed and leans against the headboard. The hair on my neck raises at his proximity. His tousled hair and sleepy eyes make him look young and boyish. Innocent. He laughs when Joey asks Chandler if he *could be wearing any more clothes*, and right now, as I sit here, I wish Matt wasn't wearing any clothes at all. Staring at his lips, I remember how soft they were, how they tasted like peppermint Altoids, and I have never craved a mint so desperately.

He slides down on the bed, bunching a pillow underneath his head. I know every *Friends* episode by heart, but right now, I couldn't tell you Ross from Rachel from Monica because all my brain power is focused on staying on my side. His cheek is resting on his stretched-out arm and his hand is an inch away from my thigh. So close yet so far away.

When the episode finishes, I dare a glance over at Matt and find that he's fast asleep. Like the creep I am, I watch as his steady breath moves in and out, staring at his long and dark eyelashes fanning across the tops of his cheeks. He looks peaceful, and while I knew being this close would be a risk (self-control? Meet the brink), I don't have the heart to wake him up and make him sleep on the tiny couch.

I quietly get up, change into the oversized T-shirt I usually sleep in, and brush my teeth. I search for an extra blanket so I can take the couch, but yet again, our hotel delivers nothing. I'm left with two choices: sleep on the stiff loveseat with no blanket, or sleep in the warm, cozy, big, soft bed with Matt.

I climb back under the covers. Matt being on top of them places a physical barrier between us, so this will work. It'll be like we aren't even in the same bed, right? Totally. It doesn't take me long to drift off as the rhythm of his breaths lulls me to sleep.

I wake up wrapped in warmth. Heat cocoons my back as I nestle into it. The cobwebs in my brain start to clear when I feel a large hand splayed across my stomach. For a split second, I have no idea where I am, but then my eyes pop open and I realize whose arm is holding me.

Somehow, over the course of the night, he slid under the covers and we ended up tangled together. His jeans are gone and only the thin fabric of his boxers separates us. I feel his hard length against me and... I don't hate it. I lean forward to slip out of bed and head to the couch, but his arm tightens, pulling me back to fit against him. His nose trails down my neck as he softly groans and pushes against me. It's still dark out so I snuggle in, content to stay in this bubble for a little longer.

My alarm buzzes, and this time he loosens his grip enough for me to snooze it. I stretch and roll to my back, not trusting myself to resist curling back into his arms. I'm staring at the ceiling, amping myself up to get out of bed when I hear Matt stir.

"Morning," he mumbles as he sinks his head deeper into the pillow.

"Good morning." I turn to look at him, putting both hands under my head so my fingers can't reach out to run through his sleep-mussed hair.

"Did you sleep all right?" His eyes are still shut.

"Like a rock. You?"

"Same. I don't remember passing out."

"You didn't even make it through the full episode." He takes a big breath in and stretches, forcing the sheet to drop down. His briefs must have shifted during the night because all I see is the sculpted V of his abs and that damn tuft of hair that had me cross-eyed last night. I didn't realize he opened his eyes, meaning they're now watching me watch his happy trail. Busted, I cover my face with my hands and try to fake a yawn, failing so miserably I definitely won't be thanking the Academy anytime soon.

"I'm sorry I fell asleep in the bed. You should have woken me up and sent me to the couch."

"It's a big bed. It's fine. Plus, we need you well-rested and at the top of your game today."

"Well, I feel great." He yawns, stretching again, and I close my eyes this time. "How are you feeling?" he asks me.

"Good. There's been so much anticipation, I'm ready to just do it already."

"That's what she said." Matt gives me a wicked grin.

I roll my eyes, laughing, "Ugh, you're such a guy sometimes."

He chuckles, burying his head back in his pillow.

"I'm going to jump in the shower and get ready, then you can have the bathroom." I take advantage of his closed eyes and make a run for it. Stepping in the steamy shower, I try to focus on the day ahead instead of how close I was to straddling Matt in that tiny, cramped, overheated bed just now. The man needs a *Stop in case of an emergency* button. Stop being so goddamn attractive. Stop making goose bumps appear on my skin by your mere proximity. And for the love of all things holy, please stop smelling so freaking good at any time of the day. I scrub my hair extra hard with the towel to knock some sense into myself and wrap the puffy white robe around my body.

When I open the bathroom door, Matt's sitting on the couch, mercifully more clothed than earlier, although there's his bicep, doing things again. He's the epitome of "calm, cool, collected," holding a steamy cup of coffee in one hand while he scrolls through his phone. Another cup is on the coffee table in front of him.

"Is that for me?" I nod toward the cup.

"It's not your regular vanilla latte, but yes, it's all yours."

I walk over and inhale the delicious scent of fresh, hot coffee. One of my favorite things in the world. I close my eyes and mumble, "I could kiss you right now for this," over the rim as I take a few steps backward to put some breathing room between us.

It clearly wasn't as soft a mumble as I intended, because Matt's eyes shoot up to mine.

"Can you repeat that please?"

"Uh." Stumbling over what to say, I buy time by taking a sip, humming in appreciation for the liquid gold. I sit down on the coffee table. "Um, I'm just grateful… for the coffee."

He chuckles, then stands up and stretches tall. "That's what I thought."

He ruffles my hair as he passes me on his way to the bathroom.

Forty minutes later, we're getting into the rental car. We arrive at Imperial HQ fifteen minutes prior to our meeting, where we sign in with security and are escorted up to the twenty-fifth floor. Dallas doesn't compare to back home when it comes to skyscrapers, but the view from here is amazing. It's a clear, crisp day with the sun shining bright and the ball of Reunion Tower dominating the skyline. White puffy clouds in the sky confirm that spring is without a doubt here.

I discreetly glance around as an intern takes us to the conference room and Matt hooks up his laptop so Roger can join us virtually again. The slides are working, and we have a few more minutes to get situated. This is the exact moment when the panic starts to set in. I start scrolling through the checklist in my head. Notebook, check. Pen, check. I scribble a circle in the corner of one piece of paper for an extra dose of confidence. Water bottle unscrewed so I don't have to fight it, check. Phone muted and on *Do not disturb,* check. Notes of pages with key pieces of info for backup. It's all here. It's exactly as I've played it out in my head too many times to count.

I start worrying about all the what-ifs. What if someone asks a question we didn't think of? What if they want something we didn't prepare? So many things could go wrong, and this feeling of not being able to control what happens outside of our presentation is causing my breaths to speed up and a drum to pound in my head.

I snap back to the stuffy room when Hunter, Nolan, and a few other people I don't recognize file in. Everyone sits, Nolan gives a brief introduction of the team, and then everyone looks expectantly at Matt and me. Matt eyes me, giving me the floor, and I freeze. I forget how to speak. Beads of sweat form on my hairline and my silk blouse clings to my back. Matt's hand finds mine under the table and squeezes. I squeeze back and he holds tight, pouring life into me and giving me courage. I take a deep breath and feel my chest loosen as my script begins to spill out of me.

♥

"If there aren't any more questions, we'd like to thank you for your time and attention today," I say as I forward to the end slide. By this point, my voice has evened out but my foot is rapidly shaking underneath the table. My armpits are swamplands, so I keep them glued to my side.

Everyone is silent. Nolan looks to Hunter, expecting him to speak. We hear Roger clear this throat and shuffle some papers over the speakers. Matt presses his foot against mine under the table. This is it.

"I will admit," Hunter starts, looking directly at me. "I didn't think a female-focused campaign made sense. While I'm still not entirely sure it does, you delivered a very compelling presentation here. I'm willing to test this out to see if it works. Impressive work, you two."

Holy. Shit.

He likes it. He wants our idea. We fucking did it. Matt taps my foot a few times under the table and I kick him back, hard, because *holy shit!* I sit up straight and press my lips together in an attempt to look professional, but I'm well aware I probably look like a lipless loon with big buggy eyes.

Nolan pipes in with his agreement and adds, "The two of you are a great team, and the ideas balance each other perfectly. It helped me realize that men would be open to these campaign messages as well—that most of us know how much the women in our lives reign over major purchases and decisions." That earns a few chuckles around the room, and I let a smile slip myself. "I think you both will be great for Imperial's business. I look forward to getting started with DMG."

Hunter stands and walks to the door, stopping to lean in by the speakerphone. "Roger, you sent the right team here, they did well. I'll call you later to discuss next steps."

You sent the right team. Damn straight he did. And it's true. I look at Matt for the first time since Hunter started speaking and find him smiling like the weight of the world was just lifted off his shoulders. We did it. Together, just like Matt said. I'm happy. I'm so happy... right? This weird, slightly nauseous feeling in my stomach is normal. Adrenaline influx and all that. It can't be because I'm not sure if Matt will stay at DMG. Or that I'm wondering if he'll decide to go back to school and leave the city before he's even fully unboxed. This is what I wanted, so why do I feel so conflicted?

Roger's voice crackles over the speaker. "Sounds good, Hunter. Thank you. Nice work, Matthew and Emily."

I startle at the sound of Matt's proper name, remembering how he reacted when I called him Matthew the night we met. Maybe Roger didn't even know who Matt was and just assumed? Nolan interrupts my ruminating around that when he turns to us.

"Y'all ready for some fun?" He motions for us to follow him and leads us to the lobby.

EMILY

The same intern who escorted us to the conference room is waiting to take us down to an underground tunnel. It feels eerily quiet and insulated from the world until a deep rumble and roaring above us shakes the walls. Nerves dance in my belly as I ascend a flight of stairs and am immediately blinded by the sun and the strong smell of fuel.

We're facing a racetrack. No bleachers. No pit. Just a small open-air garage to our right. A sleek sports car is parked in front of it. Cars are very low on my list of interests, but even I can appreciate this beautiful piece of machinery as it emits power and speed just while parked here. Blood red and low to the ground, you can feel its soul raring to go.

An older gentleman in well-worn jeans and a flannel shirt approaches us. "I'm Chris. We're happy to have you here today." He holds his hand out to me and I shake it. "Emily Cooper. We're happy to be here."

He leans over to Matt who stands mesmerized by the car, gazing at it with wonder. I laugh and nudge him. "You look like a kid on Christmas morning." He smiles deep—eyes crinkling, dimples popping, a face of pure joy.

Chris hands Matt a set of keys. "Well, it's holiday time now for y'all. Want to take Ol' Miss Ruby Rae out for a spin?"

"Ruby Rae? Do you name the cars?" I ask Chris.

"Sure do. These here are unique specimens and warrant the honor."

"So, uh, really?" Matt asks incredulously, holding up the keys. "We can drive her?"

"Yes, sir. Nolan called and said y'all would be working with the company and he wanted you to have a chance to experience what driving Imperial really means. Not that many folks will be driving a Ruby Rae, but this is more fun." He winks at me and guides us toward the car.

"I'll grab helmets then show you how to get buckled in." He looks at Matt. "I assume you can drive a stick?"

Matt gives a furious nod. As Chris steps into the garage to grab what we need, Matt turns to me, silently mouthing, "Holy shit! This is amazing!"

Sparks ignite in my belly as I watch Matt in his element. It's lust mixed with something else. His unadulterated bliss at the prospect of driving Ruby Rae is intoxicating on its own, but it's more than that. I haven't seen him this joyful, this relaxed, since the first weekend we were together. He's usually always in good spirits around the office and when we socialize as a team, but this... It's a moment of pure happiness, and I feel lucky I get to experience this with him.

Chris comes out with our helmets and we walk to the car. It's even more impressive up close, elegant curves and sleek lines, purring like a kitten. No, scratch that, this car is way too powerful. This is Mufasa roaring at the top of a cliff. The ground beneath me is trembling as I approach it. Chris hands me my helmet and waits for me to clip it on and buckle up before closing the door. He motions for Matt to follow him to the driver's-side door and hands him his helmet. They lean through the open window and Chris explains a few things, then he opens the door for Matt to get in. He taps the top of the roof with a "Y'all enjoy this," and walks away.

All my senses are vibrating with the car, slow and quiet but un-mistakably there. I completely trust Matt. I'm not worried about his capability to drive this car or if he's going to be reckless. He'd never do anything to risk our well-being. *My* well-being. It hits me like a gut punch that while I've been watching and waiting for him to mess up, to prove me wrong in some way, he's been building the case right in front of me of how solid and reliable he is.

Matt leans back on the headrest and closes his eyes. Taking a big inhale, he murmurs, "Em, is there anything better than that new car smell? The soft leather, the pristine interior. This car is more than a machine, it's a piece of art." He drags his hands across the top of the dashboard, and I envision him giving the same appreciative rubdown to my body. "I don't know if I'll ever be able to drive a regular car again."

"I never knew you were such a car guy."

"Yeah, I've always loved cars. I used to build model car after model car, watch the racing on TV... I even test drove a Lamborghini in college. I gravitated toward auto accounts when I went into advertising after school, but honestly, that's what ended up kind of ruining cars for me. It was too tied up with work, and my love for them fizzled. But this beauty may pull me back in."

I watch as he gets familiar with the dashboard, pushing buttons and turning knobs to adjust his seat and mirrors. He turns to me with the biggest grin and wiggles his eyebrows. "Ready to go for a ride?"

I laugh and shake my head. "Let's see what you got, Meyer. Take me for a spin."

He revs the engine a few times and then shifts into first gear, carefully pulling out and instinctually looking for cars behind him. *See, he's safe.* He lets himself get acclimated to the gears, then cautiously brings us to the straightaway, dropping the gear and accelerating around the corner flawlessly. Once we round the bend, he punches it, and we speed up so quickly I half expect to see the Hyper Drive lights of the Millennium Falcon appear outside the car. This is not your normal burst of power. This is the equivalent of an airplane taking off—but on the ground, so actually great for me. I grab the holy shit handle as the speed keeps climbing, my adrenaline surging as we head to the next corner.

His confidence doesn't surprise me but my physical reaction to it does. I can't take my eyes off how controlled he is in commanding this machine. His roped arm effortlessly switches gears and pulls my eyes away from his thigh as he pushes and releases the clutch. The car doesn't jolt once, and I imagine that thigh in between mine, nudging my legs open and rubbing against me. I think of those long fingers, so relaxed as he drives, curling around my neck and holding me as he captures me in a deep kiss. I lick my lips, noticing every move he makes, the speed and his control revving me up at the thought of him driving my body wild instead of this machine.

"You good over there?" Matt asks, giving me a quick glance as he slows a bit.

"Yep." My cheeks burn, wondering if he could sense what I was thinking, and I squeeze my thighs together for the friction I'm craving. I'm ready to unbuckle and straddle him as he drums his fingers against the gear stick. Instead, I sink back into the supple leather and just let it all go. The pressure of the past few weeks. The weight of worrying about my apartment. The exhaustion of battling my feelings for Matt. All I want to think about right now is this gorgeous man beside me, driving this gorgeous car. I want to fly and leave it all in our dust. "But I thought you said you could drive. I feel like I'm with a sixteen-year-old taking their permit test. Is this all you got?"

Matt's eyes twinkle with the challenge. "That's my girl. I knew you had some daredevil in you. Hold on, Goldie. It's time for the big leagues."

Matt hits the gas and we fly around the corner. This is joy. Freedom. Nothing exists right now except for us in this car. I close my eyes and let out a big scream. Not from fear but exhilaration. It's an out-of-body experience. No thoughts, just emotion. The world blurs around us and my cheeks start to hurt from smiling so much. Every now and then, Matt and I glance at each other, and he looks as alive as I feel. Not one crease of worry on his forehead. Not one line of distress.

This moment is a gift—literally flying on the ground, leaving worries and tension and competition, and needing to be perfect behind us. Screaming with joy and not second-guessing it. Laughing loud and soaking it all up without having to strategize two or three steps ahead to make sure I can be as close to perfect as possible. This isn't happening solely because we're in this car. It's happening because I'm in this car with Matt.

It's the juxtaposition of feeling safe, yet free to take chances. To do something I would probably never do on my own. This sweet, sexy man has done nothing but try to take care of me, be a friend to me, encourage me. No matter how much animosity and attitude I've tossed his way, he's never faltered. Behind that sculpted chest is a big heart. A heart I can trust. With every fiber of my being, I know that Matt won't hurt me, and for the first time, I allow myself to think of the possibility of being with him. Now that the pitch is over, now that we won the account, maybe I can take that leap and land on two feet.

After a few more laps, Matt pulls in by the garage and parks the car. Our chests are rising in sync like we just ran a marathon, our faces beaming and our bodies relaxed.

"That was incredible, Em." He tilts his head back on the headrest and closes his eyes. "I'll always remember this experience." He leans over, squeezing my thigh. "I'm glad it was with you."

"Same," I choke out, my heart in my throat, suddenly overcome with emotion from the ride and all the realizations that came with it. I look out the window so he won't see that my eyes are watering.

"Stay there. I'll come help you out," Matt tells me as he unclicks his seat belt. He walks around the hood and opens my door, leaning in with a hand for me to grab. My legs are shaking and a bit unsteady. Matt doesn't let go of my hand as we walk toward Chris.

"That was incredible! It felt like flying."

"You're not the first to say something like that. Glad you kids enjoyed yourselves." Matt finally releases my hand to take off his helmet and return the keys to Chris. I take mine off and shake my hair out, awareness prickling through me at the possibility of what happens next.

Matt intertwines our fingers together again as he talks more with Chris about the car. I quickly glance around to see if there's anyone around who could recognize us, or more importantly, our hands twisted together. Nolan and Hunter left for New York after our presentation, and the offices are too far to see such detail, so I tighten my grip, loving the feeling of his hand enveloping mine.

"Thanks so much, Chris. This was such a treat." I tell him.

"My pleasure. Hopefully we'll see you out here again real soon.

Take care, Emily."

I give a slight wave as Matt turns us toward the tunnel to exit the racetrack. It feels like a game of chicken now—who will let go first? He's talking animatedly about the drive and the torque and all of these car terms that I will have to learn very quickly. All I know is that I'm wholeheartedly content just being *here*.

CHAPTER 27

EMILY

We drive back to the hotel amid Matt's nonstop chatter about the car, his childlike enthusiasm punctuating every sentence. When we're at the top of the circular drive, Matt puts the car in park and jumps out, tossing the keys to the valet. There's a lightness in his step that's contagious. The air humming between us—it's adrenaline from the day and anticipation of where we go from here.

I'm in that rare state of bliss where I can only see good things ahead. I'm optimistic. My entire body is generating those feel-good vibes people at yoga are always going on about. I want to bottle up this feeling and sell it to single people on Valentine's Day.

Matt grabs my hand as we merge from our respective ends of the car. It feels so natural to do this, like he's mine to keep. Once inside, he steers us toward the bar. "We need to celebrate. One drink to toast to how kick-ass we were today."

I laugh as I follow him. I already feel effervescent and full of happy carbonated bubbles. A glass of some real bubbly sounds like the perfect complement.

It's that in-between period after lunch but before happy hour so we mostly have the place to ourselves. We grab two seats at the bar and Matt immediately swings his seat my way, hooking his legs on my stool. The internal battle from Smith's Cave is déjà vu all over again. Blocking. Preventing. But none of those guardrails are up right now. The last thing I want to do is get away from his man.

He orders two shots of Patron gold and two draft beers. The bartender drops off our drinks and Matt hands me a shot.

"To you, Emily Cooper. You were fan-fucking-tastic today. I know you were nervous, but no one else could tell. You..." He stops talking and points his finger at me. "You won this account for DMG. Not just today with your stellar performance, but all along. This is a win for DMG, but this is *your* win and *your* doing. This was never anyone else's pitch to win—it was yours before it was even given to you. I hope you're as proud of yourself as I am of you."

He clinks my glass and downs the shot. I quickly toss mine back, immediately feeling my body warm up. It starts in my throat, then slowly flows through my ribcage, finally settling in my belly. Is the heat from the drink or from Matt's words?

Matt's phone buzzes on the bar and he swipes it open quickly, frowning. I see "Dad" on the notification before he pulls the phone closer. His jaw ticks as he reads the text. It's not good. It's taking obvious effort to rein in his anger, so I give him a moment and look up to watch the screens above. He exhales loudly and mutes his phone before putting it face down on the bar.

"So." Matt looks at me, a smile on his face that doesn't quite reach his eyes after checking his phone. "How are you feeling about everything?"

"I am *so* glad it's all over. This has been the most stressful few weeks I've ever had at work. I think I'm still in a little bit of a shock. It's all I've been thinking about the past few weeks and part of me is wondering how I do real life again."

Matt takes a long sip of his beer and leans in. I can see the small scar on his right eyebrow and the navy rim around his eyes, contrasting with the periwinkle sparkle they usually have. I feel the featherlight scrape of his stubble against my cheek and I can't stop myself from taking a deep inhale of his masculine smell. His soft murmur all but does me in.

"Is it really *all* you've been thinking about? Because I haven't stopped thinking about you for one moment, Emily. You've owned me since the first time I laid eyes on you."

All he does is lean toward me and every nerve in my body is on high alert, the internal red emergency light spinning and blaring in my subconscious to proceed with caution. Because I know there are two ways this can go. In my dreamlike haze, I see the lines blurring between Matt the sweet, tender, sexy-as-fuck man I met in a bar a few weeks ago, and Matt, my opponent in a competition that is now over, completed, won and done. If I admit that he, too, has dominated my thoughts, there will be no turning back from this. If I deny it, I know he'll let me go. He'll put me first and take care of me before thinking about himself.

An involuntary shiver runs through me as he remains in that position. I pull slightly away, trying to hide myself with my hair as I stare at his feet resting on the bottom of my stool. I am overwhelmed with the closeness of him, the way my body instinctually shifts closer to him. He places his thumb on my chin. Ever so gently, he lifts my face so I can't look away. His eyes have morphed into a dark, stormy blue, merging seamlessly with his pupils. "Emily," he whispers, so close I feel his breath on my skin.

Our eyes lock. His thumb moves up from my chin to trace my lips in a delicate circle. His long fingers roam across my skin. First my temple, then stroking down the shell of my ear, then ever so slowly up again. He's hypnotizing me and I'm done fighting it.

"Emily, tell me what you want." He stops and pulls back to make sure I'm listening. "I want this. I want *you*. If you don't want it, we can stop right here, right now. But if you want me too, you have to know already that I'm all yours."

My heart is throwing a tantrum in my chest, stomping, and pounding. I'm waiting for it to bust through my skin like Mr. Kool-Aid from those old commercials. All I've ever wanted was for someone to choose me. My father didn't. Greg didn't. But here's Matt, who has seen me at some of my worst moments, and he is *choosing* me.

"Matt," I whisper back, biting my lip and hoping it'll help

me gain some composure. He pulls it out from my teeth with his thumb. I feel tears start to pool in my eyes. I have no idea why they're doing that. I'm not unhappy. I'm the opposite, but they're not tears of joy. I'm feeling so many things... I can't think straight. But as much as my mind is a mess of feelings, I do know whatever I answer will chart the course for Matt and me. The feelings start to peel away bit by bit until there's only one staring me down.

Fear.

Fear of letting myself fall again. Fear of trusting someone with my heart. Fear of not being enough. Fear that I'm not worthy. Fear that this won't last. Fear that I'll fuck it all up somehow. Fear that if I don't do something now, I'll regret it for the rest of my life.

"I'm scared," I whisper, studying his feet again and closing my eyes, rogue tears spilling down my cheek.

Matt cups my cheeks with both hands, his thumbs brushing away the moisture. Always so gentle. "I know, Em. I know. I am too. I'm so scared."

I look up at him as I place my hands over his. "You are?" I sniff in surprise.

"Of course. My heart's in your hands.

His eyes never stray from mine, silently reassuring me that if my heart were in his hands, he'd take care of it. "I'm most scared of doing nothing though. Of not telling you how I feel and watching you walk away and always wondering *what if*. Life isn't long enough to live in the what-if."

I nod. A heavy nod carrying with so many decisions. A nod telling Matt that I understand what he's saying. A nod confirming that I know what that fear feels like. A confirmation that he has my heart too.

I take a deep breath, accepting the same truth. Despite only knowing Matt a short time, somewhere deep down, I know he could hurt me more than Greg ever did. Yet, as petrified as I am, not knowing would be even worse. I squeeze his hands as they are still holding my face. Protecting it.

"Want to take a chance with me?" he softly asks me.

I nod once.

"Yeah?" he whispers.

I nod again. "Yeah." Another sniffly laugh sneaks out of me.

He exhales, and only then do I realize how big a breath he was holding. "Fuck, yeah." He smiles at me. Dimples out, creases outlining his eyes. *Happy.*

He leans in and places a feather-soft kiss on my lips before pulling back to make eye contact with me. I smile and keep nodding, urging him to continue. His lips meet mine again, with more pressure this time. He has a firm hold on the back of my neck, and I feel his smile as he bites my bottom lip, silently asking me to open my mouth. I obey with a soft moan, welcoming the intrusion of his tongue tangling with mine. Welcoming him into my heart. He pulls me closer as he deepens the kiss, and for the first time since he kissed me when we were wrapped in the covers of his bed as the snow blanketed the sky, stopping time, all feels right in my world.

Our make-out session continues for a few more minutes before the scrape of a chair on the hardwood floor reminds us we're in public. I didn't even realize the bartender dropped off the bill by our empty glasses.

He drags his nose against mine. "I need to get you upstairs and undressed before I get us arrested for public indecency."

"Not a fan of having an audience?" I tease.

"Not right now. I want the first time all to myself."

"Yeah?" I'm so breathy I don't even recognize my own voice. This commanding side of Matt has me panting and purring, bringing out a new side of me.

"Yes. When I finally get you alone and strip you down I'm going to worship every inch of your body to make up for all the nights I couldn't sleep. All the hours craving your skin, imagining the things I wanted to do to you."

"Are you in charge now?"

"You have no fucking clue how in charge I am." Matt stands and throws a couple of twenty-dollar bills on the bar top and grabs my hand. He's sprint-walking through the lobby, and I have to basically skip to keep up with him.

An elevator opens as soon as he hits the Up button and he pulls me in, pressing to close the door before anyone else can enter. As soon as it shuts, he pushes me against the back wall, hands tangling in my hair. There's urgency in his kiss. The sweetness has given way to something else, something primal, and he groans as he leans into me, leaving no question about how turned on he is already.

"Emily, you have no idea how many times I've thought of this. How you have tortured my dreams."

I step up on my toes, pulling his head down and pressing my leg against his outer thigh. His eyes widen as he wraps my leg around his waist, then the other, hitching me up. The ease with which he lifts me matches the lightness I feel. Now that we're here and this is actually happening, I can't get close enough. I tighten my grip and deepen the kiss, needing more. He slants harder into me, releasing my lips to kiss my jaw, my neck, and then biting that same spot just hard enough to make me gasp. I rock against him and he kisses over his bite mark, lightly sucking and marking me as his.

The doors open and again we're jolted from our bubble. Matt steps back, hands gripping my waist as he gently places me on the floor. His hand presses on my lower back, guiding me out of the elevator and directly to our room. He pulls me in for another kiss once we're at the door, all the while fumbling to pull the key card out of his wallet. We stumble into the room, our lips still locked as Matt kicks the door closed with the back of his foot, finally blocking out the rest of the world.

Our lips stay connected as he walks me backward into the room. We reach the end of the bed, chests rising as we both try to catch our breath. His fingers slip into my hair and his thumb finds my bottom lip again, stroking over it like he's warming it up for another round of bruising kisses. I catch it and pull it into my mouth, twirling my tongue around the tip. We stand there, unmoving, and I finally raise my eyes to his.

"Hi," he whispers.

"Hi, back."

"You still with me?"

"Yeah," I breathe out.

My stomach feels like it's hosting the gymnastic Olympic trials, but yeah—I'm with him. When Matt puts one of his hands on my waist and squeezes, all of my blood rushes to the spot, immediately burning at his touch. My entire body feels like it's emerging from sleep, pins and needles floating up and down my arms and legs, and I close my eyes. He gives my waist a gentle shake, almost as if he knows I need to stop focusing on all the sensations coursing through me and decide where I want this to go.

I drag my hands up his chest, tracing a path to his heart, and stop when I feel a steady strum beating in time with my own. My fingers toy with one of his buttons, my mind looking for a reprieve from all the sensations pulsing through my body.

"I don't know why, but all of a sudden I'm kind of nervous." I continue to inspect his buttons.

Matt exhales and chuckles. He's rubbing his hands up and down my arms and my skin, igniting my skin. "Trust me, I understand." He brushes my hair away from my face with a trembling hand. He holds me there, cradling my head like it's something precious to behold. "I've thought of this moment so many times, imagined it so many different ways. I feel like a rookie lining up for his first jump ball and the entire fate of the season is on me. I don't want to mess this up. I want this to be perfect for you.

For us."

He tilts my head and presses his lips to mine as I tug him once, twice, eliminating all space between us. He answers with a groan, stroking my lips with his tongue until they open all the way. He explores my mouth with his, capturing my bottom lip with his teeth, and the dam breaks.

He shrugs out of his jacket and I paw at his shirt, pulling it out of his pants, needing to feel his skin. My nails scrape his back, the warmth of him torching my entire body, gentleness be damned as desperation drives us. He deepens our kiss as I fumble with his buttons. Once they're free, I lean back to slide his shirt off his shoulders and he takes advantage of my exposed neck, nipping my jaw and dragging his teeth down it, biting and kissing along the way.

I crane my neck, taking a moment to appreciate the beauty of his man. My fingers graze across the tops of his shoulders and trace down his biceps to the toned and flexed forearms that have been taunting me for weeks. They roam from his wrists to his chest, tracing the planes of his pecs, scratching against the small tuft of hair between them. I draw a nail around his nipple and lean in to kiss it.

"Em, if you're trying to torture me, you're doing a solid job of it. A+ work." I look up and grin, feeling bold with his admission, and flick my tongue over his nipple. I'm not thinking or analyzing. I'm running on pure lust for this man.

I shrug my shoulders and press my mouth to the other nipple before kissing my way down his stomach, pausing at each toned ridge I find. I fall to my knees, hands resting on his firm ass, and kiss right above his pants, right where a trail of dark hair begins and then disappears below. I pull at his belt buckle, undo the button, and hear him exhale a curse. He's straining against his boxers, and I heat up thinking about his arousal.

"No. Not yet." He grips my shoulders, lifts me up, and turns me around. He moves all of my hair to one side, kissing behind my ear and sucking on the lobe. "So beautiful." He slowly—torturously—undoes the zipper to my dress, following it with his hot mouth and kissing my skin as he goes. "So soft."

Stopping right above my ass when the zipper ends, he slowly meanders his way up again until he's standing. My breath trips when he peels the dress off my body and pushes it to the floor, the material grazing my ankles. He slips one finger under my bra strap and inches it down it so it's resting above my elbow, his hands caressing my arms. His soft lips meet the back of my shoulder and he moves my hair to the other side, following the same routine there. *Finger. Strap. Caress. Kiss.* This guy is straight out of a regency romance, ruining me for all others. He finally unclasps my bra and lets it fall away.

I turn around and face him. He trails a finger across my collarbone and then down between my breasts. "Better than those dreams," he whispers reverently. The same finger finds my nipple and slowly circles it, watching as it tightens in response to his touch. He drags his finger to my other nipple and repeats the same routine.

"You like that, don't you, Goldie? You like my hands on your body?"

I feel myself arch into his touch and can barely talk when I whimper, "Matt, please." I'm not sure what I'm even specifically pleading for, but I need more of him, his touch, his mouth—and I need it now.

He smiles at me—a wicked, flirty, *dirty* smile—and he keeps eye contact as he leans down and licks my nipple. I close my eyes, overwhelmed by sensation, and drop my head back. My hand instinctively comes up to cover my breast and he playfully swats it away, replacing it with his mouth, feasting on it like it's his last meal.

"This tit is mine tonight. Don't you dare cover it up."

There is no longer blood flow to my brain. All the heat in my body is in my nipple and pooling between my legs. I feel a rush of wetness and need *more*. Everywhere. All at once.

After devouring my other breast, he glides his tongue down until he gets to my navel. He's on his knees in front of me and I'm self-conscious of my soft belly, so I suck in and try to cover up what I can with my hand.

He links his fingers with mine and steadies me. "Don't do that, Emily. Don't cover yourself up." He kisses above my belly button. Matt stands, his hands on my hips. "You are *exquisite*. You are a sexy, powerful woman, and if you don't believe the words I'm saying, I can prove to you how much my body wants you. I don't think I've ever been this hard in my life." He presses my hand to the tent in his jeans, emphasizing his point. "You are everything I want. I don't know what you see, but to me, you're perfect."

Perfect. Never in my life have I come close to feeling that way despite my endless attempts. Never have I felt comfortable in my own skin, proud of my accomplishments, or peaceful with who I am. It's why my anxiety rules so much of my life. Why I want to run from situations that swerve out of my control and make sure everything I touch, everything I do, is flawless. Impeccable. I always fall short—my voice shakes in presentations, I panic when there's a lull in a conversation. Perfect people don't do that. They have a handle on these things.

Yet right now, seeing myself through Matt's eyes, I allow myself to believe it. Just this once. I want to believe it.

I squeeze his hand and whisper, "Okay." *I will try to believe it. For you, for me, I will try.*

My efforts are rewarded with the most brilliant of Matt's smiles. "That's my girl." He squeezes my hand before dropping it, then returns to kissing my soft, warm, *perfect* tummy.

"Now I finally get to find out if you taste as good as you do in my dreams." He fingers the bottom edge of my underwear and pulls them to one side. I feel the cold air mix with my wetness and I throb under his inspection.

Matt doesn't hesitate to put his lips on me. It's reminiscent of our initial kisses—soft, testing, exploratory. He drags his tongue through my slit and his licks slowly get more insistent. Sparks crackle where his lips meet me, cascading out to every inch of my body. My hands tangle in his hair and I arch into him, pulsing against his tongue as he lifts one of my legs over his shoulder.

"God damn, you are delicious."

His hand circles my other leg and digs into my ass, holding me steady so I don't fall. Through all of this, he doesn't stop licking and sucking and probing with his tongue, lapping against me like the first drink of water after days spent in the desert. I feel his finger trace my entrance and press harder into his mouth, moaning his name and gripping his hair tighter for support when he inserts one then two fingers inside me.

"Matt, I can't... I don't... I..." I can't form coherent sentences because all of my energy is focused on soaking in the euphoria, in the buzzing sensations that are threatening to bubble over. His fingers press into me and curl, hitting the spot that'll drive me over the edge. He sucks hard and I yell out his name as pleasure ripples up my legs and explodes through me, launching me over a cliff to the most exquisite free fall.

His pressure eases but he continues kissing and humming against my sensitive skin, rocking me down until I land softly on the ground. "That's my girl. So greedy. So gorgeous with my name on your lips."

Matt leans in and gives me one more kiss as he gingerly takes my leg from his shoulder and places it on the floor, holding my waist in case my legs choose this moment to surrender. He kisses up my body, starting at my stomach. Kiss. Stopping at my belly button. Kiss. Dragging his tongue up between my breasts, then to my collarbone. Kiss. He rakes his teeth from my left shoulder—kiss—to my right. He licks up my neck and then cups my face with his palms. I'm still floating when I meet his gaze through half-lidded eyes and he finally kisses my mouth, telling me so much more with his touch than words could ever convey.

CHAPTER 28

MATT

We pause for a moment, foreheads connected, just absorbing the moment.

"You good?"

She nods and my heart swells. This woman. She's incredible. And she's here. *Finally,* she's here.

I can't remember a time I felt so... complete. Yes, I was married, and it was great with Stella for a while. But then things faded, like an old T-shirt that had been washed one too many times. It was comfortable, sure, but the passion was the first to go.

But now, here is something—*someone*—beyond anything I had with Stella. It isn't just her beauty. Yes, that got my attention the first time I saw her. But it's been discovering who she really is, peeling back the layers through late nights at the office and conversations when her guard is down. Her drive and determination mixes with humility and compassion. And I got to this place—this prize of her attention and affection—all on my own.

I skim my nose against her cheek, savoring the moment. I kiss the corner of her mouth, the bottom of her cheek, the underside of her jaw. I commit the taste and scent of her skin to memory, hoping like hell I can relive this every day for the rest of my life. My lips move to the hollow of her throat and I feel her hands in my hair.

"Matt." She sighs as she pulls my head away so I can look at her. "Please."

Her eyes have turned a deep evergreen, emboldened with the passion we both feel. If this is the stuff of sappy romance novels, I believe the hype.

"Please what, Emily?" I refocus my attention to her collarbone and she moans as her head falls back. "Tell me what you want."

She tugs my hair a bit harder now, forcing me to focus on her face, her words. "You, Matt. I want you. Inside me."

You know that moment on a hot summer day… the clouds are an ominous gray and you're aware a storm is coming but you don't know exactly when? Then, in a split second, the sky turns almost black, a lightning bolt crackles, and it opens up to the most intense pounding rain that seemingly came out of no-where? It's a rush, a release, as the oppressive humidity breaks, relief in the form of heavy slanted raindrops that cool you off and make you laugh at the complete surprise of it all?

Take that and multiply it by infinity. Desire drives through me and the switch is flipped. Patience gives way to need. Tenderness gives way to lust. Adoration gives way to a carnal urge for possession and pleasure.

Stepping back from Emily, I don't take my eyes off her as I push down my jeans and boxers, stepping out of them and removing my socks in the process. My body is vibrating with need and I feel immediate relief as I stroke myself. We face each other, adjusting to how exposed we are, accepting the vulnerability we're each offering. Then we rush forward and it's instinct and desire and want.

I fist her soft strands and pull her head back to press my lips on hers, tasting a moan deep in her throat. Her hands on my waist, pinching and pulling me closer, hips pressing against me, seeking friction. I turn so the backs of Emily's knees hit the bed and hold her tight against me as I place one knee down and lay her on the mattress. I force myself back and take her in. She's angelic against the white sheets, and this moment surpasses all of the fantasies that have dominated my thoughts for weeks. My cock is throbbing, begging for release, but I refuse to rush this. I don't think I've ever been this hard in my life, and the intensity of my arousal is only matched by the swelling of my heart.

I land a bruising kiss on her mouth then flicker my tongue down her throat to the top of her breast, taking one nipple in my mouth and sucking hard. She growls as she pushes into me and tugs my hair. One of my hands is working her other nipple, circling, pinching, kneading as I devour this one with my mouth. Emily's legs wrap around my waist and pull me closer so we're flush, grinding her hips against me.

I drag my mouth to her other nipple as my hand slides down

her ribcage and over her hip, settling on her gorgeous, round ass. I grip the flesh and squeeze. Hard. She lets out a curse and rubs against me again in response. I hike her leg higher on my hip as I press into her, dragging my fingers from her backside to reach the spot where I know she wants me most, my hand covered in her wetness when I find it.

"Jesus, Emily, you're soaked."

Circling my thumb as I dip my fingers into her warmth, feeling her stretch around me, I think to myself that if I die now, I will die a happy man.

Emily's breaths quicken as she unravels, chasing her pleasure with abandon. Her hair is spread on the bed like rays of sunshine, her cheeks a rosy pink, and her eyes flutter close.

"Matt, don't stop. Please."

"Good girl." She continues to grind against my hand, and I feel her walls tightening around my fingers, telling me she's close. She's so close to letting go, and I want her to feel all the satisfaction I'm capable of giving her. I press my thumb down harder and that's her breaking point.

She cries out and I hold her as her body shakes. I don't let go as her nails dig into my shoulders. "That's it, baby. Take it all." Her nails carve down my back. "So fucking beautiful."

I keep holding her close until her eyes flutter open, confessing every thought running through my head. "The things you do to me. How you respond. You're amazing." She's the picture of ecstasy as I crash my lips to hers, submitting to the need to be connected to her in as many ways as possible.

She stretches her arms above her head, inadvertently serving me her chest, and I kiss the underside of her breast. "A+ yourself, Matt Meyer. That's never worked two times in a row for me before."

I lift my head, smiling wickedly at her. "Is that so?" She nods, still smiling. "Well, then, challenge accepted, Emily Cooper." I stroke her where she's still warm and wet and feel a shiver run through her.

"Challenge?"

I lick her jaw; my voice is hoarse when I whisper in her ear, "You know what they say... Third time's a charm." Sucking on her lobe, I lean over her, caging her head between my elbows and press into her. I have never been so aroused, and her slightest movement against me threatens a repeat of the first night we were together. Her legs wrap around me again and I'm surrounded by her wetness. My restraint is spiraling. "Em, stop moving," I plead, my hands circling the crown of her head to get her attention. "This is the sweetest torture, but unless you want me to blow all over you like a clumsy teenager again, you need to. Please. Stop. Moving."

Bracing her hands on my shoulders, she pulls herself up and kisses me. It's her turn to whisper in my ear, and I shiver from her breath before she even says a word. "Then I suggest you get a condom and fuck me before that happens."

I never was someone who had to be told something twice. Limbs flail as I fumble for my jeans on the floor, grabbing my wallet and taking out a condom with the careful urgency of locating a winning lotto ticket. Right now, right here, sweet Emily's dirty mouth asking me to fuck her is better than winning the lotto. This is grown Matt and teenage Matt's dreams all rolled into one.

I walk over to Emily on my knees, condom in mouth, gripping myself as she watches me. I tear the package open and take her hand, using it to roll the condom down. When we're finished, I lift her hand and kiss her palm before placing it down on the bed. I'm back in position, rubbing my tip against her. I pause, staring at her, and she strokes my hair and kisses me. I slowly push in, watching where we're joined, hearing her purr as I fill her up. I'm surrounded by her heat, and *nothing* has ever felt this good. She's so tight, so perfect, and I start reciting the starting line-up of the 1970 Knicks championship squad to buy me some time, any amount of time, to get myself under control. Emily squeezes around me and pulls me down for an open-mouthed kiss, biting my bottom lip in the process.

Time is overrated.

I quicken my pace where I'm touching her, pushing her knees towards her chest to give me leverage to fill her deeper. I thrust into her, filling her to the hilt, pushing harder when she begs me to. My hand reaches between us and I circle her swollen skin, right where she liked it before. Her breath hitches, her legs gripping me tighter.

"Matt, I'm going to—" She pants and squirms, not able to finish the sentence.

I press down on the spot I know will get her there and she cries out as she squeezes everywhere—inside around my cock, outside around my hips, all while small spasms rock her body. I pump into her once more and find my own release, seeing stars when I close my eyes, heat coursing through my veins and my body pulsing with the most intense relief I've ever felt.

We lie there until our heavy breaths even out and I push up on my elbows, stroking her hair away from her face. She caresses my cheek, a sated glaze sheathing her eyes. We're sweaty and sticky and in need of a shower. I sit up and tell her to stay put as I step into the bathroom to take care of the condom. I turn on the shower and walk back to the bed, my chest tightening at the sight.

"Shower time." She grabs my outstretched hands as I pull her up and wrap my arms around her.

"Then some food? I'm starving."

I nod. "Anything for you, Goldie. I'll lasso the moon if that's what you want."

We take the time to learn each other's bodies when we shower, the nooks that spark a giggle, the spots that illicit moans. Leisurely, languidly, soaping and massaging each other until our fingers are wrinkled and the water turns cold. I wrap Emily in one of the hotel's fluffy white robes and seat her on the floor between my legs while I dry her hair with a towel. We order chocolate milkshakes and french fries from room service and eat facing each other cross-legged on the bed, laughing through a game of *Would You Rather* until our sides hurt.

Emily tries to stifle a yawn, but her eyes are heavy and I know the rush of today, of the past several weeks, is finally catching up.

"That's enough yawning for you. Time for bed." I stand up and grab the room service tray from the desk, bringing it to the bed to collect our empty plates.

"Normally I would say you can't tell me what to do..." Emily responds, a challenging smile immediately morphing into another yawn as she places our utensils on the tray. "But I am having trouble keeping my eyes open. Bed sounds perfect."

I place the tray outside our door and double check the Do Not Disturb sign is on the handle. Returning to where Emily is sitting on the bed, I hold out my hands to help her stand. I kiss the crown of her head, her temple. She looks radiant, all freshly washed, not a lick of makeup on her face. I feel a pull in my chest.

"I think this is the prettiest you've ever been." I release her hand to tuck a piece of hair behind her hair, caressing her cheek.

Pink spots tint her cheeks. "Thank you," she whispers.

The pressure in my chest intensifies as she lays her head against me. It's such an unexpected show of affection. "Come on, let's go to sleep."

She takes the robe off and climbs into bed, shifting under the sheets and holding them up for me to follow her in. I lie on my back and scoot close to her. Her head is splayed on my chest, leg hooked over my knee, and I lazily stroke up and down her back until her breaths are long and steady and I know she's asleep.

My chest tugs thinking about how many times I thought about a moment like this. How many nights my arms ached for her. How I was terrified I would never get to feel her mold against me like this again. Gratitude courses through my veins as I feel my own eyes get heavy, and my last thought before surrendering to sleep is *finally*.

CHAPTER 29

MATT

The sun is warming my face as I start to wake up, smiling at the gorgeous creature draped across the top of me, warming the rest of my body. Cheeks tight, I roll my lips between my teeth to stifle a chuckle as I think back to our failed attempts to not ravish each other when we both stirred in our sleep.

I woke up a few hours after we climbed into bed, needing to touch her everywhere, taste her, feel her on top of and below me. After the second time I covered her skin with my lips and my hands, we fell back onto rumpled sheets, chests heaving and fingers intertwined. Spent and satiated, we finally surrendered to sleep.

I skim my fingers up and down her back until Emily awakes beside me. She whimpers, burying her face deeper into my chest, and then rolls over to do a full-body stretch. I take advantage of her limbs facing every direction to suck on her neck and caress her breast until her nipple is a taut bud.

"Good morning to you too." Emily giggles and lowers her hands to my head, playing with my hair.

"How did you sleep?" I pepper her torso with kisses.

"I don't think I've slept that soundly in years. You are a human furnace and it was glorious absorbing all your heat for myself."

"I'm at your service. Bedtime heating available to you for a very low price."

As Emily settles onto her back, I lay my head on her stomach, looking at her through the valley of her chest. *Now that's a view.*

"Is that so? Maybe I'll talk you up on that, save some money on my heating bills. Lord knows it would be nice not to have to keep my apartment at an arctic level so I can swing more nights out with my friends." She tries to laugh it off, but there's a strain in her voice.

I sit up and shift so I'm leaning on my elbow, facing her. "Care to elaborate on that?"

Emily looks at the ceiling. She looks conflicted, unsure if she should say anything, and then lets out a heavy sigh, almost in defeat.

"You know I was engaged to Greg."

Sketching shapes on her stomach with my finger, I nod but remain silent, letting her decide where this goes.

"Right after we got engaged, we decided to move in together. My lease was up. He was able to break his early, and we found the apartment I still live in now. I know it sounds silly, but seeing this apartment was love at first sight. The minute I stepped into inside, something just clicked. I could literally *see* myself—us, at the time—living there. It was pricey, but with both our incomes, we could afford it. I put so much time and energy into decorating it and making it a perfect home."

"I bet it's perfect if you worked that hard on it," I say, knowing it has to be true with her attention to detail.

"Well, I thought it was. But I got a lot of things wrong apparently." She frowns and takes a deep breath before continuing.

"We started planning the wedding shortly after moving in together, and as more details got confirmed, Greg started pulling away. He'd work late or go out with clients almost every night of the week. When he wasn't out with clients, he was at the gym or meeting up with friends. We started growing apart, and anytime I would ask if we could spend time together, he always had an excuse. The harder I tried to find things we could do together or make special plans, the more he withdrew. He would get annoyed at every little thing I did. Like if I asked him about his plans, he would accuse me of not trusting him or trying to rule his life.

"I should have seen the red flags, but I didn't. I just tried harder and harder until it became a vicious cycle. Then one night he didn't show up for our dinner reservations. His brother Jack was in London, and Greg said Jack asked him to check on the dog. Jack's apartment is close to DMG so I usually handled the dog in the afternoon. I hadn't been able to make it that day, so I went by to make sure nothing was wrong. The dog was fine, and Greg was... even better, I guess. His client—completely naked and on her knees in front of him—was making sure of that as an empty tequila bottle and shot glasses lay knocked over on the coffee table. He was so out of it when he saw me, he casually said, 'Hey, Em,' as if I was supposed to be there."

I focus on Emily to tame the rage. I knew Greg was a world-class douchebag the minute I met him, but hearing how he treated her makes my blood boil. I think about Emily trusting him, trying so hard for pebbles of his attention, and I want to simultaneously wrap her tight in my arms and take those same arms and wrap them around Greg's neck.

"Jesus, Emily." I distinctly remember how she paled at the bar when Greg mentioned he was with clients.

I pull her closer to me, trying to shield her from this memory. I don't trust myself to say anything right now I'm so livid.

"The decision felt easy because I was so angry in the moment, but once the anger passed, I just felt really sad. After being sad, I started wondering if maybe he was right. Maybe I was clingy, or crazy, or annoying. Maybe life with me was boring and dull. Maybe I wasn't enough."

I rest my hand on her hip and give it a good squeeze. "I get why you might have felt that way..." I tug her hip to get her full attention. "But that's the biggest load of shit I've ever heard. You are more than enough in all the right ways, and everything you're telling me about Greg confirms that he not only made the biggest mistake of his life letting you go, but he never deserved you in the first place. Your heart is too precious to waste on someone like that. Even when you hated me, I thanked the stars above that I was lucky enough to have even a moment of your attention."

I mean every word I said to Emily, but keeping my cool isn't easy considering the inside of my brain is cataloging the ways I could hurt Greg. *What a fucking tool.* I mean, he did us both a favor showing his true colors because I'm here with her now, but the fact that she had to suffer in the process makes me want to throttle him.

She reaches out and touches my cheek. "Thank you. I know on some level you're right, and it's taken a lot of therapy for me to start to believe that again. I think what hurts the most is that he lied to me. He knew how important honesty is to me, how much I value it, and rather than him just manning up and telling me he didn't want to get married, he cheated so I'd call it off. It was like I was reliving the nightmare we went through when my dad left—the cheating, the leaving. It ripped open old wounds."

My stomach bottoms out at her words. I'm lying to her right now, so how am I any different than Greg or her dad? *But it is different. I'm protecting her. I didn't want her to worry about the pitch and will clear it all up this weekend when I talk to my dad.*

"Anyway." She blows out another breath. "When Greg moved out, I had to carry the apartment on my own. I've been digging into savings to cover it, but I'm tapped out. I refuse to ask my mom for help. She'd give it to me in an instant, but she's done enough for me over the years and is finally able to reap the rewards of her hard work. If I get this promotion, the bump will help me keep my sanctuary. I'm this close"—she holds her pointer and thumb about an inch apart—"to getting evicted because

I've been late with the rent one too many times. If I miss it one more time, I'm not sure what will happen. My credit is shot, and I don't have money for a new deposit. I'm sure I can stay on Josie or Lucy's couch for a while, but that isn't a realistic solution."

I swallow the lump in my throat. *Fuck.* I can't let that happen. We won the account, so my debt should be paid off—regardless of what tricks my dad tries to pull—and the promotion should be hers. I'll do whatever I can to make damn sure that's the case.

Thankfully the line at security is quick, and I hold Emily's clammy hand as soon as we grab our stuff. I do whatever I can to distract her—stopping to browse in a bookstore, buying extra snacks, pulling her into the corner of an empty gate and whispering dirty things in her ear that make her blush and giggle.

Once we're boarded and our suitcases are stowed, I place an encouraging hand on the small of her back. "Aisle or window?"

She looks up, trying to put on a brave smile, and ducks to take the window seat. After we buckle our seat belts, I lift the arm rest between us and she immediately edges closer to me.

"Hey," I say, and she turns to me with wide, worried eyes. "I'll be with you the whole time. We'll get through it together." She answers with a nod and burrows into my chest.

Together. It feels so right to say that about us. Last night obviously changed a lot of things, all for the better, and solidified how much I want this, how much I want her, in my life. I hate to see Emily nervous, but I revel in the fact that I get to hold her and take care of her now. I stroke her back and feel her breathing start to even out.

"I got you," I whisper. I keep rubbing her back as the remaining passengers board. She tightens her hold and relaxes against me. I grabbed Dramamine from the hotel gift shop before we left for the airport, then convinced her to give it another try. Her heavy eyelids show it's starting to kick in. "Try to sleep if you can."

By the time the captain asks the flight attendants to prepare for take-off, Emily's sleeping soundly. I'd like to think it's my presence that brings her comfort, but I know it's because we hardly slept last night.

I let my head fall back against the seat and look out Emily's window. For the first time, I let my mind wander to the text my father sent yesterday. I wanted to throw my phone across the bar when I read it. I'm going to have to deal with it once we land in the city, so I open my phone to read it again.

> **Dad:** Good work, son. I knew if I gave you the right circumstances, you'd get back on track. Here's to your fresh start at DMG and managing the Imperial account. We'll announce it on Monday.

You don't need a therapist to analyze the passive-aggressive bullshit packed into those few sentences. I couldn't give a shit about him thinking I'll get a fresh start at DMG. I did what he needed me to do and now I can move on. No, what's making my frustration tip over is that he wants to announce that *I'll* be leading the Imperial account. Everyone knows Emily deserves to run it, and I'll be damned if misplaced nepotism denies her of it.

The only problem is I've been a jackass coward and now have to figure out how to tell her who my dad is and what's going on. Oh, and also somehow manage not to lose her. How did I fuck this up so much? She won't ever trust me again. But how could I have told her who my dad was without her hating me even more? She hardly spoke to me as it was. I couldn't risk being permanently shut out or judged simply for my bloodline. Regardless, this is a colossal disaster, and I need to figure out how to get to my dad before he gets to anyone else.

Emily stirs against my chest and lifts her head. "Hi."

"Hey, sleepy head. Welcome back." A few loose strands frame her face, and I tuck them behind her ears.

"I didn't snore, did I?" Emily asks, holding her hand over her mouth.

"Nope, but I bet it would be cute if you did." I tap my finger on her nose.

"How long was I out?"

"Since before we took off. Probably a couple of hours. I think we're close." I peek out the window above her to see if anything on the ground is visible. Emily rises up, stretching her shirt up her stomach to reveal a sliver of skin, and I lick my lips.

"I saw that look. You're thinking dirty thoughts, aren't you?" Emily teases as she lowers her arms and shifts to fully face me, her hands in her lap.

"Just thinking about how delicious you tasted." I quirk an eyebrow. "What are *you* thinking?"

She blows out a weighted sigh. "I'm so glad the work portion of this is over, but I'm kind of not ready to leave this little bubble we've been in."

"I know, I feel the same." I link my fingers with hers and kiss the back of her hand.

"We'll have to figure out how this will all play out once we get back to the office." She's talking to herself more than me, her eyes bouncing from my face to her lap where she's tracing my palm lines. "I don't know how it's all going to work, but I..." She closes her eyes and takes a deep breath, a war raging in her head, fear holding her back. I squeeze her hand, hopefully reassuring her that she can take that leap with me. "I want to figure it out, Matt. I know I've been brushing you off, but I want to see what this is between us." She holds my eyes, backing her words with her look. "I'm in."

She's so beautiful. Knowing how hard it is for her to put herself out there clogs my throat with emotion. She's being brave for me, and fuck if it doesn't make my heart beat a little stronger. I'm so damn proud of her. With everything she's overcome, she could have been bitter or angry, but she's not. More than how proud I am, I'm fucking happy—relieved—that she's saying these words to me. I've been falling for her since I met her, and there's no turning back for me.

I love her. Clear as the bright cerulean sky behind her, I realize this with a start. *I am so in love with this woman.*

I rest my forehead against hers and stroke her cheeks. "I'm in too, Em." I kiss her again, pouring my truth into it, willing her to believe in me no matter what happens. "I'm all in."

She settles back into me and we sit in comfortable silence for the rest of the trip. As we deplane, my smile lingers but my stomach sinks when I think about how this is going to all go down.

CHAPTER 30

EMILY

Everything feels foreign to me as we get off the plane. It's the same airport, the same hustle and bustle we left only a few days ago, but so much feels different. Everything is a little bit brighter, sounds are a bit louder—life in general seems a lot clearer than when we left.

Matt holds my hand through the airport and baggage claim and while we wait for our Uber to pick us up. "Two stops?" the driver asks as we climb into the back seat. Matt looks at me, giving me the choice.

"Yes, please." I suddenly feel shy, learning to navigate this new space between us. "Is that okay? I like to get home to unpack, shower, and settle back in after being away."

He squeezes my shoulder. "Of course. I'll miss you the minute we say goodbye, but I get it and don't want you to feel like you have to explain yourself."

"Old habits die hard, I guess." I turn my attention out the window, watching the city buildings blur together as we drive. An anxious ache pulls deep in my belly. *Is this when it starts to go wrong?*

"Hey." Matt leans down to catch my eyes, his brows pulled together. "I can feel how hard you're thinking over there. Talk to me."

I expel a deep breath. "Let's just say Greg didn't like my routines." Matt's jaw pulses as he quietly listens. "In case you haven't noticed," I say with a self-deprecating chucking, "I like structure. I like being prepared and feeling like things are in order. I guess it suffocated him, and he blamed a lot of what went wrong between us on that. On me."

Matt forcefully exhales and finally breaks eye contact to look out the window. I watch him curl and unfist his hand resting on the door before he finally looks back at me.

"Emily, I need you to hear me." His tone is more serious than I've ever heard it. "He was wrong. Thoroughly, completely, outrageously wrong. Not only that, but he's also possibly the most idiotic man alive for not seeing what a gift you are. How all your habits and needs make you so special and, in my eyes, extraordinary. I'd love nothing more than to knock him out if I ever see him again. But I won't. Because as much as he'd deserve that for treating you as anything but precious, I'm glad he let you go. His loss is the biggest gain of my life."

I feel my eyes well and I bite my bottom lip. I know Matt believes the things he said, and I know I need to believe them too.

I'm getting there.

I nod silently and he brushes his lips against mine. He starts to pull me closer when the car stops and I realize we're already in front of my apartment building. Matt exits the cab first and holds the door for me as I climb out. The driver places my luggage next to us and gets back into the car, giving us a moment alone.

"So, this is me." I tilt my head toward the building.

Matt steps closer, wrapping his arms around me. "You really were spectacular these past few days. In the meeting. With the clients. With me." He tightens his hold. "I'm following your lead here. I'm all in, but I'll take this as fast or as slow as you want, yeah?" I stand on my tiptoes and nod, burying my face in his neck, allowing myself to be held by this remarkable man.

His breath caresses my skin as he tenderly kisses my forehead and then scans my face like he's trying to memorize it. Long fingers graze my cheeks and in slow motion, soft lips meet mine.

His delicate touches increase in pressure as he palms the back of my head, tilting to get better access. He playfully bites my lip and a hoarse groan escapes him, his tongue quickly following to soothe it before sinking into my mouth and tangling with mine.

The kiss scorches every part of my brain and my body, erasing every kiss before it and setting a new bar that only his mouth— and his lips—can meet again. This might be the best kiss of my life. I hum, caught in a whirlwind of sensation, all of my thoughts taken out with the current, leaving nothing but desire. Passion. Affection. An intense burst of euphoria spreads from my core, through my limbs, heating my body. Then, just as quickly, he retreats. Nuzzling my head, his nose in my hair, he mutters, "Don't be a stranger."

I watch as he gets back in the Uber, and it's then when I realize how much I don't want him to go.

Once upstairs, I robotically work through my usual routine. Unpack, shower, start laundry. Finally in my softest pink flannel pajamas pants, a white tank top, gray hoodie, and fuzzy black socks, I plop down on my couch with a cup of peppermint tea.

Me: Guess who's back, bitches

Josie: Hiiiii! How was it!?!? All you gave us was a thumbs up. Did you win them over with your brilliance?

Me: LOL, not sure about that, BUT we won the account!

Lucy: <celebration face emoji> <hands up emoji> YES!!!! Congrats, Em! So thrilled for you. Not that we didn't know you would nail it!

Me: Thanks! It couldn't have gone better. I'm really happy.

Josie: Did you nail him too?

Me: Um...

Josie: Spill it, sister.

Me: Yes, you could say the account wasn't the only thing I nailed this week.

Lucy: whooooaaaa

Josie: WHAT THE WHAT?

Me: <laughing emoji> <eggplant emoji> <shrug emoji>

Josie: Eggplant, huh? Nice, my friend. <Fist bump emoji>

Lucy: Need the SparkNotes version. Meeting my trainer for a late workout in five minutes.

Me: We pitched, we drove a super fast car, we had a few drinks, we took our clothes off.

Lucy: And what does that mean now?

Me: We're both open to see where it goes. Head. Is. Spinning.

Josie: Ok, this definitely calls for a deep dive over drinks. Brunch tomorrow?

Me: Can we go to Barbetta for prix fixe?

Lucy: Done.

Josie: Sweet. We'll figure out deets later. So happy for you, Em. Love you, mean it!

I settle in under a blanket and pick up my Kindle. The new Meghan Quinn book just dropped and I can't get enough of those Vancouver Agitators. I'm a few chapters in when my phone buzzes. My stomach swirls hoping it might be Matt and I fail to bite back my smile as I swipe to open the text.

Magic Matt: Hi

Me: Hi back.

Magic Matt: How's it going? You all unpacked and settled in?

Me: Yes. Feels good to be home. I'm snuggled under a blanket and it may take a bulldozer to get me off of this couch. Why am I so tired!?

Magic Matt: I can think of a few reasons <kiss emoji>

Me: <blushing smiley emoji> True, true.

Me: What are you up to?

Magic Matt: I unpacked, had something to eat. I'm sitting here with the TV on but not paying attention because I keep thinking about this girl I know.

Me: Yeah? What about her?

Sitting up, I can only imagine the silly grin I must be wearing.

Magic Matt: Well, it's fairly new, but I miss her more than I expected to.

Me: Interesting.

Magic Matt: Very. My hoodie smells like her shampoo because she slept on me, and now I don't want to wash it. Is that weird?

I giggle. *Is it weird how hard I'm smiling right now?*

Me: Only if it smells bad.

Magic Matt: It's my new favorite smell, actually.

Magic Matt: Is it strange that I miss her when I only left her a few hours ago?

Same, dude, same.

Me: She sounds pretty special.

Magic Matt: The most special. Do you think she might miss me?

Me: I bet she does. More than she wants to admit.

Magic Matt: Do you think she wants to see me? Or is it too much too soon?

Not too much. I think about how badly I want to see him. *Definitely not too much.*

Me: I think she probably does want to see you but is also worried about the same thing. Coming on too strong and all that.

Magic Matt: That's not something she should worry about.

Me: If that's the case, then yes, she kind of wishes you were snuggled under a blanket with her.

Magic Matt: Only kind of?

Me: Maybe a little more than kind of?

Magic Matt: Enough to get up and look out her window?

I reread the last text and jump up to the window that looks out the front of my building. Matt is standing across the street, looking up at my apartment. He lifts a hand and waves. I smile so hard my cheeks hurt and wave back.

Magic Matt: Hi.

Me: I thought you were sitting on your couch?

Magic Matt: I lied. <shrug emoji>

Me: Probably the only time I'll excuse a lie.

Me: Get up here. Apartment 6H.

I run to the bathroom and quickly brush my hair, pulling it into a tangled bun. I swish some mouthwash around and am rinsing the sink when I hear a few knocks on my door. I'm so anxious to get it I slip across the wood floor Risky Business-style. I take a deep breath before opening it.

"Hi!"

"Hi, yourself." He greets me with two adorable dimples on display.

I step back from the door, putting my hand out to welcome him in. "Come on in."

Matt steps inside and closes the door behind him. Before I have the chance to move, he grabs my waist and turns me to him. Cupping my face, he leans his forehead against mine and closes his eyes, taking a deep breath.

"Are you smelling me?"

Smiling, he opens his eyes and whispers, "The real thing is so much better than the sweatshirt."

I'm laughing at his ridiculousness until he cuts me off with a kiss. Feeling bold, I trace his bottom lip with my tongue, and it undoes him. He growls and deepens the kiss, putting one hand on my waist and tugging me to him, the other hand caught in my hair and holding the back of my neck. I answer by latching my hands behind his head and pulling myself up to wrap my legs around his waist. Our lips never leave each other as he walks further into my apartment and wanders until he finds my bedroom.

"I thought you wanted to snuggle under the blanket."

"This blanket is better. It's on your bed." He winks at me as he puts me down.

"When did you get so smart?" I watch as he unzips his jacket and pushes it off his shoulders. I grab the hem of his T-shirt and tug it over his head, openly gawking at his perfection. The ridges of his abs, the V at his hips, the trail of hair from his belly button. I lick my lips and he scratches his stomach, enjoying my reaction.

"When I finally made a move on you," he says, eyes never leaving mine.

He steps closer to me. My hands trail down the planes of his torso and settle on his belt buckle as I undo it and pull down his zipper. He shimmies his hips to help me get his jeans off. His black boxer briefs don't hide much, and I shiver seeing his physical reaction to me, knowing mine is the same. "Emily," his voice is rough and smoky as I stroke him over the cotton. He stops me with his hand. "Not yet. I need to see you first."

He unzips my hoodie and pulls my tank top off, then kneels in front of me, kissing my stomach, the underside of my breast, down beneath my belly button as his hands carefully slide my pajama pants off. He mutters a swear under his breath when he sees I'm not wearing any underwear and pulls me closer to him. "Perfection," he whispers. He kisses up my body as he stands and then steps back, taking his boxers off.

The moment is quiet, intimate, and I want to bask in it. His fingers graze up and down my body. I'm exposed and vulnerable, but I *know* I'm safe. He cradles my head against his chest where I can feel his heart beating as fast as mine, and I wrap my hands around his waist. I don't know how long we stand there, but as seems to be the case with Matt lately, he knew this was exactly what I needed.

He breaks the hug and shifts from appraising me like a piece of precious art to studying me like a piece of meat he wants to chew up, pupils dilating into a midnight sky. Gently pushing me down on the bed, he rolls above me and anchors my head be-tween his elbows, peppering me with kisses, dragging his nose against mine, nibbling along my jaw. We stay like this for a while as his body heat envelops me and he slowly starts rocking his arousal against me. He groans as he feels my response and trails his teeth down my neck, sucking on my shoulder.

"Emily," he sighs into my neck, almost as a prayer. "What are you doing to me?"

I pull his head up to look at me. "Only good things, I hope?" I whisper back.

He strokes my hair off my face as he hovers close. "Only the best things, Goldie. Only the best." He kisses me again as his hands roam all over my body, firing me up with every touch until the need for him burns through me.

I stretch my arm toward the nightstand. "Top drawer."

He nods, understanding what I'm directing him to, and leans in to retrieve a condom. Sitting back on his legs, he rips it open and sheaths himself, settling above me again. Pulling the blankets up to cocoon us in our own little world, we take our time, nowhere else to be. He slides in, his lips caressing mine, his hands continually massaging through my hair.

"Fuck, Emily. Nothing has ever felt this good. It's like you were made for me."

I've always laughed a bit at the term "making love," but that's the only way I can describe what's happening here. Something is electric between us, a force pulling more than our bodies together. More than our legs tangling, more than our arms wrapped around each other. Our hearts are spinning outside of us, merging, looping together. The burning in my belly, the tingle in my toes, the constriction of my chest—the only word that makes sense is love.

CHAPTER 31

EMILY

I wake up to a warm body spooning me, a strong forearm around my stomach, tight enough to let me know he's there, but not overbearing. I curl my back to stretch and the arm tightens to prevent me from moving too far away. Then a leg snakes over my ankle, holding me in place, and a pair of delicious lips land on my shoulder. I scoot my ass back into the warmth of Matt's body heat and place my hands on top of the one now lightly stroking my stomach.

"Morning," Matt's deep, husky voice greets me, sounding like he's half asleep. I could definitely get used to waking up like this.

We linger in bed, talking about nothing in particular, just soaking up a lazy Saturday morning. He tells stories of the trouble he, Ryan, and Ben got into growing up, and they were so ridiculous my sides hurt from laughing. Their closeness is evident, and Ben may as well have been an honorary Meyer with how much time he spent at their house. I could listen to these stories all day—I always longed for siblings. I eventually found that sense of belonging with Josie and Lucy, but I never had people who were there for me no matter what growing up.

Reality interrupts us as my phone vibrates on my nightstand, and I see it's Lucy confirming our reservation. I stretch my arms and legs as far as they go and groan. "I hate to get out of bed, but I have to shower. I'm meeting Josie and Lucy for brunch."

Matt's response is to pull the covers over his head, and I hear him mumble, "Maybe if she doesn't see me, I can stay in this bed all day."

I laugh and push at his shoulders under the blanket, then head to the bathroom. I take a steaming hot shower and think about how much I like Matt in my space. How effortlessly he fits, how natural it feels. I'm excited for brunch but could easily be just as content climbing back into bed and spending the day there with him.

I emerge wrapped in my dark pink terrycloth robe with my hair wrapped in a towel. The scrumptious smell of brewing coffee greets me. Matt is leaning against my kitchen counter, mug in hand, scrolling through his phone. He's half-dressed, jeans on but bare feet crossed at the ankles and shirtless chest on display. My breath hitches at how handsome he is.

He puts his phone down when he sees me and reaches back, handing me a full mug of coffee identical to his. I wrap my hands around it, close my eyes, and inhale. "Is there anything better than that smell in the morning?"

He smiles mischievously at me and cocks a brow. "I can think of a few things, starting with your naked body underneath mine."

I stifle my laugh with a sip of coffee. He's not wrong, but I'm trying to play it cool here. Everything feels magnified, too big for me to process. The pitch. Winning the account. Matt. His flawless body in front of me which, by the way, is draining me of all willpower to not climb him like a tree.

He tugs on the belt of my robe, pulling me closer to him. Carefully taking the hot mug from my hands, he puts it on the counter and cradles my face. "This is definitely how I like you best... natural." He places a soft kiss on my forehead. "Relaxed." Another kiss on my neck, right above the collar of my robe. "Naked." The mischievous smile is back as he gives my robe another tug and wraps his arms around my bare waist. Ducking his head, he nips at my collarbone, moving his hands down to squeeze my ass.

"Keep doing that and I'll never make it to brunch."

I ended up texting Josie and Lucy to push back our meeting time by an hour (#sorrynotsorry) and when I finally met up with them at the restaurant, my hair was damp from another shower.

I cherish these weekend brunches with the girls. Barbetta has been our go-to place since these get togethers became part of our regular routine. It's casual but chic, with large palm plants filling the corners, plush cream booths, and weathered oak tables. It has an industrial-meets-farmhouse vibe, and they're used to people staying a while for their famous frittatas and bottomless mimosas. The energy is upbeat, and the high ceilings make it so you feel like you can breathe a little easier in this city that is oftentimes congested and crowded.

Lucy and Josie are sitting at our regular corner table when I walk in, watching for me to arrive and ready to give the third degree. Three mimosas sit untouched on the table, but they've already picked through the bread basket.

"Hi." I sound breathless as I approach the table. "Sorry I'm late."

"Mhmm." Josie nods and sucks in her lips, eyes sparkling.

"And, um, why exactly did we have to change the time?" Lucy raises an eyebrow at me to spill the tea.

I feel a blush creep up my neck and stain my cheeks. Laughing, I fall into the chair and drop my head back, groaning, "You guys! I cannot believe this week."

Josie leans forward, rubbing her hands together like a mad scientist. "I need all the details."

"But first, a toast." Lucy hands us each a stemmed glass then raises hers in the air. "To Emily, kicking ass and winning the Imperial account for DMG. We knew you'd slay it, and you did. Congrats!"

We clink glasses and I take a long sip, reveling in the cool bubbles drifting down my throat. *Life is good.* Immediately, a whisper of dread washes over me, thinking the other shoe has to drop at some point. I tame it down though, because for once, I want to enjoy this feeling.

"All right, now we're ready." Josie sits back, takes another sip of her drink, and then points her glass at me. "Go."

A grin overtakes my face thinking about the past few days. "I don't even know what to say. It feels so surreal in some ways, like the stars are aligning. But it's also scary as shit, because it just all feels so right. Is it real? Can it last? Am I setting myself up to get hurt again?"

Lucy leans over and grips my forearm. "Em, that's because it's your time. Finally. You deserve good things. You deserve happiness. I wish you could see it from our point of view. No one handed this to you. You earned all of it, powering through the tough times and not giving up."

I feel my eyes well. I'm grateful to these girls who have become my family, both of them always at the ready to offer support. Lucy's my little nurturer, and I know Josie's ready for me to start inviting good things into my life.

"I know you're right, and I'm trying to tell myself that but it all just seems too good to be true."

"I'm waiting for the 'too good' part. Come on, Em. What happened in Texas?" Josie whines. She'd never had much patience.

I launch into a breakdown of the last two weeks. From the all-nighter to the game room to prepping and flying down to Texas. How Matt helped me through the flight to the test drive and the kiss in the bar. I don't tell them everything, but just enough that they can see I'm falling for him.

"*Em.*" Lucy sighs and looks at the ceiling with cartoon hearts flying out of her eyes. "It sounds so perfect."

"It feels like it is. Sometimes I have to pinch myself to make sure it's not a dream."

Josie nods. "Oh, it's real. Trust me. Ryan said he hasn't ever seen Matt this smitten. Even with his ex-wife."

We both turn to Josie and I'm relieved my turn on the witness stand is over. "Ryan? Is he no longer 'feeling like a kissing cousin'?" I lift my hands from my mimosa to make obnoxious air quotes.

"Don't get your panties in a bunch. There's no chance of a double wedding. We're still mutually and happily in the friend zone."

"And you're still talking to him?" Lucy asks, skeptical.

"Yes! I really like him. As. A. Friend."

Lucy and I stare at each other, mouths gaping in shock. Platonic is not Josie's style, so Ryan must have made quite an impression if she's still hanging out with him.

"Wow, Jose, that sounds… quite mature of both of you." I giggle after polishing off my mimosa, and Josie signals to the waiter to bring us another round.

"It is, and I'm proud of myself. Plus, I have a Tinder date tonight, so life goes on."

The waiter brings three fresh mimosas, and we pick up our glasses and cheers again. "Life goes on," we all say in unison.

"What's the latest with you, Luce?" I ask.

Her face falls as she puts her glass down. "Everything is fine with me. Same old—work, sleep, repeat. But I'm worried about Luke."

Lucy and Luke are as tight as twins can get. Lucy was born five

288

minutes before Luke and takes her role as older sister very seriously. Luke was looking at engagement rings to propose to his college girlfriend when she broke up with him out of nowhere. It shocked us all, but it turns out she was being mentored by her boss outside of the office as well.

Lucy is an empath to begin with, and when it comes to Luke, everything is multiplied. There's no doubt her heart is breaking alongside his because she can't fix it for him, and I worry about Lucy shouldering so much as Luke navigates through this new normal.

"He's just been in such a funk since she cheated on him. But now it's gotten worse because he found out he's up for partner, meaning there will be so many events this summer that he'll have to show up at alone now."

"I'll go with him." We both turn to Josie, surprised at her suggestion.

"What?" she says matter-of-factly. "If he needs a date, I'll go with him. Luke and I are friends too, you know."

Lucy's eyes light up. "You mean that?"

"Of course I do. I'd do anything to help you, and Luke is an extension of you."

"That actually may help. I'm seeing him later this week for dinner—I'll let him know."

I eye Josie closely. Lucy is too close to the situation to notice that Josie's now fidgeting and avoiding eye contact. I'm curious if there's something she's not being honest about—with us or with herself.

My phone beeps with a text message and I look down. My cheeks heat when I see "Magic Matt" in the notification, and the girls immediately call me on it.

"Ohhh, is that from your *boyfriend*?" Josie makes kissing sounds.

"Will you guys stop it? He's not my boyfriend." Despite my best efforts, I can't hide a big grin.

"I don't know, Em," Lucy chimes in. "You're beaming. That lovesick smile may be giving away more than your words."

After another hour of catching up, I excuse myself to the restroom and check my phone.

Magic Matt: How's brunch?

Me: Really good, actually. Much needed.

Me: What are you up to?

Magic Matt: Ryan and I played basketball and then grabbed lunch, but he had to run into work.

Magic Matt: So now I'm here, watching some college hoops and thinking about you.

I don't think I'll ever get tired of hearing that.

Me: Yeah?

Me: Whatcha thinking?

Magic Matt: How nice it was to wake up with you this morning… and how much I enjoyed falling sleep with you last night.

Me: Just the falling asleep part?

Magic Matt: That and how much I enjoyed being inside you last night before we fell asleep.

My core clenches reading his words.

Me: <blushing emoji>

Magic Matt: And if I'm honest, I can't stop thinking about how badly I want to do it all again. My lips didn't get to explore your body nearly as much as I wanted to, especially this morning with you wearing that scandalizing fluffy robe.

Me: Hmmmm

Magic Matt: ?

Me: Just thinking about your lips. We're paying the bill now, and then I'm heading home. Alone. And I don't know, then I'll be home. By myself. And maybe lonely.

Magic Matt: I could help with that.

Me: I'll be home in 15.

Magic Matt: I'll be there in 10 waiting for you.

MATT

My mother taught me never to show up at someone's house empty-handed. So, on the way to Emily's, I stop to pick up a bunch of white lilies from the corner bodega and grab a large Gatorade just in case she might need it

Surprisingly, I beat her back to her place so I'm sitting on her stoop when she turns the corner. Her smile beams like rays of sunshine shooting through a break in the clouds. I smile back and feel my stomach twist, knowing I can greet her like I've been wanting to the past few weeks.

I stand up as she approaches. She stops at the bottom of the steps and grabs the railing with both hands. She sways ever so slightly, revealing she may have taken full advantage of bottomless mimosas.

"Hi." She lets out a giggle as she looks up. I'm mesmerized by her eyes as they focus on mine—irises the color of pine needles and golden honey. She looks so damn adorable I have to grip the flowers tighter so I don't rush and sweep her up in my arms. *Where the fuck is your chill, dude?*

"Hi." I match her with a small laugh.

She swings around the bottom post of the railing and takes the first step toward me. "Fancy meeting you here."

"Right? I was in the neighborhood. Figured I'd stop by."

"Is that so?" She takes another step up. "You just happened to have that stuff too?" She juts her chin out at the flowers and the paper bag in my hand.

I shrug. "I like to be prepared."

She takes another step up so she's only one below me now. I move around her and down a step so we're almost eye-level and she places her hands on my shoulder, leans in, and whispers, "Tell me, Matt Meyer, were you a boy scout?"

My hand curls around her waist. She's swaying a little bit more than I realized. Her cheeks are flushed, darkening the freckles across her nose, and up close like this, even a little off balance, she's so fucking beautiful. I love that she's letting herself be carefree with me.

"Tell me, Emily Cooper, do you like boy scouts?"

"Well, you can never be too prepared. And it's nice that they're so helpful. Taking care of people and stuff."

Squeezing her waist, my voice rough against her ear, I mutter, "I'm prepared to take care of you, right now and all night."

I feel her take a sharp inhale and she leans back to search my face. The last thing I want is for Emily to overthink any of this and let the playful spark drift away. So I lean in and claim her lips, softly at first and then with more pressure after she curves her body into mine. My arm snakes tighter around her and I hum when she scrapes her nails in my hair.

"Come on, my little tipsy one. Let's get you inside and rehydrated."

The sky is turning a mix of deep orange and pink as Emily quietly sleeps with her head on my lap. Thankfully she drank the Gatorade when we came upstairs, so I'm hopeful she won't wake up feeling too bad.

For now, I'm content to sit here, listen to her relaxed breathing, and run my fingers through her hair with the Knicks game on mute in the background. I'm hardly paying attention to it, which is crazy. But that's how much this woman consumes me. When I'm not with her, all I want to do is find her. When I'm with her, I need to touch her and be connected to her in any way I can. I know we've only known each other for a few weeks, but she has a gravitational pull on me, as if she's a magnet and I'm a copper penny, powerless to my attraction to her.

The more she opens up to me, the more in awe I am of her grace and her heart. She has every reason to be bitter or angry, but instead of closing within herself and stewing in it, she channels that energy into hard work and helping others succeed. And now it's her turn to reap the benefits of that hard work. She deserves the Imperial win and more.

The thought makes my gut churn. Anger—at my father, at the situation, and mostly at myself—pulses through my veins. Closing my eyes, I drop my head on the back of the couch, wanting yet again to kick my own ass for the second time since I moved back to New York.

As usual, Roger Davis looms overhead, the dark cloud blocking my sunlight. I shouldn't be surprised he pulled this shit. Our deal was that I would help him with the Imperial account, and then I was *done*. He's held this honest mistake I made years ago over my head long enough. I don't think even winning Imperial will change how he sees me anyway. I'm realizing that now, and maybe I needed Emily to show me that I'll be okay with or without his approval.

Emily stirs in my lap but doesn't wake up. A solid night of sleep will do us both good, so I cradle her in my arms and take her to the bedroom. I slowly undress her, slipping on a silk tank and shorts I find in her drawer, and carefully tuck her under the duvet. Then I quickly discard my Henley and jeans, leaving my boxers on, and climb into bed beside her. Curling my body around her, I inhale the coconut scent of her hair and wrap my feet around hers to keep them warm.

"Good night," I whisper in her ear. "I'm falling in love with you," I whisper to myself.

With my eyes closed, I stretch my hands forward, hoping to feel Emily's warm body, but nope, it's just me in the bed. I roll over onto my back and inhale the smell of coffee and hear the toaster pop. Stretching, I climb out of bed and head to the bathroom, using the toothbrush Emily left on the sink, its cardboard wrapper sticking out of the trash can. I have an hour to get home, shower, and head to my parents for brunch, so while it's the last thing I want to do, I dress before heading to the kitchen.

Emily's buttering a slice of toast when I turn the corner, her back to me as she shakes her hips to the low music playing from her phone. I take the dancing as a good sign that she's not hungover and I lean against the table, crossing my arms and enjoying the show. Her long chestnut hair is braided to the side, and she's wearing a pair of leggings and a wide-neck shirt that falls off her shoulder, exposing her delectable skin. I inwardly groan to keep myself from startling her. Her ass is pure, round perfection, and thinking about how soft it felt in my hand, how perfectly she fit curled against me, makes my cock crowd the zipper of my jeans. Something possessive comes to life deep inside of me and snarls *Mine.*

My groan must not be as silent as I thought because Emily turns around and her eyes light up when they find mine. They cloud over as she notices I'm fully dressed, but she recovers by pouring some coffee into an empty mug.

This is my favorite version of Emily: freshly showered, relaxed, in her element. I want so badly to climb back in bed and block out the rest of the world. Snuggle under a blanket and watch movie marathons with her while the snow comes down. I imagine sitting across the table and working on the Sunday crossword together, making lists for the grocery store, and arguing over bills. And when we're done, I'd strip her bare and explore every crevice of her body, reveling in the way she comes undone, how she pants and purrs when she finally allows herself to let go. I want all of that and more with her. The good, the bad, the ugly— which is what I know I will get after I finally confront my dad. My dad... Brunch. *Aaaand just like that, space frees up in my pants.*

"Morning!" she chirps, but it sounds forced, almost nervous. I can see the wheels start to crank in her head. "Sorry I fell asleep so early last night." She cringes and hides her eyes.

"Don't apologize. It seemed like you had a great brunch with the girls."

A broad smile unravels across her face. "I did." She picks up the coffee and walks it over to me, placing it on the counter between us. It feels like she's using the space as a physical barrier, and I sense her guard going up again. "Thank you for getting me into bed."

I take a long sip of the coffee, savoring the liquid gold warming my throat. "This was the only place I wanted to be." I hold her eyes to make sure she understands how much I mean that.

She gives me a flat smile and looks down, scratching an imaginary stain on the counter. She's retreating into thoughts I know can't be productive. I circle the counter to stand before her. Her irises are a warm amber darkening the specks of green as she worries her bottom lip. "Emily, I mean it." I pull at her bottom lip and release it from her teeth. Stroking her lips, I emphasize, "This. Is. Where. I. Want. To. Be." I move my hand to grasp her neck and stroke the pulse point in her throat. "I have to go meet my father, and while leaving you is the last thing I want to do, I need to have an important conversation with him and it has to be today."

"What's going on? Is everything okay?" Her demeanor shifts, fully focused on me. She rolls her shoulders back and stands taller, as if prepping herself for battle on my behalf.

My stomach warms at this fiery warrior before me, displacing her own discomfort on a moment's notice to make sure I'm good. I don't deserve this type of loyalty. My stomach lurches at the thought of confronting him, but I'm distracted when Emily lays her fingertips across my morning scruff. "Matt, what's going on?" she asks, nothing but care and concern in her voice. "Did your dad do something to upset you?

I pull her into my chest and kiss the crown of her head. "You're something else, Emily, you know that? Do you know how lucky it feels to be part of your world? I wish you could believe it as much as I know it's true."

Reaching up on her toes, she buries her face in my neck and inhales. "The same can be said for you, Matt. I think I'm the lucky one here."

I squeeze her tight, knowing how wrong she is but begging a bigger force than me—God, the universe, karma, anyone who will listen—to please let me figure this out before I lose her forever.

CHAPTER 33

MATT

I made plans to meet my dad at his apartment, knowing this conversation might get heated. I kept Ryan updated on the pitch, Emily, and the text from my dad all in real-time, so I'm surprised to see him sitting by the island with a mug of coffee in his hand when I enter the kitchen. My mom's sorting bagels next to an elaborate tray of spreads. Freshly squeezed orange juice fills a glass pitcher, and empty mugs are waiting by the espresso machine for my dad and me.

"Matt, sweetie, it's so good to see you." My mom drops the bagels and surrounds me in a big hug. I hunch down to return it, squeezing her tightly, needing the comfort before I face my father.

"Thanks, Mom." I straighten up. "How are you doing?"

She huffs and waves a hand through the air. "Oh, I'm fine. Same as usual. But I don't want to talk about me. How are you? I heard the pitch was a big success."

I tug on my lips and look down, feeling my shoulders sag. "Yeah, it went well. We got the account."

"So why do you sound like someone just ran over your brand-new puppy? Isn't this a good thing?"

"It is," I concede, "but I don't think it's going to end up the way Dad wants it to."

"The way I want what to?" my dad asks as he passes me and places a hand on my mother's shoulder before heading for the coffee maker.

"I was just asking Matt about the pitch and getting ready to tell him how proud we are of him." My mom's eyes are scanning my face, trying to decipher what I'm not saying.

My dad points his chin toward Ryan as he pours his coffee. "Matthew, did Ryan tell you about the huge acquisition he's leading now? Could make his firm close to $100 million when all is said and done. Those are the types of deals that get your name on the wall."

Ryan just shakes his head and looks down. None of us miss the shade thrown my way by ignoring my mom's comment about being proud. He didn't even acknowledge the win, which gives me the ammunition I need now more than ever.

He walks around the island and slaps Ryan on the shoulder. He winces under the pressure, but my dad misses it since he's looking at me, trying to drive home his point. "That's the way things get done."

Ryan looks over at me with an apology in his eyes. He hates

this as much as I do. While my dad withholds all positive reinforcement with me, I know the way Ryan is constantly praised makes him uncomfortable.

"So, Matthew, are you ready for tomorrow?" my father asks as he takes a stool next to Ryan.

"Well, that's what I wanted to talk to you about." I glance at my mom and her brows are pulled together, hearing the uncertainty in my voice.

"The plan is to announce it in the all-hands meeting tomorrow afternoon. Josh and I will gather everyone, announce the win and what it means in terms of staffing and project load, review some key timelines, and then introduce you as lead account director. You and Josh can work out specifics about who will lead each of the teams under you. I'm sure we can find something for Emily."

Heat courses through my veins. I'm furious at how my father can callously toss her aside like no big deal after she laid it all out for the project. A protectiveness storms through me and I feel my clenched jaw pulsing in an effort to keep calm. My dad continues, tapping the counter. "This is how karma works, Matthew. I cleaned up your mess, and now my agency will be managing the biggest auto account on the market. Good deeds get rewarded."

I ignore his lecture. "Emily has been at DMG for 5 years. She's one of Josh's most trusted team members and probably the one person who is universally liked and respected at the office. She's the reason DMG has the Imperial account. She came up with the strategy, she led the creative examples, and she pitched the idea in Texas. You were in all the big meetings. Maybe you should pay better attention." My words are a low growl and my knuckles are white from gripping the counter.

My dad pulls back and glances at Ryan, an incredulous look of shock and amusement on his face. "Matthew, what's gotten into you? So she helped you win. It's not surprising considering we know you always need a little help to pull out the big ones. Am I right, Ry?"

Ryan stands up, ignoring my father's question. "And I'm out." He places his mug in the sink and gives my mom a quick hug, kissing the top of her head. "I'll call you later," he says to her and as he passes me to the door, he squeezes my shoulder. "Call me when you're done here," he mumbles.

I don't blame Ryan for leaving. He hates being stuck in the middle, and while he's always playing the part of the light-hearted, fun-loving brother to defuse the tension between the three of us, I know it weighs on him. Under that class-clown exterior is a guy with a big heart who just wants everyone around him to be happy.

"Why are you so worked up over this girl? Do you have a little crush? Don't tell me I'm going to need to bail you out of something else now."

"Emily should lead the account, not me. She deserves it. She's the reason DMG won Imperial in the first place."

"Well, *she* is not the CEO's child, so I don't give a flying fuck if she deserves it or spent all her free time in the office." He's turning bright red, spitting as he yells. "*You* are doing this job.

When Hunter told me he was putting the Imperial account on review, he indicated that if you were at DMG, he'd be interested in potentially working with us. He's expecting *you*. So you'll fucking do the job—and do it flawlessly—because you owe your entire career to me."

"Roger, please, calm down." In comes my mother as usual, trying to tame the situation. I appreciate her help, but shame and guilt spread at her witnessing all of this.

"No, I won't calm down. Matthew's never appreciated anything he's been given, all the opportunities, all the successes." He turns to me. "Well, whether or not you appreciate it, payback is now."

He will never let it go. In some way, shape, or form, he will find a way to drag this out and hold it over my head for as long as possible. He will always change the terms as long as they benefit him.

He dumps his remaining coffee into the sink and kisses my mother's cheek as he passes her. "I'll see you tomorrow morning in the office."

Anger seethes within me. I scrub my fingers over my face and through my hair as I hang my head back.

"Matt, honey, are you all right?"

"No, I'm not, Mom. How the hell could you think I'd be fine after that?" I flinch at the harshness in my voice.

"Maybe this time it will be different. He'll see how capable and smart and wonderful you are—simply because of who you are and no other reason."

I walk over to give her a hug goodbye and mumble into her hair, "I love your endless optimism, but we know that's never going to happen. I'll have to figure something out."

I turn to leave but stop when I hear her call my name. "Matt, is she worth it?"

"She?"

"Emily. It's obvious to me you care for her. Are you sure she's worth it? Because if you don't do this for your dad when he needs it, I don't know how you two will mend things."

A montage of Emily flashes through my mind—her beaming laughter as she hustled Ryan in pool; her flushed cheeks as she gasped underneath me in bed, nails scratching down my back; her sleeping peacefully on my chest, her tipsy and giggling on the steps last night. My body heats as each image sears into my brain. My stomach flutters like a goddamn hummingbird as I picture holding Emily in my arms. I think about how much this will all hurt her tomorrow, and it's like a punch to the gut.

My throat goes dry as I face my mom, trying to answer over the lump in it. "I've never been more sure of anything in my life."

CHAPTER 34

MATT

After I leave my parents, I walk aimlessly around the city, playing out every scenario in my head of how I can make things right with Emily. Not only did I hide my connection to my dad, but now he wants to give me the job she wants. It doesn't matter that I don't want it. It won't make a difference that I'm not going to take it. Emily is too proud to be a runner-up and get the job—even if it's rightfully hers—by default.

I don't know how long I wander but the sun is starting to set when I get home. I'm both exhausted and restless, unable to sit still but my mind and my body so completely drained from the emotional roller coaster of this past week. There's only one person I want to talk to, and she's the one person I may lose. The only person that counts.

Me: Hi

Emily: Hiya.

Me: How was your day?

Emily: Okay. I went for a run, did some laundry, and now catching up on the atrocity known as the Real Housewives.

Me: Interesting, I never pegged you for a reality TV girl.

Emily: What can I say? It makes me feel better about my life watching the train wreck they live every day. Everyone has their guilty pleasures, Mr. Meyer<wink emoji>

Me: I'll be happy to help with the pleasure part anytime, Ms. Cooper

Emily: I'll keep that top of mind

So far, so good. But something feels off and it's making my mind spin, trying to decipher if I'm projecting my fears onto Emily or if she senses it too.

Emily: How was brunch with your dad?

Me: As expected. Brutal. Unproductive. We are the purest definition of oil and water.

Emily: I'm sorry it didn't go well.

Emily: Do you want to talk about it?

This woman. Pure goodness. It's a punch to my solar plexus thinking about how I might hurt her.

Me: Yes... and no. This is probably the messiest situation to date. I feel like this one could permanently alter our relationship.

Emily: Sounds pretty serious.

Me: Serious. And complicated, if I haven't mentioned that already

Emily: Is there any way to make it less complicated? A compromise? Is what's causing the rift worth it?

Me: Funny you say that. My mom asked me if it was worth it too.

Emily: She sounds like a very smart woman.

I hope you'll meet her one day.

Me: She is. The best.

Emily: What was your answer?

Me: The truth. This is worth it all. I just wish my father could see that.

Emily: Maybe he'll come around.

Me: I don't know. Maybe. But it's a long shot.

Emily: Well, you've pulled one of those off before. Look where we are now

Me: My biggest win of all.

Emily: Aww I bet you say that to all the girls.

I know she's joking, but at this moment nothing is more important than her realizing that I don't. I don't say it to all the girls. I don't care about any other girl.

Me: I don't, Emily. I definitely don't.

Emily: <smiling blushing emoji>

Me: I mean it. This isn't a fling or something casual for me. I need you to understand that. Even if you don't feel the same way. I meant it when I said I'm all in.

Silence. I'm on the edge of a cliff here.

Me: Do you believe me?

Nothing, until *finally* three dots appear.

Emily: I believe you.

Me: Good. Because after today, the only thing I know for certain is how I feel about you. About us. About how much I want to be an us.

Emily: Us.

Me: Yes, us. I've been yours since the moment I saw you. You claimed my heart and I don't want it back.

Emily: I'll take good care of it. Just promise me you'll take good care of mine, too.

I exhale the biggest breath of relief. I've always prided myself on doing the right thing. Helping the underdog. Growing up with a father like mine amplified the difference that simple kindness can make and how much respect matters. Respect for all—not just the rich or powerful. How important honesty is.

All of these things matter to me, and yet, at the most critical moments, I caved. I hid. I risked everything to protect the wrong person. I chose myself over Emily. I was so focused on making sure we had a chance, so scared to lose her before we'd be able to explore the possibility of us, that I disregarded the one thing that means the most to her: the truth.

How do I tell her I'll take care of her heart when it may break tomorrow?

Me: You and your heart are precious to me.

Just please give me a chance to explain everything.

Me: I need to take care of a few things before heading to bed, so I'm going to say goodnight now.

Emily: Ok

Me: Sweet dreams xx

Emily: You too xo

CHAPTER 35

EMILY

Even with Matt's reassurance this morning that he wished he could stay, an uncertainty has taken shelter in my gut that I can't shake. I can't really explain it, but I feel some distance and it's making me uneasy.

After a hot bath, I pull the lapels of my fuzzy robe tight and pad over to my desk to sort through the pile of mail that collected when I was gone. I start separating the junk mail from the rest when I see a bright pink Post-it attached to one of the envelopes. I recognize Matt's block handwriting and smile.

**If I'm not here when you see this, know that
I'm missing you from wherever I am. XO.**

I bite my bottom lip as I read it again. That gnawing, constant thought of it feeling too good to be true reappears like a cold gust of wind, making the hairs on the back of my neck stand. What if it *is* too good to be true?

God, I loved the sight of him walking out of my bedroom with mussed-up hair and a sleepy grin this morning. It scares me how easily I could get used to sharing coffee and early morning kisses with him. After feeling so raw with how things ended with Greg, the difference of how safe I feel with Matt is eye-opening.

Relax, Emily. Maybe it's about time you had someone be good to you. I shake my head and put the note aside so it doesn't get mixed up in the junk pile.

I sort through the rest of the envelopes until I see the last one. It wasn't sent through the mail. There's no stamp, no return address. Just "EMILY COOPER, APT 6H" written in all caps. This time my stomach sinks from pure dread because I also recognize this handwriting. This isn't a love note. I know before I flip it around to open it that my time has finally, officially run out.

"No, no, no," I plead as I tear the envelope open. I unfold the paper inside and find a copy of my rent portal statement. Last month's rent is circled in red sharpie and "BOUNCED" is under-lined with two exclamation points.

"Shit!" I spit out in a forceful whisper. I quickly move the bills aside and log in to my bank account. My hand slams on my desk before I drop my head in it. The numbers don't lie. The payment bounced because I don't have enough in my account to cover it. And this time, my connected savings account doesn't have enough to cover the difference either.

I pull out the note, immediately feeling sick to my stomach.

Emily,
This is your second bounced payment, which means
you're at risk of breaking your lease. If you're not
whole by the next rent cycle—including late fees—
you will be evicted.
Mr. Marino

"Shit, shit, *shit*," I mumble as I grab my calendar so I can piece the timing together. I paid it last Monday, and this letter was left on Wednesday when I was in Texas with Matt. Between the trip and not thinking about anything but Matt since we got home, it's been five days since I looked at the mail. I have less than two weeks to come up with the money. I've never needed something to go my way as much as this promotion.

I wake up weighed down with worry. I try to shed it as I dress in one of my favorite spring dresses and knee-high boots. It's warming up now, so tights aren't necessary. I add my comfort gold hoops, my leather bomber jacket, and my darkest sunglasses to shield my "cold, dead eyes" vibe.

My nerves are buzzing as I take some deep breaths and try to focus on the music in my ears. I've been through enough therapy that I can rationalize that my fears don't automatically equate to reality. But what does it say that I'm still looking around every corner, wondering where the next disappointment in my life will be? The reminder of how far I am from mastering self-doubt and self-sabotage is not what I need on a Monday morning.

As if on cue, the elevator doors open on my floor and I blow out a big breath, trying to clear these thoughts from my head. Today is not the day.

Not surprising, the floor is eerily quiet. We have our monthly all-hands meeting this afternoon in place of Josh's usual meeting, but he and Sheila asked us to come in early to iron out our plan. Given how big the Imperial win is for DMG, I'm sure this morning will be dedicated to tackling how we'll staff that team and where we might have gaps.

I open my office door and smile at the fresh cup of coffee waiting for me. My body relaxes knowing Matt is already here and that he started the day thinking of me.

I drop my bag on a chair and walk around my desk to see if he left a note with the coffee. There's no note from Matt, but a note stuck to my monitor catches my eye.

Emily–
The meeting moved to Roger's office.
Come down as soon as you get in.
–Josh

I read Josh's note three times to make sure I'm not hallucinating. I've never been to Roger's office. Hell, I've never even met Roger in person despite working here for five years. Is this good news? Why would Josh be asking me to meet him there? People usually get fired on a Friday, right? My key card worked this morning so it can't—

Emily. Get a grip.

I grab a notebook and walk to my door, stopping to make sure I don't have lipstick on my teeth. *Sure, he's the CEO, but he puts his pants on one leg at a time and shits after Taco Bell like the rest of us.*

"Okay, okay," I breathe, coaching myself in the mirror. "You're just going to see Josh."

I head to the opposite side of the floor, finding the big corner office I've only glanced into when walking by. Roger's assistant notices me and smiles warmly. "Emily?"

I nod, unsure my voice actually works, and she continues. "Hi, I'm Susan, Roger's assistant. They're expecting you. Feel free to go on in."

I walk to the door with heavy legs. Voices carry from the other side and I take a fortifying breath before my hand touches the cold handle and opens the door.

The office is expansive, with floor-to-ceiling windows offering an unobstructed view of the Manhattan skyline. Everything is sleek and modern. Roger Davis is sitting behind his desk wearing a gray suit, white shirt, and no tie. An oversized glass-top desk sits on black steel legs, with just a computer monitor and a few files neatly piled up in a corner. Two low-back leather swivel chairs face the desk. Immediately to my right is a steel cabinet with a huge flat-screen TV mounted above it and a bookcase lined with industry awards, including a few Emmys and Cannes Lions statues. On my left is a black leather couch and two matching black chairs situated around a glass coffee table. I'm surprised to see both Sheila and Matt occupying it. Apparently I'm late, even though I had no idea this was even happening.

Josh sits in one of the chairs, one leg crossed on his opposite knee, scrolling through his phone. Sheila's across from him and gives me a warm smile and a low, "Hey, Emily," when she spots me.

My eyes skim past them both and land on Matt, agitation radiating off of him and suffocating the room. He's leaning forward, elbows on his knees and hands clenched between them. His back is stiff, tense, and his head is hanging low, studying his fingernails. He's so preoccupied that he hasn't noticed I entered the room.

I stand in the corner, waiting for someone to give me a hint of what I'm supposed to be doing, when Roger stands. "Emily, so glad you could join us." He walks around his desk and offers me his hand. He gives me the limpest handshake I've ever received and his palm is clammy. Letting go, he opens his arm toward the couch. "Please, come in, have a seat."

Feeling uncomfortable, I look to Sheila for reassurance, but she only gives me a very slight nod, not-so-subtly eyeing the empty chair opposite Josh. Roger comes around to lean on the front of his desk, facing us.

"Uh, thanks, Mr. Davis."

"Josh, do you want to kick us off?"

Josh looks up from his phone and gives me a warm smile that doesn't meet his eyes. It feels like a funeral in here, everyone so formal and stiff. The air feels heavy and awkward, but I can't pinpoint with what exactly.

"Hey, Em."

"Hi, Josh."

Matt's head lifts when I speak, as if he's just realizing I'm here, and the look on his face makes me lean back. His eyes are blood-shot and tired. They're a stormy dark blue, almost black. More than that is the pained gaze he pierces me with though.

Josh's eyes bounce between Matt and me and he sits up, clearing his throat. "Em, you and Matt were incredible down in Texas, and as you know, we won the Imperial pitch. We're announcing today that DMG will officially be their new agency. We know we couldn't have gotten here without all of your leadership, hard work, and strategic thinking."

The words are compliments, but his delivery sounds empty. Am I supposed to thank him? The hair on the back of my neck prickles. Something isn't right.

"Thanks, Josh." I give him a closed-lip smile and sit up straighter.

"We know how much you put into the account, and how much you've contributed to DMG all these years. You are a core and critical part of the team. There's no question about that."

I nod, not trusting my voice because I know a "but" is coming.

"We are going to announce Imperial team assignments later today, and we wanted to let you know ahead of time that Matt is going to be named the Account Director."

The room is deathly silent. I'm sure they can hear my heart pounding in my chest, my temples aching as all the blood rushes to my head.

I shake my head to clear it. "I'm sorry, did you say Matt is going to be AD?"

Josh looks at me with remorseful eyes and just nods.

Matt's head is down again. He can't even look at me. The fog around me starts to clear and my shock at this entire exchange starts to simmer, threatening to boil into rage.

"Matt?" I will him to look up, to tell me this is all a mistake, to comfort me. His shoulders are hunched over, his body defeated, and the fact that he won't make eye contact with me confirms that this nightmare is actually my reality.

I look to Sheila and Josh. "I don't understand. He"—I raise my arm toward Matt—"just got here. I've been working here, with this team, for five years. He's only been here a few weeks." I'm conscious that I'm sputtering and not demonstrating my usual control, but I don't give a damn.

Roger stands up, drawing my attention back to him after I forgot he was even there. "Emily, it's true that Matthew has only been here a few weeks. But in that time, he helped us win this pitch, and he has far more experience in the auto industry."

Matthew. No one calls him Matthew, but now Roger has called him that twice.

Matt told me he hates being called Matthew because it's what his father calls him.

His father.

I look at Roger and see familiar blue eyes studying me.

I feel like I'm going to be sick. The room blurs around me and I have to grip the side of the chair to steady myself.

"Matthew?" I whisper loudly, staring at him. I turn to Roger. "Did you just call him Matthew?"

Matt finally looks up, and I see it now. The pained expression is regret. Guilt. Shame.

Confirmation.

I look from Matt to Roger and back at Matt. The same face, one young version and one older.

"Matt?" He doesn't say anything. "Matt?" I ask a little more forcefully. "What's going on here? Are you related to him?"

He shifts his eyes from me to Roger, hatred shooting out of them.

"Matthew is my son, Emily," Roger says.

The words register, but it feels like I'm underwater, making them sound muffled. Anger seethes through me. I turn to Matt again. "He's your *father*."

Matt doesn't say a word. He glances through me, like looking at me will burn his eyes, but he nods in defeat.

"Are you fucking kidding me?" Sheila flinches at my outburst, but I focus on Matt as my body vibrates with anger.

"Did you, I don't know, think that might have been something you could have told me? Or was it fun watching me all this time, thinking I had a shot at the AD job? Was this a joke to you?"

Matt finally speaks up. "Emily, no. Nothing—"

"Oh, now you talk? Now you say something?" I stand up. "Too little too late. Go to hell."

Without acknowledging anyone else, I storm out of the office, eyes blurring with tears I refuse to shed.

CHAPTER 36

MATT

Emily is sprinting to her office as I try to catch up with her. Self-loathing floods through me from the cold, hard glower she sent my way when she put the pieces together. I expected anger, rage even, but the intensity of betrayal clouding her eyes was a spear through my heart knowing I put it there.

She reaches her office by the time I finally catch up to her. "Emily," I plead. "Please, I can explain."

She whips around and snarls, "Famous fucking last words, *Matthew*. Save them. I'm not interested." She's so angry she doesn't register the stares directed our way.

She tries to slam the door behind her but I catch it. Stepping in, I quietly shut it to avoid the attention directed our way. Leaning back on it for support, my voice is shaking as I beg. "Please, can you just hear me out?" An overwhelming sense of dread overtakes me. I am not a religious man, but I'd gladly bargain my life to any god who will listen if I can just get the chance to explain.

She turns to me, seething, marching so close to me that I can feel how heavy she's breathing.

"I already told you." She pushes a finger into my chest for emphasis. "I don't give a shit what you have to say."

I grab her finger, clinging to it like it's my lifeline. "I know how this all looks, but please just listen for five minutes." Deja-vu from my first day, standing just like this, washes over me. But this is far worse. My chest aches seeing her in pain. Pain I caused.

She crosses her arms over her chest. Her brows draw together, emphasizing her moist eyes, clouded with pain. Her voice cracks, and my heart fractures knowing this is all my fault. "How could you lie to me like that?"

"Emily, I know." I rake my hands through my hair, trying to mute their trembling. "Everything I told you about my relationship with my father is true. Things *are* complicated, and he is an asshole to me 99.9% of the time."

She rolls her eyes and sarcasm seeps out of her as she mocks me. "Poor little Matthew."

I press on, knowing I deserve all of that and more. "And I know... I know I don't deserve for you to understand it right now. But please, *please,* just listen."

She doesn't move, so I launch in. "What I didn't share is that when I was going through my divorce, I was working on an account for Falcon, and they were pouring their entire marketing budget into the Super Bowl. One commercial. A year's worth of work and budget. They had their entire annual strategy riding on this commercial and how it would come to life in the dealerships through the summer.

"I was distracted and depressed with everything going so wrong with Stella. I was also covering another account for someone who went on last-minute medical leave. Things were chaotic. I know it's not an excuse, but my head wasn't in the game to start with, and then the work just doubled, all with the most important advertising project of my career looming."

Her posture is closed off but she hasn't moved, which I'll take as a win that she's at least listening. I press on, praying I can get through to her.

"Anyway, I ended up trafficking the wrong ad to the network. The unmixed version ran. Audio was off, it had the wrong copy. It was a total and complete disaster. My client was Hunter Holt. He went ballistic. Called me screaming. Told me he was pulling the account from the agency and making sure I got fired. My dad knew the minute he saw the commercial that something went wrong. He called me and I was a mess, confessing everything Hunter said. I didn't care about my job, but it would cost so many others their jobs if the agency lost Falcon, and that was what killed me the most.

"I didn't want to, but I had to ask my dad for help. After all the bullshit, all the backhanded comments he's made my entire life, how hard I'd always tried to avoid ever asking him for anything... I groveled. Asked him to pick up the pieces. I was a fucking grown man asking my daddy to help. I hated myself. But

I could live with that if it meant no one else would lose their job."

Tension is reverberating between us. I want to touch her, reassure her this will never happen again, rekindle our connection. But I need to get the full story out, so I lean back on my hands and continue.

"My dad called Hunter and talked him off the ledge."

Bitterness drips off her lips as she sneers, "Isn't that nice that it all worked out for you then."

My gaze drops to the floor as guilt overwhelms me. She's right. It doesn't matter if it was the one and only time I asked for his help.

"He didn't tell him it was my fault. DMG was in the process of acquiring the agency where I worked, and my father said he would personally cover the cost of the media. Millions of dollars. The agency kept the account and no one—not even me—was fired. My dad never let me forget how he saved the day. Since then, he's always reminded me that one day I'd have to do him a favor instead of paying back the millions of dollars a Super Bowl commercial is worth."

I hang my head against the door, clamping my eyes shut. Drawing my brows together, I drop my head and look at Emily. She's still there, not moving. Our eyes lock, and I only hope she can see how sorry I am. Feel my remorse. Taste the anguish that is clogging my throat.

"When Imperial was up for review, Hunter told my dad he wanted to work with me again, that if I was with DMG, it would be almost a no-brainer. So, my dad called in his favor. I told him

I would help with the pitch, but that I didn't want to stay afterward. I told him I was done with advertising. He just told me yesterday at brunch that he was making me AD. Staying on was never part of the deal. Emily, you deserve the job. I told him that, but he wasn't hearing it. He was gloating too much about how karma has been good to him."

She's listening, but I have no idea if my explanation is reaching her or pushing her further away. I'm desperate for any sign that she believes me, but she's not giving anything away.

"Emily, I need you to hear me. Regardless of what happens, *you* are what matters to me. You. Not this account. Not the job. Not my father or what he thinks. You brought me back to life. I didn't think it would be possible for me to ever feel anything close to what you've given me. I feel everything so much more than I ever did with Stella, more than I have any right. From the minute I saw your emerald eyes across Smith's Cave, you've dominated all my thoughts. I'm gone for you, and I need you to believe that. I know I messed up, but nothing is more important than having you in my life. I *need* you in my life." I hear my voice catch as the thought of losing her makes my body run cold.

Fire sparks in her eyes as she stands tall, erecting a barrier between us. "Actions speak louder than words, Matt. You waltzed in here and simply because of your last name and DNA, you took away everything I've worked toward for the past five years. Because of you..." Her resolve finally breaks as tears slide down her cheek. "I can't even stay here."

I reach out and grip her arms, pleading. "Emily, no. We can

figure something out. I'll leave. I'll talk to Hunter myself. I'll do whatever I need to do so you can stay here, so that you get the AD position." My willpower disappears and I wrap her face in my hands, wiping at her tears, desperately hoping they can help wash my betrayal away.

"It's too late. You should have thought of that all the times you chose to keep your mouth shut about what was really going on." She steps back out of my grasp and chides herself. "How could I be so fucking stupid?" She sits on her chair, sniffling as she pulls herself together and gains composure.

"Matt, the only thing I want right now is for you to leave. The least you can do is that." She swivels to face the wall, ending the conversation and shutting me out.

With thin lips and a nod she can't see, I exit and quietly shut the door behind me.

CHAPTER 37

EMILY

Me: SOS

Lucy: I'm here. What's up?

Me: I don't even know where to start. It's bad. Can you guys meet me at my apartment as soon as you get off work?

Lucy: Do I need to kick anyone's ass on the way over?

Me: Maybe Matt's. And his dad. Who, by the way, is Roger fucking Davis - as in CEO of Davis Media Group.

Lucy: Wait, what?!!!

Josie: Holy shit. OK, kids dismiss at 3:10. I'll grab wine and be there by 4.

Lucy: I can sneak out around 3. Hang in there. We got you.

♥

My chest squeezes as I look around my office. Five years of my life took place in here. The random scribbles on my whiteboard. A row of branded tumblers collecting dust on top of a bookshelf with a handful of binders and CEO memoirs on how to be an effective leader. Framed *Ad Age* articles line the wall, and a few pictures of adventures the girls and I have had are scattered in between.

I stare at the couch across from me that has been an escape for so many. Priya took naps on it when she had morning sickness with her first kid. Jose and Jeremy flipping coins on who could lie down on it during conference calls when nursing hangovers. Naomi and Rachel on either side of me rubbing my back as I held my head between my knees, hyperventilating after things ended with Greg.

A lot of memories were made here, almost all of them good. Matt's in here too. The coffee he left me every morning. The random times he sat on the couch during debriefs when all the conference rooms were booked. The football-shaped stress ball that he'd toss in the air sitting on the arm of the couch.

Thinking about how he was so casual, so calm about everything makes perfect sense now. How he wouldn't stress about changing deadlines or client pushback. How the mention of Roger wouldn't rattle him. How did I miss all of that?I hear a soft knock on my door and murmur a low, "Yeah?"

The door slowly opens and Sheila pops her head in. "Hey, Em. Can I come in?"

My eyes suddenly fill with tears again as I nod at her. She comes around my desk with her arms spread and pulls me into a hug. I let the tears stream down as she rubs my back.

Sheila sits on the corner of my desk. "Are you okay?"

I laugh bitterly and shake my head. "No, I'm actually not okay."

"Em, you need to know Josh and I had no idea Roger was going to assign the account to Matt."

"But you knew who he was? This whole time?"

Sheila nods regretfully. "I'm sorry, Emily. I truly am. But Roger asked Josh and I not to let anyone know, to give Matt a fair chance to get settled in. I didn't think it would end up like this. We all know the job should be yours. Matt, especially."

I scoff at that. "I'm sure."

"I don't know what's going on between you two, and I don't know if this will mean anything, but this morning in Roger's office before you came in, Matt was furious. He said it was your job to have. That you deserved it."

"He doesn't even want it, which is the worst part considering it's all I've ever wanted. And on top of that, he lied to me. He never said a thing. Just sat there acting like he was one of us and lied about it every single day."

"We can figure out the best place for you outside of Imperial so you won't have to cross paths with him so much."

I shake my head. "Sheila, I'm done with DMG. I can't thank you or Josh enough for everything you've done for me, but I can't stay here. Not after this."

Reaching out to rub my arm, she tries to console me. "I know you're upset, but let's sleep on everything and reevaluate when it's not so raw."

"I appreciate that, but I'm not going to change my mind. I'll check in with you once I'm done processing all of this." I stand up, signaling that the conversation is over.

Sheila rises with me and gives me another hug. "I'm here when you want to talk."

I feel the walls of the office starting to suffocate me, so I grab my coat and purse. I leave my laptop and work phone behind—I need a clean break from this office and everyone in it.

I decide to walk home, confident Sheila and Josh will let me have a few hours to clear my office once my head stops spinning.

It's a gorgeous, early spring day. The bright sun reflects off the buildings and creates a magical glow over the city. People are eating outside, sitting on ledges by fountains and benches that line courtyard areas. I love the buzz of days of like this. Coats coming off, sleeves being rolled up. I catch a few people with their heads back and eyes closed, faces turned upward, accepting the glorious warmth.

This was my Disneyland when I was younger. I dreamed of life in the big city, working at a big advertising agency, and while I'm proud of how far I've come, I know deep down I'm not ready to leave. The city feels more like home than my hometown. I came here with nothing and carved out a life for myself. Found my passion, made a family with Josie and Lucy. In a city this big, the five city blocks around my apartment now feel like my village. Marco my pizza guy on the corner. Maria at the diner who always laughs with me when I stumble in at two in the morning for an order of cheese fries. Jay at the bodega who always has my coffee ready for me after my run.

I feel a pang in my chest when I think about my apartment. The place where I fell apart and put myself back together. My balcony overlooking the courtyard, my kitchen where I spent so many nights eating and drinking with the girls. The sweat that went into revamping the whole thing myself. If I thought begging Mr. Marino for another chance would make a difference, I would. The thought of packing makes my bottom lip tremble and new tears form in my eyes, but I don't know how to make it work anymore.

Josie and Lucy show up at four p.m. on the dot, each of them holding a bottle of wine. Josie pours generous glasses and raises hers in a toast. They sit on the couch across from where I am on the floor, leaning against the coffee table.

"To Emily. And to the three of us. I love you like my sisters, and we're stuck together forever." Josie looks at me pointedly. "No. Matter. What."

"Josie, I've cried enough today. Don't make me cry more."

"We love you. Whatever you need, we're here." Lucy squeezes my hand as she raises her glass to Josie's.

"Thanks." I feel my throat sting for the hundredth time today and I drop my head back, closing my eyes.

Josie tucks her legs underneath her. "Can we start with hearing about what the actual fuck happened?"

I blow out a resigned breath and open my eyes as I start filling them in. I'm still so angry at Matt, but the loss of him is already hitting me. I'm disoriented as I try to balance the fact that he caused this hollowness in the first place but I want him to comfort me from it.

"Anyway," I blow out a deep breath. "He didn't want anyone to know. But I didn't think I was just anyone. He was telling me how much he liked me and wanted to be with me, all the while he was keeping this huge secret that he had to have known would blow up in my face. How can I trust anything he says? How do I believe any of the things he told me?"

The girls are silent, none of us able to reconcile it.

"This morning, they told me Matt got the AD job. And for me, it's not just about losing the job. Without the promotion, I can't afford this apartment. I have no more savings. I have horrible credit." I pause, soaking in my list of failures. "I guess this is what rock bottom feels like. Nothing to show for it but a broken heart."

Lucy scoots down and wraps her arms around me, lending me her strength as I cry into her shoulder. "Emily, you can stay with either one of us. You know that. You don't have to leave altogether."

Josie joins us and rubs my back. "I know, but you're both in studios and I'm too old to couch surf at this point. I have to get my entire life together."

"Could your mom help?" Josie asks softly, knowing asking her is the last thing I want to do.

I sigh. "I mean, technically yes. But do I want to ask her? No. She's going on vacation in a few weeks with Steve, so I'm going to drive up there tomorrow and talk to her, as much as I hate the thought of it." I hardly go home anymore because my mom usually visits me in the city. I couldn't get out of my hometown fast enough once I graduated, equating every extra day I was there as a day being further from my dreams. Returning feels like conceding defeat.

Our attention is pulled toward the coffee table where my phone has been vibrating nonstop since our conversation started.

Josie nods her. "Are you going to check that? I could probably get off on it at the rate that it's buzzing."

I sit up and laugh despite myself. "I'm actually not. You two are here and I told my mom I'd explain everything when I see her. I don't want to talk to anyone else." I stand. "I need to start packing so I can leave first thing in the morning." I walk to my entry closet to grab my suitcase, and when I pass the couch to head to my bedroom, I see Josie scrolling through my phone.

"Josie, seriously!"

"Em, I'm sorry, but you have twenty-five texts and eight missed calls from Matt. Aren't you the least bit curious what he has to say?"

"No. I don't want to hear any more of his bullshit. The sooner I can get away from him the better."

My phone buzzes again. "It's another text," Josie announces.

"Please just ignore it."

We hear yet another beep, but this time it's Josie's phone. She picks it up and curls her lip. "Ryan's texting me." She scans it and looks up at me.

I blow out an exacerbated breath and roll my eyes. "Fine, tell us what he said."

Josie clears her throat and reads, "I'm not entirely sure what the fuck is going on, but Matt is trying, rather desperately I might add, to get in touch with Emily, and she's gone MIA. He asked me to ask you (see above: desperation) if you can help?"

"Am I supposed to feel bad for him? Well, I don't. Let him feel desperate. It's a familiar feeling for me now. I should have learned my lesson with Greg. Hell, I should have learned my lesson with my dad."

I grab my phone from the table. My fingers are shaking as I quickly work them over the screen.

"Em, what are you doing?" Lucy asks.

"Turning my phone off. I don't care what he has to say."

We finish the two bottles of wine and order a pizza, throwing on a movie in an effort to distract me. My body aches, depleted and weary from all that transpired today. The sun is starting to set just as I'm in need of fresh air.

"I have to move my car for street cleaning, so I'll walk you out." A car in Manhattan doesn't make sense, but I've had it since I got my license and it works well enough to take the three of us on adventures outside the city. I worked my butt off in high school to buy it, and it's chock full of sentimental value. An Imperial it's not, but it's mine.

We stop outside my building and they both wrap me tightly in their arms. The thought of leaving them and our adopted home completely guts me. Am I really going to give up so easily? Regret burns through me when I think about walking away without trying to figure something out.

I step back and wipe my eyes.

"I'll keep you posted. I love you guys."

CHAPTER 38

MATT

Three Hours Earlier

Me: Did you text Josie?

Ryan: Yes, just like I said I would.

Me: Did she answer?

Ryan: Not yet.

Me: When did you send it?

Ryan: Five minutes ago.

Me: Did she read it?

Ryan: Matt.

Me: Ryan.

Ryan: Where are you?

Me: Two blocks from Emily's apartment.

Ryan: Stalker much?

Ryan: Turn around. Take a deep breath and walk away.

Meet me at Gannon's in 20.

I'm halfway through my first beer when Ryan walks into the pub. When he opens the door, the sun is shockingly bright, illuminating dust streams and disrupting the dark ambiance. This place is an old school dive, with a weathered bar and wood stools, hunter green walls with faded posters, and TVs hanging from the ceiling permanently stuck on ESPN and horse racing. It smells of stale beer, and there are only a few people here. Ryan slaps my shoulder and takes the stool next to me, nodding to the bartender and pointing to my drink.

The bartender brings over a fresh pint for Ryan as I stare at the foam in my half-empty glass.

"You look positively like shit, my brother." Ryan smacks his lips as he finishes the first sip of his beer.

"You can thank Roger."

"I was afraid of something like that." Ryan shakes his head in disappointment. "What happened?"

"What always happens. It's only about what Roger wants. I can't do this anymore, Ryan. I've tried to keep my head down and deal with it for Mom's sake, but he pushed too far this time."

Ryan looks at me. "Is this because of Hunter?"

"Yes! He told Hunter if DMG won the account, then I'd be leading it. But that was never part of our deal. I reminded him of that, and that Emily deserved it way more than me anyway. He lost his fucking mind, calling me ungrateful and a disappointment. Of course he threw in his favorite line that I'm always 'looking a gift horse in the mouth.'" I rock my shoulders and use the world's worst accent to portray my father's stupid words.

"Please don't ever do that again," Ryan deadpans. I don't laugh, but I do appreciate his attempt to infuse levity into the situation.

"I'm out though, Ryan. There's no way I can work for him. I shouldn't have to in order to keep the peace. I know it'll destroy Mom because it feels like the final straw between us, but I'm done living my life vying for his approval. Nothing I do will ever be good enough. He moves the goal posts every time so that I can never get close to succeeding. I helped him win the biggest fucking auto account out there, and it's still not good enough."

I draw zigzag lines in the condensation on my now empty glass. "I'm just done." I say it more quietly now, exhaustion from the past two days seeping in. "I can't keep trying and always hearing how I fall short. There's no question she would have gotten the job if my last name wasn't Davis. But he's so thick-headed that he won't consider her at all."

"Is it just about Emily not getting the job?"

I face him. "What do you mean?"

Ryan sighs. "I mean, is this just about Emily and the job, or is this about something bigger with Emily?"

I scoff out an exhale. "Even if it is, it doesn't matter. She won't talk to me. She won't forgive me for lying to her and basically told me to fuck off."

"Does that surprise you?"

The question makes me pause. The reasons why I didn't say

anything before felt very valid to me, but if I put myself in Emily's shoes—Emily who has been hurt too many times by lying men—I can't really blame her. I'm not proud of myself, even though whatever I did was with the best intentions and to protect Emily.

Did she need protecting? No. She's much stronger than she gives herself credit for. Did I give her enough credit? Definitely not. Was I protecting myself instead? Yeah, from losing my shot with her.

I shake my head and click my tongue. "No, but what the hell was I supposed to do? If I divulged who Dad was at any point during the pitch, she would have completely shut me down and shut me out. The pitch process would have been unbearable and unsuccessful. When was I supposed to tell her? When she was already blocking me at every chance? Or when we were making out in the hotel bar like horny teenagers? There was never a right time."

"You made out in the hotel bar? So cliché, man." Ryan shakes his head, and this time I can't hide my smile.

"Shut the fuck up. When was the last time you made out with anyone? Because I know Josie didn't pan out for you."

Ryan laughs at my clapback. "Yeah, it's been a while. Nothing I'm ashamed of."

"You never really told me what exactly happened with her. I just know it was over before it even got started."

"That's a story for another day. Anyway, Josie said Emily was pretty upset earlier today. She and Lucy were going to help her pack."

"Wait, what? Pack? Why is she packing?"

"I guess she's heading to her mom's place upstate."

"Why the fuck didn't you start with that?" I stand up, rushing to grab my phone off the bar, my voice raising enough that the few patrons in the bar turn toward us.

"Dude, I thought you knew!"

"No, I didn't. I have to go. She can't leave. She can't go home. I have to stop her."

I turn to leave and Ryan grabs my arm. "Matt. Wait. Just answer this: if you fight Dad on this and ultimately walk away, will you still be able to say Emily was worth all of this?"

"Why does everyone keep asking me that?"

"Because we saw what Stella did to you and how long it took to piece yourself back together. None of us want to see you go through that again."

"Ry, this isn't even in the same stratosphere as Stella. This is so much more. Emily is so much more. She's..." I stop, taking a deep breath. "She's everything, man. I'm in love with her." I feel a pang in my chest. "I can't lose her."

Ryan stands, dropping a few bills on the bar. "Then let's fucking go! Why are we just standing here?"

I don't even bother trying to hail a cab, I have to keep moving. I'm five blocks away from Emily's apartment and God help anyone or anything that blocks my path. I weave around pedestrians and dogs being walked, bumping more than a few shoulders and looking back with quick apologies as I keep my pace. Ryan is on my heels and slams into my back when I stop short after turning the corner. Emily's down the block, hugging Josie and Lucy. Ryan grabs both my arms from behind to steady us.

"What the hell, why did you stop?"

He follows my gaze and drops his hands from my arms. We silently watch the girls as they huddle close. The three of them are wiping their eyes and laughing now as they break apart. They remain in a tight circle as I start to jog over. Josie notices me first and shifts to stand in front of Emily. Lucy lines up next to Josie, and I can see Emily standing on her toes between them like she's trying to see the stage from the back of a mosh pit.

She freezes when she spots me. Ryan and I are shoulder to shoulder as we slow to a walk and greet them.

Josie widens her stance and glares at me. "What do you want, *Davis*?"

I ignore her, focused only on Emily. "Emily, please, can we talk?"

"She has nothing to say to you," Lucy chimes in as Josie steps forward, blocking her completely from my view.

"Josie." I turn to look at her. "Please, let me talk to her."

"Stop talking about me like I'm not here." Emily pushes between them. Her hands are fisted at her side and her eyes are bloodshot. They're welling up, but the disappointment is clear as day. "I told you I have nothing to say to you. If you care about me at all like you say you do, then leave me alone." Her bottom lip starts to tremble and she bites down on it.

Big, desolate eyes look up at me. I try to swallow around my throat thickening, not trusting myself to speak. We stand toe to toe, not blinking, and I try to convey my apology through my eyes.

"Emily," I croak out.

"Please." She chokes down a sob and turns toward her building without looking back at any of us. All I can do is watch as she walks away, taking my breath and my heart with her.

Once she disappears behind her foyer doors, Ryan squeezes my shoulder. I feel my own eyes get glassy and turn to Josie, who looks crestfallen as she watches her best friend walk away.

"Josie—"

She puts a hand up to stop me. "Matt, for Emily's sake, I want to believe this is some kind of terrible misunderstanding and there's an acceptable explanation for what happened."

I exhale in relief and step toward her. Josie sticks her hand out further.

"But all I'm feeling right now is Emily's heartbreak over losing everything in one day. So the best thing right now is to turn around and walk away."

Silently nodding, I turn around and start walking away. I hear Ryan mumbling something to Josie but can't make out what it is. I don't even try, too consumed by how empty I feel leaving behind the best thing to ever come into my life.

CHAPTER 39

EMILY

I shuffle slowly up the stairs to my apartment, my body aching, exhaustion deep in my bones. I can't really get my head around everything that's happened. From waking up in Matt's arms to not wanting them anywhere near me. From feeling excited about the possibilities at work to walking out for good. I'm in shock—numb, hollow, lost. The biggest loss of all? The hope that had finally started to peek its head out again. I thought I was taking it slow, keeping it in check, but I apparently pulled the wool over my own eyes.

Now, reflecting on the past few weeks with Matt, I feel nothing but shame and self-loathing. Disappointment with myself. Frustration that I got distracted from my work. Annoyance that all my effort the past few years could be swept away with one intense storm, swirling down the drain like the last of the dirty bathwater.

I thought Matt was different. He felt different. For the most part, he *was*. But it was all a lie.

My breath catches when I enter my apartment and see the New York City skyline under a mosaic sky of purple, gold, and burnt orange as the sun disappears for the day. This is the view that whispered "home" to me the first time I walked through this door. The view that never let me down. The view that I'll have to give up if I don't figure out a plan.

I chug a large glass of water and shut off the lights in the kitchen and living room, barely registering when I undress and unceremoniously climb into bed. For now, I just want to close my eyes and pretend this day never happened.

I wake up in the exact same spot I remember closing my eyes. So, while I know I slept soundly, I have to dig deep to find the energy to get out of bed. My eyes are puffy and dry and I blink a few times to combat the dryness. My muscles complain the entire time I take a cold shower to wake up. There's no use prolonging the inevitable, and I'm suddenly itching to get away from it all. Leave the city in my rearview mirror, if only for a week or so.

Hours later, I take the familiar exit from the highway. I remember how badly I wanted out of this town. How I swore I'd never come back, determined to start anew and carve out the life I imagined. But with more life experience under my belt the town doesn't feel as claustrophobic. Time has faded the bleak outlook that invaded my thoughts during high school.

Two minutes later, I've already made it through Main Street and all there is to see in Oakwood, population 4,500. I pass the high school and worn-in football field and reach the entrance to Colony Park, known for the best small homes money can buy.

I twist the doorknob to check if it's open and lean my head in, calling out to my mom. Her entire face lights up as she wipes her hands on a dishtowel and opens her arms for the best hug known to mankind.

"Emily, it's so good to see you, sweetheart."

"You too, Mom." I squeeze her back and hold on for an extra beat or two, inhaling her familiar vanilla scent and relishing the comfort you can only get from someone who loves you unconditionally.

I take a deep, appreciative inhale as I follow her to the kitchen. My mom didn't cook much when I was growing up because she worked two jobs. She sacrificed so much of her own life, to the point of neglecting herself in some instances. But when she did cook, our kitchen rivaled any of the best five-star places in Rome or Syracuse, the closest "cities" to Oakwood.

I know immediately from the lingering scent of onions browning in olive oil that she's making her famous sauce. The smells swirl around me as I take in the sight of my favorite ingredients on the counter—bright green basil, ripe red tomatoes, and a mound of buffalo mozzarella. My senses are being invaded by every sight, sound, and scent of home and I exhale, feeling cocooned amid all the warring thoughts and emotions that have racked my body for days.

"How was the drive? You must be exhausted." She pulls out a stool for me by the counter. "Come sit, I'm almost done with dinner." She pours me a generous glass of wine before she drains the pasta and sets out two plates. "Steve is out for the night. He wanted to give us some time to catch up."

After a very long string of bad boyfriends, my mom finally hit the jackpot with Steve. At first, I was wary, because she doesn't have the best track record, but Steve kept showing up, kept caring, and five years after they met, he still looks at her with the same mix of love and appreciation she deserves so much.

We bring our plates to the square four-person table by the kitchen, and I pour my mom an equally large glass of wine. Raising her glass, my mom holds my eyes and toasts, "To coming home."

We catch up on all the little things as we eat dinner: her job at the local grocery store where she has moved up to morning shift manager, Steve's job at the Home Depot two towns over, their upcoming RV trip out west to camp for a few weeks. She avoids asking me anything about work or the city, giving me the space to open up when I'm ready.

After we clear our plates, I pour us more wine as my mom grabs a Tupperware full of my favorite brownies and brings it to the table. We each take one, but instead of taking a big bite, I leave it on my plate and pick at the corners.

"So, are you going to pick at that all night, or are you going to finally tell me what's going on?"

CHAPTER 40

EMILY

I let out a deep sigh, releasing the heaviness weighing over me. "Well, let's see. I got my heart shattered into a million pieces and then I quit a job I loved all on the same day. All my fault for being a blind idiot."

My mom doesn't say anything. She keeps her eyes steady on me, slowly nodding and encouraging me to continue.

"What's the saying? Fool me once, shame on you. Fool me twice, shame on me. What happens when you're completely fooled a third time? You would think I'd have learned my lesson that no man can be trusted, but what do I do? I go ahead and believe that I might be wrong, that maybe there could be some good guys left. Ha. I was wrong, alright, but not about there being good guys left. Just that they're all liars who can't be trusted. I've seen it happen all my life."

At that last statement, my mom turns her head in surprise.

"Oh, Emily. Do you really think that?" I nod, looking down at my hands. "Why, honey?"

"Well, for starters, Dad. He left and didn't look back. He showed up for what, one of my birthdays after he split? Then ignored every card, every call, every time I ever reached out to him? It was like he wanted to erase me from existence. Move on with his shiny new family. And I saw how it made you cry. How it hurt you. You didn't have the best luck with boyfriends after that. All I saw was you getting upset over and over again. All the men in our lives disappointed us. You didn't have to explicitly say it for me to realize it."

I remember swearing to myself that I'd never rely on someone else for my happiness, I'd never give my heart away. Risking the pain wasn't worth it. I learned the hard way as an adult with Greg. What surprises me most though, is realizing that the pain with Greg felt like a superficial cut compared to what I'm feeling now. This hurt is slicing me in half, like a hot knife through butter.

My mom keeps her eyes on the stem of her wineglass as I talk. When I finish, she looks up at me, her eyes shining. "I cried for *you* all those times your father let you down, Emily. Not for him. I hated him for how he disappointed you and eventually, you're right, how he just erased you from his life. I didn't care about any of that for myself; I knew it was a lost cause with your father loving me. But you," she strokes my hair. "You were wonderful and didn't deserve any of it."

I've given up on trying to wipe my tears, opting to just let them fall as I wait for her to continue.

"As for all the other men... I made a lot of bad choices. I was scared, and lonely, and didn't have the best judge of character because of that. I should have been a better role model for you. I should have kept most of those men away so you wouldn't have to witness them leaving. I can see how it would reinforce your thoughts that no man is reliable, and for that, I'm so, so sorry." She squeezes my hand. "But Emily, those men and their decision to leave had nothing to do with you. Especially your father. Those are their issues, their faults and downfalls. I should have been more forceful in drilling that into you. None of those men left because of who you were. They left because of who they were not."

I never thought my mom would be upset for me. "Maybe you're right about the deadbeat boyfriends, but my own father didn't care about me enough to make any effort, not even a birthday card or phone call once a year. How could I not think it was me? I tried so hard. Straight A's. Girl Scouts. Soccer. Spelling Bees. No matter how good I was at anything, it never made a difference." I choke out a sob. "Why didn't he love me?"

My mom shifts her chair closer and puts her arm around me as I rest my head on her shoulder. "And then look what happened with Greg." I drop my head back and groan, anger now replacing the tears. "I ignored the warning signs, just wanting someone to finally love me. But he never did. And then I finally get over it, and Matt fucking Meyer—Davis? Who the hell knows what his name really is—had to come along."

"Do you want to tell me what happened with Matt?" my mom asks softly.

"It was me being stupid all over again." My voice rises in frustration, mostly at myself. "Worse than ever, because I fell hard for him in such a short time." I drop my head, shame washing over me through my tears. I take a deep breath, wipe my face, and look at my mom.

"When I found out I was going to lead one of the pitches for Imperial, I was so excited." The first genuine smile I've managed in days shows up. "It felt like my work was finally paying off. I was finally good at something, I was *worthy* of something good. I went out with Josie and Lucy one night and just so happened to meet Matt. He took my breath away, his looks, his charm... and he seemed genuinely interested in me. We didn't really talk about work, so I was completely blindsided when he was introduced as the lead for the other pitch team."

"He never mentioned it?"

I spill the full story—meeting Matt that first weekend, working on the pitch, everything up until Texas. It's cathartic and heartbreaking at the same time and I need a minute to keep going.

"But that all sounds good, Em... What went wrong?"

"It *was* good. We ended up winning the pitch. He gave me all the credit and was my biggest cheerleader. We both thought for sure I would get promoted to lead the account, and I needed that promotion more than anyone knew."

"Why? Why did you need it so badly?" Her question has a bit of an edge to it now.

I blow out a resigned breath and tell her everything about the apartment.

"Well, the worst part is that even though I deserved the promotion, I didn't get it, because Matt's dad is the CEO of the agency. I never had a chance."

My mom sits back in shock. I finish the rest of the story, revealing how bad Matt's relationship is with his dad and how his father basically cornered him into taking the job. How he begged me not to leave and was texting me pretty much nonstop after I quit and walked out.

The front door opens and Steve walks in. He must feel the heaviness in the room because his first question is, "Who died?"

"My career. My love life. My dignity."

Steve walks over to my mom and kisses the crown of her head as she squeezes his forearm. He then turns to me, giving me the same kiss on my head. "Hi, kiddo. It's good to see you."

I adore Steve, and more importantly, he adores my mom. Tall and slender, Steve is the epitome of kindness. Patient, reliable. With his short salt-and-pepper hair and broad smile, it's easy to see why my mom fell for him.

"Do I need to hurt anyone? It's not that dumbass Greg again, is it?"

Steve lived through a lot of teary nights and weepy phone calls when Greg and I first broke up. He told me afterward that he never liked him, that he felt slimy and too weak for me.

My mom turns back to me. "Emily, do you think Matt was maybe telling the truth? That he didn't know how to tell you everything in the middle of the pitch, and that his dad was pressuring him about the job? It doesn't sound like he even wants it."

"You're right, he doesn't. But he still lied to me about who he was. He lied to me every time I talked about the promotion."

"But he didn't want it or know he was going to get it... so maybe it wasn't really lying."

"Even then, how could I trust anything he tells me now? It would be impossible to believe anything he says. Plus, he didn't turn the job down. Don't you see, Mom? When it's between me and something or someone else, I'm never enough." I bite my bottom lip as it starts to tremble, a heaviness taking over my limbs from admitting that truth out loud.

"Look at me." My mother turns to me and cups my cheeks. "You are enough, Emily. You are *more* than enough. I can say it until the sun comes up—and I will if that's what it takes—but there comes a point where you're going to have to believe it yourself. You are perfectly you, and you're perfect the way you are. I pray for the day you realize it and let yourself off the hook. All this pressure to be flawless, to never make a mistake—no one expects that but you. Life is imperfect. People are imperfect, sweetheart. Even the ones who love you. Josie and Lucy make mistakes, but do you love them any less? Would you push them out of your life if they messed up?"

She looks at me and I shake my head. She knows I can't argue with that. I don't expect them to be perfect, and it wouldn't matter if one of us messed up because we know all the bad parts about each other and still choose to stick around. Could I have that type of loyalty, that solidarity, with Matt in such a short time? Is that even possible?

"It's okay to be messy, to make mistakes, and to forgive people for their mistakes. Loving the people in your life, loving yourself through the mess, is the glue that binds all the pieces of life together. There's beauty in the mess if you look hard enough."

A new set of tears soaks my cheeks thinking about how much time and energy I've committed to avoiding mess. To avoiding anything going wrong. To holding myself to such a high standard that it's impossible to have a cup of coffee with someone for fear of not having anything to say or speak to a group of people without my voice shaking enough to activate the Richter scale.

"Do you think Matt set out to betray you?" she asks.

I shrug, not wanting to answer because deep down I know he didn't. "Only you know if Matt is a good person who was maybe put in an impossible situation and did the best he could. It's all we can really ask of ourselves and those we love—to do the best we can with what we have."

I nod, sniffling as my tears finally stop flowing.

"As for your apartment and financial situation, I wish you came to me sooner with this, but I understand you were trying to figure it out on your own. I am going to loan you the money you need." I start shaking my head to protest and she puts her hand out to stop me. "Because I am your mother, and no matter how old you are, I will always take care of you. You can pay me back once you're on track. Take the money so you can focus on finding a new job. Sometimes the best things have a way of showing up in the hardest times."

I stand, bringing my empty wineglass and my uneaten brownie to the sink. "Okay."

My mom comes over and gives me a long, tight hug.

"I'm exhausted from the drive. I think I'm going to turn in."

She pulls back, squeezing my shoulders. "Of course. Get some sleep. Everything will feel better in the morning."

"Yeah, let's hope so," I mumble, unconvinced. "Night, Steve."

Settled in my childhood bedroom, I lie awake thinking about everything my mom said and recounting my last few conversations with Matt. I reach for my phone and turn it on. I click the Messages square at the bottom of my screen and the pit of my stomach rolls, not sure of what I'll see.

CHAPTER 41

EMILY

Monday 11:02am: Magic Matt: I understand how upset you are right now and you have every right to be but Emily, please don't shut me out. I fucked up in the biggest way possible but I'm begging you to give me a chance to make it up to you.

Monday 12:42pm: I know you don't want to talk to me but I don't know where you went and I just want to make sure you're ok. Please let me know.

Monday 3:52pm: I'm so sorry. If you only knew how much I hate myself right now. You are the most amazing person I know and you didn't deserve this. I know I messed up but baby, please, please just talk to me.

Monday 4:12pm: How can I make this up to you? I'm going out of my mind here. If I could go back and redo everything I would. I wouldn't be a coward, I wouldn't hide the truth from you. How can I fix this? Please tell me there is something I can do to fix this. I'll do anything. I can't lose you.

Monday 8:12pm: Nothing has ever hurt as much as knowing I hurt you. Seeing your face just now, the pain I caused, knowing how badly I hurt you wrecked me. It took all my willpower to not run after you. You are the one good thing in my life. The light. The joy. The laughter. I wish I could talk to you but I'm going give you the space you need. I'm so sorry. I thought I was doing the right thing but I made it so much worse because now I may have lost you forever. Just know I'm not going anywhere. I will wait for you as long as I need to. Please don't give up on us.

CHAPTER 42

MATT

I lie awake all night, thinking about how wrong it felt to walk away from Emily. Regret consumes me. My arms ache to hold her and I'm going out of my mind not being able to talk to her. The sun is just peeking through the darkness and I'm already up and dressed, knotting my shoelaces for a run. Maybe I can physically force some of this regret out of me through sweat and sheer determination. Physical pain is a welcome salve at this point. I want to feel anything but this overwhelming guilt.

I'm dripping like I just emerged from a pool when I walk back into my apartment. My dad has already texted me to meet him in his office ASAP. The grueling run did nothing to temper the fire kindling inside of me. I jump in the shower, shame soaking me with the water as I think about walking into that office knowing Emily isn't going to be there.

It's eerily quiet for a Tuesday morning, and I take that to mean people have intuitively stayed away. I take the elevator to my father's floor, nodding to Susan as I knock once and walk into his office.

He's sitting at his desk, leaning back in his chair and flipping through a file as if he doesn't have a care in the world. Why would he? Roger Davis doesn't think beyond himself, what he wants, and how to get it. He looks up from his file and shuts it, standing up and rounding the corner of his desk to greet me.

"Son, come in. Have a seat." He gestures to one of the black chairs facing his desk as he takes his seat behind the desk.

"I heard Emily didn't take the news so well and decided to leave the agency. She won't go far if that's how she reacts to unfortunate news in professional settings."

"She left because she was wrongly passed over for a role she should have gotten. I don't blame her. I'd leave too."

"Yes, but we know that's not an option for you."

"Are you seriously going to resort to blackmail to keep me around? It's no secret what a disappointment I am to you, so why bother? DMG won Imperial. I held up my end of the deal and won the account. We never talked about me having to run it."

"Things change. The terms of the deal have changed. Hunter expects you to run the account."

"You can't just change the terms on a whim. It's not what we agreed on."

My dad sits up and punctuates his words by jabbing his desk with his finger. "If I remember correctly, the terms were mine to adjust when I covered a seven-figure mistake you made and kept us from both being humiliated."

"And I paid you back with Imperial."

"Matthew, you don't want to fight me on this."

"Oh, but I do. I don't give a flying fuck who knows about"—I raise my hands to make air quotes—"my big mistake."

"You'll never work in advertising again if that gets out."

"Have you ever asked me if I even want to work in advertising? News flash: I've never wanted to. The last thing I want to do is be stuck to a desk, commuting to an office every day. I should have stood up to you years ago, but stupidly, I thought maybe, just maybe, if I followed in your footsteps, if we had something in common, you might start seeing me for me. Not for every single misstep I've ever made in my life."

My dad rolls his eyes. "Can we move on please?

"You're making a big mistake." My eyes drill into his to drive my point home. "Emily should be running this account."

"It's admirable how much you stand up for her, Matthew, but this is my decision. Hunter expects you."

"Are you sure about that?"

My father stands, clearly exasperated. "Why are you pushing this so hard? You should be thankful I'm even giving you a chance, that you have this opportunity in the first place. When will you stop being so ungrateful?" He's trembling as he tries to reel in his anger.

"It's not being ungrateful if I don't want or ask for it!" I roar. "This is what you want, not what I want. I said I would help with the pitch, but I never committed to staying or running the account. And I'll be damned if I subject myself to being in the same office as you every day, only to be reminded how much I fall short of your unattainable expectations."

I stand up, unable to sit still any longer. I shake my head, realizing once and for all nothing will ever change. "I'm not staying here. If you don't want to give the job to Emily, that's an enormous mistake. But either way, I'm not taking it. I'm done."

"Don't be ridiculous, Matthew. I don't have time for your tantrum."

"This isn't a tantrum, Dad. I'm done. I *quit*."

My dad scoffs at that. "You quit? Yeah, okay. If you quit, you have nowhere to go. No options. No one else will hire you once word gets out about this."

"Is that how you see me?" I whisper.

"Please." He sits down aggressively in his chair, rolling his eyes. "How will you pay me back? You don't have that type of cash."

I grind my teeth, venom filtering through my snarl. "I paid you back with Imperial. But if that's not enough I'll figure it out. I'll work myself to the bone making sure you are paid back every single penny, but it sure as hell won't be here under your control."

"And who will run Imperial?"

Without looking back, I say, "Not my fucking problem."

I walk out of my father's office, straight to the elevators, and leave the DMG building for the last time. While I'm still full of regret for how things went down with Emily, I immediately feel a hundred pounds lighter. I head straight to see my mom, knowing I'm going to have to do some damage control.

She doesn't seem surprised when she sees me. Silently turning to the side to let me pass her, I give her a kiss on the cheek.

"Coffee?" she asks as we walk to the kitchen, like me showing up at eleven a.m. on a Tuesday is a normal occurrence.

I shake my head. Blowing out a breath, I jump in. "I quit DMG."

She looks up from filling the carafe with water, stunned.

"Matt…" she starts to soothe me, but I hold my hand up to stop her.

"He's toxic. I'm done trying to convince him to love me. That's not my job."

Her shoulders sag as she puts the coffee pot down and her voice cracks. "I'm so sorry. I should have been stronger. I should have been a better shield for you."

"Mom." I reach out and hug her tight. "I don't blame you." And I don't. I know she did the best she could to balance him out, she loved Ryan and me enough for the both of them. But a tiger can't change their stripes, and Roger is the most stubborn of all. If anything, I love her more for all the times she tried. "I can't even imagine working with him, let alone being his wife."

She pulls back and wipes her eyes. "So what will you do?"

I scrub my hands down my face. "Well, I have to pay him back for the Super Bowl."

"Excuse me?" Disbelief funnels through my mom's question. "He said that?"

"Yep." I nod my head a few times. "I have some money saved up from selling the apartment in Chicago. Instead of buying a place here, maybe I can crash with Ryan for a little while. It's not nearly enough, but it's a start. I'll have to figure the rest out."

"But the agency covered that, not your father. And they didn't even feel the loss. They had credits from the network that they just transferred over to Hunter."

My eyes widen. "What!?"

My mom slowly inhales a deep breath. "He never told you, did he?" I feel the fury reverberating off of her. She mumbles a "God-dammit, Roger" under her breath.

"I told him he had to tell you. The way he held that mistake over your head was infuriating, and I threatened him with a sep-aration if he didn't tell you that the agency was able to cover it."

I lean into my hands on the counter and hang my head, a bit-ter laugh escaping me. "He really is a piece of work."

My mom's face is drained of all color. "I'm so sorry, Matt. I thought you knew."

I push off from the granite surface and walk over to give my mom another hug as she sobs into my shoulder. Her regret is palpable as she apologies to me over and over.

When she lets go, she leaves one hand on my shoulder and cradles my cheek with the other. "What now for you?"

"I don't know, but I have some ideas. I want to become a phys-ical therapist and work with athletes. I have a lot of credits from my undergrad, and it wouldn't take long to get the rest to apply to grad school. It feels like it could be a good fit for me." Saying it out loud to her for the first time cements my resolve to finally do this. It feels right as excitement coils in my stomach.

Her eyes fill with tears, pride bursting through as she squeezes my shoulder. "You've thought this through."

I let out a shaky laugh. "Yeah, I guess I have. I never admitted it because all I heard was Dad's voice telling me I'd fail."

She pulls me into another hug. "He's wrong, Matt. You're going to be a huge success, and I can't wait to finally see a real smile on your face again."

Nolan: Congrats, man. It's going to be great to work together.

Matt: Just the man I wanted to talk to.

Nolan: Yeah? What's up?

Matt: Any chance you and Hunter are around tomorrow? I need to talk to both of you. I'll fly down to do it in person.

Nolan: Is everything okay?

Matt: It will be.

"And so—" I release a big exhale. "That's why I won't be working on Imperial." I turn toward Hunter. "You've always been upfront and fair with me, and I wanted to return the gesture. This has nothing to do with you or your business. It's all a personal decision."

Hunter is leaning back in his chair, hands steepled under his chin. "That's quite a story, Matt." He shakes his head as he sits up. "I had no idea all of that was happening behind the scenes."

Nolan adds, "I'm sorry you were put through all that."

"Well, I did mess up the campaign, and for that I'm truly sorry. I'd like to think my father thought he was protecting me, but who knows anymore. That being said, the team at DMG is phenomenal, and Imperial will be in good hands."

"But both you and Emily are gone. You two were why we picked DMG," Hunter says.

Nolan turns toward Hunter. "Maybe we revisit the possibility of bringing it all in-house instead of an agency."

"Have you been thinking about that?" I ask Nolan.

"It's always been a possibility. Before we put out the review, we did a deep analysis of the pros and cons. We even interviewed a few potential candidates to lead the in-house team, but no one fit the bill. It's true what Hunter just said about you and Emily and the comfort we felt with the account in your hands."

"So hire Emily to run the team in-house," I suggest to them. "She was the heart and soul of it. The idea to pitch to women was all her."

Hunter drills his fingers on his desk as he looks out his window. "You know, that's an interesting idea. I've been toying around with the idea of focusing more on women and STEM overall. Emily has the right passion and energy to help with that too."

A panicked thought pops in my head. "Would she have to

move here to do the job?"

Nolan shakes his head. "No, that wouldn't be necessary. We know the talent we need is probably in New York, so we were going to base the team there anyway."

Hunter looks at me. "Do you think Emily would be interested?"

I can't stop my smile as my heart expands in my chest, knowing without a doubt she would be amazing in the role. "I don't know what she's thinking about doing next but if you go that route, I would definitely give her a call and ask."

I'm back after a whirlwind trip to Texas. Ironically, I'm at Smith's Cave, sitting with Ryan and Ben and staring at the door even though I know Emily won't be walking in. I texted the guys from the airport with a condensed summary of the past few days, and we decided to meet for a drink. I'm finally done rehashing it all and sit back to take a long swig of my beer.

"So, what now?" Ryan asks.

"Uh, were you not just listening? I quit DMG. I cleared the air with Hunter, once and for all."

"Yeah, yeah, I heard all that." Ryan waves his hand impatiently at me. "What about the girl?"

"The girl?"

Ben leans forward. "Yeah, man. How are you going to get Emily back? It's grand gesture time."

I look at Ben like he just suggested we braid each other's hair. "What the fuck is grand gesture time?"

Ryan snaps his fingers and points at Ben. "Yes, yes, you're right. You were always the smart one."

Ben nods his head toward Ryan, accepting the compliment and sipping his beer.

"What the fuck are you two talking about? Did you hear when I said Emily won't talk to me?"

Ben looks at me. "Dude, what do you expect? Your crushed her heart. You lied to her." I sit up to defend myself, but Ben holds his hand up. "With good reason, I know. But it's hard to turn off feelings that quickly and we hope she realizes that when the dust finally settles. In the meantime, you need a grand gesture. Something big to let her know how sorry you are and how much she means to you. A last-ditch effort. A do or die."

"A fucking Hail Mary, Matty. That's what you need," Ryan says, tapping his fingers on the table for emphasis.

"Okay, fine. If this *Hail Mary* somehow works, what are the chances she'll even listen to what I have to say?"

"You'll never know unless you try," Ben whispers, shaking his head back and forth, spewing wisdom on me. "Do you want to always look back and ask yourself *What if*? Or do you want to look back and say, *Hell yes I went for it.*"

Me: Josie, this is Matt.

No response.

Me: I need your help.

Josie: Excuse me?

Me: Emily won't talk to me.

Josie: Shocking.

I drop my hands to my side and look to the sky, swallowing the scream I want to let out.

Me: I know. But I can't make things right if I can't reach her.

Silence.

I stare at my phone like its water on the stove refusing to boil. *Come on, throw me a bone, Josie.*

Me: I fucked up, Josie. Big time. And I know that. I need to talk to her.

More silence.

Me: I love her. More than anything in my life. I'm not giving up on her, but she won't know that unless I can reach her.

Josie: I'm listening.

CHAPTER 43

EMILY

I've been in my hometown for a week now. Sleep has evaded me, but the long walks with my mom and the home-cooked meals have soothed some of the initial burn. Besides the walks, I've mostly hibernated, huddled under a crocheted afghan on the couch, reading my favorite romance novels and challenging Steve to *Jeopardy* every night after dinner. I've been contemplating staying here, daydreaming about working at the supermarket with my mom or at the local bookstore, coming back to this couch every night and residing in this carefully curated haven.

That idea blows up when my mom gets home from work today and joins me on the couch, nudging my socked feet to make room for her to sit. I close my book and sit up against the couch arm, hugging my bent legs and resting my chin on my knee.

"Honey," my mom starts, twisting toward me and leaning her head on her hand, arm bent on the couch cushion. Steve is in the kitchen prepping food to grill for dinner.

"You know I love having you home, and you are welcome to stay here as long as you need—even when Steve and I head on our trip in a few weeks. But at some point, you need to figure out what comes next."

I drop my head, lightly tapping my forehead on my knees, and groan. "But I don't even know where to begin." I sigh and straighten out my legs so my feet are on my mother's lap.

She squeezes my toes. "I understand it's overwhelming, but why not think of this as a do-over? A blank slate. You can try anything, be anything."

I watch my fingers explore the holes between the granny squares of the blanket. "When you say it like that, you make it sound so easy."

"Well, let's pretend it is easy. What would you do?"

This has dominated my thoughts on the rare occasions I'm not thinking about Matt. What do I want to do? What would make me happy? What excites me? The solitude has helped me sift through those questions, and while it's intimidating to say them out loud, I tell her anyway. "I want to run my own accounts. Imperial was actually going to be fun because the entire campaign was going to focus on women, which would have been a first for them."

"So run your own accounts," she says, as if she's deciding what's for dinner. *As if it's that easy.*

"If anyone can do it, you can, kiddo," Steve adds from the sink as he washes his hands.

Just then we hear a knock on the door. Steve looks to my mom. "Are you expecting anyone?"

She stands and heads toward the front door. "No, I have no idea who that could be."

I pick up my book to start reading again as my mom opens the door.

"Hi, is Emily home?"

I freeze at the greeting. I would know that voice anywhere. It's been in my dreams every night since I left the city. It swirls in my head in the quiet moments during my morning walks. It's the voice of every hero in my books as I read.

I put the book down and slowly lower my feet to the floor. I watch Steve wipe his hands on a towel and meet my mom by the door, his palm on her shoulder.

How did he know where to find me? I rub my fingers through my hair, wondering when I last washed it. It gives a whole new meaning to messy bun. My black leggings and gray hoodie are fine, but the fuzzy Rugrats socks I found in my old dresser aren't exactly screaming sophistication. *Perfectly imperfect, right?*

"May I ask who's looking for her?" my mom inquires, curiosity piqued.

"Mrs. Cooper?" Matt asks with a question in his voice. My mother nods. "Hi, I'm Matt... Davis. I'm hoping to talk to Emily, if that's alright." I see my mom and then Steve each shake Matt's hand. *Classic boy next door.*

I hardly recognize my voice as I say, "Mom, it's okay. I'm coming." My legs are shaking and my stomach is a Tilt-A-Whirl, but an unexpected rush of relief overtakes me when Steve steps away and I have a full view of Matt at our door.

He's in the same dark jeans from that first night at Smith's Cave. His long-sleeve tee hugs his chest and loosens down his torso, accentuating his tapered waist. Of course his sleeves are pushed back, forearms taunting me. His hair, however, is mussed, like he spent the better part of the trip here running his fingers through it. Dark circles rim his eyes, and they brighten as they connect with mine.

"Emily," he whispers with reverence, almost like a prayer. His glassy eyes close and he takes a deep breath, exhaling slowly. Opening them, he looks at me, and he may as well be looking at my soul as he says exactly what I'm thinking. "It's so good to see you."

I hear Steve step behind my mother's back to grab the tray of burgers and walk out the door to the backyard. My mom turns to face me and squeezes my arm before she follows the same path as Steve. "We'll be out back if you need anything."

I nod and take her spot, leaning my head against the door. "Hey," I say in a soft greeting.

"Can we talk?" The air between us swirls with tension and regret, pulled taut like the skin of a drum. "Please." Matt's voice cracks with his request, and his torment is so clear across his features I can't say no. I don't *want* to say no.

"Sure." I step around him and close the door, sitting on the top step of our porch. I fold my arms on my legs and look forward. Matt sits next to me, and I fight the gravitational pull he has on me to keep some distance between us. Otherwise, I'd be sitting on his lap.

"How did you know where to find me?"

"Josie."

I nod once, pursing my lips. The silence extends a beat, then another.

"It wasn't easy getting it out of her." Matt looks down, smiling and shaking his head. "She can be vicious."

A small laugh escapes me. "She definitely protects the one she loves. You must have said something right to get her attention."

"Emily..." He turns his body toward me as words rush from his mouth. "Emily, I'm so sorry I didn't tell you about my dad. About the situation. It was wrong, and I'm not about to excuse it. It was selfish. I knew if I told you I'd lose any chance of reviving the connection we had the first weekend we met."

I keep my gaze forward, my arms now wrapped around my middle, but give a small nod to let him know I'm listening.

"You were so shocked when I showed up at DMG, and rightfully so. I knew telling you my dad was Roger would be the final nail in the coffin, and I couldn't risk it. My entire life I've been judged by who my dad is, by being Ryan's younger brother. There's no way I would have had a chance of fitting in at DMG if anyone knew the connection. I needed you to know me just for me. Then, when I learned how important everything was for you—the promotion, your apartment—I didn't want to you to get distracted. I wanted the Imperial win for you. I meant it when I said you were the heart of the entire team, the reason we won the pitch.

"And my deal with my father was for me to help bring Imperial to DMG. Between my time working with Hunter and my history with Nolan, it felt like it would be a slam dunk. I could repay my big debt to my dad and finally move on."

I look at Matt for the first time since we sat down. His eyes are etched with worry, lines creasing his forehead.

"But my dad changed the terms, surprising all of us. Normally I probably would have accepted it. Quietly dealt with my resentment. But that's because normally it would only be affecting me. But this time..." His voice is hoarse as he continues, "This time it wasn't only me. There was so much more on the line that I couldn't silently stand by this time."

He pauses, waiting for me to look at him.

"So, I quit yesterday."

"You did?" I ask, eyes wide and mouth open.

"Yep." He pops the "p" at the end. "I basically told my dad to fuck off."

The visual of Matt doing that stuns me. My hand covers the laugh escaping my mouth.

Matt grins at my reaction. "That's not even the best part. I left DMG and went to talk to my mom, knowing this would all upset her. She told me my dad used credits from the agency to fix the mistake from the Super Bowl. The payout never even came out of his own pocket. She demanded he tell me and believed that he had, but he never did. This mistake haunted me for years. I stayed in this industry for *years* thinking I had to prove that I wasn't a fuck-up. And none of it was necessary. He was lying to me this entire time."

This quickly sobers me. "Sucks being lied to, huh?"

He presses his lips together and stares ahead. "It does." Nodding his head in agreement, he continues, "And if I could go back, I would do everything differently, Emily. I don't know if you'll be able to forgive me. I'm so worried I've shattered the possibility for you to trust me again. But please know this, anything I kept from you wasn't malicious or to hurt you. I was trying to shield you but it all just... backfired." He stops and picks up a twig from the step and rolls it between his hands.

"The thing is, Emily..." He pauses, eyes locking with mine. "You never needed protecting. You are so much stronger than you give yourself credit for. I've watched you be hard on yourself for things no one would even notice or consider a flaw. There were so many times I wanted to pull you in my arms and tell you how amazing you were. How amazing you *are*. I want to protect your generous heart, your kind spirit, and your beautiful soul from any harm. That's what you are, Emily. As precious as a rare gem and as strong as a diamond. And I'm so sorry—" Matt's voice catches. "I'm so sorry I hurt you."

His anguish is evident, and my heart softens as my mom's words play back in my mind.

It's okay to be messy, to make mistakes, and to forgive people for their mistakes. There's beauty in the mess if you look hard enough.

"How do I know..." My voice shakes as tears threaten to fall. "How do I know you won't do it again? You might think you're protecting me and doing the right thing, but what if you end up holding back and leaving me in the dark?"

"Because, Emily..." He waits for me to turn toward him and then he grabs my hands. "If I were lucky enough to get another chance with you, I'd do whatever it takes to build up that trust again. I would prove it to you over and over and over again. I'm not perfect, but I'm not going anywhere. I'm in it to win *you*, Emily.

"You brought light back into my life. You made my heart beat again. These past few days have been exponentially worse than any day during or after my divorce. This makes my relationship with Stella look like child's play." He slowly reaches out to tuck a lone curl behind my ear, softly smiling. "If you could only see yourself like I do, you would know that nothing could have stopped me from falling in love with you."

I sniff and wipe my nose with the back of my hand. "You love me?"

"More than I ever thought I could love someone. More than I ever knew I was capable of loving someone. It's all just so much *more*."

I curl my hands in the sleeves of my hoodie. More tears fall as I cover my mouth again, a quiet laugh escaping me.

He reaches out to cup my cheek. His thumb lightly caressing me before dropping his hand.

"I love you too," I blurt out. And I do. I can't deny it. And maybe I'm a fool, but I'd rather be a fool and take a leap of faith on Matt than miss any more days with him.

"Yeah?" His eyes are shining as he blows out a shaky breath.

He wipes the tears from my cheeks, showing me the tenderness he's promising.

I nod, sniffling again. "I do. I love you too."

Matt gives me a watery, playful grin. "Fuck, yeah, you do." I laugh as he holds my face in his warm hands. "Emily, I will spend the rest of my life proving to you how much I love you, and I promise I will always be honest with you. Always."

"Okay, then I have a question."

He gazes at me with eyes so bright, so full of love. "Ask me anything."

"Meyer? Davis? What is your real last name?"

"It's Davis." He pauses, watching me for a reaction. "Meyer is my middle name. It's my mom's maiden name. I knew I'd never have a shot at fitting in at the company if I was a Davis, so I told my dad I'd only do this if I was Matt Meyer. Surprisingly, he agreed to it."

"Matt Meyer Davis," I softly say as I caress his cheek.

He leans against my palm and turns slightly to kiss it. He starts to pull away and I wrap my arms around his neck and pull him back to me. Our lips connect, and it's the first time the world has felt right in days.

Every fiber of my being is telling me it's okay to jump. To give him another chance. That he'll catch me. It may be messy, but it'll be our mess. *Together.* There's nothing more beautiful in the world to me than that.

CHAPTER 44

MATT

I smile against Emily's lips and pull her onto my lap, wrapping my arms tightly around her. I graze my tongue along her bottom lip and she opens her mouth, letting me taste her. Pulling her tighter, I deepen the kiss, the desperation I felt at the thought of losing her powering me. She responds with equal emotion and relief rumbles deep in my throat. I trail kisses along her cheeks and jaw, burrowing my head in her neck as my hands lower and playfully squeeze her ass. She yelps and gives me the most beautiful smile. My heart hurts seeing the obvious pain she's been feeling—her dry eyes, her red-tipped nose—especially knowing I caused it. I say a silent prayer of thanks to the universe for giving me another chance with her.

She leans back, arms still snaked around my neck. "Wait, you said you quit. What are you going to do now?"

"I'm going to do what I always wanted to do. I'm going back to school to become a physical therapist. It'll take some time, but I'm good with that."

She kisses me, cradling my face with her hands. "I'm proud of you."

"I love you," I say with fierceness as I pull her close. She's giggling into my neck when my phone buzzes in my pocket, and she pulls back.

"Ignore it." I lean in and kiss her. It buzzes again, then a third and fourth time.

"It sounds like it might be important."

I let out an impatient curse and shift to grab my phone, keeping a tight hold on Emily. She's leaning her head against my temple as the screen lights up, revealing all the notifications.

Nolan: Hey Matt.

Nolan: Sorry to bother you.

Nolan: I'm trying to reach Emily and just want to make sure I have the right number.

Nolan: Can you send it to me or have her call me?

Emily pulls her brows together and narrows her eyes at me. "What's that all about?"

I kiss the crown of her head. She watches the screen as I type out a text to him.

Me: Hey, I'm actually with her now. I'll give her my phone to call you.

With that, I hit the phone icon next to Nolan's name. When it starts ringing, I hand Emily the phone. She stands up but remains between my legs as she stares at me. I hear Nolan's voice as he picks up.

"Hello?"

"Hi, Nolan. This is Emily Cooper. Matt mentioned you wanted to talk to me?"

"Hi, Emily! Yes, I've been trying to reach you. Hunter and I have been talking and wanted to run something by you."

Emily turns and steps down to her front yard, putting a finger in her free ear to hear better. She's nodding and tracing her foot in an arc in front of her. They talk for ten minutes before she holds the phone out to end the call. She walks toward me with a startled but very happy look on her face.

"Did you have anything to do with that?" she demands.

"With what?" I try to act innocent, but I can't hide my smile.

"The fact that Nolan just offered me a job running an in-house media department at Imperial."

"He did?!" I feign an exaggerated shock.

"Matt." Emily fists her hands on her hips like she's talking to a toddler.

"Okay, okay." I hold my hands up in surrender. "I didn't have anything to do with their decision, but I may have known they were thinking about it."

"Continue, please."

Her arms drop as she walks toward me. I grab her hips and pull her between my legs, the need to touch her overtaking me. I explain how I flew down to Dallas to tell Hunter and Nolan that I was leaving DMG and confessed the whole story from the Super Bowl until today. Hunter wasn't surprised.

"Turns out he's not a huge fan of my dad, but he liked our idea—*your* idea, Em—and it made him start thinking about how he could support women in STEM overall. Nolan mentioned they had been toying with the idea of bringing media in-house, and he wondered if you'd be interested in the role. I said I couldn't speak for you, but I encouraged him to get in touch with you if they chose to go in that direction."

Emily places her hands on my shoulders. "It's kind of impossible to turn down. I'd get to hire my own team. Work on Imperial and other initiatives. And with the salary they're offering, I could actually stay in my apartment, at least until I find something more affordable so I can build my savings up again."

"So you're going to say yes?" I ask, full of awe and pride at the woman in my arms, feeling so damn lucky and grateful I have another shot with her.

Emily nods. "I'm going to take it."

I pull her into a tight hug and she squeezes my neck hard. "I'm so proud of you." I pull back to catch her eyes. "I love you. So much."

She smiles at me. "I love you, too."

"How are you feeling?"

"Like I won it all."

EPILOGUE

EMILY

FOUR MONTHS LATER

"Flight attendants, prepare for takeoff."

My stomach reflexively drops at the words and my foot starts shaking as the plane turns the corner of the runway. I grip the arm rest before I feel a warm set of fingers link with mine.

"Are you alright?" Matt asks, squeezing my hand.

I nod and squeeze back. I pick up the half-full champagne glass from the small tabletop between us and drain it. "Much better now." A small hiccup escapes as I put the glass down. I've never sat in first class before, but I could definitely get used to this.

Matt laughs and leans forward to place a kiss by my temple. "That's my girl."

I will never get tired of hearing him say that.

"I still can't believe you were able to pull this off," I say as I giggle after another hiccup.

Matt winks at me and I playfully roll my eyes at him. "How were you able to plan an entire trip to Paris without me knowing?"

"It was a team effort." He picks up our joined hands and kisses the back of mine. "The girls packed for you, and I took advantage of the fact that I could ask your boss to release you for a few days."

An unexpected bonus of taking the job with Imperial was Matt and Nolan reconnecting. Nolan's been to New York a few times to help us open the office and they've hung out quite a bit. Nolan's wife even flew out for a weekend and the four of us had dinner. Turns out Stella also grew tired of Ava when she stopped wanting to close down the bars on a Friday night. Ava hasn't heard from her since they moved to Texas, and it sounds like that's not necessarily such a bad thing.

"But what about school?" I ask Matt, knowing he has finals coming up.

"I'll be fine. I told my professors I need to be out for a few days and was able to get one of my papers done before we left. It's all under control." His free hand cups my cheek and his soft lips land on mine, momentarily distracting me from our conversation.

His kisses are soft and sweet, light touches against my lips as I taste the lingering peppermint from one of his Altoids. His other hand slides through the strands of my hair, stroking until his palm cups the back of my neck and tilts my head for deeper access. His tongue slides across my bottom lip, then playfully nips at it to pull it down.

Taking advantage of my parted lips to tangle his tongue with mine, he swallows my small moan—or maybe I swallow his, I can't really tell as we remain fused together. I grab a fistful of his T-shirt and pull him closer. We stay connected by our hands and lips, and I have some vague recollection that we are in plain sight of others, but it's impossible to separate myself from him. Matt finally pulls back but not until we're in the air and the fasten seat belt sign dings off.

"I see what you did there," I tell him, smiling wide and marveling at how Matt is always one step ahead of me, taking care of everything. He gets up to use the restroom and I pinch his firm ass as he steps in front of me.

"Hey now, is that a request to join me?" He wiggles his eyebrows. I laugh and swat his ass before he walks to the front of the plane. I take a moment to breathe now that we're in the air. The champagne relaxed me, but I know I'm calmer than I normally would be simply because of Matt. The past few months have been like a dream I never want to wake up from.

Matt seamlessly slipped into my life, and quickly became my biggest champion and strongest supporter. He embraces my need for order, often trying to anticipate what I need before I even know myself, and making sure I embrace the mess that inevitably gets thrown our way. It took some time to redeem himself, but Josie and Lucy adore him now, and we have had many fun nights out with Ryan and Ben.

Matt returns and stops in front of my seat, facing me. He grins down at me with a look of pure adoration, stroking my cheek as I gaze up at him. "I love you," he mouths as I place my hand over his.

"I love you back," I respond as my entire body floods with warmth and affection.

He sits down and fastens his seat belt. "So, is this the weekend Josie's going away with Luke on their big fat, fake dating adventure?"

I laugh. Matt playfully teased me about all my romance novels at first, but once I explained how tropes work, he loves to tie them into any conversation we have about our friends' love lives.

"Yes, this is the weekend. Josie's been a bit cagey with the details. I think she's more nervous than she's letting on."

"Josie... nervous?" He shakes his head. "Not buying it. My money is on her maybe not wanting it to be that fake."

"Really?" I pull back and squint at him.

He confidently nods. "And I've seen the way Luke can't take his eyes off of her when she's not looking. This is the summer of Josie and Luke, trust me."

I shrug my shoulders. "Maybe." I let that settle in. "You know, it wouldn't be the worst thing."

The flight attendant comes by and refills our champagne. I take a big sip and the bubbles break down my filter a bit.

"Once I knew what was going on with the trip, Josie told me she bet Ryan that you would propose this weekend." *Did I really just say that?* Holy hell, Emily. No more champagne.

We've talked a little bit here and there about the future, but not in any specific terms or timelines. I have zero doubts or concerns about Matt and I can't imagine any day without him, but it's too soon to be blurting anything out about proposals or weddings. I want to crawl into the overhead compartment and hide.

I try to avoid Matt by turning my head away, but he isn't having any of that. "Excuse me?" he enunciates, bending to catch my attention.

I lean down and start digging through my bag, pretending to search for something, but unfortunately my rewind time button isn't in there.

"Emily, look at me." I continue ignoring him. "Emily," he says more forcefully, with the tone I envision him using on his children one day when he's trying to discipline them but knowing he's so far wrapped around their fingers that there's no use trying. "Emily. Rose. Cooper."

I huff out a big sigh, blow some loose strands of hair away from my face, and sit up, willing the embarrassed tears welling in my eyes not to fall.

Matt grabs my chin and turns me to face him, his expression tender, loving, and pure. His eyes study me, gazing over my features like I'm a masterpiece worthy of a spotlight in the Louvre. Every day this man tells me how much he loves me. Every day he shows me by making me feel protected, safe. Every day he does everything he can to make sure I know I'm cherished. All of me. Every perfectly imperfect part of me.

"Emily," he says softly, wiping away a rogue tear. "When—not if, but *when* I propose, the last two people on earth I will tell are Ryan and Josie. When—not if, but *when* I do it, no one will know but you and me. And when—not if, but *when* I propose, I will be a nervous wreck until I hear you say that yes, you'll be mine forever. I don't want to think about a day without you in my life. The most important thing for you to know is that ring or not, I. Choose. You. Yesterday, today, tomorrow, and the day after that. I choose you over, and over, and over again. Forever."

About the author

Ali Curtis lives an overly fulfilled life with her husband, three young daughters and two dogs. When she's not avoiding stepping on Legos or searching desperately for Barbie's other shoe, she works full time in Corporate America. In theory, her free time is spent voraciously reading romance and daydreaming about love, but in reality, she's an uber driver to and from her daughters' activities, secretly listening to audiobooks and hoping her blush isn't too obvious when she hits the steamy parts. You can find her at @authoralicurtis and @herefortheHEA on Instagram.

Acknowledgements

I always dreamed that one day I'd get to write acknowledgements and it's been a winding road so the list is long. Please stick around until the music plays me off.

Writing a romance – a steamy romance – was scary. I worried what people would think of me, of the book and how I might be judged. But I learned through this process that the romance reading community is one of the most inclusive, acceptive and supportive group of people. We watch romance, we sing and talk about it, but for some reason reading it is still stigmatized. In a world where there is so much bad news, so much heartbreak, romance can make you smile, provide an escape, and give us hope. Love really is all around if we just look for it. Let's celebrate it in all forms, for all people.

My first thank you is to you, the reader. Thank you for making a dream come true. The fact that you took time to read my book is a true pinch-me moment. I hope it brought you joy in some way.

Dawn Alexander, without your guidance this would have still been scraps of paper scattered around. Thank you for your patience, your kindness and your mentorship. Britt, you are a shining star and working with you was a highlight of this process. Enni, you brought Emily and Matt to life in the most perfect way. Brooke, thank you for your meticulous eye and attention to detail.

My heartfelt appreciation to my beta readers and romance connoisseurs: Carolyn Russo, Molly Cesario, Joanne Darmanin and Linda Shapiro. Your thoughtful feedback was critical to Emily and Matt's story. Thank you.

To Bonnie Callahan, Norah Pritchard, Jessica Booth, and Sarah Estep - authors who so kindly answered my questions and gave sage advice - thank you from the bottom of my heart.

To the Emilys – you continuously blow me away and this book would have never reached anyone without your help. Overwhelmed will always be an understatement. Every indie author or content creator out there needs them. @bookedwiththeemilys

Find your tribe and love them hard, they say. I'm blessed to have two without whom this never would have happened.

V8: there are no words for how much you all mean to me. Thirty something years later and stronger than ever. You keep me sane and laughing. Love you, mean it.

AOTM Book Club: whoever says you can make real friends online has never been on bookstagram. Thank you for being **the best** cheerleaders and for your endless patience with my grandma/ weakest link status. I can't wait to hug you all in person.

Nicky: It took me thirty-something years but I did it. Thank you for being my first fan and the voice in my head encouraging me to go for it.

Jojo: You were such an integral part of this. I treasure our shared love of reading and couldn't have done this without your endless support. My romance ride or die. In your next life may you find Will Sumner and marry him (sorry, John).

Jenny: My soul sister. You are stuck with me, 1500 miles be damned. I don't have words but when I find them I'll be sure to text and not call you.

I'm also blessed with a loud, loving family that always has my back and always pushes me forward. Life is so much better with all of you in it. Thank you for believing in me even when I didn't believe in myself.

Nanny – my #1 fan always. Always there for me, even when I used to drunk dial you at 2am after a bad night. Thank you for the wise words about Em, too. She owes you big time.

Mom & Dad – please don't read the sections I black out for you. Thank you for always encouraging me even when I made crazy decisions, for loving me through my mood swings, for being there no matter what, and for always telling me to go for it because you were there to catch me if I fell.

Last, but definitely not least: S, R and E – my most important dreams come true. Thank you for all the times you let me write and for all the times you interrupted me for hugs. You are my heart beating outside my chest.

And finally, D. Without you, none of this would have happened. Romance would only exist in books. I hope we never stop kissing in the kitchen no matter how much the girls whine about it. Forever UATW.